D0070674

The Kingsley House

The Kingsley House

Arliss Ryan

St. Martin's Press ✻ New York

THE KINGSLEY HOUSE. Copyright © 2000 by Arliss Ryan. All rights reserved. Printed in the United States of America. No part of this book may be used or reproduced in any manner whatsoever without written permission except in the case of brief quotations embodied in critical articles or reviews. For information, address St. Martin's Press, 175 Fifth Avenue, New York, N.Y. 10010.

Design by Nancy Resnick

Library of Congress Cataloging-in-Publication Data

Ryan, Arliss.
    The Kingsley House : a novel / by Arliss Ryan.—1st ed.
      p. cm.
    ISBN 0-312-24209-3
      1. Kingsley family—Fiction. 2. Livonia (Mich.)—Fiction. I. Title.
PS3568.Y262 K56 2000
813'.54—dc21

                                99-089772

10 9 8 7 6 5 4 3 2

For my mother and father

Acknowledgments

It took the help and encouragement of many people to make this first novel a reality.

My agent, Olivia Blumer of the Karpfinger Agency, believed in the book and persisted until a publisher said yes. Senior editor Hope Dellon and assistant editor Maureen Drum of St. Martin's Press treated me and my manuscript with care and respect. I am eternally grateful to all three for their willingness to take a chance on a new author.

For information on Livonia and Kingsley family history, I am much indebted to Suzanne Daniel, chairman of the Livonia Historical Commission. My thanks to pilot David Goetzinger, Murray and Jane Randall of Aero Ads, Mike Collins of *AOPA Pilot* magazine and Henry Bergen of the Aircraft Owners and Pilots Association, and to Tom Zwemke of Cessna Aircraft Company for technical information and wonderful stories of 1940s aviation. Reginald Cooper of Aquidneck Building Movers & Riggers Inc. explained to me the mechanics of house moving. Any factual errors in the text regarding these topics are mine alone.

The feedback from my fellow writers at our weekly meetings was invaluable in keeping the novel on track. I thank Florence Archambault, Clint Hull, Jim Huston, Jack Galvin, Anita McAndrews, Carmel McGill, Susan Nichols, Judie Porter, Jan Shapin, Sylvia Smith, Tom Storey, David Tornquist, Amy Weintraub, Rosalind Wiggins, and Joan Zeller for their friendship and insightful contributions.

Most important, I thank my family. In addition to giving me the story, my mother, Laura, served as my on-site researcher in Michigan, visiting the Kingsley House, the library, the cemetery—whatever it took to dig up the information I needed. My husband, Eric, and our children, Kira and Dane, lived with the book almost as much as I did—you are my rock and my magic.

And to my late father Barry, I return that special hug.

The Kingsley House

Prologue

1977

Laura Millard Gorman hugged her arms tight in her gray wool jacket, shivering in the bitter November cold. The wind snapped at her face. She'd lost the feeling in her feet some time ago. *Why is this taking so long?* she pleaded as the minutes crawled by, and instantly recanted, *No, no, take whatever time you need.* All around her, people pointed and chattered, and she wished she could ask them to be quiet. She needed to listen for other sounds: the agonized crack of wood frames, the crumble of collapsing walls, a shout or cry that something had gone wrong. This was the seventh day she'd stood vigil, the last and most precarious day, and for a minute she shut her eyes. She couldn't watch. It was too hard. But her inner voice spoke back stronger: *You must watch. You are the witness to the end.* Laura pressed her lips, opened her eyes, and forced herself to look squarely at the Kingsley House as the truck prepared to haul it off its land.

Yet still the house did not move. Although she was tall and stood at the front of the crowd, Laura couldn't make out the action around the base of the building. There were too many men and vehicles in the way. And despite the fact that this was the house she'd grown up in, the house built by her great-great-grandfather Nathan Kingsley in 1843, she, like all the other spectators, had been confined at a safe distance behind the police lines on the opposite side of the street. At the start of the week, the owner of the moving company had briefed her on the operation. Holes knocked in the stone foundation. Crossbeams and runners inserted under the floor. Hydraulic jacks positioned to lift from below. The jacking had occurred yesterday, smoothly but so slowly it became an inch-by-inch, all-day affair. She'd intended to stick it out,

1

until her husband Barry and her own chattering teeth convinced her that at age fifty-eight she was no match for the frigid weather.

Laura shivered and pulled the hood of her jacket close around her salt-and-pepper curls. Today felt even colder, but today she would not budge. She stared at the house, and her heart took up an odd, painful beat. Elevated above-ground level, the support beams obscured from view, the house resembled a strange vision, as if suspended by enchantment in the air. It wasn't right for a house to float like that, disembodied. Surely any minute it would thump back to earth with the jolt of an awakened dream. One of the men called out, and Laura's heart leaped. Was something wrong? What was happening? Was this what her father would have wanted? What would Nathan have said?

Laura sighed, envying the festive air of the crowd. Far from complaining about the blocked-off road and the loss of utilities as the phone and electric crews disconnected impeding lines, the business owners and residents along the street were cheerfully braving the unseasonable weather to exclaim and snap photos in an atmosphere of unexpected holiday. Laura tried to catch their mood—this was exciting, after all—but when she looked at the house, tears came to her eyes.

The Kingsley House was neither fancy nor large, but its Greek Revival style had been the height of architectural fashion when twenty-two-year-old Nathan built it in the fledgling farm community of Livonia, Michigan. It had a Doric portico with six stately pillars, a full-length dormer on the second story, and a simple harmony and balance of design. Yet as it sat stranded on the support beams, the once proud and dignified house appeared shabby and forlorn. Worse, it looked unwanted, its weathered white clapboards and boarded windows adding to its deserted aspect. In the beginning, the house had anchored the northeast corner of forty acres of virgin forest, soon to be cleared and planted as a prosperous farm. Now, torn from its foundation, it was diminished and powerless, out of place and out of time.

Put it back! Laura wanted to shut out the scene around her, the squat brick travel agency and real estate office next door to the Kingsley House, the civic center plaza, bank, and hamburger stand at the busy intersection down the road, the modern residential developments to the north. She wanted to picture instead the house her parents had inherited when she was six years old, when the back porch still looked out on a barn and orchard and acres of open land, and back further, before her birth, when Emma and Joe had fallen in love and Horace the Wicked

2

lived across the road, and back to the beginning when young Nathan Kingsley had brought Mary, his bride—

"Look!"

A shout and hubbub among the crowd startled her eyes open, and she let out a gasped, "Oh!" Amid a great rumble of gears, the truck backed up to the front of the house, to be hitched to a yoke on the beams, and they'd put rollers or wheels or something of that nature under the runners—in the excitement of the moment, Laura couldn't remember exactly what the owner of the moving company had told her a week ago. The spectators jostled forward, everyone talking, the self-appointed experts giving play-by-play descriptions of what they saw. Laura scanned for Barry, hoping he was getting good photos. Their daughter, living in England with her husband, would want copies. So would their elder son, away at college. Their youngest boy had begged to skip high school today to watch, but a geometry exam was scheduled, and Laura, a former teacher, had packed him off to class. He'd catch up with them when the test was done.

Around the house, men and equipment were in motion, and Laura strained for a clear view. She had to see, to satisfy herself that no detail had been overlooked, no precaution neglected, although precisely what instructions she would have given these professional movers she could not have said. Her mind simply cried, *Please, be careful!* and she reminded herself, not for the first time, that the house was strong. Nathan had laid on every board, every shingle, by hand, and were it not for the press of commercial development, the six-lane highway at the door, the Kingsley House would have sat unmoving on its stone foundation for another hundred years. She glimpsed Barry in the crowd. Since his retirement from General Motors, her husband had grown a neat silver mustache to complement his thinning hair, and he had a habit of smoothing the debonair growth with his forefinger while he gazed at some intriguing scene. If she asked what he was doing, he'd reply, "Oh, just watching the world go by." He was in that pose now, enjoying the spectacle, and Laura thought sadly, ruefully, *I'm watching the past go by.* To separate the house from its land, no matter how small a plot remained, felt like severing body from soul.

"All clear!"

The truck driver's vigorous shout made everyone jump, and the grumble of the engine filled the air. Laura clasped her hand to her chest. The house was in open view now, and it sat behind the truck like an ungainly float looking to join a parade. A fresh plague of worries assailed her. What if the house were too wide, too tall for the route? What if the roof became entangled in overhanging trees? What if the driver were careless and turned a corner too sharply, and the house slid off the flatbed and thudded onto the street? She plucked at her gloves. She would have felt so much happier if only she could have shrunk the house to miniature size and carried it safely in her hands.

Then the house *moved,* it came forward, and the sensation was so startling Laura imagined she felt the ground vibrate under her feet.

The truck edged down the curb with its burden, swung wide into the street, and straightened. The onlookers fell silent. For a long moment, the house sat smack in the middle of the road. A police car, lights flashing, moved into position ahead of the truck; a second cruiser took up duty at the rear. The truck driver shifted gears, the lead police car moved forward, and as the unlikely procession began to crawl away, a spontaneous cheer arose from the crowd.

Laura cast a last glance after the Kingsley House. On the now-empty lot, only the cellar remained, a gaping hole in the ground. In a few days the old foundation would be removed and construction of a medical clinic would begin on the site. No one would know the house had ever been there. People would pass by and never guess what came before. *I'm the last one to know this piece of history,* Laura thought, *and even I don't know the whole of it, where the truth and memories converge, where they take separate paths.* She had assembled in an album the few early photographs and family documents about the Kingsley House—a faded marriage license, an old quitclaim, a series of sad death notices, a letter of inheritance. To these, she had added her father's stories and some slight information gleaned from the public records. Yet it hardly gave a full picture, not for a hundred and thirty-four years, not for the tale of so many lives. No one in the family had ever kept a journal; no great deeds had ever brought them fame. You had to use your imagination to tell their stories. . . .

Her eyes were wide open, but Laura no longer saw the city block before her or the empty plot of land. She saw the house, back on its stone foundation, painted fresh white, sunlight reflecting off the windowpanes. And over there was the barn, and the greenhouse, and all around ripening fields of corn and wheat pushed up to meet the blue sky. She saw red apples and cherries in the orchard, heard the chickens clucking in the coop, smelled the scents of moist, plowed earth and sweet, mown hay. Most of all she saw the people, summoning them to life from the old black-and-white pictures that captured who they had been for one second in their lives.

Once this land had been a promising farm, where a handsome young settler named Nathan Kingsley built a fine, strong house to welcome his new bride. . . .

Book One

1844

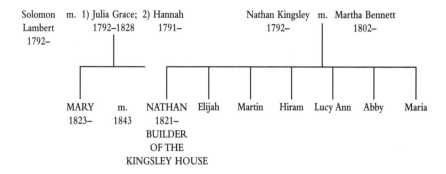

Solomon   m. 1) Julia Grace; 2) Hannah   Nathan Kingsley   m.   Martha Bennett
Lambert   1792–1828   1791–   1792–   1802–
1792–

MARY   m.   NATHAN   Elijah   Martin   Hiram   Lucy Ann   Abby   Maria
1823–   1843   1821–
                      BUILDER
                      OF THE
                      KINGSLEY HOUSE

One

At first, glancing out the living-room window, Mary Kingsley thought it was ashes falling from the sky, delicate black flakes sifting down through the winter grayness, landing softly on pure white snow. Ashes? Falling from the sky? Who would be lighting a fire outdoors in January? She gazed toward the barn but caught no sight of her husband Nathan. Then she peered upward into the bare limbs of the maple tree, retracing the path of the descending flakes. She could see nothing, yet the ashes continued to fall, curling in an elegant dance. A movement in the topmost branches caught her eye, a huge crow. He seemed to be preening himself with his beak, and when Mary gazed downward again she recognized the black objects on the snow as feathers. But the dark plumes kept dropping, each clump growing larger—too many; the crow would strip itself bare. Suddenly three bright red splotches hit the snow. Mary gasped and started back, then pressed forward to stare through the pane. In the treetop, the crow continued its stroking movements, only now she realized it wasn't preening, no. It was tearing at something pinned to the branch beneath its claws, some poor small bird. The feathers fluttered down in deathly quiet, while Mary stared, aghast, at the crimson-splattered snow.

"Stop that! Stop that!" She pounded on the pane with her fist, but the crow, high in the tree, paid her no heed, and already she knew it was too late.

Mary turned from the window with a shiver. Death was a daily occurrence on a farm, chickens slaughtered for Sunday dinner, rabbits shot and skinned for the stewpot and to provide fur for mittens and muffs, cows and hogs butchered for meat and hides. But at home her father and stepbrothers had seen to that work, and since her marriage, Nathan, though he laughingly chided her tenderheartedness, had taken over the job of wringing the chickens' necks.

"I must take extra good care of you now," he had promised, kissing her.

Mary smiled. Even in this frosty cold, Nathan was out in the barn, smoothing planks for a cradle that would not be needed for another six months. Hadn't she married a good, hard-working man? And this new house he had built, all for her, his bride—Mary glanced happily over the rooms. As yet, the furnishings were sparse: a horsehair sofa, a doily-covered table, a few straight-backed chairs. But that was only to be expected at the start, and come spring she would have pretty wallpaper, vases of flowers, a rag rug on the pegged wood floor. Really, it was one of the finest houses in Livonia Township, and Mary loved the sense of order and rightness that defined every room.

She went to the small shelf Nathan had made for the wall and ran her finger over the spines of their three books. If it were Sunday, she would have to choose the Bible, and although she tried to select the most exciting stories—David and Goliath, Samson and Delilah—she and Nathan both exhaled a little sigh of relief when this duty was done. But this being midweek, Mary's finger skipped quickly to the second and third volumes, a book of fairy tales and a collection of poetry, and she tapped back and forth between them. Both were well worn, treasured from the lonely days after her mother's death when her grief-stricken father Solomon had pulled his five-year-old daughter onto his lap and taught her to read to assuage his own sense of emptiness. Her step-mother Hannah, however, considered such reading matter conducive to dillydallying and was glad to have Mary take the books with her when she had married Nathan in November.

Mary's finger settled on the poetry, and she carried it back to the kitchen. In winter, the best place to stay warm was beside the big wood-burning stove, and after dinner, with Nathan's arms curled around her, they would sit by the stove's heat and she would read aloud to him. But first she had the meal to cook. Mary smoothed her apron over the full skirt of her plum-colored dress. A cornbread was already baking in the oven. Now she poured a little water from the wood bucket beside the sink and began scrubbing potatoes to go in the roasting pan with the beef. At home Hannah had her own strict way of doing things, and whatever Mary's efforts—washing the clothes, mending, cooking, churning butter, cleaning, spinning, weaving, making candles and soap—there was always some flaw to be found in the method, the result, or both. Meanwhile, Martha Kingsley, her new mother-in-law, was equally adamant about how each household chore should be accomplished. The problem was that where Hannah said, "Do it this way," Martha said, "Do it that," so that Mary often felt buffeted between two opposing gusts of wind.

"But this is *my* house," she said aloud. "My house. My husband. My home." She couldn't help the smile that crossed her lips. Mary was just twenty and not a little proud of her new status. It did not hurt either to have brown doe eyes, auburn curls, dimpled cheeks, and just enough height to tuck her head beneath her husband's chin. As she set the scrubbed potatoes in the pan, her mind leafed through the pages of the poetry book, mentally marking the sonnets that were Nathan's favorites.

Footsteps sounded on the back porch, and she turned to greet her husband. But instantly her smile froze. Nathan's left hand, swathed in a rag, dripped blood, and his face wore a grimace of pain.

"What happened? Are you cut?" She hurried toward him, wiping her hands on her apron. The rag was fast becoming blood-soaked, and as Nathan unwrapped the cloth, she recoiled from the ugly gash in his palm.

"My fingers grew cold, and the plane slipped." He tipped water from the bucket into a washbasin and began to bathe the wound. Already his tone sounded more irritated than hurt, as if the pain bothered him less than the interruption to his work.

"You must have a bandage." Mary reached to the cupboard where they kept a small stock of medicinals—sarsaparilla, chamomile, licorice root, pennyroyal—along with a roll of clean white cloth. She sheared off a long strip, folded it into a pad, and pressed it against Nathan's palm.

"Hold this," she commanded. She cut another strip of cloth, wrapped it around the pad, and tied the ends of the bandage in a neat knot. "You must be careful, Nathan. Whatever would I do if you were hurt? I should be lost without you." She gave him a pouting, half-worried smile, and with a laugh he cupped her chin and drew her toward him. His dark blue eyes in his sharp, handsome face, glinted into hers.

"I will always take care of you. Now stay warm in your little nest while I go back to work." He kissed her and headed for the back door. "Call me when dinner is ready."

He left, and through the window Mary watched him crunch across the snow to the barn. Nathan was tall and lean and loved to work outdoors with his hands. She loved to watch him, imagining the lithe movement of muscles beneath his clothes. Her thoughts drifted back, recalling how diligently Nathan had labored throughout the hot summer to have the house ready for their November wedding. On several occasions, she and her family had traveled by buggy from their farm three miles distant to observe his progress. Her father Solomon approved of Nathan.

"Nothing sways him," he remarked to Hannah as they watched the husband-to-be cut boards for the sturdy frame beginning to rise from the stone foundation. Solomon Lambert owned one hundred sixty acres, whereas Nathan's farm, deeded to him by his father, encompassed only forty. But as Mary's father gazed over the fields of corn and wheat, newly cleared from surrounding timber, he declared expansively that there was "plenty of room to grow." Like most of the early settlers in Livonia, the Lamberts themselves had lived in a one-room log cabin for many years before they were finally able to afford sawed lumber and a frame house. So it was a matter of pride throughout the community whenever a fine new home like Nathan Kingsley's was erected.

Hannah had her own reasons for approving of Mary's fiancé. "The eldest of seven. He will be of some use when the babies arrive," she averred through pursed lips. She retied her straw bonnet under her chin and lifted her arms for Solomon to help her down from the buggy.

Mary followed, blushing. Intent on his work, Nathan had not heard their approach along the dirt road. He wore old trousers, powdered in sawdust, and his shirt had been cast off in the July heat. Seeing the Lamberts, he grabbed it and hastily buttoned it on, but not before Mary took in the taut, bare chest, sun-browned skin, dark nipples, and thatch of black hair under each arm. She had never seen Nathan unclothed before, and the sudden sight, coupled with her stepmother's casual remark about babies, made her cheeks burn. Nathan, too, seemed embarrassed, shaking Solomon's hand and apologizing to the women for his untidy state. For several minutes, he and Mary avoided each other's direct gaze, until the redness faded from her face.

Four months later they were married, and now . . . the baby had happened so quickly, perhaps even on their wedding night. A little too much wine at the festive dinner following Reverend Swift's marriage service. The gay talk of family and neighbors crowded into the new house. The glow of candles illuminating the rooms. Her pretty cream lace dress and kid leather shoes. Surrounded by a knot of pipe-smoking men, Nathan had talked exuberantly of his plans for the farm, pulling unconsciously at the stiff collar of his formal suit. Eyes shining, Mary received the attentions of her guests and sipped another glass of wine. The company departed late amidst a swell of congratulations, and the good feeling carried the newlyweds upstairs to the bedroom. Then the wine must have taken over and caused a blank, for the next sensation Mary felt was the awkward lump of white nightgown bunched at her waist, frigid sheets against her bare thighs, and Nathan plunging into her a part of his body she had never seen. She shocked awake then—every thrust seemed to fill and choke her—and all she could envision was her father's black stallion, his huge maleness vividly erect, as he clambered to mount the roan mare. It went on and on, though she knew he never meant to hurt her, until finally he pulled out and her insides collapsed in relief. Nathan murmured awkwardly and kissed her, but the bed was wet and sticky, and they had to sleep on opposites sides. Repeat episodes had been less painful and more pleasurable, but they stopped altogether once her second monthly cycle had been missed and she confided her condition to her husband.

"Then we must not do anything that might harm the baby," he said, as if stating a well-known fact, and from then on, he simply snuggled her against him, blew out the candle, and so they fell asleep. Mary would have liked to ask some woman if this were indeed true, that relations between her and Nathan must now cease, but she hardly dared pose such a question to Hannah or Martha, and since she had only stepbrothers and Nathan's three sisters were but little girls, she was bereft of female advice. Still, Nathan, although only two years older than Mary, was always so sure of what must be done that she bit back her curiosity and trusted that he was right.

A warm smell of baking interrupted her thoughts, and she peeked into the oven. The cornbread had gone a rich golden color, and the edges had browned and pulled away from the sides of the pan—ha! Even Martha, who had passed on the recipe from her New England forebears, could not have done better than that. Mary drew out the pan and set it atop the stove to keep warm. She was turning toward the cellar, to fetch sweet apples to stew with cinnamon, when she saw out the window that Nathan had emerged from the barn and stood conferring with a man in a buggy. She recognized Old Bess, a big gray-white mare, then knew the hunched figure on the seat to be Reverend Swift. Mary stopped, puzzled. What was he doing out paying social calls on a Wednesday?

Mary pulled off her apron. She must open the parlor, heat cider, and then—she sighed—she and Nathan must sit and listen patiently while the good reverend declaimed about his latest crusade. Marcus Swift, one of the first Livonia settlers, was the circuit preacher for the township, and since no one had gotten around to building a church yet, he delivered his holy message in homes, barns, schoolhouses, or wherever else space could be found. A thin, pinch-nosed man of fifty, he was tireless in his duties and admirable in all his beliefs, but so long-winded. Nothing could be said or done without a Biblical reference, and at Mary's wedding he had droned interminably about the marriage at Cana when it was her own happy future about which she wanted to hear. Afterward, at the festive dinner, he had spoken long and passionately for the abolition of slavery, his favorite cause. And always there was a new mission to pursue, an evil to defeat, a heavenly edict to uphold. The other townspeople, Mary noticed, endured his sermons with the same fortitude they exhibited during blizzards or drought. Religion and morals were necessary to a fledgling community, but Reverend Swift did tend to flagellate his congregation with the whip of perpetual goodness.

But now, she saw, Reverend Swift was gesturing toward Nathan's parents' house, a half mile down the road. He seemed agitated, and Mary frowned. Father Kingsley, also named Nathan, had been ill this past week, running a high fever and coughing spasmodically, but though still weak, he had seemed to be recovering. Could his health have turned poorly again?

Nathan broke off talking and came quickly toward the back door. He blew in, bringing a gust of cold air that made her clasp her arms to warm her chest.

"Some work needs doing at the Jasper's place, Mary. Reverend Swift has asked the neighbors to ride over and help." He took his hat and scarf from a peg on the wall, his bandaged hand moving stiffly as he wound the wool muffler around his neck.

"Work? What work? How long will you be gone?"

"A few hours, no more."

"But you will miss your dinner." Mary caught his arm as he stepped toward the door. "Should you not eat first?"

"There is no time, Mary. I must go now." Nathan placed his hands firmly on her shoulders, a gesture that both stopped her forward movement and set her irrevocably in her place. He pressed his lips, as if more words urged to be spoken, then a tender look softened his face. "There is no cause for you to worry, dearest. Stay here and you will be safe until I return."

He strode out the door, leaving Mary perplexed. What could be so urgent? Although Nathan was better acquainted, she hardly knew the Jaspers, a prim Quaker couple who thee'd and thou'd her whenever they met. And, *several hours*, Nathan had said. What a topsy-turvy turn the day had taken. She had planned such a lovely dinner. She had worn her plum-colored dress, which Nathan, usually indifferent to clothes, had actually complimented her on during their courtship. And their special time together . . . Mary glanced ruefully at the waiting poetry book, then bucked herself up. In a pioneer community people must stick together and help one another, and perhaps their evening together would be more special for the wait. She recalled Nathan's tender look and his protectiveness toward her and the baby, and her glance went to the warm cornbread. Nathan would get hungry, and Reverend Swift as well. She cut two thick squares of the yellow bread, wrapped each in a blue cloth, and took her cloak from its peg. She swirled it on and checked out the window just as Nathan appeared from the barn leading their brown horse Jake. In his good hand, he gripped his shotgun.

"Nathan?"

For a second she stood disconcerted, hardly realizing she had spoken aloud. Nathan used the gun to hunt wild turkeys, rabbits, deer in the wood. Why would he need it at Jasper's farm? And what else had he said? *Stay here and you will be safe.* Safe from what? Mary snatched up the cornbread and hurried out the door.

"Nathan!" Her voice vaporized, thin and ineffectual in the cold winter air. Reverend Swift slapped the reins on Old Bess, and the big mare bolted off smartly. Nathan had already mounted, and a kick of his heels sent Jake snorting after the buggy. His back was toward her, and Mary called again, louder, but to no avail. Then because she could not shout and run at the same time, she gave up calling and plunged after the departing men. Her cloak dragged in the snow and her high-laced boots threatened to slip on hidden patches of ice. Indians! It must be Indians! Though the few red men left in these parts acted peacefully, she had heard stories of their atrocities elsewhere. Who knew what horror might be brewing?

"Nathan!"

This time she screamed it, and at that instant her heel caught in the hem of her cloak, the cord jerked back around her neck, and she pitched, choking, into the snow beneath the maple tree. It took several seconds for her to lift her face from the prickling frost and grope to a sitting position, her left arm instinctively covering her belly. She closed her eyes and swallowed painfully, massaging her throat, to reassure herself she could still breathe. When her gaze refocused, she saw the receding figure of her husband, galloping away down the road. Then she saw something else, tufts of soft, bloody feathers, clinging to the front of her dress.

"Oh!"

Mary scrambled up and frantically brushed and shook herself clean. But a nameless fear had embraced her, a chill like ice on her spine. Something was wrong! Nathan was riding into danger! She must go after him, but how? The Jasper's farm was several miles distant, and he had taken their only horse. Then she remembered the way Reverend Swift had gestured down the road to her in-laws' house. They must know what was happening. They had extra horses. And there she could get Lij, Nathan's brother Elijah, to help her.

Teeth chattering, Mary hiked up her cloak and began to run, two neat blue packages abandoned in the snow.

Two

Nathan bent forward in the saddle, his good hand cramped around the reins. Just ahead, Reverend Swift's buggy flew over the snow. Cold rarely bothered Nathan Kingsley, but he did wish he had taken the time to pull on a pair of gloves. The gash in his left hand was growing painful again, and his fingertips felt numb.

At twenty-two, Nathan was tall and keen-faced, a straightforward man who never wasted movements and never questioned much that came his way. Why should he, when the good Lord had made things so simple? Work hard, earn your bread, love your wife, raise your children, honor your parents, respect your neighbor. He could neither read nor write and had little call to do so, although Mary's sweet voice lilting sonnets in his ear was an unexpected pleasure. He also enjoyed the music and storytelling at gatherings. Still, these were amusements that had no real bearing on his needs or his sense of happiness. For Nathan Kingsley, everything was concentrated in the physical, the here and now of plowing a field, planing a cradle, galloping a horse through the grayness of a January afternoon.

He scanned the fields to either side of the road where an occasional farmhouse stood in winter quiet. The land was flat, blanketed in soft whiteness, thick with patches of forest. Nathan's property was at the center of the township, but although the crossroads there was aptly named Livonia Center, there was no town as yet, no bustling main street of blacksmith shop, livery stable, general store. Instead, the few small mills, stores, and taverns in Livonia were scattered at crossroads throughout the thirty-six square mile community, as if the settlers preferred a widespread sense of independence to the benefits of a centralized town. That suited Nathan fine. Who needed a city when you had land? Though his younger brother Elijah thought otherwise. Lij, summoned from his parents' house, was already somewhere ahead of him on the road to the Jaspers', as were men from a half dozen other farms Reverend Swift had visited. Nathan's thoughts circled back to Mary, picturing her safe at home. Yes, it was better not to have worried her with Reverend Swift's news.

In a few miles they reached the Jasper's place, a simple clapboard house fronted by two large pines. Reverend Swift reined in Old Bess, and Nathan dismounted from Jake and rubbed his stiff fingers. As they walked toward the porch, he tucked his bandaged hand under his good arm, as if by sharing the wound with the rest of is body, he could absorb and heal it more quickly.

Garrett Jasper opened the door at their knock. "Enter, friends, enter. Our thanks to thee for coming, Nathan." His round face lit briefly in welcome, then resumed its anxious lines. "Everyone else is here, Reverend. William, run see to the horses." He beckoned into the house behind him, and a boy of twelve darted out, piping, "Yes, Father." Nathan set his shotgun amongst a row of others on the porch and followed Reverend Swift into the living room. The Jaspers had come to the new state of Michigan some three years before, and though their Quaker beliefs and austere dress set them apart from the other families, Nathan admired their honesty and industriousness. Their home was plainly furnished, and the few times Nathan had been inside, it had always presented a vigorously scrubbed look, as if Lucretia Jasper had just put away her mop and pail after vanquishing every last speck of dirt.

But today there was no time for more than a quick impression of cleanliness. Eight or so men, including Elijah, stood in tight conference before the fireplace, and as they parted to admit him, Nathan saw Lucretia on her knees before a rocking chair. In the chair huddled a girl of about fifteen, wrapped in a down comforter, and though Reverend Swift had forewarned him, Nathan stopped at the sight. She was Negro, her skin as bitter dark as molasses, and the sense of her blackness was so out of place in this white house, in this pale winter world, that Nathan was at a loss to react. His eyes went to the plaits of soot-black hair that crisscrossed her scalp like chicken tracks, and she bowed her head as if she could no longer endure the weight of so many stares. Lucretia tucked the comforter more securely about her knees, but the girl shivered nonetheless. Nathan averted his gaze, knowing his eyes had only added to her burden.

"Have any more arrived?" asked Reverend Swift.

Garrett shook his head. His broad face and clean-shaven upper lip were framed by a shaggy brown beard and hair, and he wore his usual garb of plain gray suit and white shirt.

"We have had no sight of them," he replied. "The children are posted at the upstairs windows as lookouts."

"Then we must organize a search at once."

"Begging your pardon, Reverend." Samuel Millard, a frowning, burly man, stepped forward. "But now we are gathered, some fuller explanation of this incident is needed. All you told us in your summons was that some slaves seeking freedom were attacked and became lost yesternight in the woods. Who attacked them and why? How did this girl alone come to be here? And what concern have you and the Jaspers with this business?"

The other men murmured agreement, and Nathan nodded. Reverend Swift had given him few details of the commotion, and but for the startling presence of the Negro girl, he would have deemed it an unlikely tale. No such event had ever intruded here before.

Lucretia rose from beside the rocking chair. She was a small, resolute woman, dressed in homespun gray with a white kerchief knotted around her neck, brown moles dotting her face, and Nathan thought how she and Garrett matched each other like a set of salt-and-pepper shakers. Lucretia spoke calmly, but one hand went back toward the slave girl as if both to shield her and to motion her to silence.

"The girl is frightened and confused, but I have most of the story and can tell thee what is necessary to know. She escaped from a plantation in Kentucky with her sister, who carried along her six-month-old babe. A sympathetic ferryman gave them safe passage across the Ohio River. Once on the free shore, they joined four others, fugitives like themselves, and the party continued northward, their hope being to reach Canada. They managed well enough until last night when they were attacked and put to flight. In the darkness and turmoil, the girl became separated from her companions. She struggled through the woods alone and arrived this morning on our doorstep. Garrett and the children have searched the near edge of the forest, but no more of the party did they find. That is when Reverend Swift determined to ask thy help. We know not if the lost ones be injured or alive, but we fear they cannot survive another night out-of-doors."

Lucretia paused, and in spite of himself Nathan's gaze returned to the Negro girl. He had seen black people before on his few visits to Detroit, freed men and women going about their business, storekeepers, cobblers, coach hands, families with children. But he had had no occasion to speak to them or to learn more than his eyes could see. The girl hunched by Lucretia's fire was pretty but so thin, the whites of her frightened eyes haunted by yellow. She clutched the comforter in scratched fingers, and every so often Nathan heard a clacking sound as her teeth clamped together.

Elijah strode forward, eyes sparkling in excitement. "Who attacked them?" he demanded.

"A band of slave hunters," answered Lucretia. "The girl believes there were five or six pursuers."

"Where did this trouble occur?" Ephraim Peck asked on Nathan's right.

"South of the river, sometime after midnight."

"Then how can we be sure they crossed to this side?" demanded George Chilson. "They may have been chased south again, or east or west."

A clamor of talk broke out, the small room filling with questions and debate. Nathan knew all those present, farmers like himself, though most were older, seasoned men of cautious bent. Their holdings of forty, eighty, or a hundred sixty acres represented a small measure of prosperity in a state that was still a vast wilderness. They would not be satisfied until each had his say.

Samuel Millard's burly figure asserted itself, and the men stepped back to let him speak. "You numbered six yet lost," he said to Lucretia, his frown deepening. "This girl's sister, her babe, plus four more fugitives. Are they men? Women? Children?"

"Four men," answered Lucretia. "Two young brothers, a single male of about thirty, an old man with a crooked leg." Her mouth quirked in a wry smile. "I think that any Negro thou finds wandering these woods shall be one of our missing."

Elijah chuckled, and Millard sent him a warning glare. "They travel on foot then? All six together?" he persisted.

"That is uncertain." Lucretia paused, as if weighing how much to reveal. "At their last station, a horse and wagon were provided. But when their pursuers neared, the men jumped down to offer resistance so the women and child might escape. This girl heard shots and a scuffle, then the hunters galloped after the wagon. Her sister pushed her from the seat, crying her to flee, then she lashed the horse onward, the hunters closing behind. When this girl crawled from the bushes where she had landed, all sight of her sister was gone."

Lucretia folded her hands, and Nathan regarded the slave girl. Her dark head was bowed again, and in the light from the fire a trickle of tears glistened on the slope of her cheeks.

"What is her name?"

It was the first time he had spoken, and the other men turned to look at him. The question sounded odd to his ears also, and if asked, he could not have said exactly why he wanted to know.

"We find it best to use no names," said Garrett gently. "That way, should anyone ask if thou hast seen a particular Negro, thou mayst in truth say no."

"And what does the law say?" Frank Noble stepped forward. He was a thoughtful man, respected for his efforts to help organize the community's first school, and his expression grew troubled as he spoke. "I do not like the idea of slavery. Reverend Swift has railed against it often enough in his sermons. But by the law, this girl is someone's property, and if her master comes to claim her, are we not legally bound to restore his goods?"

"Aye," chimed Ephraim Peck. "I have heard of folks fined, imprisoned, their lands and houses forfeit for giving aid to runaway Negroes."

"And what of the slave hunters?" George Chilson demanded. "Are we likely to cross paths with them?"

"Then we shall make them turn tail and run!" Elijah cried.

"Neighbors! Neighbors!" Reverend Swift's voice, thin and weedy like himself, tried to sprout above the crowd as the men debated. Nathan shook his head. The winter afternoon was already dwindling, and with each minute lost, their search area shrank smaller and smaller. His gaze went to the slave girl, forgotten in the din. She had buried her face in her hands, mutely sobbing, while Lucretia enfolded her, murmuring, "Hush, child, have courage. I promise no one shall harm thee."

"Friends!" Garrett boomed, and the room grudgingly quieted. A grim, weary expression etched the Quaker's face. "What thou sayst is true, and no small risk is run by those who join us. We have asked thee here to break the law, an earthly law that calls this girl and all like her chattel, to be worked and whipped and denied unto death the right to draw one breath in freedom. But there is a higher law that must be obeyed, and we would not have summoned thee without believing thou would answer the same."

Lucretia rose and stood beside her husband. "What hope is there for any of us, if good men such as thou, when faced with evil, stand aside and do nothing?"

"Do nothing?" Samuel Millard's chest huffed in indignation. He glared from Garrett to Reverend Swift to Lucretia. "I need no man, nor no preacher, nor no woman either, to tell me my conscience. Six souls are lost in the woods, and not one man in this room, I hope, would turn his back on another in need." An angry murmur of assent rippled through the crowd, and Millard raised his hands for calm. "All I say, Jasper, is that you and your wife have a way of speaking that is both plain and not plain. I have heard tell of this Underground Railroad that spirits slaves out of the South, hiding and provisioning them at stations along the way. If your house is part of this line, I think you owe your neighbors some knowledge of your activities."

"On the contrary," Reverend Swift interrupted, "the less you know, the safer everyone will be." He paused for his words to take hold. "Now, will you help us search?"

"Aye!" The chorus rose from all present.

Elijah came to Nathan's side. "At last," he whispered. "Those old men would talk forever. May I never become like them! Well, brother, shall we search together? I think we shall find our strays as easily as snaring rabbits in the woods."

"I hope so." Nathan glanced out the window where the boy William was leading their horses from the barn. Reverend Swift began assigning search areas, two pairs of men to the south bank of the river, Millard and Peck to the west, Nathan and Elijah to the east. Lucretia brought hastily wrapped packages of bread and meat from the kitchen, and as the men filed out, they retrieved their guns from the porch.

"Bring any wanderers you find here to the Jasper's," Reverend Swift instructed. "But if you find no one by sunset, return to your homes. We can accomplish little in the dark and may only obscure their trails."

"What did you do to your hand?" Elijah asked, as he and Nathan rode off in their assigned direction.

"Cut it. Planing a cradle."

"Ah. That is what comes of sowing seed, brother."

"That is no way to speak of my wife, Lij."

"I am sorry." Elijah's face showed momentary contrition, then he flashed another grin. "But must you always be so serious, Nathan? If you cannot enjoy life and the pleasures of a beautiful bride, you will grow as gruff and grim as our father."

Nathan smiled in spite of himself, but he had no intention of divulging private details of his marriage, even to Elijah. That was between husband and wife, and although he had promised himself he would not touch Mary now that she was with child, some nights holding back seemed the hardest duty on earth. That this soft, warm creature had consented to be his still slightly amazed him, and he minded not at all if his dinner was sometimes a little burnt or the gravy had lumps. Just thinking of Mary filled a space in his heart he had not known existed. Elijah was sending him a curious look, and realizing the smile must have lingered on his face, Nathan abruptly changed the subject.

"It is good to be out hunting again, just us two, eh? I wish it were only rabbits we were after."

"Why?" Elijah sat jauntily in his saddle, eyeing the approaching woods with an eager glance. "This is far more exciting, Nathan. When do we ever have the chance, out in this lonely country, to be part of such a drama?" He threw out his arms in exuberance, his breath puffing white in the cold air.

"It is not a game, brother. You saw that poor girl shivering. Somewhere in these woods a mother and babe are lost, and an old man hobbling on a bent leg. It sobers me to think that all we may find is a frozen corpse."

They had come to a gully, and as Nathan slowed to ease his horse through it, Elijah plunged down and up again. Nathan shook his head. Lij was twenty-one, a proper age for a man to be married and working his own farm, but though he flirted with every girl he met, he showed no interest in settling down. More often he talked of going to Detroit and finding employment in the city. Nathan had been to Detroit a handful of times—once with his father in 1839 to record the deed to their property at the newly opened federal land office, another visit or two to purchase equipment or fancy goods—and found it crowded and noisy. Yet he could halfway picture Elijah there, parading in a fashionable suit, partaking of whatever dubious activities such a place might afford.

"It is no game, Lij," he repeated.

"Ha!" Elijah spurred his horse. "There is a game in everything, brother. Race me to the woods!"

He took off at a gallop, and Nathan bolted after him. A few minutes' hard riding brought them to the edge of the forest, Elijah still in the lead. He dismounted, laughing, and with a grunt Nathan slid from Jake's back. His injured hand was cold again, and he took Lucretia's bread and meat from his pocket and munched on it as they walked through the snow. The grayness was deeper in the woods, as if a shadow had fallen between the bare trees, and the stillness was almost church-like. No bird chirped, no deer glided past. Once, hunting alone in spring twilight, Nathan had been startled by a procession of Indians threading their way along the opposite bank of the river. Their dark eyes recorded him, their faces expressionless, as if they recognized something in him unknown to himself. He had stood rooted to the spot, half in fear, half amazed. Though Indians were still known to roam these parts, they were rarely seen by white men. The procession struck Nathan as a migration, the band moving westward in steady steps, single file. No child cried, no twig snapped beneath their feet. Not until the last brave disappeared did Nathan feel the thrill through his body and the breath of relief exhale from his lungs. He was almost unsure if what he had seen was real or a vision, and he had told no one, pondering it to himself.

"Which way will they have gone, do you think?" Elijah asked, breaking into the memory. "The river is frozen, so they may have crossed at any point. If their destination is Canada, as Lucretia said, they have only to follow the river east, and it will take them to Detroit."

"*If* any among them had a map or knew the route." Nathan paused and studied the forest, the same in all directions. "That may be too much to hope for, especially if they scattered in the dark."

"Yet they managed to get this far from Kentucky. They must have had directions or guides along the way." Elijah kicked through a knee-high drift. "Do you know anything of this Underground Railroad?"

"No, though the Jaspers seem to."

"And Reverend Swift. Well, I say we take parallel tracks, within sight of each other, and follow the river. With luck, the snow will give us some footprints." He descended the slope toward the riverbank, leading his horse.

For an hour they tramped eastward, their progress slow. The ground was uneven, and the snow reached Nathan's ankles in one step, over his boot top the next. From time to time, Elijah offered a joke or a remark, but gradually their silences lengthened, the words futile and unwanted in the vast quiet. Nathan felt his heartbeat change, become less insistent, less real. On the farm, on the flat open land he had cleared with his two hands, he knew what a man was meant to be and do. He felt the strength of the contract between himself and the Creator, the agreement that he should till, sow, reap the bounty of the earth, and in return, believe. But here in the forest, another power tugged at him, whispered in his ears, stretched his sight, caught his breath. Here in this undisturbed world, where owls watched through ancient eyes and great bears slept in hidden dens, a man's senses loosened, contracts dissolved, and acreage meant nothing at all. He walked in a realm of soft white snow that engulfed the ground and powdered the trees, and the air held a taste of wetness that melted sweet on his tongue. Tall trunks of sentinel oaks, maples, and beech stretched before him like endless pillars of some ruined temple, and all around him the misty grayness grew imperceptibly darker as forgotten minutes sighed by. If he paused and looked straight up, he saw only more gray sky, and though his mind knew sun and blue heaven still existed, they were like a dream of some other place. Here all was enveloped in isolation, and Nathan's purposefulness drained away to be replaced by a steady, unconscious will that moved him on. He no longer felt cold. He forgot to think. And with each step forward, time moved with him, so he was always in the present, surrounded by the same moment, unchanging.

Once in a while, his eyes picked up tracks: a deer, a fox, a leaping hare. But no human footprints other than his own and Elijah's marred the pristine snow. Nathan's mind traveled back to the slave girl. He could not imagine her life; it felt dishonest even to try. Now, wherever she had come from, whatever home she had known was irrevocably gone. She had flung herself into a void, clutching at the hope of a better life, and beside that he placed a memory of himself when his family departed New York State for the new land of opportunity in Michigan Territory. The trip had had its perils: unknown roads, harsh storms, the threat of accident or illness far from help. Yet to a ten-year-old boy it had been a great adventure, where the slave girl's journey was a desperate flight. Nathan lifted his foot, stepped slowly forward, watched his boot sink into the snow. *I have the right to step anywhere,* he thought, and the idea was so powerful it caused a pain in his chest. How could it ever be otherwise? How could one human being own another? It came to him that once or twice before he had heard vague rumors of events at the Jasper's farm or someone had sighted Garrett out driving his creaking wagon long after dark. Samuel Millard and Elijah were both right: some greater drama had overtaken them, and now no man could turn his back. It was enough to keep Nathan pressing onward until twilight fell.

"Nathan!" Elijah trudged up from the riverbank, leading his horse. His jaunty step was long gone, his face showed disenchantment, and he clapped his hands together to warm them. "Nothing, Nathan. Not a print nor a sign. They cannot have come this way."

"No." Nathan let out his breath in reluctant agreement.

"Shall we start home?"

"You go. I want to ride back to the Jaspers' to learn if any have been found. After you stop home, ride on and tell Mary I am coming, will you? She will be worried I am so late."

"My pleasure." Elijah's spirits grew lively again. "Yes, a visit to Miss Mary is just the thought to speed me on my way. Then back I shall hie to Mother's good supper of roast pumpkin and mutton stew. A little beer would not go amiss either, if I can pry a glass from Father's keg."

Nathan chuckled. "Let us get out of this forest and onto solid ground. My legs ache, and the sooner I climb on Jake again, the better."

He rubbed the horse's nose, and they headed northward. By the time they emerged from the trees, darkness had settled over the fields, and the white snow cast up an answering paleness to meet the descending night. The brothers mounted their horses and rode off, Elijah to the north, Nathan skirting the woods to the west. His feet inside his boots were numb, he realized now, and his fingers were stiff with cold.

"Go, Jake." He clicked his tongue and urged the stallion to a gallop, and the horse, sensing their long trek was ending, put on good speed toward the Jasper's farm. Nathan let his mind fly homeward ahead of him, away from the solitude of the winter forest, back to Mary and the solid things he cherished, house and land. So fixed was he on his path that he was almost upon the group of mounted men before he saw them.

"Whoa, stranger!"

Nathan reined in his horse. For a fleeting moment, he had taken the figures to be Reverend Swift and the other searchers, but the next instant his mind rejected the shapes as unfamiliar, and the word "stranger," harshly spoken, confirmed it. Cautiously, Nathan trotted Jake forward. He counted five men, and though it was difficult to read their features in the deepening dark, he had an impression of surly faces, rough clothes, and hard-ridden horses. The man who had first accosted him spoke again, and his voice this time strove to be ingratiating.

"Good evening to you, traveler. Might you be from hereabouts?"

"A ways yonder." Nathan shrugged and waved vaguely behind him.

The man nudged his horse closer. Even in the saddle, he was more than common tall and dressed like a frontiersman in a Western hat and fringed buckskin jacket. His square jaw bore a stubble of beard, and straw-colored hair hung lankly across his shoulders. Among the other four riders, Nathan picked out a young man near his own age, the possessor of a fine-boned face and a well-cut coat.

"Hurry up, Burke!" he ordered the leader. "It is damned cold, and I am tired of delays."

"Then perhaps you should have stayed behind and let me handle this," Burke replied with gritted politeness. "It may be this traveler can provide us some useful information." He gestured toward Nathan, and a smile parted his lips. "Now, sir, my associates and I are on a bit of business in your territory, and we would be obliged for your assistance. Can you direct us to the home of a man named Jasper?"

For a moment, Nathan did not reply. It was strange, he thought, how a man's language could betray him, how Burke's genteel words sat ill upon him, like a suit of clothes he had borrowed without permission from his betters. Now he had to make everything else fit the words, adopting an easy posture, smoothing a pleasant expression onto his hard-bitten face. It was as if one deception put the whole man out of alignment, made of him a crooked person, never quite right to the eye.

"Jasper?" said Nathan. "Yes, I have heard of a farmer by that name. He lives," Nathan thumbed over his shoulder toward the east, "that way."

"Far?" asked Burke.

"Quite a few miles, as I recall."

"Damn it!" The young gentleman pranced his horse forward, and in the pale aura from the snow, Nathan saw curly chestnut hair, a handsome mouth, and straight nose. "Enough of this talk, Burke. You let my man slip through your fingers last night, you ignored my orders to raise a general alarm. When my father hears how this affair has been mishandled—"

"Maybe he will keep you home where you belong," Burke muttered, so low only Nathan heard. Two of the other men began to grumble also, calling for bed and supper and a fresh start in the morning, while the one remaining, a small, sniveling creature, whined at them to shut up or forgo their reward.

"You can see my associates are travel-weary," said Burke to Nathan through clenched teeth. "We would be obliged if you could guide us to our destination."

"But my route lies in the opposite direction." Nathan shrugged apologetically, but his nerves had begun to tighten. He was bone-cold and tired, and his mind urged the party to ride eastward on the false heading he had provided while he covered the last mile westward to warn Garrett and Lucretia of the slave hunters' presence. Then at last he could gallop home to Mary, to a hot supper and a soft bed. He stroked Jake, whose labored breathing attested to the stallion's need for rest.

"Surely you would not wish a party of gentlemen travelers to wander astray in the dark?" said Burke. "What business might you be on yourself, alone at this hour?" Suspicion edged his voice, and Nathan's hopes sank. But before he could muster a reply, the haughty youth spurred his horse between them.

"Enough, Burke! You have mismanaged this job from the start. I shall take charge now, and matters will move more quickly." He drew a pistol from his belt and aimed it at Nathan's chest.

"Damn it, Pendleton, put that away!" Burke commanded. "There are better ways to—"

A shot blasted between the front legs of Burke's horse. The animal reared, men shouted, and in the confusion, Nathan dug his heels into Jake's side and tried to wheel away. But before his numb hands could control the reins, they were ripped from his grasp.

"Going somewhere?" Pendleton pointed his pistol squarely at Nathan's chest. "I think not. Now, Burke, you call yourself a professional, but I will show you how this affair ought to proceed." He called over his shoulder to the other men, ignoring Burke's growls of protest. "Anyone who expects a slice of my father's reward will obey me, is that clear?" A disgruntled mumble replied. Pendleton poked his gun against Nathan's heart and tossed back the reins. "To the Jasper's farm, sir, smartly, if you please."

Silently, Nathan turned Jake eastward.

Three

Trapped. Mary was trapped. She must escape and find Nathan. She would sneak to the barn, saddle a horse—

"Now, you must always wash the diapers in hot water and lye soap. Do not dream of feeding porridge until the infant is at least three months old. Avoid onions, cabbage, and beans while nursing so the little one will not suffer from gas. And chop those carrots smaller before you put them in the stew!"

"Yes, Mother Kingsley. No, Mother Kingsley. Yes, Mother Kingsley," Mary replied, though her jaw clenched with the effort of maintaining a smile.

She had arrived at her in-laws' out of breath and with a painful stitch in her side from running, only to learn from Martha that Nathan and Elijah as well were gone to search for escaped slaves. Escaped slaves? Here? But how? Why? Were they dangerous? Were they armed? To which her mother-in-law responded with a few bare details and a firm admonition not to upset the younger children by further questions. "Now, as long as you are here, you may make yourself useful," Martha had decreed, handing her a basket of darning. Pressing the stitch in her side, Mary sat down and obeyed. Better to stay a while and rest than risk hurting the baby. Besides, Nathan would probably stop here with Elijah on his way home. But as the afternoon wore on and neither Nathan nor Lij reappeared, Mary's fears returned.

"I will ride to the Jaspers' and ask for news," she offered, a mistake, she saw at once by the look on Martha's face.

"Nonsense! You will only put yourself in the way," Martha scoffed. Then she set Mary to more work, sweeping the floor and carrying broth to Father Kingsley, still recuperating from his illness in an upstairs bedroom. Mary shrank from encounters with her father-in-law, whose bristling gray eyebrows and beard made him look like a raging windstorm, though in fact he had never treated her unkindly. He simply ignored her, except to mutter now and then that she had "too many curls." So Mary delivered the soup as politely and quickly as possible and hurried back downstairs. As for her mother-in-law, perhaps Martha meant well by keeping her occupied, but the truth, Mary suspected, was that any sight of idleness was an affront to her Yankee soul.

Meanwhile, the five younger Kingsley children shrieked and bounded through the rooms in an endless series of squabbles and games, fighting over toys, clattering dominoes on the floor, singing nursery rhymes. Every so often, Father Kingsley's bellow would reverberate from upstairs, "Quiet, you lot! A man can't rest!" The children would hush and squirm, then gradually the volume would climb again. How, Mary wondered, amidst this unremitting pandemonium, had Nathan grown up so calm? It only made her more jumpy, and she started at every creak of the door and imagined the crack of a gunshot when a dead limb snapped in a tree. Now that it was dark, even her vision played her tricks. Only a few minutes ago, glancing toward the kitchen window, she had gasped to see a pair of faceless eyes staring in at her. By the time she blinked, the apparition was gone, and calming her pounding heart she went on chopping the carrots. At least Mother Kingsley had not caught her in such a foolish moment.

"I will see to the baby," she offered, as yet another wail came from the living room. There she found two-year-old Maria in tears as four-year-old Abby tried to tug away her doll. Mary pulled the baby onto her lap and caressed her silky blond hair. Now, how to get away and where to go? Was it too late to trudge in the dark to the Jaspers'? Perhaps she should try the Millard's house, which was closer, for Martha had mentioned that Samuel Millard was among the searchers and his wife Lucinda might know more. Should she slip out the front door while Martha was occupied or stand up to her mother-in-law and declare, "I am going to find my husband!" She had just nerved herself for the latter course and was on her feet when the back door slammed and in through the kitchen tromped Elijah.

"Lij!" His name leaped gladly from Mary's lips.

"Home is the hunter, the seeker, the prodigal son," Elijah proclaimed. He laughed heartily, and Abby and seven-year-old Lucy Ann ran squealing to meet him and threw their arms around his legs.

"Play with us, Lij! Play!" they cried.

He pried them loose from his limbs. "I think you are two little cock-leburs to snag me so tightly," he teased. "Ah, it is good to be home. I am exhausted." He slumped into an armchair, dangled his elbows over its sides, and stretched his legs out before him.

"Where is Nathan? Is he all right?" Mary demanded.

"He is on his way. But what are you doing here, Mary? Your husband is expecting to find you at home. I had better escort you. Pull me up quickly, or I shall never rise from this chair!"

He held out his hands, and with a laugh she pulled him upright while he groaned about his aches and pains. From the corner of her eye, Mary caught the disapproving look on Martha's face. No doubt Martha thought a young married woman should display more decorum, but Mary was too glad at having the worrisome afternoon end to care much for her mother-in-law's proprieties.

"Did you find what you sought?" Martha asked coolly.

"No luck," Elijah replied. "Nathan has ridden back to the Jaspers' to see how the rest of our search party fared. Come, Mary, don your cloak while I fetch a lantern to light our way."

He steered her toward the door, the little girls shrieking after him to stay. He fended them off, until at last he and Mary escaped into the cold night.

"Thank heaven," she breathed.

Elijah laughed. "It was bedlam as usual, then?"

"A madhouse! How is it you are not all deaf from the din? And I always feel your parents disapprove of me. They think I am frivolous."

"Exactly their opinion of me. You are therefore in excellent company."

He bowed and offered his arm, and Mary accepted with a touch of pleasure. When she first met the two brothers, she had flattered herself that Elijah was in love with her, and she had weighed him against Nathan in her mind. Most women would say Nathan was handsomer, clean-featured and sharp-eyed, where Elijah resembled a second imprint from the same press, a shade softer and less distinct. But Lij was dashing, quick-witted, ready to take chances his elder brother would shun as unwise. It was always Elijah, Nathan had told her, who returned from their boyhood expeditions bloody-kneed and black-eyed, while Nathan endured a scolding for not restraining his brother's impetuosity. In the same way, Elijah was careless toward love, flirting with every woman from fifteen to thirty-five. He made all the girls feel pretty and the matrons feel young again, and although one could not help falling a little in love with Lij in return, it was a fancy and nothing more. Elijah was a bold adventure tale, Nathan a quiet volume of hidden pages, and Mary's heart had chosen the deeper reading. As they crossed the snow, her brother-in-law regaled her with the story of the slave girl at the Jaspers' and the fruitless excursion through the woods. To hear him tell it, he had been the hero of the day, rallying the doubters to join the search, laying out the course along the river. Later, when Nathan returned and she pried loose his version, it would sound very different, and her husband would take no credit at all.

Elijah opened the back door with a sweep of his hand. "Now to prove my usefulness, I will come in and help you fill the lamps."

"Thank you, Lij. I should never have left the house in such haste, everything untended."

He set the lantern on the kitchen table, and they set about lighting the lamps and rekindling the fire in the stove. As the room began to warm, Mary breathed a deep sigh, and only now did she feel her shoulders truly ease and her mind relax. *My house. My husband. Our child.* She smoothed her hand over her belly, although only a slight roundness showed, then stopped as she saw Elijah register the motion. His flippant mood slipped away, and he drew his finger in a careful line across the table.

"So, Mary, my brother makes you happy?"

"Yes." She paused. It was not quite true. There were times Nathan made her unhappy, because he guarded his feelings and she did not always understand him, because nothing ever turned out as perfectly as you dreamed. But how could she not feel lucky and optimistic when life had so favored her with blessings? She glanced over her house, symbol of all that was safe and good. "I know you think a home and marriage are dull, Elijah, but what else could happiness mean?"

He shrugged. "When I find it, I will tell you. I only know it is not here, not for me. Cook a good supper, Mary. Your husband will be hungry."

He lifted the lantern and nodded a goodnight. Mary waited until his footsteps disappeared, then she turned to the stove. All was as she had left it, the beef and potatoes waiting to go in the oven, the cornbread, long grown cold, sitting in its pan. She regretted the chunks she had dropped in the snow. She did not remember having cut such large pieces, but the bread was half gone. The poetry book still lay on the table, and she had been heading to the cellar to fetch apples. . . . Mary took one of the lamps and a small basket and cautiously descended the steep cellar stairs. Chill and darkness enclosed her, and the glow from the lamp penetrated only a few feet ahead. Mary patted her way past the brick chimney and across the uneven stone floor, ducking under the rough-hewn ceiling beams. The cellar was one large space except for the northeast corner where Nathan had built a small storage room. Inside was their stock of apples, potatoes, carrots, onions, turnips, and pumpkins to last through the winter. Mary pushed open the door.

In the brief instant before the man loomed out of the shadows, she saw the whites of his eyes like milky marbles in a midnight face. Then the lamp flew from her hand and crashed out, and she screamed as powerful arms closed around her in the blackness. A thick voice moaned in her ear, "No, missus, no," but she kicked and shrieked until the arms crushed her to an unseen body and the breath gasped from her rib cage. Her head knocked against the doorway as the man dragged her out of the fruit cellar and across the floor. In her faintness Mary felt her toes tripping over the uneven stones, and her mind grasped at an image of a stumbling monster from her old book of fairy tales. "No, missus, no," the voice kept groaning, as if it were desperately unhappy at the havoc it wreaked. Mary twisted and pried at the imprisoning arms, but the power of speech had left her. As the man lumbered with her up the stairs, she put out her hands to feel the steps and to keep from being dropped and crushed beneath him. By the time they spilled into the kitchen, Mary on her knees, the shape crumpling over her yet struggling to hold them both upright, she had lost the will to fight.

But at the same time she sensed no further struggle was necessary. The man had released his crushing grip and now seemed only to be trying to protect her from more harm. She heard him panting in her ear, and when she crawled away, he let her go and stayed unmoving behind her. She groped a few feet more to the kitchen table and pulled herself upright. A second lamp still burned on the table, and holding it aloft, Mary turned to face her assailant.

What she saw was a woolly-headed figure in a dirty coat, bowed to the floor as if praying, a hunched shape defined by ill-fitting clothes. Broad shoulders had split the seam of the jacket, and bare wrists extended from the cuffs. A pair of dark, large-knuckled hands was clasped before his head. From the unseen mouth came the same agonized murmur, "Please, missus, no, missus, I never had no thought to scare you."

"Scare me?" Mary's fear revived, then flushed into anger. "You hurt me! You might have hurt my baby!" Tears wet her eyes as she pressed her hand to her bruised ribs and her mind relived those few terrifying moments. "Who are you? What are you doing here? Oh, go away! Go away!" She kicked at him, though she was not near enough for her feet to touch him, and he cringed, though with his head still bowed he could not have seen the gesture. A last shudder rolled over Mary, and she inhaled several slow, deep breaths. She knew who he was now, of course—one of the escaped slaves Nathan and Elijah had been seeking. She felt only scant comfort in the knowledge. Having sat through Reverend Swift's abolitionist preachings, Mary had pitied the oppressed in her heart. But now here was just such a being in her kitchen, and she had no idea what to do about it. The man said he would not hurt her, but intentionally or not, he already had. Thank heaven Nathan was on his way, would be here any minute. Mary took courage at the thought. She had only to protect the baby and herself until he arrived. The Negro still had not raised his eyes from the floor, and Mary tried to put authority into her voice.

"Who are you? Why did you grab me?"

"I didn't know it be you, missus. I heard footsteps, and I feared them slave hunters comin'."

"Why did you trespass in my house?"

"I didn't know where else to go. When I peeked in your window, it didn't seem like anybody home."

"Well, you should not have come in. You had no right to enter my house unbidden. Stop crouching there. Stand up and face me."

She had spoken rashly, and instantly she regretted it. As the slave rose onto one knee and slowly straightened, he grew bigger and taller than she had guessed, and his face held none of the obeisance and docility his voice had led her to believe. Anger and pride smoldered in his eyes, and Mary felt herself shrink at the advantage his size alone gave him. How did anyone dare keep a slave? How could you ever feel safe owning a being who must hate you? Yet he could have killed her there in the cellar, she reminded herself, twisted her neck, plundered the house, and stolen away. That he had not done so renewed her courage.

"You ate my cornbread. You must be hungry. You must be starving." Her mind pulled together Elijah's story, and she began to grasp what must be done. She gestured to the kitchen table. "Sit down. I will feed you. I will not hurt you," she said, though the statement was ludicrous, for of course he was in a far better position to hurt her. Yet the assurance seemed to level the ground between them, and Mary felt a little of the tension dissipate.

"Thank you, missus."

The slave glanced toward the doors, then sat hesitantly at the table. While Mary heated water and made coffee, his eyes kept up an anxious surveillance and his ears pricked at tiny sounds in the house. Mary cut a wedge from a fat orange cheese and another chunk of cornbread. She put the food on a plate, set it before him, and sat in the chair opposite. His pupils widened gratefully at the golden feast, and he looked one more time around the kitchen, as if questioning that no one else would appear.

"I am alone," Mary said, "though my husband will return shortly. He is a good man and will know what to do. Go on, eat."

Slowly, the slave reached toward the plate. When his fingers touched the food, he hurried it to his mouth. He had no manners, clutching the cheese and bread in both hands, gulping the hot coffee though it must have burned his throat, never lifting his eyes from the plate. Instead of slowing after the first few bites, he ate more ravenously, as if the hunger he had suppressed all night had suddenly been released, as if he feared the food might run out before he had swallowed his fill. Mary pushed more cheese and cornbread toward him until all of it was gone.

"Now," she said softly. "Tell me who you are."

Four

For Nathan, a gun at his back, everything had become very clear. He could not lead the slave catchers to the Jasper's farm where the Negro girl was sheltered. He could not divert them to the Millards' or Pecks' or to any other of the nearby homes where wives and children might be endangered. The same thought for his mother and sisters eliminated his parents' house, though he might have counted on help from his father and Elijah. Last, but most surely, he could not allow them to come anywhere near Mary.

"I say we find an inn and stop for the night," grumbled one of the party, a snub-nosed, red-bearded fellow. He pulled a metal flask from his coat pocket, unscrewed the cap, and tipped it to his mouth.

"Giving up already?" sneered the little man, the one who had spoken earlier of pursuing the reward. He had a scruffy look, as if he had rubbed shoulders with all the wrong company, and he sidled his horse closer to Pendleton and Burke, insinuating himself into their circle. "This is no skylarking expedition, and you knew it, Reynolds. Next time stay home with the women."

"Snipes, you miserable toady—" Reynolds began.

The explosion of a gunshot into the air sent Nathan's heart thudding against his ribs, and he clutched Jake's reins just in time to prevent the stallion from bolting. If they had been nearer the woods, he might have made a break for it, but here on open ground his line of flight was too exposed.

"And I say you all be quiet!" Pendleton leveled his pistol at Reynolds. "Put away the whiskey, you fool. Do you think you will be any use to us drunk?"

For answer, Reynolds tipped the bottle to his mouth and swallowed noisily. Satisfied, he stowed the flask in his pocket.

"Now move on," Pendleton ordered. He trotted his horse, a fine bay stallion, alongside Jake and glanced backward in distaste. "Tavern scum," he confided to Nathan. "We picked them out of their cups some twenty miles south when it seemed we had our prey within our grasp. I was all for bringing a full hunting party from the plantation, but Burke, who is a professional, decreed we would travel faster unencumbered and recruit our posse along the way."

Sarcasm tinted his voice, and Nathan cast a sideways look at the tall hunter. Since the young slave owner had taken charge, Burke had maintained silence, but his eye glinted and his lips pulled tight across his teeth in a suppressed snarl. He seemed to be awaiting an opportunity to resume command, and Nathan's instincts told him to remain neutral for the time being. The men reminded him of a pack of dogs snapping at each other's flanks, bound together by mutual need but each coveting the chance to move up in the pack.

"Take us to this Jasper's place," Pendleton whispered in Nathan's ear, "and if we recover my property there, you shall share in the reward. A slice of five hundred dollars, how does that sound?"

"Fine," Nathan agreed. "But you have not said exactly what it is you seek."

"Why, a nigger, a runaway nigger, a prize field hand that my family has fed, clothed, and housed since the day he was born. Rest assured, sir, I mean to have that ungrateful devil back and flay him to the bone. Not only is he a runaway but a thief."

Pendleton gestured with his pistol, and Nathan glanced to his own shotgun, stowed in the saddle holster. There was scant hope of pulling it out and using it to any effect against the five.

"Well, as I say, I do not know Jasper personally," he apologized. "I should be sorry to take you on a wrong turn. An inn tonight and an early morning start might serve you better."

"No!" Vehemently, Pendleton shook his head. "Night is the very time these fugitives travel, station to station on their damned Underground Railroad. The closer they get to Detroit, the less my chances of securing my man. I can see you are unfamiliar with these matters, sir. Let me enlighten you."

Gravely and earnestly, Pendleton began to explain the proper procedure for pursuit and capture of Negroes, when to employ federal marshals, how to word the advertisement of reward, when to unleash hounds. Nathan tried not to listen, yet he knew he should pay heed in case Pendleton dropped some remark he could use to extricate himself.

"Once this past summer," Pendleton continued, "Burke here did prove his worth. He used to be a frontier scout, you see, tracking Indians for the Army, and the cunning of those savages far surpasses the dim understanding of the blacks. So when Mother's mulatto girl ran off, Burke overtook her before she had covered ten miles. We had her stripped and beaten, and the other slaves were summoned to look on. If Father had been home, he would have stopped it—he's gone to rum and sentimentality in his old age—but the whip is the only way the niggers learn. It is a pity God made them with any brains at all, since they have no cause to think."

He threw up his hands in chagrin at the Creator's practical joke, and the little man Snipes guffawed close behind. Nathan managed to say nothing, alternately tucking one hand, then the other, under the opposite armpit to warm them.

"Burke, give my friend here your gloves," Pendleton ordered. "He will ride faster with warm fingers."

Burke started to protest, and Nathan almost uttered his own denial. Burke's gloves were leather, thickly lined in soft fur, but much as Nathan's hands ached with cold, there was something repulsive to him about slipping the slave hunter's gloves over his fingers. Yet he dared not refuse. In the last half hour Pendleton had gone from pointing a gun at his chest to adopting him as an ally and confidant, though he still waved his revolver for emphasis as he spoke. Burke also apparently deemed it best to humor the young slave owner. He pulled off his gloves and passed them over, but his face kept its shrewd look. Nathan scanned the empty darkness ahead. He had continued to lead them parallel to the woods, avoiding all the homesteads he knew of, but still no plan had come to him how to end this charade safely, and as his weariness increased, his mind grew only more blank.

"How is it you injured your hand, by the way?" Pendleton inquired as Nathan slipped on the gloves.

"Planing a cradle," he replied without thinking. He had not meant to give any hint of Mary, but the answer only set Pendleton off on a discourse about his fiancée and his imminent inheritance of his father's tobacco plantation. His lady, he said, was a rose of delicate color and many accomplishments, and he spent some minutes in praise of her virtues. Then he turned to the subject of farming.

"We are too heavily committed to tobacco," he informed Nathan, "and when the auction prices are low so is my income. It is my intention to diversify. Hemp is well suited to our Kentucky climate, and the market for whiskey grains increases every year. With new equipment and modern production methods I could realize a profitable yield per acre. Tell me, sir, how is the soil in these parts?"

"A little sandy, but good enough." Nathan shook his head to clear his ears. Pendleton had begun to sound much like any other ambitious young farmer. He had begun to sound like Nathan himself. *If I had been born in Kentucky, would I be him?* Nathan wondered. The thought disturbed him, but he could not shake it, and as Pendleton talked on engagingly of the latest agricultural advances and his hopes for his family, Nathan found himself responding in kind. By an effort of will, he recalled what separated them.

"Your plantation sounds large and prosperous," he ventured. "With fifty slaves, will you really miss one Negro, especially a thief and troublemaker such as you describe? Perhaps you are well rid of him."

"If he were aged and used up," Pendleton shrugged, "I would agree. In fact, it is smart business to set them free and turn them out when they grow old. It saves the cost of clothing and feeding them when no more work is forthcoming. But this runaway is a thirty-year-old male in prime condition, worth sixteen hundred dollars on the auction block. Would you let your money walk away? No, sir! Besides, it is the insubordination I cannot tolerate. Let one escape and the others may take it into their thick skulls to follow. Why, do you know how hard it is to make those niggers do an honest day's work? Turn your back one minute and they lean on their hoes. Teach them a dozen times to black your boots or saddle your horse, and still they cannot get it right. If your Northern abolitionists knew the true worthlessness of the blacks, they would thank us for taking on the burden of providing for them."

Nathan did not reply. They had been heading northeast, and in another mile they would reach a broad arm of the forest. There, among the trees, he might spur Jake to an escape. He peered ahead, hoping to discern on the horizon the darker shapes that signaled the outer edge of trees.

"I quit!"

Nathan turned. Reynolds had reined in his horse and was holding his whiskey flask upside down to show the last drops trickling out. "My belly is empty, my feet are froze, and we ain't seen a cent of money for fightin' them niggers last night."

"Because you let mine get away!" Pendleton swung his horse around, brandishing his gun. "There will be no reward to anyone until my man is in chains."

"But we got the ma and the baby," protested the fifth man, a slouching character, silent until now. He brought his horse beside Reynolds, the two of them forming a sullen pair. Nathan could feel the pack splitting, the dogs arching the fur on their backs. He nudged Jake a step backward.

"Then let their owner pay you when he comes to collect them from jail." Pendleton gritted his teeth. "Now shut up and move!"

Reynolds and his ally stood their ground, muttering but unwilling to turn tail with Pendleton's gun cocked. Burke had moved silently into place on the young slave owner's left, and Nathan tried to anticipate the hunter's next move. On the fringe of the confrontation, Snipes shifted in his saddle, his weaselly face darting glances side to side, judging where his best advantage lay. Nathan backed Jake another step.

"Drop it!" ordered Burke suddenly, and in one swift movement he snatched Pendleton's gun. Shouting curses, Pendleton lunged to recover it. The moment was all Nathan needed. As the two men grappled for the weapon, he dug his heels into Jake's flanks and whirled the stallion away. Over his shoulder he saw Reynolds and his partner fleeing in the opposite direction while Snipes's horse pranced fretfully against the reins. More cries and shouting rose in the dark, but Nathan bent low in the saddle and prayed for speed. All the tension of the last hour, fear he had not let himself feel, released and flowed off him, and the rush of night air on his face revived every longing for Mary and home. Then a gun fired, and a pain hit his lower back. In an instant, it bloomed from a small hard sensation to a fire that burned up his spine and collapsed him against Jake's neck. His head dropped forward, and numbness radiated down his arms. As the reins fell from his hands, he squeezed his thighs tightly against the saddle in a last effort to stay on. Jake slowed. In the darkness overtaking him, Nathan heard horses galloping closer.

"I got him! I got him!" shrilled a high little voice. "Now for my reward!"

"Snipes, you idiot! He was leading us to my property! If you have killed him, your reward is gone! And you, Burke, when my father hears how—"

"Our friend is not dead." Burke's voice brushed close to Nathan's ear, and though Nathan could not lift his head, he managed to focus on the slave hunter's face. He made out the stubbled jaw and glinting eyes star-

ing at him, but his vision was growing glassy and the weight of his eyelids brought them down. His hands jerked as the gloves were stripped
from his fingers. For a last time, before he slipped into unconsciousness,
Nathan heard the slave catcher's voice.

"Let Reynolds and his friend go. We are better off without them. But
this one knows more than he has told us, and dead or alive, he can still
be of some use. Planing a cradle, isn't that what he said? Tie his hands
beneath the horse's neck, then give the animal its head. Somewhere
nearby a tender wife is waiting, and I never knew a trusty horse that
could not find its way home."

Five

Now tell me who you are.

The black man seated at Mary Kingsley's kitchen table looked at her in mute apology. A name was all she wanted. She would think him stupid or untrustworthy or both if he did not reply. Yet she had no idea how difficult her question was to answer. A month ago he had been a slave with a slave's name bestowed by his master. When he reached the land of Canada, he would be a free man able to call himself whatever he pleased. But for the past four weeks he had been neither, a shadow on the run. "We call thee 'freight,' " said the kind man in Cincinnati who had first set him on this Underground Railroad. Another woman who had sheltered the party of escapees referred to her fugitive guests as "packages." "Do not give us your name," several others cautioned along the way. So he had become nameless, his identity a puzzle to himself. And where was he? He had no sure grasp of how far he had traveled or which towns marked their route. Hidden by day, spirited to the next station in the blackness of night, perhaps he was a dead man walking, as in the stories old Mammy Wata had told when he was a child. But the white woman required an answer, and he needed her help, so he licked his lips and plucked a name from the air.

"Robert," he said. "Robert Rivers." The instant the surname left his mouth he felt satisfaction and a tiny jolt of surprise. *Rivers.* First he had rowed across the Ohio River to make his escape. Then last night he had traversed a smaller, frozen river in the woods to elude his pursuers and come safely to this house. Now only one more river, in Detroit, so he had been told, separated him from the promised land. Somehow, without exactly pondering it, his brain had picked the one word that symbolized the story of his flight. Robert smiled, satisfied. Denied schooling, laboring in the field most of his thirty years, he had had few opportunities to use his head. But these past few weeks on the run, he had several times been startled by the way his mind leaped and danced ahead of him, making connections all by itself, almost as if it had got free as well.

The white woman made a small curve of her lips, returning his smile. She was soft and pretty, and he was deeply sorry he had hurt her. Already a red welt had raised on her forehead, and one of the jet buttons on her purple dress had been torn off in their struggle; he would be in trouble when she noticed. He remembered now he had seen her in the previous house into whose kitchen window he had peeked. But there had been too many people in that dwelling for him to dare knock, too many to fight off if they chose to restrain him. This house, unlit and deserted, had seemed the answer to his need. He had been in the kitchen, gobbling cornbread, when the sound of voices approaching from outside sent him bolting down the cellar stairs. When the steps pursued him there, he had panicked and attacked, then not known how to extricate himself when he discovered to his shame the feel of a woman in his arms.

"I am Mary Kingsley," she said.

"Yes, missus."

They paused, and Robert considered. The woman's willing exchange of names meant she was probably not one of those who called themselves conductors nor was her home one of the Underground Railroad stations. Perhaps that was good. It might throw the slave catchers off his track. If only she would let him stay here a few hours to recover. He would offer to sleep in the barn, leave at midnight if they would point the direction to Detroit. He could walk the rest of the way.

"I know a little about you," the woman said. "My husband and his brother were searching for you in the woods. Searching to help you, I mean," she added hastily as Robert started up. He sat again, slowly, while the woman eyed him anxiously. She looked as if she wanted to help, yet he saw the flash of fear that for an instant had blanched her face.

"My brother-in-law says you came from Kentucky." Her fingers smoothed the hollow of her throat, as if to steady her voice.

"That's right, missus."

"I suppose you ran away because you were treated badly?"

"Yes'm."

It was not exactly true. By the standards of what many slaves endured, his lot had not been unbearable. He had had a peck of corn plus a small ration of salt pork and molasses every week, three coarse shirts, and a pair of shoes each year. Only three other men shared his one-room log shack, and they had contrived mattresses of rags and corn shucks to lie above the dirt floor. Robert had never been sold and had been beaten only twice when the overseer was in a foul mood. In fact, he had been all but forgotten, a silent, seemingly obedient field hand, a bent back among the rest hunched over the rows of tobacco plants. But it was that very emptiness, the anonymity of his life, that he wished he could express. Robert rubbed his coarse knuckles. He had never spoken much to any white person before, and the past few weeks among them had made him painfully conscious of his backwardness. He wanted to sound smart, wear fancy clothes, live in a fine house such as this one. He gazed around the kitchen. A sturdy wood-burning stove to sit by all evening and be warm. A pantry stocked with good things to eat. Cupboards and drawers full of china dishes and metal spoons. It was not half as grand as the big house on the plantation he had left, yet surely it had everything a man wanted. Compared to his low hut in the lice-infested slave quarters, it was a palace.

"Was it your family who escaped with you? Elijah said a young girl from your party made it to the Jasper's farm."

"No, missus. We ain't related. Them others already in Ohio when I come, so the Quaker man say we be one package goin' north."

Robert's tongue felt looser, but the words still echoed clumsily to his ears. He dipped his hand into his pocket and fingered the pearl necklace that lay curled at the bottom, like a riverbed of cool stones. When he got to Canada, he planned to forget he had ever been a slave. Maybe if he told his past to the white woman, here and now, it would stay behind in this house and not follow him to his new life. Then he would truly be free.

"Ain't got no family, missus. My mama died when I was born. Mammy Wata raised me up, got me fed."

He did not try to describe old Mammy Wata, though the shriveled, toothless woman, dead these twenty years, came clearly to mind. Mammy Wata had been born in Africa and had come on a slave ship long ago, captured and sold to white traders during a war between tribes. She could read the rings around the moon, and she knew which herbs made a man go speechless and a barren woman conceive. At night, she cast bones by her fire and told the slaves' fates. Some of the other slaves declared she was crazy, and it was whispered she had poisoned two of her children when a former master tried to sell them away. Too ancient for field work, Mammy Wata minded the youngest children while their parents toiled, feeding them scraps from her cook pot and spinning them stories from the deep caverns in her mind. She said the white God was powerful but evil, and the African gods could not cross the great water to defeat him. Sometimes she let Robert curl up in the crook of her arm, where he fell asleep, dreaming.

"What sort of work were you made to do?" Mary Kingsley asked, and he blinked back to the present.

"Plowin', plantin', splittin' fence rails, pickin' crops. Last few months, they let me work some in the blacksmith shop."

The woman nodded at the common-sounding tasks. Young and strong, Robert had not found the labor hard. Except that it did not stop. Every year, every month, every day, every hour dissolved into minutes that were all the same. Even when the seasons and chores changed, the work went on all day under the sun, at night when the moon was full. So like the other slaves, Robert learned to steal the minutes back. If he walked a little more slowly to get his noontime drink of water, that was one minute of his own. If he feigned a cramp in his leg that needed to be rubbed out, there were two minutes he had claimed for himself. If he hit the plow against a rock and broke the blade, there was an hour he must trudge to the blacksmith shop to have it repaired. And all around him, all the black people silently did the same, while Young Master Pendleton fumed to the overseer that they were the slowest, laziest creatures on earth. Yet even at the end of a day when he had filched more minutes than he had dared to hope, what did he have in his hands? Nothing. He had minutes of nothing that mocked him with their emptiness.

"Reverend Swift says slave families have no protection," said Mary Kingsley. "They may be sold apart on the auction block, never to see each other again."

She rose, visibly upset by the idea, and began to pace, arms pressed against her belly. Robert nodded. He had never witnessed such a scene himself, but he had heard of it and many stories more. Of the slave girl who drowned herself when her little boy was sold away. Of the handsome young women sold to the brothel trade. Of the gray-headed old folks, hair blackened with soot, who were made to jump and dance for buyers to prove they were still fit. Other stories Robert knew firsthand, like the way Jim, a rebellious field hand, got his shred of ear: A former master had him nailed to a tree by its flesh and ordered him whipped until his writhings tore him free. He knew, too, who had fathered many of the mulatto children on their plantation and that Old Master Pendleton was drinking heavily and moaning in his sleep of repentance.

"I think you were very brave to run away." The white woman walked to the window, her hands twisted in a knot. "I am not brave at all. I wish my husband would come. He should have been here by now."

They fell silent. Robert felt in his pocket, and the smooth roundness of the pearls rebuked his rough fingers. Looking at the soft curve of Mary Kingsley's back, he knew he had satisfied her questions, but he had not told the full story. Brave? It was because of him the others had been pursued and attacked. He had heard the hoofbeats gaining on their wagon, recognized in dismay Young Master's voice crying, "Halt!" Then his brain had leaped ahead—this time in a way that did not make him proud—and the next instant his body followed, jumping from the wagon and rolling down a gully to flee. Behind him rose the furious cries of the two brothers, "Stay! Help us fight!" But Robert had run, crashed away through a thicket, raced across a field. He ran and ran, and by the time his terror and his legs were spent, all was quiet and he was lost.

He searched for the North Star, the slave's beacon, and began to trudge northward. The star's steady light reminded him it was Christmas Eve when he had run away. He had not expected much from the holiday, though the white preacher who came monthly at Old Master's request had that very Sunday exhorted them to share in the joy of the season. At least it was a change from his usual sermon, "Servants, Obey Your Masters," and standing in the chilly December morning, Robert and his fellow slaves cried their "amens." When the preacher left, Robert spat on the ground as Mammy Wata had taught him. But at least Christmas meant a day off from the fields, and it was rumored Old Master would give a dollar to everyone who had served him well that year. Robert had heard of some masters who hired out their slaves and let them keep a portion of their earnings, and by diligent saving they had eventually bought their freedom. But Robert had always been kept to work in the field, and at a dollar a year for Christmas, he would be dead long before he was free. As for running away, twice that he could recall, slaves had vanished from their plantation and news drifted back that they had reached a place called Canada. But how did you get there? How did you live? All he knew was field work, and the overseer said it was so cold in the North that few crops grew and the niggers froze in the ice. Some Northerners, said the overseer, boiled black people alive and ate them.

And what if he didn't make it? He remembered all too well the recapture of Mistress's mulatto girl Sally. They stripped her naked, even her private parts, and tied her wrists to a stake. She managed to bite back her cries for the first three lashes, so the overseer laid on harder until the screaming broke from her throat. It did not stop for what seemed hours as Sally writhed at the base of the post and huddled there trying to cover what parts of her body she could. Young Master ordered two of the men to pull out her legs so she lay spread facedown in the dust. As more blows ripped open her thighs and buttocks, the screaming stopped and Sally began to bite great mouthfuls of dirt. She buried her face in the earth, chomping, and Robert understood that she was trying to choke herself. When the overseer kicked her in the head to make her stop, her eyes closed and she moved no more. Young Master and the other white men walked away, and the slaves gathered around Sally's bleeding body. Some said let her finish dying, but she still breathed so they untied her and carried her to her hut where an old woman bathed her wounds. Old Master was away when it happened, and when he returned, the slaves in the big house said he threatened to lash his son. But instead he drank himself a bottle of rum and groaned that his end was near. Lately, the house slaves had heard Old Master declare he would free all his slaves on his deathbed, but though Robert knew cases of a few favorite Negroes being set free on such an occasion, more often it was a ploy to keep black folks docile, hopelessly waiting for an event that would never come. Sally's body healed, but her mind had gone out like a light. As for Young Master, he never seemed to realize that mulatto girl was halfway his sister.

Robert's fingers closed around the pearls. Sally's beating had revived talk in the slave quarters about running away. Follow the North Star. Go to the Quakers who help the blacks. Steal everything you can from Master before you leave. But none went. Once when he was a child, crazy old Mammy Wata had whispered to him the secret of escape. "You git li'l bird in your heart. He put wings on your back." For a week afterward, Robert had earnestly studied every sparrow and robin that hopped by, wondering how to entice them to enter his chest. Sometimes, even after he was grown, he would awaken before sunrise to the birds' chatter and try to imagine what it felt like to fly.

But he did not go. Besides, soon after Sally's beating, his own lot had improved, because Zeke the blacksmith broke his arm and Robert was detailed to help him. Now Zeke was teaching him the blacksmith trade, and Robert found he was good at metal work. That was how, on Christmas Eve, he had come to be in the big house for the first time in his life. Old Master had given Zeke a pass to visit his wife on a neighboring plantation, and in his absence, Robert was called to fix a fireplace damper in the bedroom of Young Mistress. Led into the main hall by Nell, the senior house servant, he gaped at the warmth and luminescence that surrounded him. Glowing lights, polished floors, golden yellow paper on the walls—he felt as if he had stepped into the center of the sun. Nell said the Pendleton house was not the largest in their part of Kentucky, but to his eyes it was immeasurably grand. From a glittering room ahead floated laughter and music, and through the open doors he glimpsed a rainbow swirl of ladies' gowns. A Christmas ball, Nell explained, as she led him up the stairs.

She took him to a bedroom spun of sugar, and he stared at the bed, a strange thing with a frilly canopy stretched over four tall poles. Dainty, feminine items decorated the room, and on a mirrored table, china boxes and crystal bottles sat on a silver tray. Nell pointed him to the fireplace and tapped her foot while he wedged himself to look up the chimney. The problem was simple—the damper had jumped its socket—but Nell grew impatient while he grunted and tried to shove it back in place. Worried that the kitchen slaves would not serve the ball guests properly, she hurried away, muttering that Jenny would come watch him. No sooner had she left than the damper popped into place, and Robert backed out of the chimney, covered in soot. He looked again around the beautiful room. Maybe this was what heaven was like. He felt a powerful urge to touch things and make sure they were real. He wiped his hands on his pants. Young Mistress, who was sixteen, had left several dresses lying across a chair, and Robert's fingers stroked rose silk, green satin, pink velvet ribbons and bows.

On the dressing table, his eye caught the carelessly draped strand of pearls. He caressed the pale moonlike shapes, and he wondered, half shocked at the thought, if this was how a white woman felt, how Young Mistress might feel if he touched her. Smooth and round, no sharp joints, no broken teeth or cracked fingernails. Plump and full, no bones poking through thin flesh. Lustrous milky skin that smelled of bath oils and scents, not a dirty, whip-scarred back. Robert knew of slaves who were white enough to pass, and he thought of Sally, the mulatto girl. Had her white half felt the pain alongside the black? If just one drop of Negro blood made you black, why couldn't all that whiteness make you white?

He put the pearls in his pocket, not knowing exactly why. He had never stolen anything in his life before, except for all those minutes of empty time. But the instant the necklace was in his pocket he knew a fatal act had been done. His heart pounded as if a bird had dived into it, and he could almost feel his back sprout wings. He could still pull out the necklace, replace it on the table, for Jenny had not yet come. But he did not want to, he clung to it in stubborn joy. Then Jenny arrived and shooed him away, and he hurried back to his hut, pocketed his few belongings, turned his face toward the North Star, and ran. At times along the way, rowing across the Ohio River, joining the other packages on the Underground Railroad, he tried to understand why he had chosen that moment and that impetus to flee. But all he knew for sure was that in a single minute of selfishness, of grasping something tangible for himself, he had changed from a slave to a human being.

Robert let out a breath. The white woman still watched anxiously out the window, her hand pressing her hurt forehead. No, he was not brave, and he was not proud that he had run off and left the others to fight. But he had never been a human being before, he was so new at it, and if he had not told Mary Kingsley the whole story, at least he had thought it, and now it stood outside him like a spirit delivered to this house for safekeeping. His first answer to her had been right after all. Yes, he was treated badly. He had been enslaved from the day of his birth. He would never go back; he would die to be free. Only one shackle remained. He drew the pearls from his pocket, cradling the luminous white globes in his rough black palm.

"I hear a horse coming! Out front! Nathan!"

The white woman gave a clap of joy and hurried from the kitchen, and Robert jumped up, heart pounding, and hastened after her. She peered out the living-room window, her voice growing puzzled.

"There seem to be several riders. . . ."

He looked out beside her. In the pale light cast up by the snow he saw four horses approaching. On one rode a tall figure in buckskin, on another a young man waving a gun.

"Master! Slave catchers!" Robert cried out and whirled away from the window, his voice choked. Mary Kingsley stared at him with horrified eyes.

"Oh no, what shall we do?"

She clasped her hands at him, but this time Robert's new brain froze. The next instant a heavy tramp of boots mounted the porch steps.

"Hide! Hide quickly!" the white woman gasped. She shoved him toward the kitchen, and, as he stumbled for the cellar stairs, she turned back to the window and he heard her cry.

"Oh, my God! Nathan!"

Six

Mary flew to the front door and yanked it open.

"Nathan!"

Three men pushed her back into the room. The tallest carried her husband's body over his shoulder like a sack of meal.

"Put him down! What happened? Who are you?"

For answer, the tall man bent and dumped Nathan onto the sofa. Mary dropped to his side.

"Nathan! Nathan!" She stroked his face, but he made no sound, his eyes closed, his jaw slack. His skin was bluish with cold. Frantically, Mary felt for the pulse in his neck, and when a faint beat rose beneath her fingers, she let out a sob. She patted over his shoulders and chest, trying to locate the source of his injury, pleading, "What have you done to him? Oh!" Her hands encountered the small of Nathan's back, his jacket wet and stained with blood.

"I regret an injury has befallen your husband." The tall stranger stroked his stubbled chin. "Perhaps you have been expecting us?"

"No! Go away!" Mary cried.

"Maybe you could tell us the whereabouts of an escaped slave, or of a man named Jasper?"

"What would I know of any slave?" Her mind shoved aside the questions, too consumed with fear for Nathan to think straight. What to do? What to do? Run to her in-laws. Fetch Martha, Lij, the doctor. And Nathan must be warmed . . . she scrambled to her feet, intending to fetch a blanket, but as she whirled around the tall man caught her wrist.

"As I said, ma'am, we would be obliged for your assistance."

"Let me go!" She kicked him, and he grabbed her other arm, slowly tightening his grip around the slender bones.

A snicker of laughter broke from another of the men, and Mary darted an angry glance across the room. She had registered a brief impression of the other two when they burst in her door: a small, twitchy, rat-like man and a well-dressed youth who might have been a gentleman. He seemed out of place amidst his companions, but Mary had no time to puzzle about it. The tall man appeared to be in charge, and she must convince him to let her secure help for Nathan.

"Please, let me go," she whispered.

For a moment longer, the slave hunter imprisoned her wrists. His pale blue eyes studied her, as if a woman were an object of curiosity for which he had little use or interest. It made Mary tremble, and as if sensing he had sufficiently intimidated her, he released her arms. She backed to the sofa and sat on the edge, shielding Nathan. Slowly, she raised her finger and pointed to the small bedroom that led off the living room.

"I just want to get a blanket."

"And I want my property!" The young gentleman pushed forward and began an outraged tale of the escaped slave, a stolen necklace, and the punishment he planned to exact. "You Northerners know full well the law is on my side. Just because a slave crosses into a free state does not make him a free man. If your horse strayed into your neighbor's barn, you would still be the rightful owner, and if your neighbor refused to return the beast, you would arrest him for a thief. It is exactly the same for a nigger and more so, for unlike a horse, the devils know they have no right to run away. And all who help them escape, like your husband there, are traitors and liars!"

He pointed scornfully at Nathan, and Mary felt a hot burst in her chest. She jumped to her feet.

"My husband would never help the likes of you!" she cried.

The little man chuckled, and as Mary snapped her head toward him, he lifted one of the lamps and slunk away into the parlor. She heard the heavy scrape of furniture shoved across the floor. Mary willed silent messages: to the slave to sneak up the stairs and flee out the rear door; to Nathan to stay warm and alive; to Elijah to show up whistling for no good reason. The tall slave hunter had looked bored during the young owner's tirade. He helped himself to a chair and stared lazily at Mary, studying first her forehead, then her chest. A chill crawled over her skin, and when she glanced down at her bodice, she saw a tear and a loose thread where a jet button should have been.

"I am going to get a blanket," she said, and this time he let her circle around him to the bedroom. As she grabbed the cover from the bed, a loud creak on the cellar stairs froze her heart. She ran back to Nathan and began tucking the blanket around him with shaking fingers.

"Snipes, keep searching!" the young master ordered, pointing the rat-man toward the kitchen while he snatched a lamp and bounded upstairs. Mary chafed Nathan's hands and pressed her warm fingers to his face, trying to block out the growing commotion in her house. Burke's voice, gravelly and unpleasant, drifted over her shoulder.

"You can understand my employer is distressed at the loss of valuable property. But that is all the more reason not to let personal feelings interfere with one's judgment. In my profession a man should always be patient, observe small details, stop to listen and sniff the wind. A clumsy approach only puts your quarry to flight." He paused, and Mary started at the thud of overturned furniture upstairs. "You see, prey has a way of coming to you in its own time. It thinks it is running away, but have you ever tried to run with your head always turned back over your shoulder? Not easy, ma'am. You stumble, you trip, you veer off course. Why, I have known prey to make a full circle and rush right back to my arms. But a hunter always looks straight ahead, and that is my advantage. That, and fear, of course. Being scared does not make a man run faster, except in his mind. Truth is, ma'am, it puts wood in his legs."

"Let me get help!" Mary turned and pleaded. "Take anything we have. Just go!"

Burke shrugged. He reached up his hand, clamped it over the crown of his hat, and set the hat on the table beside him, as if chagrined he had temporarily neglected his manners. "Like I said, ma'am, for me this is purely business. I used to hunt Indians for the army out West. I confess to some admiration for the red men. They know how to blend into the territory. But they have no loyalty to one another, and it is easy enough to hire a scout from another tribe to track them. Then you lure them in with treaty talk and firewater. But I got weary of generals telling me what to do. So I turned my hand to slave catching, and I find the work suits me. Still, I have no personal grudge against any Negro, or you, or your husband there."

"Then why did you shoot him?" Mary begged. "Please, let me get the doctor! There is no slave here."

The tall man's cool blue eyes probed her, and her heart stopped on the words. But of course there was a slave here, and if she turned over the fugitive, these people would go. Her head spun at the solution. Yes, she had pledged to help Robert Rivers, as Nathan must have tried to do. But suppose she gave the man up in exchange for a promise not to hurt him, only put him back to work in the fields as he had done before. Would that be so bad? Was not her first duty to save her husband? What was the good of drawing this out when Nathan's life might be ebbing away?

"No, ma'am, I did not shoot your husband. That was Snipes's doing and would not have been my choice." Burke dragged his fingers through his stringy blond hair to straighten it. "You can fetch a doctor after we have what we came for. I would think that a woman in your condition would want to be cooperative."

He lowered his gaze respectfully to her abdomen, and Mary sucked in a gasp of fright. It was no use. He knew everything. The rat-man would find their quarry in a minute anyway. She could hear him in the kitchen, twitching his way across the floor, tapping walls and sliding furniture, as if he expected to find some hidden compartment. Now it might be even worse when they did discover the slave, for they would know she had lied. The words of betrayal rushed to her lips.

"Damn it! Nothing!" The young master burst down from upstairs. "None of this would even have been necessary if your husband had led us straight to the man called Jasper."

"Jasper?" Mary snatched at the name. Yes, that was it! Send them to the Quakers! Garrett, Lucretia, and Reverend Swift were already on the lookout and would know what to do. Some of the men from the search party might have returned there as well. Together, they would be more than a match for these men.

"You know him." Burke nodded, pleased.

"Yes, yes!" Mary jumped to her feet. In her eagerness she grabbed his buckskin sleeve and pulled him toward the door. Once the slave catchers were on their way, Robert Rivers could fly and she could run to her in-laws, send Elijah galloping for the doctor and then off to aid the Jaspers, while Martha came to help her save Nathan. "They live two miles southwest, a clapboard house near the woods. I will point you to the road."

"Well, well, looky what I found. Some people are pretty careless what they drop on the floor."

The rat-man spoke from the kitchen doorway, his face creased in a delighted grin. From his fingers dangled a string of softly glowing pearls.

"My sister's necklace! He's here! He's here!" The young gentleman sprang forward, and even in her confusion at the appearance of the jewelry, Mary felt a desperate flash of anger at his triumph.

"No, it's my necklace!" she cried. "Mine! Give it back!" She dashed at the rat-man and snatched at the pearls, but he only sidestepped into the living room and dangled them above his head, chuckling. Mary turned in the doorway. Even through the thickness of walls and floors, the slave must have heard this commotion. Surely he knew his only chance now was to flee. She clenched her fists and shrieked full force, "Get out—!"

Her voice died as if sliced through by a knife. The slave hunter stood beside the sofa, his cocked pistol pointed at Nathan's head.

"Where is he, ma'am?" The blue eyes were cold as a frozen lake. His finger squeezed slowly on the trigger.

"In the cellar," she whispered.

She straightened in the doorway, an absurdly small obstacle to the three men. As Burke stepped toward her, her arms crossed instinctively in front of her and she locked her jaw, expecting her end had come. The next instant two strong hands gripped her upper arms, and she was lifted off her feet and set aside almost as gently as if she were a doll. The slave hunter passed by her without a word, the young master and Snipes crowding after him. But before they reached the cellar door, a bellowing figure burst upon them.

"Freedom! Freedom!" Robert Rivers charged like a whirlwind, swinging wildly at his attackers. Pots clattered from the counters, the rat-man stumbled to the floor. Mary fled to Nathan, the fight exploding like a storm on her heels. She buried her head on Nathan's chest and threw her arms over him, shuddering at the crashing of tables and chairs. A cry of pain sounded, and she hoped viciously that the slave had hurt someone and might still reach the back door. But the fight was subsiding. Mary heard sickening blows into flesh, a body toppling to the floor. A minute of panting silence followed, then grunts and heaving sounds. She raised her head to see the tall slave catcher reappear in the doorway, dragging the body of Robert Rivers by his bound feet. The rat-man came second, then the young master wincing and dabbing his sleeve to his bloody nose. Mary stared at the Negro. His hands were shackled before him, and there was no resistance in his body as it dragged across the floor. But his eyes were open and fixed with a dull light, as if asking death to come find him.

"Thank you for your assistance, ma'am." Burke clapped his hat on his head. There was no irony in his voice, and he seemed neither excited nor elated at the capture of the fugitive. "You can fetch a doctor for your husband now." He motioned the other two to open the front door, and they went out, the young master cursing and gingerly tending his nose. A trail of blood from the slave's skull streaked across the floor like an untidy length of crimson ribbon.

Mary let out a sob and turned to feel for Nathan's pulse, so faint it seemed no more than a thread beneath her touch. She clambered to her feet, tugged her skirt out of the way, and ran to the front door. The men had mounted, and she saw the Negro's body dangling over the saddle of the tall man's horse. They galloped away southward, leaving Jake tied to the porch railing, and Mary spied Nathan's shotgun in the saddle holster. She ran and drew it out, heedless of the cold night air that slipped frigid arms around her. Mary pointed the gun skyward and fired into the night. She dropped the gun, shaking from the explosion in her ears, her teeth chattering, "Please, please, someone come!"

Seven

On Sunday when Reverend Marcus Swift stepped to the front of the crowded schoolhouse, he knew his sermon by heart. It had begun to compose itself in his head even before the episode of the escaped slaves was over and the fate of all involved had become known. I should have been a writer, he sighed, not for the first time, and he wondered if his favorite author, the blind poet Milton, was also guilty of converting life into a story while it was still going on around him. He only wished he possessed more physical presence to impart authority to his words. Reverend Swift was a hearty eater who enjoyed his beef and brown-gravy dumplings, smacked his lips over second helpings of sugared fruits and honey cake. Yet the pounds refused to stay put on his spare frame, and his black suit and clerical collar only accentuated his thinness. But what the body lacked, Reverend Swift more than compensated for in mental energy and passion. He had every confidence that today's sermon would resonate to the rafters with righteous affirmation and the ringing truth of his beliefs. The text was perhaps a trifle long, but he could not find it in his heart to prune a single flower from his oratorical bouquet. Every blossom seemed essential to the fullness of the whole.

"Friends and neighbors, a great calamity has befallen us, or so at first glance it must seem. This past week we have been confronted by events that have shaken and dismayed us, threatened the peace and security of our families and our homes. Who can doubt that our community has been severely tested? Which of us ever dreamed to encounter the villainy of slavery on our very doorsteps? Who did not feel a pang of fear at the prowl of the slave catchers on our cherished land? At such a time, well might we throw up our hands to heaven and cry, What have we done to deserve this?"

Reverend Swift thrust his hands toward the ceiling. Inspiration flowed like spring sap in his veins. He wished, just this once, Garrett and Lucretia had accepted his invitation to hear his sermon, but they held a steadfast preference for their own form of worship and he respected them far too much to impose on their friendship. Still, it was gratifying that his congregation should know at last how he had worked in concert with the Quakers, the free blacks, and all the men and women of conscience on the Underground Railroad. Though like most conductors he kept no records, by mental count he reckoned some sixty slaves of all ages and conditions had so far passed through his hands to freedom, and all with such commendable dispatch and secrecy that few in the community had even suspected his labors. If not for this one mishap, he, the Jaspers, and their fellow conspirators might have gone on undetected for years. Reverend Swift knew full well that his parishioners viewed him as a good-hearted but long-winded soul, spouting heroic words unmatched by any deeds. He had caught them nodding off in their chairs while he preached, though afterward they thanked him robustly for the sermon. But today, after the tragedy in their neighborhood, every face in every seat was alert. So perhaps the Lord would forgive his devoted servant if he enjoyed his moment of recognition. It was good to be humble, but it was also very nice to be appreciated.

"Yes, what have we done to deserve this? Yet even as we plead so with heaven, our first duty is to give thanks to the Lord and rejoice. Last night I received word from friends in Detroit that the young Negro girl who first struggled through the snow to the Jaspers', along with the two brothers and the old man found by members of our search party, have made safe passage by boat to Canada. There they alighted on free soil with joyous cries of thanksgiving, and all four bent to kiss the ground beneath their feet."

Reverend Swift cast a nod toward Samuel Millard and Ephraim Peck. They had ignored his warning to end their search at twilight and were still stubbornly tramping the woods an hour after sunset when they picked up a faint movement in the darkness ahead. There they came upon the Negro brothers, stumping along on half-frozen feet and carrying between them on a makeshift litter the lame elderly man. After fending off the slave-hunting party the previous night, the trio had continued northward by hunch and instinct. When the old man's strength failed and he begged the brothers to leave him behind, they crafted the litter out of two stout branches and their jackets and carried him onward despite his protests. It was a story to bring tears to every eye, and though most of his congregation had heard it already, Reverend Swift retold it with all the drama at his command. Besides, it did not hurt to give Millard and Peck their moment of glory. Both men straightened proudly in their seats as he mentioned their names.

"Let us also give thanks for the valiant efforts of all those who joined the search and especially for the recovery of our brother Nathan Kingsley, who imperiled his own life in a courageous attempt to lead the hunters astray. No less did his wife Mary, whose bravery would put many a man to shame."

A sympathetic murmur ran through the crowd, and Lucinda Millard, sitting next to Mary, reached over to pat her hand. Elijah, on Mary's other side, put his arm protectively around her shoulder. Mary smiled faintly at the tribute, although her face, Reverend Swift noted, was still haggard and pale. Poor girl! Martha Kingsley had stayed by her son's bedside today, insisting Mary come out for the sunshine and fresh air. The weather had warmed considerably the last few days, and the mere sight of cerulean sky was a tonic to Livonia's winter-weary souls. Not that anyone expected the thaw to last. Michigan would be locked in snow and ice a good two months yet, all the more reason to savor these few days of respite. But Mary seemed less cheered than his other parishioners at this blessing of sunshine and blue sky, and Reverend Swift guessed she had passed another cruel night.

"Nightmares," Martha Kingsley had confided to him when he called at the house on Friday and heard the full story of Mary's ordeal. Her firing of Nathan's shotgun had brought Elijah, who rode to Dr. Shaw, rousting him from bed. By the time the doctor had extracted the bullet, declaring it a miracle the steel had lodged against but had not broken Nathan's spine, it was near midnight. Nathan was tucked into a warm bed; meanwhile, Elijah had ridden on to the Jaspers' to spread the news of Robert Rivers's capture. But the slave hunters had gained several hours' lead, and though Garrett rode urgently southward to alert friends along the Underground Railroad, the party had not been located. At least, Reverend Swift reminded himself, there was some hope of rescuing the last two fugitives, the mother and baby captured in the wagon. They were lodged in a jail some miles to the south pending the arrival of their owner to claim them, and the local abolitionists had put forward a lawyer to argue for their release. If the matter could not be done by law, supporters were prepared to storm the jail and free mother and child. All of which news he had imparted to the Kingsleys on Friday, glad to see Nathan cheerful and already much recovered, though still in pain. Then Martha had drawn him aside to convey her worries about her daughter-in-law.

"She cries and struggles in her sleep, Reverend, and wakes up shaking in fright. I have tried warm milk, chamomile tea, even a little whiskey at bedtime, but nothing soothes her. Perhaps you could speak to her?"

"Certainly, certainly," he had replied, never reluctant to dispense comforting advice.

Martha led him to the living room where Mary sat by a window, a closed book in her lap. Fragile sunbeams stretched through the glass and fell onto her idle hands. He had always thought Mary a pretty young woman, but today her auburn curls were dull and bad dreams lurked in the purple shadows beneath her eyes. Her pale blue dress gave her an appearance of iciness. The instant Martha left and Reverend Swift sat down, she jumped up and began speaking vehemently, as if the need to empty herself of her thoughts had become oppressive.

"I tried, Reverend! I tried! But everything went wrong!"

"Now, now, Mary, be calm. You were alone against three armed men. You acted the best you could."

"Did I?" Her expression was half scornful, half longing to be reassured.

"Of course. Everyone will say so. You faced a desperate situation, and although it is natural afterward to agonize over what you might have said or done differently, I think you showed great courage and strength of mind."

He paused to let her speak, but she only refused his praise by a shake of her head. Reverend Swift tried a coaxing tone.

"Please, Mary, do not berate yourself. Neither you nor anyone else can say whether this word or that action might have brought a happier outcome. Any other step might have turned out worse. Give thanks that Nathan will recover and do not blame yourself that you could not save the slave."

"But I could have, and brought help for Nathan sooner, too! Do you not see how simply it should have been done? If I had sent the slave away the minute I found him in the house, those men would have left us alone!" She picked up the book lying on her chair, stared at it a moment as if it were some foreign object, then hurled it to the floor. Reverend Swift, confounded, dropped his jaw. "But no, he was cold and hungry, so I fed him and let him stay. I delayed. Nathan promised he would always take care of me, and I trusted to that. I waited for him to come. How could I know he was injured? And when that awful man dropped him on the couch, I thought he was dead, and then I could not think straight." An anguished cry escaped her lips, and she pressed her hand to her forehead as if in pain. "Every minute might have been fatal for Nathan, losing blood, a bullet pressing on his spine. What if he had been crippled or paralyzed? How should we have managed then with a baby on the way and no money to hire anyone to help work the farm? Or what if Nathan had died? They put a gun to his head—how could I not tell them? Was not my first duty to save my husband? Who was I trying to protect?"

"The greater good, Mary. Without knowing it, you were striving to protect the greater good. Just as Nathan did when he took upon himself the risk of leading the hunters astray."

"But how shall that comfort me when I cannot even pretend to understand?" She turned to him, hands outspread, and spoke in a pleading tone. "What good would it have added to the world for Nathan to die so one slave might go free? For me to grieve, so another might rejoice? Where is the gain in that?" Wetness brimmed in her eyes. "And it is all to no purpose since the man is recaptured anyway. Please, is this heavenly justice?"

"No, Mary. It is not just at all. But you and Nathan and everyone in this community did as your hearts dictated, and you cannot change what happened."

Mary's shoulders drooped, and she returned wearily to her chair, as if wishing his words could persuade her. How many times already, Reverend Swift wondered, had she relived the event, trying to make it come out right? And when her conscious mind could not solve it to her satisfaction, her dreams plagued her with failed attempts.

"You cannot change what happened, Mary," he repeated. "You and Nathan and everyone else did the utmost within their power. Now you must look forward with happiness to springtime and the birth of your baby."

At the mention of the baby, a flicker of hope crossed Mary's face. Swift picked up the book lying on the floor, a volume of poetry, he saw, and set it on her lap. Mary placed her hands over the cover, and the wetness that had gathered in her eyes turned into a trickle of tears.

"You do not understand, Reverend. Why has this happened to us? How can one event so alter your life? Two days ago I did not have to try to be happy. I *was*. I had my husband, my baby, my house. Everything was safe and well tended and fine. Now I step in the kitchen, and I see the black man by lamplight at the table. I sit here in the living room, and the slave hunter stares at me from your very chair. I know the images will fade in time, but what other unhappiness might take their place? I never expected hurt could come to me. I always trusted things to turn out beautiful and right. Now I cannot believe that any longer, no matter how selfish or foolish it was to begin. You may say I should take heart at the discovery, that I should cherish what I have for the very knowledge that at any minute it might be taken away. Is that the only answer?" She searched his face, and he could not tell if she was begging him to say yes or to say no.

"Not the only answer, perhaps, but as good a one as I could give."

Mary was silent a long minute, contemplating. Then she drew in a breath and pulled herself straight. "I shall try," she whispered. "For Nathan, for the baby, I shall try."

Now, as he gazed at Mary in the front row of the congregation, Reverend Swift reminded himself to speak to her when his sermon ended. To thank her, for it was her very questions, her need to reconcile and understand, that had shaped his message today. His flock was waiting, and his meager chest swelled in pride at the glorious words to come. Perhaps he should dig out his past sermons, burnish them to a divine glow, and seek a publisher in Detroit. Was it too much to hope that he might shine forth as the Milton of the New World?

"Friends and neighbors, I ask again: What have we done to deserve this? But this time I raise the question not as a wail against an unjust fate but as a joyful cry of thanks at the opportunity for enlightenment. For see what we have learned of good and evil. Who among us did not shudder to see firsthand the oppression of our Negro brethren? What soul here did not burn with indignation at the wickedness of the laws by which black men, women, and children are enslaved? Let us translate this new knowledge into words and deeds, not only on behalf of those enchained by reason of their color, but in aid of any abused person who cries out to us. Each time we assist another, be he poor, sick, hungry, or without a roof above his head, that man becomes a brother who will help us in our turn."

From the congregation came murmurs of agreement. Thank you, Lord, Reverend Swift prayed silently, for giving me this chance to show them what we can be. Next week or the week after, their enthusiasm would wane. Farm chores, winter cold, and all the daily dramas of snow-storms and foxes in the chicken coop would occupy their minds. But for this moment, he had been allowed to reach into their hearts and make his words answer to an event they were still struggling to comprehend. Might it even prompt them to move speedily toward the construction of a real church? Reverend Swift's soul sang.

"Friends! What have we done to deserve this blessing? For look now how we ourselves have stood forth. We have been tested and not found wanting. We have acted with strength, compassion, and true presence of mind. We have been granted an experience that might have split our community asunder, driven a wedge between good people over an issue that already divides our good nation. Instead, it has brought us closer together, acting with one heart and one mind. If we can do so in a time of trial and adversity, what can we not achieve in the years of progress and prosperity to come? Let us thank the Lord! Let us praise Him! Amen!"

As the people chorused their answer, Reverend Swift exuded a great sigh of content. Even Mary's face had brightened at last. Bless these people, Lord, he added silently, for they have done well. And hear especially my prayer for Nathan and Mary Kingsley. Let them heal from the hurt they have suffered and cling to each other as husband and wife ought. Let their union be fruitful, the coming child healthy and strong. Let their farm prosper and their new house bring them joy. Let them, as Mary said, be happy. Or at least, Reverend Swift closed his Bible, as happy as any of us have a right to wish.

Book Two

1863

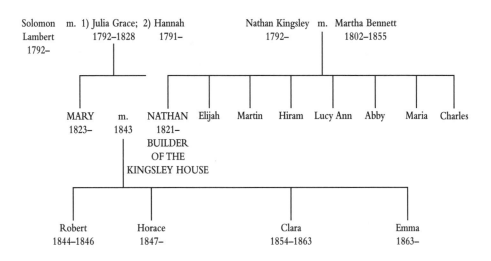

Solomon   m. 1) Julia Grace; 2) Hannah   Nathan Kingsley   m. Martha Bennett
Lambert   1792–1828   1791–   1792–   1802–1855
1792–

MARY   m.   NATHAN   Elijah   Martin   Hiram   Lucy Ann   Abby   Maria   Charles
1823–   1843   1821–
                  BUILDER
                  OF THE
                  KINGSLEY HOUSE

Robert   Horace   Clara   Emma
1844–1846   1847–   1854–1863   1863–

One

In the middle of the August night, sixteen-year-old Horace Kingsley awoke with a grin on his face. He sharpened his ears to catch any sound from his parents' bedroom upstairs, then he listened for noises in the yard outside. A summer night was never entirely quiet, and through his open window came the slender rustle of wheat, the faint crackling of growing green corn, the soft, dreaming grunt of the spotted hog in the sty. Horace wondered if, a half mile down the road at his grandfather's house, Maria's little poodle, Trixie, was yapping. Maria, twenty-one, was the youngest sister of Horace's father Nathan, which made her Horace's aunt. But given the slight difference in their ages, Horace preferred to think of her as his cousin, which was more convenient, because Maria was as pretty as honey and cream, and he would have kissed her lips if she'd let him. Her dog Trixie was a source of particular amusement to Horace, for the poodle's midnight yappings drove Grandfather Kingsley into a passionate uproar.

"Damn beast never shuts up!" the old man would bellow to anyone who listened. "What do we want with a fluffy topknot like that on a farm? Ridiculous name! I have a mind to shoot the blamed creature!" Then he would settle into a grumble about his sleepless nights and how he would tan Elijah the next time he came from Detroit for giving the poodle to Maria for her birthday.

Horace slipped out of bed and dressed quickly, chuckling at the memory of the old man's flusters. His was the small bedroom off the living room, and sometimes, just to liven life up a bit, he sneaked over to Grandfather's when everyone was asleep and pelted stones at the house to taunt Trixie. Then he dashed home while the frantic poodle jumped and barked and yipped like a demon. By the time Horace dove into bed, his sides would ache from running and the laughter he had to suppress to reenter his house undetected.

But perhaps tonight it was just as well if Trixie remained quiet, for Horace had other business. It was one of his fortunate talents to be instantly awake and alert at any time of night, and as he tiptoed through the kitchen and out the back door his senses prickled in anticipation of his nocturnal prowl. The night was warm, and a round, silver moon hung in the sky. Horace passed the pigsty, and in the sweet-sour muck he made out the spotted hog snoring blissfully on its side. *Sleep on, streaky bacon,* he thought, his mouth watering.

He reached the chicken coop where three dozen red hens slumbered on boxes stuffed with straw. Horace was not fond of chickens, not since it had recently become his job to collect their eggs every morning at sunrise. Women's work!

"You will gather the eggs, and I will hear no more about it!" Pa had said, his anger buckled so tightly that the muscles in his neck corded like rope. "Your mother is worn out with grief at your sister's death and the strain of the new baby coming. You will do whatever I tell you to help."

"Yes, Pa," Horace had agreed, chastened. But still, the henhouse was a girl's job, and you could bet Uncle Elijah had not been out gathering eggs in a basket when he was sixteen. Horace hoped the new baby would be a girl and would grow up quickly so the hens could peck her hands instead of his.

He knelt and examined an oblong wood and wire box in front of the chicken coop. Empty. Horace gave the contraption a kick. That made three nights now. Why wasn't it working? He bent down again and studied the clever trapdoor and spring mechanism he had devised. Maybe there were no more skunks around to catch. Maybe shooting them was just plain easier. But he had been proud of his design, and Pa had said it looked a smart device. Still, all was not lost. Horace fetched an empty meal sack from the barn, threw it over his shoulder, and set off whistling.

The night air had a summery softness, a niceness, Horace told himself, not being one for words. His nine-year-old sister Clara had been a real storyteller, and once a week she had walked to the schoolteacher Miss Polly Noble's house where the town library was kept to borrow one of the five dozen books. Clara always got stories that were too big for her, then she pestered Horace to tell her the meaning of the words.

He was sorry for her illness, sorry she had sickened and died, sorry for his parents' grief. But he was also sixteen, with a head full of plans and a mustache starting to fringe his lip, and he could not help but feel optimistic when the earth was green and the moon beamed full as a silver quarter in the sky.

Horace smiled. Quarters. He had a can of them in his bedroom, a dozen he had earned in the past three weeks alone, and he meant to get as many more as he could before the bounty ran out. He crossed the road and headed kitty-corner through the neighboring farms toward Silas Joslin's place. Silas was the town clerk, a dry, balding man with no more sense of humor or imagination than a bone, and his meticulously recorded minutes of the Town Board meetings were as lifeless as dust. All the civic records were stored in his home, but tonight Horace had no need to approach the house. His destination was a small shed near Silas's barn.

Ahhh . . . the odor alone was enough to guide Horace to the rear of the wood structure. His eyes were already well adjusted to the dark, and in the moonlight he made out the heap of furry bodies. At least a dozen skunks had accumulated—which meant Silas would never miss one or two, not that he kept track of the black-and-white corpses once they were turned over to him.

"Dump them behind the shed," he ordered Horace and the other boys when they brought in their trophies, pinching his nose and vigorously motioning them away from the house. Horace would accept his quarter per skunk bounty, deposit the furry carcasses on the pile, and head home well satisfied. The dead skunks remained by the shed until the town pound master, responsible for stray and unwanted animals, came by every few days to collect and dispose of them.

I'll take two, Horace decided now, his greed getting the better of him. He selected the pair that were the least mangled from the townspeople's efforts to trap, shoot, poison, and otherwise annihilate the pesky animals which, unusually abundant this summer, were wreaking havoc in the local chicken coops. Taking the meal sack from his shoulder, he dropped them in and started home.

Oh yes, I am clever, Horace crowed to himself. *Handsome, daring, a likely young man.* Maybe he would ask Maria to dance with him at the September social. He would don his fancy suit, polish his shoes, slick his nut-brown hair. Horace was average height, but he walked with a stride that convinced him he was taller, and what girl could resist those fine white teeth, that debonair jaw, those smoldering brown eyes? He pictured Maria beside him in a pink dress trimmed with blue ribbons, blond hair pinned and curled. He would twirl her around the dance floor and steal that kiss he had been wanting. Clara had once called Maria a "slif," and Horace had laughed.

"A slif? What's a slif? There is no such word."

"A slif," Clara insisted. "I saw it in a poem. It means like a fairy."

"That's an *elf*," Horace retorted, rocking with laughter, which only made Clara shake her pigtails in stout denial.

"No! You're not listening! I said *slif*! S-y-l-p-h!"

"That's not slif, you little ninny! It's silp, and there is no such word either! You mean slip, like when people say she is a slip of a girl."

"Slip is not what I mean at all!" Clara cried. "Slif, slif, slif!"

Horace had covered his ears and strode away laughing, much to Clara's distress. He felt a little bad about it, now that she was dead, and either way Clara had been right. Maria was a slip of a girl and rather fairylike, too, a slender beam of sunlight trapped in human form. Grandmother Martha Kingsley had died when Maria was thirteen, leaving the girl and her five-year-old brother Charles to be raised by their two older sisters. But the older girls soon married, and Maria was left to manage the house, Charles, and her crusty old father. Spotting their house on the road ahead, Horace considered detouring and provoking Trixie to a barking fit. But the risk was too great with his booty in the bag. He reached home and crept close to the house, listening. All was quiet, Pa and Ma still asleep upstairs. He stole into the kitchen, then continued on to the chicken coop with Pa's shotgun and the burlap sack. Propping the stiff skunks against a fence post, he stepped back a fair distance, raised the shotgun, and fired twice.

"Got 'em! Got 'em!" Horace whooped as the chickens flew into a panic and hurled themselves around the coop, clucking and crashing into each other. "Got two!" He snatched the clumps of smelly, blasted fur, laid them beside the coop, tossed the meal sack out of sight, and raced back to the house. Already he could hear his mother's terrified cry from the window, and by the time he reached the back door, Ma and Pa, in their nightclothes, were there to meet him.

"What happened? What happened? Are you all right?" Ma clutched her dressing gown, her face startled into disarray, her long hair fraying from its nighttime braid, belly huge with the coming child. She reached anxiously toward him. "Are you hurt?"

"No, Ma. It was skunks!"

Mary sighed, her breath ragged in relief, and Horace continued triumphantly.

"I got two, but don't go out, Pa!" He waved back his father as Nathan started toward the door. "They stink something fierce."

"Two," said Pa evenly.

"Shot 'em dead on!" Horace punched his fist into his palm.

"Lucky you had good moonlight."

"Saw 'em clear as anything!"

"Wonder why you didn't wait to let them try your trap?"

"They were headed straight for the chickens, Pa. I couldn't take the chance."

"I guess you heard them scratching at the coop and that woke you up."

"Jolted smack out of my sleep, threw on my clothes, got your gun, and saved our chickens."

"So it seems."

Pa said no more, only turned to Ma and gently helped her through the kitchen and toward the stairs. Horace strutted back to bed, a swelling pride in his chest. He was more wide-awake now than ever, and this afternoon Pa would scold him for falling asleep over his chores. But what did he care? Pulled it off again! he exulted. He flopped onto his straw mattress, and in his euphoria he began to picture Maria in a way he knew he should not. The result was a swelling in another part of his anatomy, which caused him several painful minutes until he finally scooted back outside to relieve himself with a pleasurable groan. He buttoned his fly, eased back to bed, and fell asleep. It seemed only minutes later that the rooster crowed, and he had to drag himself groggily from bed. With Pa's steely eyes on him, he set out to fetch the eggs, milk the cows, and feed the horses. After breakfast, he hauled water from the well and carried in more wood for the stove. Finally, Pa gave him leave to go turn in the skunks.

"Stop by Grandfather's house on your way," said Ma, kneading bread dough at the kitchen table. "Ask if they have any news when Elijah is coming."

"Sure, Ma."

Horace shrugged, secretly pleased at the unexpected excuse to see Maria. He retrieved the skunks from behind the barn where he had cached them. The unfortunate corpses had been stiff when he purloined them from Silas's house. Now in the midday heat they were beginning to rot. Phew! Horace dropped them by their tails into the burlap sack, tied the neck with twine, and dragged the bundle along behind him on the dusty ground. As he neared his grandfather's house he spotted Maria hanging laundry. Leaving the skunk bag beside the road, he sauntered over.

"Hello, Maria." He nodded toward the road. "Got two more skunks last night." He hooked his thumbs in his pants pockets. Some of the other young skunk hunters, obviously jealous of Horace's success, had dared to call him "Skunk Boy." Let them eat their words when they saw how impressed the girls were with Horace's prowess and rapidly accumulating wealth. He waited for Maria's approval, hoping she would also notice his new mustache, but she only smiled distractedly and said, "That's fine."

"Ma said to ask if you have any news when Uncle Elijah will visit."

"We had a letter yesterday." Maria pinned a white shirt to the line. Her face had a faraway expression, as if even while she spoke, her thoughts floated elsewhere, as if her eyes saw a white shirt while her inner gaze traveled somewhere beyond. She wore a yellow gingham dress, and in the golden sunlight, her blond hair loose around her face, she seemed almost too radiant to touch.

"So when are Uncle Lij and Aunt Lisette coming?" Horace prodded, trying to recover the conversation.

"On Friday. But the boys will stay home with their governess. Tell Mary you are all to come for dinner that night." Maria picked a lacy camisole from the laundry basket, and as she pinned the delicate garment to the line Horace felt his organ begin to rise again. "Lij and Lisette are bringing a medium with them."

"A medium what?" Horace squeezed his thighs together.

"A medium, a Spiritualist. Her name is Mrs. Gregg."

His concentration still diverted to his trousers, Horace tried once more to understand. "What is a Spiritualist?"

"Anyone who believes in the possibility of communication with the spirits of the dead. Mrs. Gregg is very well-known. Elijah writes that she even conducted a seance for the governor."

Maria shifted the laundry basket further along the ground and pegged half a dozen white handkerchiefs to the line. Horace followed, the bulge in his pants somewhat tamed.

"But why is she coming here?" he asked. He was not sure what Maria meant by a seance but decided it best not to reveal any further ignorance. Trixie, yawning in the shade beside the house, rose, stretched, and trotted over to sniff Horace's shoes.

"I asked him to bring her."

"But why?"

"Because I want to talk with Mother." Maria had moved around the end of the clothesline to start the next row, and Horace hurried after. "It would be good for Charles, too. He was only five when she died, and he has few memories of her to treasure. I want to find out if she is at peace, if there is happiness for us after this life ends. Perhaps Mrs. Gregg could help your mother also."

"Help her how?"

"By summoning Clara's spirit from beyond the veil. Would it not give your parents great comfort to know their little daughter has been received into a better world where pain is banished and earthly sorrows cannot penetrate?"

"I suppose." Horace scratched his head. How could he find out what a seance was? Who in town would be able to explain to him about a medium? This was obviously important to Maria.

"And think of all the other spirits who may even now surround us, awaiting the chance to make contact with loved ones they have left behind. The brave Ryder boys, my dear Sarah, poor little Robert who was taken so young." Maria spread her arms in a graceful motion, as if welcoming unseen guests.

Horace did not reply, and as Maria went on hanging laundry, he paused to sort out the names. John and Alfred Ryder had perished together in July at Gettysburg, two of more than a half dozen sons Livonia had lost when the Michigan 24th took the brunt of the Confederate attack on the first day of the battle. Sarah Brigham, Maria's closest girlfriend, had died three years ago in an influenza epidemic that Horace himself had barely survived. He recalled his mother's anguish as she applied cold compresses to his feverish forehead, and her crying into Pa's arms that she could not bear to lose another child. Which made him remember the final name Maria had uttered—little Robert, his parents' first child, had died at barely two years of age, a year before Horace was born.

"Trixie, no!"

Horace jerked out of his reverie as Maria started toward the road. Finished with sniffing Horace, the poodle had discovered the burlap bag and was worrying it between her teeth and paws. Horace bounded past Maria.

"Leave my skunks alone!" he shouted, closing on the dog. The meal sack still clenched in her jaw, Trixie bared her teeth and growled. "Drop it, you damn dog!"

"Horace, wait!"

But Horace did not listen. Snatching a sharp rock from the road, he took aim and let fly. Trixie yelped and dropped the bag as the missile struck her nose, then shrank away whimpering.

"Trixie! Poor Trixie!" Maria brushed past him to rescue her pet. She cast an angry look over her shoulder. "For shame, Horace!"

Cursing, Horace picked up his skunk bag. There was no damage done, but in the growing heat the stench of rotting skunk was overpowering. He glanced at Maria, who knelt beside Trixie, petting her and crooning as lovingly as if the poodle were a child. Damn dog! Horace supposed he ought to go over and apologize, but it wasn't his way to say "sorry" to anyone. Did Maria even care that Trixie might have made off with his hard-earned skunks that he had so valiantly shot in the act of robbing his family's chicken coop? That was gratitude for you! Horace stalked away, dragging the smelly bag behind him. By the time he reached Silas Joslin's house, he was feeling perfectly in the right again, and as Silas, nose pinched, paid him two shiny quarters and motioned him toward the shed, Horace's good humor returned. He had generously thought of using his money to buy Maria a present, but now he would keep it all for himself. Horace set out for home, clinking the coins in his pocket, his mind singing his own greatness.

Oh, a daring fellow, a lucky devil, a bold, handsome lover am I!

Two

You could tell something about a community, thought Nathan, by the way it buried its dead. He gazed sadly over the small cemetery, a grassy site sheltered by cool green shade trees, granite stones standing shoulder-to-shoulder in peaceful family plots. A white picket fence and gate enclosed the ground, a sign of respect more than necessity since no dwelling infringed on the burial land and there was no reason to keep anyone out. Instead, the fence bespoke an understanding that the dead should have dignity and due place, and the neighbors took it in turns to keep the pickets straight and freshly painted. When the grass grew long, sheep were let in to graze.

The stones were modest, no ornate markers, no attempt to appear better than one's neighbors at the final reckoning. Most were grayish granite with a simple inscription of name, date, and family relationship. Dear husband. Beloved wife. The smallest stones were the children, shy markers peeping from the grass, and Nathan wondered why it should be that having less history they merited less size. Shouldn't their monuments be the biggest and bravest of all, to proclaim to the world that even the shortest life would not be forgotten? Or were the children content to remain children, nestled amidst the large, protective stones of their grown-up relations?

There was no marker for Clara yet—it would take time to save enough money for a proper stone—and as he helped Mary stoop to lay a bouquet of asters and daisies on the grave, he straightened the wooden cross he had planted there the day of the burial. Beside Clara lay the smaller coffin of Robert. He would have been nineteen now, had he lived, and Nathan's imagination struggled to picture his firstborn as a smiling, grown-up man. Next to the children lay Nathan's mother Martha, a space reserved beside her for her husband when his day should come. Someday I shall lie here, too, thought Nathan, and as he glanced over the quiet cemetery other names spoke forth: Millard, Chilson, Peck. Here they brought their dead and laid them to rest, and for every fresh grave was a family who mourned—

Nathan lifted a hand to his cheek and brushed away a tear. Mary must not see him crying, not when her own grief had cut so deep. The new baby was due in less than a month, and she needed his strength to support her. He blinked back the wetness, and for each headstone in their family plot he tried to call to mind a happy memory. The tenacious way his mother had dickered with a traveling peddler to obtain a cherished copper pot. Little Robert's dimpled cheeks and head of silky auburn curls. Clara's bright-eyed insistence that she would teach him to read.

"Now repeat after me, Pa. A,B,C," she lectured in a proper schoolmarm voice. To humor her he had orated "A,B,C" while she tapped her finger to keep the beat. "You are my smartest pupil!" she proclaimed when he reached X,Y,Z, and in an outburst of pride she flung her arms around his neck.

A silent sob wracked Nathan's chest. At his feet, Mary was weeping. He stooped and laced his arms around her, and while he ordered the tears on his own cheeks to dry, Mary sobbed in his arms.

"Hush, hush, Mary. Her pain is gone."

"I know." She struggled to control herself, and she patted the flowers this way and that as she would do when arranging Clara's wayward dark hair. "I wish I were beside her, Nathan."

"Hush, Mary. That is sorrow speaking."

"But sorrow is all I am. How can my child die and my heart still beat?" She pressed her hand to the second tiny grave. "When we lost Robert I felt the world must end. To live through this again makes me think I must be granite like these stones."

"If our hearts were granite, we could not love. Come, Mary, let us go home."

He offered his hand and helped her to her feet. Their horse and buggy stood outside the cemetery gate. They spoke little during the ride, and when they reached the house he tried to persuade her to nap.

"No." She shook her head, her face wan and still blotchy from tears. She rubbed her fingers to her temples, as if to force her brain back into circulation. "I must do something, Nathan. Idleness is no relief. I will bake a cake for Maria's dinner tonight, a spice cake. Now let me see, I need flour, sugar—"

She stepped into the pantry, naming ingredients in a purposeful voice. Nathan helped her carry them to the table. He wished he had something to occupy himself, but for the past two days, in anticipation of Elijah and Lisette's arrival, he had cleared away many of the chores, and he felt disinclined to start new ones. But even as Mary was now cracking eggs, measuring milk, stirring flour and cinnamon into a blue china bowl, he needed something practical and ordinary on which to concentrate, some task that would put his hands and head at peace. He went to the barn and hitched the horse Arthur to the wagon, though the simple act cost him another stab of memory. It had been Clara who had named the big tan horse after the ancient Celtic king, though the aging beast bore little resemblance to a noble knight's steed. Now it was hard to see Arthur without Clara astride his broad back. And everywhere Nathan turned it was like that, as if Clara still lingered in the skip of the breeze, the clear beauty of the air, as if the whole bright world smarted from one little girl's absence.

Nathan mastered himself and walked the horse past fields of wheat, corn, oats, and rye. The farm was a hundred twenty acres now; he had tripled his original holding of forty. His livestock numbered four horses, nine cows, two oxen, four sheep, and one swine. Two years before he had harvested 600 bushels of potatoes, 500 of corn, and they had butter and eggs to sell and trade and honey from their hives. Yet while other farmers in Livonia had become quite well-to-do, Nathan's income and status were no more than average. In truth, his soil had proven too sandy, and when the weather failed, as it had these past two years, prosperity became an illusion.

Nathan ran a hand through his black hair, flecked with gray at the temples. He was forty-two, and he could not remember now exactly what he had envisioned for this place, and he wondered if Elijah had not been right after all to leave for the city. Who would ever have guessed his reckless brother had such a head for business? Now Lij lived in a fine house in Detroit with a fashionable wife and two handsome sons, attended by a half dozen servants. And their younger brother Hiram had gone west and farmed two hundred acres in Oklahoma Territory.

Nathan shrugged away his thoughts. He had reached a corner of his land where over the years a rock pile had accumulated from the boulders that met his plow as each new acre was tilled. Earlier in summer, before Clara fell sick, Mary had mentioned wanting a border for her flower bed. Nathan began to sort through the rocks, lifting them, feeling their heft, setting those of the most pleasing shape and texture into the wagon. Their hardness gave purpose to his hands, and ignoring the old twinge at the base of his spine that revived whenever he exerted himself, he let his muscles warm to the task. Rock after rock, he scanned and lifted and chose, aligning them in his mind's eye around the flower bed. Black-eyed Susans, blue asters, white daisies, pink columbine. The land spread wide around him, wheat gold and grass green; silk blue sky stretched above. Rhythmically he lifted and sorted, hard gray granite, bones of the earth. He thought of Mary, mixing sugar, butter, eggs. Now repeat after me, A, B, C.

Don't cry, Pa.

Arthur turned his head and nickered in curiosity at the mounting load as rock after rock passed through Nathan's hands. Yes, this was what he needed, something solid in his grasp. Something that would not skip away on the breeze, dark braids flying. He would lay the stones in a border for Mary's flowers, shoulder-to-shoulder, the large and the small, to give the flowers dignity and due place. Tall purple cosmos, day lilies, Queen Anne's lace. *Don't cry, Pa.* He had been meaning to do something about this rock pile for a long time. Cinnamon and flour in a blue china bowl. You are my smartest pupil! X,Y,Z. So many rocks poor Arthur would never budge them. Small shapes of granite, peeping through the grass.

Please, Pa, don't cry.

Three

"Horace? Hurry up! We will be late for Maria's dinner."

"Coming, Pa!"

Horace dipped his comb into the glass of water and added a final slick to his hair. Wait till Maria saw him in his dapper gabardine suit. Wait till Uncle Elijah saw how manly he had grown since Christmas. Why, he near about measured up to Pa now; at least he imagined he did not have to look up very far. Horace buttoned his jacket and stepped out the back door where his parents waited in their buggy. He wished Pa and Ma were more presentable. Ma couldn't help her belly, of course, but she had overdone her cosmetics in honor of the occasion and two rosy patches showed prominently on her hollow cheeks. Her hair was fussy as well, threaded with a pink ribbon to match the sprigged design on her beige dress—as if anyone would care. You could bet Aunt Lisette would outshine her. Now there was a woman who knew how to dress. As for Pa, though he and Uncle Elijah were but a year apart in age, in appearance the gap seemed to widen with every visit. Just look at the deep crease between Pa's eyebrows, the nicks and calluses on his hands, his skin leathered by constant exposure to sun and wind. Uncle Lij was a gentleman, smooth-featured and smartly dressed, and still one to catch the ladies' eyes. Horace climbed into the buggy, shaking his head. There was little hope of sprucing up his parents at this late stage in their lives.

"Horace, would you carry the cake, please?" asked Ma.

"Aw, do I—" A look from Pa silenced him. "Sure, Ma."

Horace accepted the covered plate and peeked under the lid. The cake looked decent, iced with fluffy white frosting, but it was still no comparison to the mouthwatering trifles and chocolate eclairs he had been served at Uncle Elijah's house. He wished Pa cared to go to the city more often. Still, a clever young man could get rich anywhere, if he put his mind to it. You had only to sniff out the opportunities and take a few risks.

They reached Grandfather's house, and Horace hopped down from the buggy and bore the covered plate to the front door.

"Look what we've brought you," he announced to Maria when she answered.

"Thank you, Horace. Would you please put it in the kitchen?" Maria held the door wide for him to enter, but instead of following him she stepped out to the porch to welcome his parents. He heard her thank Ma for the cake, and he clucked his tongue in annoyance. Wasn't he the one who had carried it safely all the way from home?

"Horace, there you are! How have you been?"

A handshake from Uncle Elijah restored his good mood as he entered the parlor where his parents were already enfolded in a circle of greetings. There was Aunt Lisette, elegant in a violet silk traveling dress, Grandfather Kingsley, gray and grizzly as an old bear, Maria's younger brother Charles, and a couple Elijah introduced as Professor and Mrs. Gregg. The medium, Horace remembered, sparing the woman a curious glance. Short, stout, a plain round face, putty nose, mousy brown hair tidied into a bun, wearing a dull blue dress with a wide hoop skirt, of an age somewhere around fifty—hardly a woman of fascination. He had expected something dark-eyed and exotic, like a gypsy or a Spanish dancer, not this dowdy matron. Her husband, thin and white-haired, seemed a decade or more older. He had pink cheeks and a neat white mustache, and he wore a black frock coat that was shiny at the elbows. Horace dismissed both Greggs as inconsequential. What he really wanted to hear about was Uncle Lij's latest business deals, but Elijah and Lisette were murmuring condolences to Ma and Pa on Clara's death, and the Greggs joined in, surrounding his parents with a soft mournful cooing. Horace was left standing beside Charles, technically his uncle, despite being four years younger. But Maria doted on the boy, so Horace assumed a jovial manner and gave him a comradely nudge in the ribs.

"Anything good for dinner?"

"Ham, sweet potatoes, biscuits, apple pie."

Charles looked wistfully toward the grown-ups, as if he wanted to join their conversation, though Horace could not imagine why. They had concluded their condolences for Clara and moved on to news of the war with Grandfather blustering about General Sickles's mistake at Gettysburg.

"I wish I could go to the war," said Charles.

"You? What would you do?"

"Be a drummer boy."

"You're not old enough."

"I'm twelve, and Freddie Norbert has gone and he is only thirteen. Why don't you go, Horace? Maria says it is a noble cause to free the slaves and fight for Lincoln and the Union."

Charles regarded him earnestly, his clear blue eyes and flaxen hair a replication of Maria's fair coloring. He was slight like her, too, a willow of a boy.

"Well, of course I would go to the war," Horace asserted, "if I were not needed on the farm." He tucked his hands in his pockets and rocked on his heels. Of course he would have marched off to war, would probably have been a hero by now, decorated by President Lincoln, not like one Livonia boy who had deserted and was drummed out of his regiment—head shaven, buttons torn off his coat—at the point of his comrades' bayonets. Horace was picturing himself in a handsome blue uniform, medals agleam on his chest, when Maria summoned them to the dinner table. She and Charles carried in a half dozen serving dishes and set the ham before Grandfather to carve. The old man poked the ruddy pink roast with the knife.

"Ho, Barney," he gloated. "You were a good fat pig, and you are a better ham!" He sawed thick juicy slices for Maria to serve while Aunt Lisette explained to Ma and Pa how she and Uncle Lij had met the Greggs.

"It was at the home of our dear friends, the Fischers. Their infant son died of smallpox in April, poor little one. They had heard of Mrs. Gregg and her powers and asked us to join them in a seance." Aunt Lisette paused and gave a slight shake of her head as if still unable to believe the story she was about to relate. "Never have I witnessed anything so remarkable. In the dark room the table danced, strange rappings broke out, then the voice of the dead child spoke through Mrs. Gregg's mouth. Truly, it was a miracle, and one we have now seen repeated on a half dozen occasions."

The medium bowed her head. "You are too kind," she murmured.

"It really is not *my* power at all. It is simply a gift I have been given to act as a channel to the spirit world. When I enter my trance, their messages pass through me, and when I awaken I cannot recall a single word my lips have uttered, though all around me are astonished by the communications." She sighed and spread a generous pat of butter onto a biscuit.

"This sensitivity to the spirit world is most predominantly a woman's gift," added Professor Gregg. "We who are serious investigators of these phenomena believe it is woman's passive nature that makes her the ideal conduit for messages from beyond. Most of those male sensitives who have demonstrated a like power are readily acknowledged to have a preponderance of the feminine in their character." He pursed his lips in deep thought, while Mrs. Gregg, Horace noticed, dug into a second helping of mashed sweet potatoes.

"The Greggs have established a foundation for the study of Spiritualism," Elijah explained. "Many men of science are interested in these occurrences."

"I thought, from what Maria told Horace, that Spiritualism was a religion," ventured Mary. She looked hesitantly from Maria to the professor.

"It is science *and* religion, dear lady," he replied. "As Christians, we believe in the immortality of the soul. As Spiritualists, we seek the scientific means to prove it. We live in an era of tremendous progress. Think, for example, of the telegraph, one of the wonders of our modern times. It has opened channels of communication undreamed of by our ancestors, sending messages from New York to California in little more time than it takes to speak the words aloud. To the uninitiated, it seems to be a miracle—words traveling through wires. Yet it is all based on clear scientific principles that can be easily understood once the explanation is given. In the same way, sensitives like my wife act as a spiritual telegraph to send and receive messages between this world and the next. Though we do not yet completely understand its operating principles, I am confident that great discovery cannot be far off."

"Mrs. Gregg has even received messages from Benjamin Franklin and William Shakespeare," said Aunt Lisette. "Think of it! To know that great minds are not silenced by death!"

An awed hush fell on the table, and Horace, seated between Charles and Grandfather, heard the old man muttering "malarkey" and "bag of tricks" beneath his breath. Pa so far had said nothing, nodding intently at the professor's description of the telegraph, while Ma bit her lower lip, as if a question trembled there that she longed to ask. Horace mused on the matter. Could living people really talk with the dead? After all, the dead could appear in dreams. Visions of Grandmother Kingsley still vexed his sleep from time to time, always lecturing him about his moral character, and once, after eating too many tart cherries, he had had a nighttime visit from George Washington who chased him with an axe. And there were plenty of ghost stories known to the boys in town. Some were pure mischief, concocted to scare the girls, but Horace knew several stout fellows who swore on the Bible to true hair-raising encounters.

"You mean you can see ghosts?" he interrupted.

"Ghosts are most often unhappy spirits," said Professor Gregg. "Murder victims or others who have met a violent end. The trauma involved in such cases causes the victim to throw off what we call a 'thought-form,' a permanent impression of their distress that lingers in the atmosphere in the vicinity of their demise. If the emotions are powerful enough, the thought-forms may be perceived even by nonsensitives. Have you ever seen a ghost, young man?"

"No, but I would chase it away if I did," Horace declared.

"Exactly what must *not* be done." Professor Gregg adamantly shook his head, and his cheeks grew pinker in his zeal. "The ghost cannot depart as long as its soul remains in torment. Mrs. Gregg and I have successfully resolved a number of these cases by allowing the unfortunate ones to express themselves through her at a seance. Once their unhappiness is made known and the blessing of the living is granted them, the ghosts are released from their earthly restraints and depart in peace to the spiritual realm."

"I have never seen a ghost," said Maria. "Yet sometimes I do feel there might be spirits around us. The air seems to shimmer and vibrate. I almost feel their caress on my face."

"It is a woman's gift indeed," sighed Mrs. Gregg, as she polished off her third slice of ham. "We mediums are needed now more than ever when so many sons and husbands have fallen in this terrible war, when children are taken in their bloom by cruel disease. My only mission is to ease the grief and suffering of the dear families left behind."

"Can you talk to Clara?" Mary begged. "Can you find her? I only want to know that she is all right."

"I will do my best." Mrs. Gregg patted Ma's hand, while Aunt Lisette passed her a lace-edged handkerchief to dab her brimming eyes. "I can promise nothing. Sometimes, for all my best endeavors, the spirits choose silence." She turned to Maria. "You also wish to contact someone, your mother, is that not so?"

"Oh yes!" breathed Maria.

"Then I must rest and prepare myself, and tomorrow night we may meet for a seance. It is a very draining experience, so I must sustain myself now. Did you say, Miss Kingsley, that you had an apple pie?"

"Yes, and Mary brought a spice cake. Let me bring you some."

Maria hurried to the kitchen, and while Professor Gregg described the investigations being conducted by their Spiritualist foundation, Horace satisfied himself with a generous helping of each dessert. Mrs. Gregg, he noted, did likewise. When the plates were cleared away, Elijah invited the men to the parlor for a cigar, and though Horace considered himself included, Pa did not.

"Your grandfather wants help rigging a pulley in the hayloft," he said. "Now is a good time."

Horace grumbled and followed Grandfather through the kitchen where Maria and Charles were washing dishes. Aunt Lisette had taken Ma and Mrs. Gregg to sit on the front porch. The old man led him to the barn, talking back at Horace over his shoulder.

"So you think you are a smart one with contraptions, making skunk cages and such. Let's see you figure out this pulley, and don't suppose just because my bones creak on the hayloft steps I couldn't do it myself. Get away, you damn dog!" Trixie had run up, frisking and yapping about Grandfather's legs, and the old man swatted as if trying to shoo away a horsefly. Horace snickered. "Think this is funny, do you?" Grandfather marched on, joints stiff from rheumatism. "Get up in that loft. Trouble with you is, your Ma spoiled you. My Martha said so from the start. She was a good woman. Did her cooking and laundry right up to the day she died."

Horace climbed the stairs to the hayloft, taking care not to soil his gabardine suit. On the one hand, he was still miffed not to be smoking the cigars Uncle Lij had brought. On the other hand, Grandfather's mood, if properly provoked, might yield some fun.

"What about the damn dog, Grandfather?" he called down.

"Damn fluff! I ought to tan Elijah's hide for giving Maria that beast. Barks at everything that moves. Here, pay attention, you lazyboots! Pull that rope! Spoiled, I say. Brought those infernal Spiritualists, too. Talk with the dead, ha! Might as well talk with my pig Barney."

"What do you think of Mrs. Gregg?"

"A boiled potato, she is. A lump! Looks set to eat me out of pantry and home. Did you see the way she gobbled up Barney? Did you?"

"I saw, Grandfather."

"And that husband of hers—Skinnyshanks!" Grandfather marched to the wall where his tools hung on pegs. He was in fine fettle now, Horace observed with a grin, the muttering he had suppressed throughout dinner finding its outlet. "Pretends to be some kind of scientific professor. Spouts ten-dollar words. Tomfoolery and poppycock! My Martha is dead as them skunks of yours, dead and gone to her reward. Drat Maria and her notions! A pretty girl has no call to fill her head with ideas. Wants Charles to go to the university in Ann Arbor soon as he gets old enough. I'll get that girl a husband if it's the last thing I do! Here, watch what you're doing!"

Horace clutched too late as the pulley fell from his hand and crashed to the barn floor a foot away from Grandfather. The way the old man threw up his hands and leaped back might have been comical if Horace had not been so distracted that he nearly lost his own footing and plummeted after the pulley.

"What do you mean about Maria?" he demanded, as he recovered and once again hauled up the control line he had rigged.

"Ate four biscuits, my pie and cake, too. If my Martha had anything more to say to me she would have said it in the thirty-five years we were married. Thought-forms, in a pig's poke. Spoiled you are, I say. A snake is a snake no matter its pattern."

"Grandfather! What about Maria getting married?"

"Tan Elijah . . . disturbing the peace of the dead . . . not a penny of mine to their damn ghost foundation!"

It was no use. Grandfather was muttering again, and as Horace finished his work on the pulley the old man marched away without so much as a thank-you. Horace descended the hayloft steps and picked the pieces of straw off his trousers. Grandfather made a lot of heartfelt threats that vanished the minute they were uttered. But more than one young swain in town had tried to court Maria. She had turned them all away, saying her place was at home caring for her father and Charles. Did Grandfather mean to encourage someone? Horace scowled. Too many things were not to his liking, and though he could not put his finger on anything in particular, a smart young fellow ought to be on his guard. Maria did not need a husband. No spirits should be caressing her face. He must get to the bottom of this, and the first thing to do was to launch his own investigation of Mrs. Potato and Professor Skinnyshanks.

Four

Mary stepped from the soapy water in the metal bathtub and wrapped herself in her dressing gown. She was alone in the kitchen; Nathan would come in later from picking the corn to take his bath. She twisted the water out of her hair and walked barefoot up the stairs. At the top of the landing she paused. To reach her bedroom at the front of the house, she had to pass the closed door of Clara's room. Just a dozen steps, yet each time she felt powerless to move forward, halted by some invisible force. Going down was better than going up. She could sit in her room and prepare herself first, though even then it was impossible to walk straight by. The door had to be acknowledged, the memories confronted. If she did not pause for at least a moment, if she tried to thwart her heart by brushing past, the ache would rush after her and force payment at the bottom of the stairs. Going up was worse, slowed by the weight of her belly and the swelling that afflicted her legs and feet, and more so now in late afternoon, when sunlight through the west window bathed the landing in soft yellow warmth. She could not advance, she could not speak, could only stand there mute and helpless before the closed door until some power released her and allowed her to move on.

She reached her bedroom and sat at the mirrored dressing table Nathan had made for her. The smooth oak top held an assortment of scents and lotions, most of them gifts brought by Lisette from the fashionable ladies' shops in Detroit. She reached her bedroom and sat at the mirrored dressing table Nathan had made for her. The smooth oak top held an assortment of scents and lotions, most of them gifts brought by Lisette from the fashionable ladies' shops in Detroit. Lisette was a banker's daughter, raised amidst servants and society, a brunette beauty possessed of clear oval features and an effortless style of dress. The first time Elijah had brought her to Livonia to meet her new relations, Mary had worried that Lisette would look down her nose at them, contemptuous of their country life. Instead, her sister-in-law embraced her warmly, offered gifts and amusing news from the city, and praised Mary's cooking before everyone as wholesome and delicious, making her blush.

Mary worked her brush through her wet hair. Lisette was wearing her glossy tresses in an elegant new style called a chignon, and for a moment Mary debated trying to copy it. But the prevailing atmosphere for tonight's seance must be purity and innocence, so perhaps the best treatment would be a simple bun covered by a white net. The baby twisted in her belly, and Mary stopped to let the ripple pass. She had been too on edge to eat much today, and though she felt a bit light-headed, she was not hungry. Much of her appetite had faded anyway since Clara's death. She rose and went to her wardrobe. Professor Gregg had instructed the men to wear dark suits to the seance, the women to appear in white dresses.

"The company must be balanced," he explained, "male and female, dark and light. By repeated scientifically controlled experiments our research has ascertained that the spirits respond most favorably to a harmonious setting in which all forces are equalized. We will require a round table, and we must seat ourselves opposite one another in such a way as to pair positive and negative personalities."

Positive and negative personalities. Mary still was not sure what that meant, though if the sitters tonight must be so identified she conceded she and Nathan were probably the negatives. Not merely for their grief or their less prosperous status than Elijah and Lisette, but because they seemed to have missed something somehow, as if they kept treading the same water while the rest of the world swam on. She felt it when Elijah detailed his latest business investment, when Lisette, at Maria's urging, recounted the entertainments they had seen in the Detroit theaters. And Nathan felt it, too, although he kept his counsel to himself. *We have a good life. We have each other,* she wanted to tell him, but she only pressed his hand and let the gesture serve where speech would not.

Footsteps tramped into the rear of the house, and stepping just outside her room, carefully avoiding the pull exerted by Clara's door, she called over the banister.

"Nathan? Nathan, could you bring my sewing basket from the living room?"

He appeared a moment later, carrying the woven basket.

"I will bathe now, Mary. Is Horace in the house?"

"I thought he was helping you pick corn."

"No, I sent him to the barn to sand and repaint the old cradle, but he has vanished and left the job undone." Nathan made a sound of disgust.

"Do not be hard on him, Nathan. He has probably gone to see Lij. You know how Horace looks forward to his visits, and the cradle is not needed for another month yet."

"As you wish." He left her the basket and went downstairs.

Mary took her sewing kit to the bed. She had one white dress, but the fit was not intended for a pregnant woman and she would have to unpick the stitches and contrive a more ample design. The dress was years out of fashion anyway, and even when not pregnant her figure no longer had the firm round curves the scooped neckline had once flattered. She envied Maria her slender waist and high breasts.

"I looked like that once," she told the mirror.

She put the past aside and bent to her sewing. All that mattered was to follow Professor Gregg's instructions as closely as possible. Nothing must interfere with the hope of contacting Clara.

The sun was lowering by the time Mary finished the alterations to the dress. Nathan had come in earlier to don his dark suit, reporting no sign yet of Horace. Mary dressed, fixed her hair, and descended slowly past Clara's room. She found Nathan on the rear porch, whittling a pair of wood whistles for Elijah's sons. For all the toys they could buy in the city, the two boys clamored for wood whistles from the farm. Mary sat down beside her husband.

"I feel I have been counting the minutes all day," she said. "Is it too early to go over, do you think?"

"A bit yet. Let us wait until the sun is down."

Mary nodded. The seance was to be preceded by a light meal Maria would prepare, but the spirits could not be summoned until full darkness had fallen. Father Kingsley had already declared he would not attend.

"Sit in the dark and talk to ghosts? Hogwash!" he had proclaimed to Nathan and Mary as they bid him goodnight the previous evening. "Your brother is a damn fool to have truck with such nonsense."

"Please, Father Kingsley!" Mary raised her finger to her lips, hoping they were far enough away on the lawn for the others not to hear. She had long ago lost her apprehension of her father-in-law, had even come to like the crusty old man. But he was not modern, not interested in scientific progress, and Elijah had proven himself anything but a fool. In the nineteen years since Lij had left for the city, the summer her first baby was due, he had gone from clerk in a mercantile store to owning a dry-goods business to partnerships in half a dozen profitable enterprises. He gambled on investments, and his luck never deserted him. When Mary had nervously inquired of Lisette, in confidence, whether the medium was to be paid for her services, Lisette assured her Elijah had already made a generous contribution to the Greggs' foundation. Surely Lij, so astute in all his dealings, was right to have faith in the Spiritualists' methods.

The sun simmered on the horizon, and as Nathan finished his whittling they sat in silence, watching the pale orange band of the sunset blur and fade. Some nights the colors were so fiery it seemed the sun had ignited the fields where it touched down, and Mary tried to envision the far westward lands that lay beyond the horizon. She would never go there, she knew. Once she had lived on a frontier; now it had passed on and left her behind. Even the sunset was tame tonight, streaks of iridescent rose and gold, soft as butterfly wings brushing the sky. A figure approached from the south, and Mary recognized her son's nonchalant stride. He arrived before them, hands in his pockets, whistling.

"I gave you a job to do," said Nathan evenly.

"I know, Pa. I'll do it tomorrow, I promise."

"Where have you been?"

"To see Silas Joslin."

"Did you catch another skunk?" asked Mary, puzzled.

"Not yet." Horace looked sly.

"Well, at least you are in time to come to your grandfather's," said Nathan. "Get dressed, Horace. I will bring the buggy for you, Mary."

Nightfall was complete by the time Arthur brought them to Father Kingsley's house. Maria welcomed them in. She had prepared a supper of vegetable soup, cold meats, and rye bread, and as Mary ate she felt relieved to note her white dress and hair net were in keeping with the other women's demure garb. Around her neck Mrs. Gregg wore a small golden cross on a chain, a reassuring sight. Old Reverend Swift had passed on, Livonia Center still had no church, and Mary and Nathan rarely heard a service. Still, if God in his wisdom had seen fit to take their child, would He not in his mercy allow her to appear one more time?

They finished their meal, and Maria invited them to the parlor. The only light was a small candle in the center of the table, which Professor Gregg took pains to illuminate and shade with a red glass globe. "Another scientific advance," he explained. "We have discovered that a subdued red light, as is used in photographic development, is the one bearable color for visitors from the spirit world." He guided the sitters to the table, and though their circle was slightly unbalanced, being nine in number, Mary found Nathan and herself seated opposite Elijah and Lisette—negative and positive—and humbly accepted her place. Maria and Charles sat close together opposite Horace while the Greggs completed the pairs at the table. Mrs. Gregg had spoken little during supper, consuming several bowls of soup and sighing often, in preparation for her ordeal.

"Friends, we are ready," said the professor, and the last shifting of chairs quieted. Soft red light from the globe warmed the darkness, and Mary stopped trying to force her eyes to adjust and let herself be drawn into its comfortable glow. She could just make out the faces around the table, shadowy as if glimpsed in a dream, and Professor Gregg's voice seemed to come from far away.

"Lay your palms flat upon the table and concentrate your thoughts. Let no stray notion distract you from the image of your departed mother Martha Kingsley. She loved this house and all in it, and we ask only some sign that she is near."

A long moment of silence passed, and Mary's heart yearned for any sound or sight. Please let Martha come, she prayed, for then Clara may, too. She glanced at Mrs. Gregg. The medium's eyes were closed, her plump cheeks slack, her body slouched in her chair. Mary closed her eyes and focused her will, as the professor spoke again.

"Martha Kingsley, are you there?"

"Mmmmm."

The sound wafted from Professor Gregg, a pleasant murmur, like a sleeper awakening from a refreshing nap. Mary opened her eyes and watched as the medium's head rotated in a gentle circle on her neck.

"Mmmmm."

"Martha?" coaxed Professor Gregg. "Martha, your family is here to speak with you. Can you hear us?"

"Yes." The word came softly from the medium's lips, then her eyes opened and her tone grew lively. "My dear ones, is it you?"

"Mother, yes!" cried Maria. "Where are you? Can you see us? Are you in this room?"

"Yes, daughter. My spirit is beside you even now."

Maria turned joyously from side to side.

I see nothing, thought Mary. Oh, where is she? She glanced to Mrs. Gregg, and started. The medium sat upright with her hands on her hips, nodding briskly as had been Martha's wont. Her round face had grown purposeful, and glancing sharp-eyed around the table she made a tsking sound with her tongue.

"Now where is your father?" she scolded. "Is he being thick-headed again?"

"I am afraid so, Mother," said Maria. "He went to bed."

"Well, I shall give you proof of my presence, and mind you tell him so."

A trembling ran under Mary's hands, a vibration that tingled her palms. Then in a slow, smooth movement, the table began to rise. She stifled the amazed cry that sprang to her lips. Beside her, Nathan gave a quick intake of breath. Across the table she saw Lisette, serene, Maria and Charles, awestruck, Horace, looking wary, as the table hovered six inches above the floor. Slowly it descended again.

"Oh, Mother," cried Maria. "What place have you come from?"

"From a lovely place called Summerland where there is no work nor illness, only health and leisure. We hear concerts by the finest musicians and eat at tables set with silver and crystal."

"Do you converse with other spirits, Mother?"

"Yes, often, and now that my earthly work is done I have many opportunities to improve my mind. One may learn French or geometry and take walks in sunny glades."

"Are you happy?"

"Yes, daughter, and now you have summoned me, my satisfaction is complete. To see how well you have managed the house makes me quite content. Clean, orderly—I could not have done better myself."

"Oh, thank you, Mother. That means so much to me! Charles is here, too. May he speak to you?"

"Of course, my dear son."

Mary ventured a glance down the table. She had paid hardly any attention to Professor Gregg, and she saw he was watching his wife intently, noting every change in her tone or posture, no doubt for his research. Charles, meanwhile, seemed tongue-tied, and Maria, her hands still on the table, gently nudged her brother with her elbow.

"What do you want me to do, Ma?" Charles blurted.

"To be a good boy and study hard as Maria tells you. She cares very much for your education."

"I want him to go to the university, Mother," said Maria.

"Yes, dear, I know. It is a fine goal."

"May I have a message for Father? Even though he is not here. . . ." Maria's voice faltered.

"Tell him I am sorry his rheumatism pains him. All will be healed when he joins me here. I must return now to Summerland. Goodbye, my dears."

"Goodbye, Mother! Goodbye!"

Maria rose from the table, arms uplifted in farewell, while Charles, mouth agape, stared round-eyed at the ceiling. Mary's shoulders trembled. Oh please, let it be her turn now. Let Clara come.

"Please," she whispered aloud, and Professor Gregg nodded as if he understood.

"Clara, beloved daughter of Nathan and Mary Kingsley. Will you join us tonight from beyond the veil?"

Mary's breath stopped. She felt such tension in her being, it seemed she must pass out from the strain. Yet minutes passed and nothing happened. Mrs. Gregg had slumped back lifeless in her chair as if exhausted from the previous effort. Across the table Elijah and Lisette held themselves in total stillness, fixed deep in meditation, and a small cry of anguish escaped Mary's lips.

"Calm yourself, dear lady," the professor urged. "Place your hands on the table and concentrate. The spirits cannot appear if the harmony of our circle becomes unbalanced."

Across the table Maria wore a blissful look, while Horace's face was smug. Charles had closed his mouth, and at Professor Gregg's instruction he screwed his face into obedience. Yes, concentrate, Mary ordered herself, feeling her heart would break to come so close and be denied.

Thunk! The table tipped to the left. Bump, bump, bump. It danced a little jig, and Mary fumbled to keep her palms on its surface. Rap, rap. A knocking sounded beneath the red globe.

"Tee-hee-hee."

The medium wiggled in her chair, a giggle on her lips.

Thunk! The table tipped to the right.

"Clara, are you there?" Professor Gregg asked.

A sudden sssst! split the air, and as the company started, the candle flame leaped in a luminous flare. For several seconds the light sparkled like a firecracker while Mary watched enthralled.

"Tee-hee-hee."

"Clara," the professor admonished good-humoredly. "You are a playful child. Will you be mannerly now and speak to your parents?"

"Yes, sir!" A little girl's voice came brightly from the medium's lips.

"Clara!" Nathan's voice cracked, and in her happiness, Mary forgot to keep her hands on the table and clutched his arm. Images of Clara rushed to her mind, joy choked her throat, and she found herself powerless to speak. "Where are you, daughter?" asked Nathan.

"I don't know, Pa, but it is a very nice place."

"What is it like?"

"I have toys and other children to play with and lots of good things to eat."

"Is your illness gone, Clara?"

"Yes, Pa, I am fine. I did so like the daisies and asters Ma put on my grave. Will you bring me some more?"

"Dearest, I will bring you more flowers than you could wish." Tears spilled down Mary's cheeks.

"And we shall have a stone for your grave, as soon as we can," said Nathan, "carved with your name and age and the date you left us."

Clara sighed, and the giggle left her voice as her tone grew soft and consoling. "Sweet Ma and Pa, you have grieved so much for me. Do not cry anymore. It says in the Bible that the good shall go to heaven, and surely that is where I am. Every day is warm and sunny, and such lovely books they have to read! I shall be quite happy here until we are all together again."

"Is it true, then, that we will be reunited?" Mary begged.

"Yes, Ma, it is sure. But you must cheer up and take care of yourself for the new little baby will need you. I must go now. Goodbye!"

The voice faded, and for a long moment Mary did not move, rapt in peace. Across the table, Maria's face shone. The medium had sunk back into her chair, and in the center of the table the candle flickered low.

"Friends," said Professor Gregg. "We have shared a most moving experience. Now my wife must return to us."

He called gently to Mrs. Gregg, who blinked her eyes and turned her head as if to clear away the cobwebs of a dream.

"Did the spirits come?" she asked faintly, and as Lisette assured her they had, the medium pressed one hand to the cross on her bosom and humbly bowed her head.

Nathan helped Mary from her chair, and she found her weak knees in need of the support. But her heart felt a balm she had not known could exist, and when she looked in her husband's eyes she saw the clearness of youth rekindled. Nathan stepped toward the professor, who was attending his wife.

"We cannot thank you enough, sir. It has been a scarce year, the rains scant, but if you would accept a small donation for your foundation . . ."

"You are too kind." Professor Gregg shook his hand. "Rest assured that every heartfelt donation, no matter its size, furthers our investigations into the realm of spiritual affairs."

"I am so glad to see your prayers answered," said Lisette to Mary, leading her from the room. "Already the veil of care has been lifted from your cheeks."

"I will drive the buggy home, Ma," offered Horace, "so you and Pa can sit comfortably in back."

They walked outside, and Mary climbed onto the buggy seat. The moon was just past full, and the silvery night shone like a blessing on her upturned face. Nathan settled beside her, and as his arms went around her, she rested in gratitude against the solid warmth of his chest. She would sleep well tonight, for the first time in weeks, and come morning she would open the door to Clara's room and let in the dawning sun.

Five

It was, thought Horace, a fine morning for singing, so as he stepped onto the front porch, he treated the world to a robust rendition of "Oh, Susanna." From inside the house came the sound of his parents' laughter. Ma had arisen so bright and happy that morning she had gone out to the chicken coop and collected the eggs before Horace even had his trousers on. After breakfast, Pa had assigned him only half the usual chores. Now he was dispatched to Grandfather's with two silver dollars wrapped in a paper for Professor Gregg. If this run of luck continued, Horace might get out of plowing the fields, picking the apples, cleaning the barn, and sanding the blasted cradle, too.

Instead of heading to Grandfather's, however, he circled away toward the rear of his parents' land, where a secluded creek ran among the trees. It was a good place to work out thorny problems, and besides, if he completed his errand too soon Pa would only set him to work on some tedious chore. He would say that the professor, grateful for Pa's generous donation, had detained him to explain at length the tenets of Spiritualism. Pleased at having an excuse so easily concocted, Horace sat down with his back to a sycamore tree.

In fact, Horace already knew a great deal about Spiritualism because yesterday afternoon, before the seance, he had set out on a scientific investigation of his own. The result was like holding a ripe, juicy fruit in his hands. *Oh yes, I am clever!* he crowed to himself. Miss Polly Noble, the schoolteacher, had used to chide him for not caring to know his facts and figures, but Miss Noble was wrong. Horace did care for knowledge—of a certain sort. After all, where was the profit in knowing the capital city of Virginia or the twelve amendments to the Constitution?

But knowing how to turn dead skunks into quarters or how to spot a snake—no matter its pattern—that was the way to get ahead in the world.

His first stop had been the library, located in Miss Noble's house. His former teacher was surprised and delighted to see him. "Even though you have graduated from eighth grade, you are never too old to learn," she avowed. She besieged him with volumes on history, literature, science, agriculture, and geography, but when Horace politely inquired for a text on the new scientific religion of Spiritualism, she conceded, crestfallen, that she had no such book. However, Miss Noble had heard of the Spiritualist movement and was able to provide a vague description of what a seance entailed. Evading her efforts to send him away with an enlightening volume of essays by Mr. Ralph Waldo Emerson, Horace thanked her and trekked back to Livonia Center, where Stringer's General Store had opened the previous year.

Several horses and wagons were tied to the hitching rack in front of the long, narrow clapboard building when he arrived, and at the counter, Abe Stringer, the store owner, was waiting on Samuel Millard and the two youngest of his ten children. Horace inspected the merchandise crowded on the shelves. Tea, flour, sugar, tobacco, beeswax, goose quills, calico, suspenders, shoes, rope, wire, nails—if it could be bought, sold, or bartered, you would find it at Stringer's General Store. Horace strolled past the pickle barrel and ambled toward the counter where a gold watch in a case caught his eye. Twenty dollars! But it sure would look fine dangling on a chain from the pocket of his vest. The Millards were departing, and before another customer could start haggling with Mr. Stringer, Horace wedged himself forward.

"My Uncle Elijah has brought two Spiritualists to visit," he announced. "One is a medium who talks with the dead, and she is to give a seance this very evening at my Grandfather's house."

The result could not have been more gratifying. Like a rock dropped in a placid pond, the news rippled to the walls of the room and lapped back to Horace, the instant center of attention. Pressed for details, he gladly obliged, being careful to stick more or less to the facts. Mr. Stringer made h'mmms of agreement as Horace spoke. The storekeeper was one of the most educated men in town and made frequent trips to Detroit to purchase inventory for his store. He was also a member of the Town Board and therefore well informed on a wide scope of affairs.

"The whole religion was started by two young sisters, Kate and Margaret Fox, in New York State," he informed his enthralled customers.

"Must have been 1848 or so. They heard a spirit rapping in their house"—he tapped three ominous beats on the counter—"and pretty soon they devised a way of spelling out messages, asking the spirits to rap when people pointed to alphabet letters on a board. Some say those two girls broke through a wall to the world beyond, and now there are mediums everywhere, calling up the dead."

"How could two children start a religion?" scoffed Ira Tuttle. He spat a jet of tobacco juice into the brass spittoon by the stove and wiped the residue from his beard. "Who would believe a pair of simple country girls?"

"Who would believe a poor carpenter's son in Galilee?" said his wife tartly. "A prophet is always scorned in his own land. Yet look how the whole world is Christian today. If one man can start a religion, why not two innocent girls?" She plucked her husband by the sleeve and towed him away.

Elizabeth Stringer turned from arranging bottles of medicine on a shelf. "And I have heard," she announced with a twinkle of mischief in her eye, "that some of these mediums say women ought to have the right to vote." The consternation provoked by this remark nearly side-railed Horace's quest for information, as vehement protests rang from the men in the one-room store.

"But what do *you* think?" Horace tapped on the counter to regain Abe Stringer's attention. The store owner had proven his best source so far. "Are these seances real?"

Mr. Stringer spread his hands and gave a measured shrug. "I don't know, Horace. I have never witnessed one, and until I do I will keep an open mind. There are miracles in the Bible after all. Why shouldn't they happen in modern times as well? But I tell you what—every time I go to Detroit I bring back the latest newspapers for the Town Board to follow the civic affairs. Go over to Silas Joslin's house and ask to have a look at them. The Spiritualist movement has grown so popular, you may well find an article or two."

So Horace had set off for the town clerk's home, though by now the sun was lowering toward the treetops, and if he were late for the seance, Pa would be fierce. Silas answered his knock by automatically pinching his nose and motioning him away toward the shed.

"No, no," Horace waved his empty hands, "I don't have any skunks today." He explained his errand and was invited inside to a small room furnished as an office. Livonia had no town hall yet, though people were already arguing over whether and where one should be built, and in the meantime Silas's bookshelves served as the central repository for all accounts and records. He pulled out a thick stack of newsprint.

"If you ask me," he peered suspiciously over his spectacles, "there's trickery in this business. It's nothing more than poor, grieving folks being taken in by confidence men."

"Could be, Mr. Joslin." Horace nodded gravely. "Though everyone knows you're not the man to be duped."

Horace rubbed his back against the bark of the sycamore and chortled at the memory. He had spent almost an hour poring through Silas's newspapers and had arrived home just in time to accompany Pa and Ma to the seance. But the delay was worth it. Near the bottom of the stack, in a year-old paper, his eyes snagged on a headline, "Medium Exposed!" Invited to witness a seance in a fashionable Detroit home, a reporter had thrown the company into an uproar by grabbing the medium's wrists just as the seance table commenced an unearthly dance. Tied to each of her arms, concealed by the long sleeves of her dress, was a steel bar slipped beneath the table's rim. Although the disgraced Spiritualist was not Mrs. Gregg, Horace had gone to the seance with a gloating heart. When the table rocked it was all he could do not to jump from his seat and tackle her. Instead, unnoticed in the excitement, he slipped one hand beneath the table and felt carefully along the underside. No steel rod, but a jacklike device met his fingers, and worming his foot across the floor, his toe encountered the edge of a bellows pump. Both Greggs had their hands in full view, faces fixed in concentration, and looking around the rapt audience, Horace felt he would burst at the seams. But Mr. Stringer's reflection on keeping an open mind had stayed his hand. Was there more advantage in exposing the Spiritualists . . . or in joining their game?

Horace unwrapped the two silver dollars Pa had entrusted to him and weighed one in each hand. Look, he counseled himself, at the advantages of exposing the charade. The whole town would acclaim his superior intelligence, his bravery and daring, his dedicated pursuit of justice. "Why those Spiritualists fooled even Elijah Kingsley," the townspeople would exclaim, "a rich businessman who surely ought to know the ways of the world. Yet our clever Horace caught them in the act. Now there is a young man destined to go far!" Horace basked for several minutes in this glowing daydream before remembering to continue his analysis.

Revealing the Spiritualists would also spare Uncle Lij and his parents any future donations they might be inclined to contribute to the Greggs' foundation, bringing Horace their long-lasting gratitude and possibly—dare he hope it?—a reward. Most important, he imagined the sheer joy, the exquisite delight of catching the tricksters red-handed. What a ruckus it would cause, a scandal, a seven day's wonder, a veritable explosion of excitement in this sleepy country town. Ma would faint, Grandfather would bellow, Aunt Lisette and Maria would cry in each other's arms. Why, Pa and Uncle Elijah might throttle Professor Gregg with their bare hands. Yes! Yes! That was what he wanted! Horace's soul swelled with the absolute drama and magnitude of the scene, and he had to restrain himself from bolting to his feet and tearing across the fields yelling his discovery at the full pitch of his lungs.

But . . . were there not also advantages to playing along?

Who had gathered the eggs today? Not Horace. Who was probably, even now, sanding the cradle? Not him. Frauds and fakers the Spiritualists might be, but Ma and Pa's newfound happiness was as genuine as that twenty-dollar gold watch. Maria was blissful, Uncle Elijah, Aunt Lisette, and Charles were well content. The only person the Greggs had failed to win over was Grandfather, and when Horace weighed the benefits of having six joyous relatives susceptible to spiritual commands versus gaining the approval of one cantankerous old man, no real contest presented itself.

Moreover, there was always the chance that these same happy relatives, far from being grateful to Horace for stripping them of their illusions, might deeply resent his intrusion, especially since they themselves would be revealed as gullible fools. Such was the very return made to that fearless newspaper reporter by his much-offended hosts. Besides, the Greggs are only spreading comfort, Horace told himself, and he nodded, liking the sound of it. After all, when Clara died hadn't all their friends and neighbors tried to do the same? "Rest assured, she is with the angels," they promised, and "Though your dear lamb is taken, her memory can never fade." The Greggs had merely taken the comfort one step further, adding physical evidence to these heartfelt beliefs. Where was the harm in that? Why, it was a very Christian undertaking of them to bring solace to Horace's dear family by conjuring forth the spirits of Grandmother and Clara. Indignation burned in his chest at the mere idea that anyone would brand the Spiritualists as frauds.

The cawing of a crow overhead abruptly stirred him from his passion, and Horace rewrapped the silver dollars, stowed the money in his pocket, and got to his feet. Well, there lay the gains and losses on both sides, though in truth he admitted he had not yet discovered Professor

Skinnyshanks and Mrs. Potato to be complete charlatans. A jack might explain the dancing table, but what had caused the candle to flare just as Clara was summoned? Anyone could see how hard Maria worked to manage the house, but how could Mrs. Gregg have known that brisk way Grandmother used to nod her head? Grandfather in his mumblings might have dropped useful tidbits about Charles's schooling or Clara's love of books, but how could the medium have described so accurately the flowers on his little sister's grave? He would have to gain the Greggs' confidence to find out.

Horace scratched his privates and headed for Grandfather's house. As he approached, he saw Maria and Charles in the yard, scattering feed for the chickens, and he shook his head at the sorry sight. Women's work. Maria would turn the boy into a sissy for sure. Horace could afford to be scornful now that he was not collecting eggs anymore.

"Morning, Maria. Hello, Charles." He strutted up beside them. Trixie was off sniffing the vegetable garden, and Horace remembered it had been some time since he had paid a nocturnal visit to rile the dog and stir up Grandfather's ire, an oversight he must rectify soon.

"Good morning, Horace." Maria threw a handful of dried corn in a graceful arc, and the hens darted in a cackle to gobble kernels from the dirt. "Isn't it a lovely day?"

"I'll say it is." Horace nodded. It was always a lovely day when things were going his way. Maria, however, paid little attention to his answer. Her long blond hair hung loose, tendrils wisping around her face like corn silk, and her print dress clung delicately to her form like the petals of a flower. She seemed impervious to the mad dash of hens squabbling around her skirt.

"I have brought a donation for the Spiritualists," said Horace. "What did you think of the seance last night?"

"It was wonderful! I felt Mother's presence so clearly, it was almost as if I could touch her. When I told Mrs. Gregg the intensity of my experience, she said it is very possible I might be a sensitive also. She said I should welcome any voices that come to me."

Horace's eyebrows slanted in skepticism, but he quickly resumed an open face. "Will Mrs. Gregg hold another seance tonight?"

"Oh no, it is much too taxing. You saw how weakened she was by last night's visitations. She must have at least a day of nourishment and rest."

"I could take her for a buggy ride," Horace offered.

"Would you? That would be so kind."

Maria clasped his arm, for once looking at him with true appreciation, and Horace straightened smugly. This was the way it should be. Respect, that was what he deserved, that and a pretty girl on his arm. It was about time Maria noticed all his admirable qualities. Why, he would kiss her right now, smack her sweet lips, if it weren't for Charles hanging about her apron.

"Do you know what meant the most to me?" said Maria, and Horace frowned because she had released her grasp and become dreamy-eyed again. "That Mother is pleased at the way I have managed the house. What a blessing to know everything is as she would have wanted." She tossed the last of the corn from her basket, and Charles shooed away the clucking hens. "Come in the house, Horace, and you may give the donation to Professor Gregg."

They went inside to the parlor where Uncle Lij, Aunt Lisette, and the Greggs were conversing over tea. Grandfather, Maria said, had stalked off to the Houghton farm to discuss buying a horse, though Horace suspected the errand was probably concocted to avoid the Spiritualists. At least it spared Grandfather the anguishing sight of Mrs. Gregg consuming a plateful of glazed cherry tarts. Horace made his donation and the offer of a buggy ride for two o'clock, which the Greggs gladly accepted.

"Lisette brought some new fabrics from Detroit," said Maria, as she led him out. "She is going to help me cut a new dress for the September social. It will be coral pink with a full hoop skirt. Lisette says the high fashion ladies in the city wear skirts nearly ten feet wide."

"Might be hard to dance in," Horace observed casually, remembering his intention to claim Maria as his partner at the party. "So you like the socials, Maria?"

"Of course. Doesn't everyone? It is fun to see all the neighbors and dance to the fiddles."

"Is there anyone in particular you want to dance with?"

"No." Maria shrugged, no hint of guile in her reply. She took a light step forward, lifting the hem of her skirt, and turned on her toe, humming a tune.

"Well, if you haven't a partner, I could fill in and give you a dance or two," Horace allowed.

But Maria did not answer. She only hummed and skipped lightly, this way and that, like a butterfly flitting on a flower. Horace was quite forgotten, and in annoyance he jammed his fists into his pockets and strode away. He was relieved to hear Maria had no special beau, but irritated she had not named him, especially considering his reputation as a fine dancer. Still, the social was three weeks off, and Horace had more pressing matters at hand. He strolled home, and when he explained to Ma and Pa his offer to take the Greggs on a buggy ride, they were so grateful they pressed him to take along a peach cobbler to help Mrs. Gregg keep up her strength.

"Do you think," Ma asked hopefully, "that we dare ask her to contact the spirit world again on our behalf? Not to find Clara—now I know she is well, I am content—but to speak with little Robert? Or will it be too late, seventeen years past his death?" She twisted her apron in her fingers.

"But Mrs. Gregg has received messages from Benjamin Franklin and William Shakespeare," recalled Pa. "Surely, then, she can reach our son."

"Yes, that's so." Ma's face flushed with new promise. "Oh, Nathan, would it not be a joy to know that Robert, too, is safe? Horace, could you ask them, please?"

"Sure, Ma," he replied.

At quarter to two, Horace finished hitching Arthur to the buggy, set the peach cobbler on the seat beside him, and drove to Grandfather's house. From an open upstairs window came dainty laughter, Maria and Aunt Lisette snipping the fabric for the new dress. Uncle Lij escorted the Greggs to the buggy, thanked Horace for his attentions, and wished them a pleasant ride. The September day was fine, sunny and tinged with the first hint of autumn coolness. A breeze stirred the leaves and rustled like a starched crinoline through the shoulder-high fields of corn. Good smells rose from the earth, sweet clover, ripening apples, the warm animal scent of grazing sheep and cows.

"It is very nice to go along the edge of the wood and look for pheasants," Horace suggested. "I can show you the beaver dam on the river and a place where elderberries grow." He did not offer to take them to Stringer's General Store or to meet Miss Noble or Silas Joslin. For now, he must keep the Spiritualists to himself. The Greggs made polite conversation as they rode along, inquiring with casual interest about the people and doings in town, and Horace answered cheerfully, embellishing when the mood took him, for a little fancying up never hurt the plain truth. By the time they reached the berry bushes and descended from the buggy, the party was quite convivial. Horace spread a blanket to sit on, and Mrs. Gregg, at his urging, started on the peach dessert. Now, he thought, let's see what I can make of Mrs. Potato and Professor Skinnyshanks.

"My Ma is wondering if you might hold another seance to call up my brother Robert," he said. "He died before he was two."

"How tragic." Professor Gregg's face lapsed into sorrow. He wore his usual black frock coat and vest, and his cheeks showed pink against his neat white hair and mustache.

"There's plenty of other folks in town would probably like to talk with their dead, too," Horace continued. "The Ryders lost both their boys at Gettysburg, and Mrs. Cates near about cried herself sick when her husband tripped over his shotgun last year and did himself a fatal injury."

"A catastrophe," sighed the professor. "So many lives taken before their time. It is precisely why I believe Spiritualism is the single most important development of our modern era, a far greater boon to mankind than such mechanical devices as the reaper or the internal combustion engine."

"But you would have to be careful," Horace warned. "I heard some folks say Spiritualism is all a trick."

He glanced quickly at the professor, alert for the slightest twitch of his mustache or start in his pose, any clue that might hint at a guilty conscience. Instead, the medium's husband ardently nodded his head.

"It is a charge we hear often," he said, deeply concerned. "Unfortunately, it is sometimes true. Some low individuals who call themselves mediums are in reality villains of the worst sort. Utterly devoid of spiritual powers, they seek to gull the unsuspecting by cheap parlor tricks. Such behavior is unforgivable! These frauds must be exposed! They do immense harm to the reputation of true sensitives such as my wife, and their shameless exploitation of the public is nothing less than a criminal offense. They infect the public with skepticism, and if even one unbeliever slinks to the seance table, it may seriously disrupt the medium's ability to communicate. If you were a spirit, Horace, would you visit a home in which you felt unwelcome, nay, threatened?"

"No, I guess not," Horace agreed, taken aback. Professor Gregg had risen and began pacing in agitation, his matchstick figure jerking at the joints as he turned, and for a moment Horace was confounded. But you . . . but I felt. . . . The words trailed away unspoken. Could he, Horace, have been wrong? He had been eager to conclude that if even one medium were a fraud, so must they all be, that if the table's dance was the Greggs' doing, the flaring candle flame must also be their prank. Yet for every twice-dead skunk Horace had delivered to Silas Joslin's pile, had not ten others in town brought a freshly killed article? And Horace himself had trapped and shot a few of his skunks fair and square. Could the Greggs be genuine after all? The idea sent a shiver up his spine for if even one physical sign were real, it meant the spirits of Grandmother and Clara had actually been present in the room. Horace shook himself to shed the icy tingle on his flesh. No. It couldn't be. Grandfather was right, dead was dead, and more important, Horace was never wrong. He had felt the device, and it was only a matter of time before he uncovered all the Greggs' tricks.

"I guess," said Horace, matching Professor Gregg's concern, "it would help you to know which of the people hereabouts don't take kindly to Spiritualism."

"Indeed, it would," he said fervently. "You can imagine how disappointed, how crushed the true believers are when their hopes of contacting their deceased loved ones are dashed by a hostile presence."

"I sure wouldn't want that to happen," Horace averred, "not after all the good you did my Ma and Pa." He snapped his fingers at a sudden idea. "If you were to stay in these parts a while, I could tell you all the folks who would be grateful for a seance, and I could warn you who to look out for and suspect."

"That is very generous, Horace." Professor Gregg's cheeks shone in appreciation. "The more seances we conduct under open-minded circumstances, the more we advance our scientific inquiry into these phenomena."

Mrs. Gregg licked buttery crumbs from her fingers. She had been too absorbed in the peach cobbler to join the conversation, ferrying the food to her mouth with single-minded dedication. Now she let out a long, contented sigh.

"Your mother is an excellent cook," she said, poking a finger into the empty dish to capture a final dab of peach syrup. "I would be so happy to help her contact your dear little brother and to offer my services to any other good, generous people you might name. We had expected to return to Detroit in a few days with your aunt and uncle, but perhaps some other arrangement can be made."

"You could stay on at Grandfather's," offered Horace. "It's a big house with plenty of room. Maria would want you to stay. And I could drive you." He gestured at Arthur, nibbling in a clover patch. "I could take you to the seances, or wherever you needed to go."

"You are a helpful, thoughtful young man," Professor Gregg declared. "We need many more like you in the Spiritualist cause."

Horace beamed. "Let's pick elderberries for my Ma," he suggested. "She makes lots of good things with them, wine and jelly and jam."

They set to work filling the empty cobbler dish with juicy berries.

Horace picked with a great goodwill. Why, already he could think of a half dozen families who would be only too grateful for a spiritual visit, and once he impressed the Greggs with how much he could help them—oh, so much more than simple buggy rides—they would make him a trusted accomplice. As for his reward, Horace tallied the possibilities. Money, perhaps—for the good-hearted people of Livonia would not send the Greggs away empty-handed. Fun and excitement, most definitely—for never before had such a wonder come to the town. But best of all—Horace felt joyous anticipation rising—here was the opportunity to pull off a deception so grand, an artifice so magnificent, it made resurrected skunks pale in comparison. Yes, deception, that was what Horace liked best, and it mattered not whether his victim was parent or relative, friend or foe. He popped a fat purple berry into his mouth, crushed it between his teeth, and slurped the sweet juice that spurted onto his tongue.

Oh yes, I am clever, he sang to himself. *A marvelous fellow, a bold handsome devil, and the whole world shall know by and by!*

Six

To curry a horse the size of Arthur, thought Nathan, was no easy task. It required vigorous, circular movements, brushing against the lay of his coat to dislodge dirt, straw, and pebbles. Arthur's hair was thick, and since the old stallion had a habit of rolling in his stall, the paddock, and any bare patch of ground he could find, his coat quickly became embedded with debris.

"Yes, you are a mess," Nathan said affectionately, giving Arthur a pat as he stroked up the horse's neck with the currycomb. "What am I to do with you?"

He paused, realizing he was once again addressing the horse as Clara used to do. It was a habit he had fallen into these past few weeks, and though he would have colored with embarrassment should anyone else have overheard, between himself and Arthur, it felt comfortable and right. It was Clara who had faithfully groomed the big tan horse, scrambling onto his docile back to ply combs and brushes around his neck, singing him songs, scolding him for his untidy behavior, and reciting stories of the king for whom she had bestowed his name. Clara had been small for her age, yet she never missed a spot on Arthur's coat and thought nothing of crawling under his belly and between his legs, oblivious of his weight. At first, Mary had fretted to see their daughter so free about the beast, but even more than Arthur's gentle nature, Clara had a fearlessness toward animals that had protected her like a charm. Now that she was gone—no, not gone, nearby—Nathan ought to have given the grooming job to Horace. But selfishly, he kept it for himself. He imagined Clara close beside him—"Watch his chest, Pa, he's ticklish!"— and heard her giggle behind his ear.

"Yes, we miss her," he said, currying along Arthur's flank. "I think even you feel her absence. But it has been a month now, and I am beginning to accept."

It had been less easy when their first child died. He had been stunned, disbelieving for weeks, going though the daily chores like a sleep-walking man. Little Robert. Mary had proposed the name out of the blue, a week before the birth, and so strong had been her preference and he so willing to accommodate her that he had never much troubled to inquire for its origins. Besides, it was a good, strong name, and so had their son been until the night they laid him in his crib and awoke the next morning to find him as beautiful and lifeless as a newly plucked flower. Now, seventeen years later, Nathan could look back on Robert's life in gratitude as short yet complete, a gift to cherish for what it was, not to mourn for what it might have been. It was a life small enough for Nathan to cradle in his two hands, and Clara's life was just big enough to encompass in a hug. And that was exactly what Nathan did with his dead children, loving their memories for their very briefness, protecting them as a father ought.

The currycomb had rubbed Arthur's coat all the wrong way, giving the horse a frowsy, comical look, loose tufts of hair, straw, and pebbles exposed everywhere on his coat. Nathan began to lift them off with smooth strokes of the body brush. Horace was taking Arthur out again tonight on the buggy, driving the Greggs to another seance, and the horse deserved a thorough grooming for all his extra journeyings of late. In the three weeks since Elijah and Lisette had returned to Detroit, the Spiritualists had experienced an incredible burst of energy, holding sittings three and even four times a week. With Horace as their attentive guide, they had crisscrossed the township, their reputation growing with each performance and eager sitters clamoring to be admitted.

At the same time, events at the seances had grown ever more miraculous. The uncanny voices, table tilting, and flaring candle flame he and Mary had witnessed had now been joined by new, amazing phenomena. At one seance, mysterious whispers had sounded on the ceiling and a music box in the room had suddenly begun to play. At the seance for the Ryder family, Mrs. Gregg, in her trance state, had so accurately revealed forgotten incidents from the two boys' childhoods that Mrs. Ryder had swooned. Even the few doubters left in town were having second thoughts, and if not convinced, were at least keeping quiet. All these events were eagerly reported by Horace, the morning after each seance.

"You say flowers appeared in Widow Cates's lap?" Nathan queried after Horace delivered the news at breakfast.

"Yes, Pa, out of nowhere!"

"But you were waiting outside with Arthur."

"That's right, Pa, I was."

"Then how did you see it?"

"Widow Cates was so taken, she was still clutching the bouquet when she came out to bid the Greggs goodnight. She told me all about it."

"What kind of flowers were they?"

"Oh, asters and black-eyed Susans and I-don't-know-what, Pa. I couldn't see them well on account of the dark."

But Nathan had seen. That sunrise, going out to milk the cows, he had paused at Mary's flower bed to rearrange one of the border stones he had laid a few weeks before. Puzzled, he had marked where a swath of flowers had been rudely cut. It could not have been Mary, for despite her fervent promise to keep Clara's grave supplied with fresh blooms, Mary had been confined to her bed for almost two weeks. So heartened had she been following Clara's spiritual visit that she had overexerted herself in the house and garden, and the swelling of her ankles and legs had become acute. "Off your feet!" Dr. Shaw had ordered. "I'll allow no more of these seances if this is the excitement they cause." Tamely, Mary had acquiesced, still hoping for a sitting to call Robert and busying herself meanwhile with knitting baby clothes from her bed. The birth was due any day now, and to ensure Mary rested as much as possible, Nathan had willingly agreed to see the flowers delivered to Clara's grave. So every few days he had clipped judiciously, a few blossoms here and there, so the loss should not be visible among the flowers Mary tended with such care. No wonder then he had noticed the stark, ravaged patch the morning after a bouquet had inexplicably appeared in Widow Cates's lap.

Nathan's brush strokes grew slower, and a shadow stole over his heart, like a cloud that passes before the sun. He did not want to examine the coincidence too closely, but how could it be ignored? Yet if he asked, Horace was sure to have an innocent explanation and would only cover his tracks more carefully the next time. Where, Nathan wondered, had he gone wrong? Had he been too easy on the boy? Ought he to have applied a birch rod, as his father had often done, instead of heeding Mary's pleas to be forgiving? Now here was Horace, in intimate company with the Spiritualists, always handy at their call, immensely pleased with himself, while at the same time astounding new phenomena manifested themselves almost nightly.

". . . and if I say she will, why then she will . . . ought to thank me for it . . . a curse it is to have daughters . . ."

Nathan straightened, waiting for his father's figure to catch up with his voice as it preceded him around the half-open door and into the barn.

"Nathan!" The old man put a hand to his bushy eyebrows and squinted into the relative darkness. He advanced with a quick, limping step, giving no quarter to the rheumatism that plagued his hips. "Nathan!"

"Here I am." Nathan stepped around Arthur's flank.

"I want turpentine. Ran short. Can you spare some?"

"There is a can on the shelf." Nathan pointed, and his father stumped toward it. "What are you up to?"

"Fixing to get that sister of yours married."

"What?"

The old man pulled down the turpentine and shook the can to his ear, estimating its contents. "Mix it up . . . varnish that chest . . ."

"What do you mean about Maria getting married?" Nathan asked, directing each word carefully to penetrate his father's muttering.

"Found her a husband, that's what I mean." His father came toward him, prepared to concentrate on the subject now the turpentine was in hand. "Pretty as Maria is, she ought to have had no trouble arranging the matter herself. Plenty of young men in town have been sweet on her. But she has no conception, not an inkling, what a woman ought to want in the world. A home and children, and let that be that!"

"Does she want to become a teacher?" Nathan mused. It was the only other possibility he could think of, though Maria had never mentioned it, and most of the teachers the town employed were, like Polly Noble, former students who graduated at the top of the class. They taught a few years before marrying and starting families of their own. Horace had reported that the spirits, speaking through the entranced Mrs. Gregg, opined that women ought to pursue careers, even become doctors and business owners, but what careers were there in a farming community other than schoolteacher or farmer's wife? Even the boys, except for those few like Elijah who took off for the city or enlisted as soldiers in the war, never doubted their destiny was to work the land as their fathers did. It was not something people thought much about.

"Maria doesn't want to do anything, there is the nuisance," his father rumbled. "Stay home taking care of Charles and me. We can manage fine, I tell you. Needs a home of her own and take that damn dog with her. So I found her a husband, Henry Houghton. Got a hundred sixty acres and a good, honest man. You'd think the girl would thank me for speaking to him on her behalf."

"But she didn't?"

"Cried, she did! Said she wasn't ready to marry anyone. But a few more years and who will be left for her? All the young men marching off dying in the war. . . ." The old man shook the turpentine can to his ear again, frowning.

Nathan moved around to Arthur's head and took the mane comb to the tangled hair on the horse's neck. Henry Houghton was five years older than Maria, a hard worker, serious about his farm, as well made a man as Maria was fair, and with a ready smile and helping hand for his neighbors. Like Maria, he was near the youngest of many children and had been the one to tend his elderly parents until their deaths the previous year. Well might he think of marrying now, and Nathan allowed that his father had made a surprisingly good match. Of course, it must be up to Maria to decide her heart and mind. But his father was right: Maria had never expressed much ambition or desire for herself at all, daydreaming through life as if a current of air might blow her away.

"Give her a little time to come around to the idea," Nathan suggested. "She is too much occupied with the Spiritualists now anyway."

"Flimflam! Damn ghost seekers are probably emptying my cupboards this very minute. Told Maria I want them out of the house by month's end . . . tears again! . . . no such thing as spirits . . . hide that apple pie where *she* can't find it . . ."

A few last mutterings trailed into the barn as his father headed away. Arthur nudged his nose against Nathan's arm.

"You want me to finish, do you?" Nathan asked. "All right, let's see to your tail and hooves."

He combed the bushy tail and took the hoof pick from a shelf. He lifted the first of Arthur's feet and scraped off the caked mud and grass, cleaning gently over the sensitive sole, then carefully slipping the pick under and around the metal shoe to scrape out the final traces of muck. Clara had been adept at even this part of Arthur's grooming ritual, and Nathan settled back into the comfort of her imagined presence beside him. For what was a spirit, after all, but the impress of one life upon another, the intertwining of two souls? So when that person was absent they were still as real to you as if they walked companionably by your side. You knew what they would say, how they would say it, their laugh, their footstep, their sigh. You knew how they polished their spectacles or fussed with their dress. You could even predict that unconscious gesture they were unaware of, like the way Clara would twine a pigtail around her finger when she was deep in a book. So although Nathan had genuinely believed in the happenings of that first seance and had gladly contributed scarce dollars to the cause, in the days following he had come to realize that to contact Clara's spirit, he did not need the Spiritualists at all. Who knew her spirit better than he and Mary? Who needed dancing tables and flaring candles when Clara's own sweet voice sang in his ear? What was the point of red lights, black suits, white dresses, and the veil of darkness, when he could picture Clara anytime in the clear light of day? So even before the incident of the butchered flowers, Nathan had begun to suspect the Spiritualists were frauds, simply because it was all so unnecessary. The power to contact Clara had been in his hands all along. It was simply a matter of love.

Now for the past three weeks Nathan had watched and observed as Horace and the Greggs made their triumphant appearances in homes throughout the town. He felt no need to betray them; oddly, he thanked them for showing him the way. But he could not let them continue much longer. As their reputation grew, each seance called for phenomena more spectacular than the last. How long before a trick went awry, especially if its execution depended on Horace? For although Nathan had not troubled to analyze and still could not logically explain each trick, it was clear enough that quite a variety of events could be produced if a third person sneaked into the seance room after the Greggs had seated everyone in the dark. Horace was careless and sloppy; it was only a matter of time. And though some might say it was Nathan's duty to expose the charlatans, by now so many people had been comforted by their message that to strip his neighbors of that solace seemed to him like killing their loved ones a second time.

No, the best he could do was to persuade the Greggs that having accomplished so much good it was time to depart and continue their mission elsewhere. If his father had now set a limit on his hospitality that would help to hasten their departure. But first they must have one more seance, so Mary could contact Robert and have her mind easy before the new baby came. Then the Spiritualists could go with his blessing, and next time he saw Elijah, he would have a private word with his brother and let Lij decide for himself whether to continue his support.

Nathan cleaned the dirt from Arthur's last hoof, and the horse whinnied softly and shook his mane as if to thank him for the job done. Now Clara would throw her arms around the horse's neck and exclaim, "I love you, Arthur!" Nathan slipped one arm over the stallion's shoulder and rested his cheek against Arthur's newly groomed neck.

I love *you,* Clara, he thought.

Seven

Horace needed to sneeze. Not a mere sniffle, not a polite little ah-choo. No, he needed a huge, convulsive explosion that would clear his head, rattle his eardrums, and expel the tortuously ticklish feeling that plagued the tip of his nose. He needed an "AH-CHOOOO!" and that was precisely what he was not going to get. Because Horace was hidden beneath Mrs. Gregg's enormous hoop skirt, and if he sneezed now the assembled company, hearing the desperately stifled sound emerge from the vicinity of the medium's ample rump, would either mistake it for a very unladylike bodily emission or come to their senses, haul him from hiding, and run Horace and the Spiritualists out of town.

"Go on, move," he whispered, though not loudly enough for anyone to hear. Tonight's seance was at the home of Mr. and Mrs. Brigham, the parents of Maria's deceased girlfriend Sarah. The other two sitters were Maria and Widow Cates, who, inspired by the floral contact from her husband, now yearned to hear from a young nephew on whom she had doted. So following the usual procedure, Horace had delivered the Greggs and Maria to the front door and casually returned toward the buggy to wait with Arthur. The minute everyone was inside, however, he crept back up the porch, pushed the door open an inch, and listened. After several minutes of pleasantries, Professor Gregg ushered the party toward the parlor for the seance, extinguishing the lamps in the living room as they left. In the bustle and darkness of their exit, it was easy for Horace to slip inside the house. A moment later came Mrs. Gregg's apologetic voice. "Dear me, I have forgotten my shawl. No, do not trouble yourself, Mr. Brigham. I shall step back to the sofa and fetch it." While the professor took pains to guide the sitters to their seats, the medium returned to the living room, collected her wrap, and Horace as well.

But Mr. Brigham, unable to resist his gentlemanly impulse, had risen again and met Mrs. Gregg in the doorway. Gallantly taking her arm, he drew her forward so briskly that the skirt had nearly whooshed off Horace's back. He scrambled to catch up, while Mrs. Gregg strove mightily to hold back, and Professor Gregg noisily scraped his chair to cover the sound of Horace's knees clopping on the floor.

"Go on, move," he whispered again, rubbing his ticklish nose. He raised his hand and gave the medium's posterior a whack to signal he was safely in place. She proceeded to the table, and as Mr. Brigham pulled out her chair, Horace scuttled between her legs and out the front of her skirt to refuge beneath the table, nearly tipping Mrs. Gregg off her feet. Unfortunately, under the table was not where Horace was supposed to be. His destination was behind the armchair in the corner, to which spot he could have crawled directly once Mrs. Gregg got him into the room, had not Mr. Brigham intervened. Horace stretched his arm to where Professor Gregg sat and tugged on his pants leg.

"Is the candle tipping?" the professor asked concernedly. He pushed back his chair and leaned over the table to minister to the wayward taper while all the company generously tried to assist. It was all the diversion Horace needed. He felt his way past the professor's empty seat and crept to his hiding place. Whew! He settled into position, glad for the cover of darkness. It had not been one of his smoother entrances, but all he had to do now was sit and await his cues. Then the tickling feeling around his nostrils began again.

"Ah-ah. . . ." He muffled the sniffs, hand clamped over his nose, and the sneeze was momentarily vanquished. Professor Gregg had begun the preliminaries, explaining how the least skepticism might deter the spirits, plus his usual rigamarole about the scientific nature of their pursuit. Horace chuckled to himself. What a lark! It had taken him but a week to prove to the Greggs what a useful accomplice he could be, scouting out advance information such as stories about the Ryder boys' childhoods and alerting them when Silas Joslin turned up at a sitting. On the latter occasion, the spirit had tried—oh, how valiantly—to penetrate from beyond the veil, gasping, "Someone hinders me! An unfriendly presence. Oh, I cannot come!" The evening had ended in great disappointment, and although the unfriendly presence had never been named, Silas had slunk away at the earliest opportunity.

"Besides," Mrs. Gregg advised Horace, "it never hurts to have a failure or two. If it came too easily, people would think *I* controlled the spirits, but when the spirits refuse to show, they take it as proof that the spirits control *me*."

Tonight, Mrs. Gregg had decreed, the visitors from beyond would surely appear but only after some suspense had mounted. In fact, it had taken some earnest pleading by the Brighams to secure the medium's services at all. She had professed to be so undone by the three seances already given that week, she feared her sensitivity might be exhausted. Which only made Sarah's parents more determined to believe their dear daughter could and would appear. When Horace had stopped by the previous afternoon to give the medium's reluctant acceptance and to inquire if the Brigham home contained a room suitable for the seance, Mrs. Brigham gladly showed him into the parlor and anxiously offered to make any changes necessary. Horace made a few helpful suggestions about the positioning of the table and chairs, which Mrs. Brigham hastened to obey. The floor plan Horace drew for the Greggs on his return noted the convenient space behind the corner armchair, the upright piano nearby, and the window in the east wall.

Professor Gregg concluded his introduction, and with many sighs Mrs. Gregg sank into her trance state. Horace patted his pockets to make sure his equipment was in place. It was Mrs. Gregg who had first taken him fully into their confidence. Several more buggy rides, complete with ample picnic lunches, had smoothed the way. Finally, as they sat one afternoon on a blanket, eating fried chicken, Horace offered a brilliant and, he thought proudly, original suggestion.

"We could go by the cemetery and take note of the names and dates," he said, still hoping to convince them of his usefulness. "Would that not give you helpful clues for contacting the dead?"

Mrs. Gregg looked him over. The corners of her mouth began to twitch. Then her shoulders shook, and she burst into such hearty laughter that she dropped her chicken leg. Tears of mirth rolled down her chubby cheeks.

"Oh, Horace," she gasped, laughing and slapping him on the shoulder. "That is exactly what we did the very day we arrived! Stop playing the innocent. It's perfectly clear you are one of us."

Horace beamed, then a bright light dawned. "So that is how you knew about the flowers on Clara's grave!"

"Of course."

"But how could you be sure it was Ma who put them there?"

The medium shrugged. "A fairly obvious guess."

Professor Gregg frowned, proper as always in his black frock coat and vest. "But what inspiration prompted that guess? Could it not have been a spirit who put the correct answer on your lips? Must it not have been Clara herself?"

"Pish-posh." Mrs. Gregg gave a disgusted snort. "Don't mind him, Horace. He has been playing his part so long he has begun to convince himself."

"That is not true." The professor's cheeks flushed. "How do you know there is no science in it? It is only that we have not yet studied enough cases to fully discover the method. Do we not get better levitation results, for example, when we use a smaller table?"

"Because a smaller table is easier to lift!"

"Easier for the spirits to inspire us to lift," her husband insisted. "And do my records not show that in many instances you have described the physical attributes of the departed individual with astonishing accuracy?" He patted his breast pocket where he kept a notebook preserving the details of each seance.

"Of course, I have," Mrs. Gregg scoffed, "whenever there was a photograph or a portrait in the house I could sneak a look at beforehand."

She waved him away, and he went off to pace under an oak tree, perplexing over scientific concerns. Horace watched, fascinated. There was no need for Professor Gregg to maintain any further pretense, yet he showed no sign that his protestations were an act.

"Naturally, the more you believe it yourself, the more will your audience," said Mrs. Gregg, as if she had followed Horace's train of thought.

"The rappings," Horace demanded. "How do you do that?"

"By knocking my shoe on the underside of the table. Or like this." Mrs. Gregg innocently crossed her hands, palms flat as on a seance table, and in a quick, almost invisible movement, she cracked her left forefinger with a loud "pop."

"The flaring candle?"

"A ring of magnesium powder around the taper before the seance begins."

"The voices—Clara's, Grandmother's. You sounded so much like them."

Mrs. Gregg drew herself up proudly, fingers to her bosom as if about to utter a dramatic speech. "I, Horace, am a great actress. If only you had seen me in my younger days on stage in New York, playing Kate in *She Stoops to Conquer* or my triumph, Lady MacBeth." She dropped the pose. "On the other hand, most nine-year-old girls sound pretty much alike, and as for your grandmother, well, I know exactly how I would feel if I had to bear eight children to that cantankerous old man."

Horace threw himself over and rolled on his back in delight.

"Let me help you," he pleaded. "I could do the tricks. I know I could!"

"Not so fast." Mrs. Gregg's careless mood vanished, and she pursed her lips. "Why should you want to fool your neighbors, your own kin?"

"Because it is fun!" Horace crowed. "It is a grand scheme!"

"And . . . ?"

"And because they *want* to be fooled. Why, it is their own fault."

"And . . . ?"

Horace fished, not quite knowing what further reply the medium required.

"And because it would prove I am smarter than they are," he decided. "Yes, it would make me smart."

"And . . . ?"

Horace blew out a perplexed breath. "Because it is our mission to do good? Ow!" he cried as Mrs. Gregg slapped him upside the head.

"Believe that, and you'll end up like my husband," she warned, nodding to the still-pacing professor. "If he gets any more addled with this science nonsense, I won't know what to do with him. Now, one more time. Why do you want to join us?"

Horace thought very hard. What had he missed?

"Because there is money in it!"

"Bravo!" Mrs. Gregg clapped her arm around him and drew him close. "Now, Horace, here is what I propose. . . ."

In the darkness behind the armchair, Horace started from his reverie. A voice was coming from the medium, faint, feminine, but insistent as if weary of repeating the same message.

"I . . . am . . . trying," the spirit said deliberately, "I . . . am . . . trying . . . to . . . come . . . through . . ."

Hastily Horace pulled from his pocket a pair of black gloves and a black hood cut with eyeholes, jammed the hood over his head and his fingers into the gloves. He got the hood on backward, and trying to switch it around he bumped the chair with an audible thud.

"I . . . am . . . trying . . ." the voice continued with a definite tinge of impatience.

Horace crept the few feet to the piano and felt for the keys. "Middle C, middle C," Mrs. Gregg had prodded him, whacking his fingers as he practiced on Maria's piano while she was out of the house. Horace located what he hoped was the right note.

"Tra-la-la-tra-la-la-*donk*," went the piano. Horace winced and tried again. "Tra-la-la-*donk*."

"I am through!" cried the spirit, mercifully ending the mangled tune, and a gasp of welcome rose around the table. As the enraptured Brighams began to question their spirit daughter Sarah, Horace crawled back behind the armchair in relief. Maria had often praised Sarah's musical ability, and though Horace had never managed to learn a single piano piece, Mrs. Gregg had assured him that even a few notes would produce excellent results. As he stripped off his hood and gloves, Horace heard the sweet-voiced Sarah spirit explaining to her parents that if her touch on an earthly piano was slightly off-key, it was only because she had become so accustomed to the divine lightness of the keyboard on her fine piano in Summerland.

Horace's nose began to twitch again. He rubbed it on his sleeve, ordering the elusive sneeze to go away and stop tormenting him. Maria and Sarah were singing a childhood song together, the spirit's voice, if one troubled to listen closely, a mere fraction of a second behind on the words. It did bother Horace a bit to deceive Maria. On the other hand, thanks to Mrs. Gregg, Sarah was even now declaiming on the bliss of eternal maidenhood, which ought to reinforce Maria's inclination to remain single. Henry Houghton indeed! Why, Horace was twice the man Henry was, and he bristled at Grandfather's match-making. In his temper, the sneeze subsided again, this time completely. Horace banished Maria's suitor from his mind and prepared for the next trick.

From his pocket he took a folding wood ruler, painted black and affixed at one end with a metal hook. On the hook he hung a toy horn painted with luminous paint. Wired to the horn's mouth was a long black rubber tube. Sarah had departed, Mrs. Gregg had slumped into her trance state, and Professor Gregg was calling forth the next spirit, Widow Cates's young nephew. In casual conversation with a few gregarious townspeople Horace had gleaned anecdotes from the boy's life, which Mrs. Gregg now put to good effect. Peeping around the armchair, Horace could just make out the medium's shadowed figure, and he shook his head in admiration. Her shoulders moved up and down in a careless, jaunty way, her voice made sudden descents from the high pitch of an adolescent to the wavering tenor of a young man whose voice had not quite dropped. Even her puffy cheeks had somehow flattened into the leaner lines of a thirteen-year-old boy.

"I am so jolly here in Summerland!" the spirit nephew declared. "I will give you a toot on my heavenly horn."

Up went the wooden ruler, out it tilted toward the table, there hung the luminous horn magically suspended in the dark. Ohs and ahs rippled among the sitters at the miraculous vision. With his free hand Horace took the end of the rubber tube, lifted it to his mouth, and prepared to blow.

"AH-CHOOO!"

The explosion threw Horace against the armchair, madly clutching the ruler, while the luminous horn dangled and bounced, the ladies gasped, and Mr. Brigham leaped from his chair.

"Stay calm! Stay calm or the spirit will depart!" cried Professor Gregg as Horace frantically regained his balance, whisked the horn back into darkness, and let the whole apparatus drop on top of his head. Heart hammering, he huddled into a ball, praying to be invisible and expecting any moment to be yanked from behind the chair. Instead, the spirit nephew began to laugh.

"Oh, auntie! Dear auntie!" he cried. "Did I startle you? I am so sorry! Just as I was about to blow my horn, a little bird flew right before my face and tickled my nose!"

"And you always did love birds!" Widow Cates exclaimed joyously, as Horace, not believing his ears, peeked over the chair. The spirit nephew was gleefully reenacting the bird's flight, and there were the Brighams, Widow Cates, and Maria chuckling together over the escapade. Horace shook his head, incredulous, and feeling about in the dark, he collected all the parts of his device. As the professor skillfully brought the seance to a close and Mrs. Gregg slowly emerged from her trance, the grateful sitters flocked about her and related, to her utter astonishment, all that had occurred.

"And you should have heard the lovely piece my Sarah played on the piano," Mrs. Brigham enthused. "I am quite sure it was by Mozart."

The voices rose and faded into the living room, and Horace tiptoed to the window and slipped out. Right about now, the Brighams and Widow Cates would be pressing Professor Gregg to accept a generous contribution, of which—Horace smacked his lips—he would receive a twenty percent share. He strolled through the night to the buggy to await his passengers.

"I tell you, Arthur," he whispered to the horse, "the world is full of fools just waiting to make me rich!"

Eight

Mary tapped her foot in time to the fiddle, clapped her hands, and smiled at the dancers swirling before her. There went Polly Noble, swinging by on Lawrence Mason's arm. How long before an announcement was made for those two? There went Nathan, squiring Widow Cates, for since Mary's belly precluded dancing, she had urged her husband to partner some of the ladies who might otherwise have spent their evening as wallflowers. There went Maria, allemande with Henry Houghton, though it troubled Mary that her young sister-in-law looked so sad. Maria was surely the prettiest girl at the social, wearing the new coral pink dress Lisette had helped her style, pearl combs pinning her blond hair. Henry Houghton was handsome and well-spoken, and all evening he had courteously attended Maria, bringing her cider and cookies and finding her a chair between songs. Yet the smile on Maria's face seemed trapped there, and she held her body rigid as if mentally shunning Henry's touch. He twirled her out of sight, and Mary smiled as another couple danced by.

She felt wonderful, almost beautiful, though her belly now loomed so huge she had joked to Nathan she could not remember what her toes looked like. More important, Mary felt at peace. The long rest ordered by Dr. Shaw had relieved much of the swelling in her legs, though she had not, of course, spent all the past few weeks tucked in bed. What woman could afford to do that? Who would make the jam while the berries were still in season? Who would wash the clothes and clean the house? Besides, Nathan, though he tried, was hopeless in the kitchen, and one more burnt porridge for breakfast was more than her stomach could take.

Mary waved as young Charles tripped by, doing his best to partner ten-year-old Annabel Lewis. The two children bumped and collided, each attempting to lead, their cheeks coloring at the missteps as they tried to regain the beat. The September night was fine, and after several days of rain, the sky had cleared to a full moon in time for the social, held outdoors on the lawn beside the school. Lanterns strung on clothesline illuminated the scene, and wrapped in a warm shawl, Mary felt comfortable enough. She caught a glimpse of Horace across the crowd, scowling intently at the couples sashaying past. Why did he not invite some young lady to dance? With a number of Livonia men and boys off to the war, the town had a surplus of eligible females. The music ended, and Mary joined the applause. As she lowered her hands, she became aware of the baby, kicking robustly.

"So you like music, do you?" she teased, smoothing her hand over her belly. Another kick and a sudden tightening of her abdominal muscles answered, and Mary frowned. Was that a contraction or merely her imagination? She hoped the latter, for tonight, after the social ended, Mrs. Gregg had promised to hold a seance at their home to contact Robert, and Mary already wore the white dress required for the occasion. She pressed her hand to her belly a minute longer, relieved when no further reaction came. Nathan appeared, laughing, and took the seat beside her.

"Either I am getting old, Mary," he panted, "or Widow Cates has discovered the fountain of youth. She led me through four dances without stopping, and she kicks her heels like a young girl."

"It is the Spiritualists," Mary replied. "Widow Cates told me she has been filled with new life since they contacted her dead husband. Is it not marvelous all the good they have done?"

"H'mmm." Nathan made a noncommittal sound, and Mary resumed stroking her belly beneath her shawl. "Mary, I hope you will not be disappointed if the seance tonight is not as . . . eventful as some that have occurred lately."

"What do you mean?" The baby was kicking again, and Mary smiled, her attention divided between her husband's words and the turmoil beneath her fingers. It felt like such a healthy baby, twisting and rolling in corkscrew turns, that she had to bite her lip to keep her hopes from soaring too high.

"I mean," said Nathan, "that I spoke to Mrs. Gregg about contacting Robert and explained he was very young when he died. So we would not want him, or her, to strain themselves simply to please us."

"Oh no," Mary agreed. "Just to speak to him, that is all I desire."

"So I told her." Nathan nodded. "This will probably be their last seance here."

"Why?" She looked up, surprised.

"Because they are leaving in a day or two. After all, they have stayed at Father's nearly a month and have held seances for almost all who requested them. And I cannot spare Horace to attend them any longer. We have crops to harvest and winter wheat to sow before the first frost comes. I told Horace that as of tonight his service to the Spiritualists must end."

"He has been so helpful to them. Thank you, Nathan, for sparing him as much as you have." Mary took his hand. "I have been so little help to you lately, being off my feet, and when the baby comes I shall only be less so."

"All I want is for you and the baby to be well." Nathan kissed her forehead and stood, offering his hand. "It is time we went home."

They walked to their buggy, bidding neighbors goodnight and fetching Horace, Maria, and Charles on the way. Horace, Mary noticed, was still scowling, while Maria seemed glad to leave. Perhaps tomorrow she should try to speak privately with the girl. Nathan had mentioned his father's unromantic meddling, and it must be hard on Maria to have no other woman at home to talk to, no sisterly ear in which to confide her hopes and dreams. Young Charles at least was in high spirits tonight, and as they rode homeward, Mary coaxed from him a bashful account of his evening with Annabel. Nathan directed the buggy first to Father Kingsley's house, where they deposited Charles and met Professor and Mrs. Gregg. Maria, who had asked to join the seance, went to change into a white dress. When she reappeared, Mary's concern grew. The coral frock must have lent a false impression of color to Maria's complexion, for now, in the silvery moonlight, her eyes shone large above the pale hollows of her cheeks, and in the white dress she shimmered like a specter. Mary stayed her husband's hands on the reins.

"Maria, you do look tired," she offered. "Are you sure you want to attend?"

"Yes, Mary." Maria nodded, composed and faintly reserved. "It would do me good to be in contact with the spirits tonight."

The buggy traveled the short distance home, and while Nathan led Arthur to the barn, Mary brought her guests inside. She had cleaned the house thoroughly that morning, and Horace had moved into the parlor a small round table and comfortable chairs. Professor Gregg carried a satchel, and opening it he set a candle upon the table and covered it with a red globe. A small Bible came next from his bag.

"A scientific experiment, with your permission," he said to Mary. "Given the tender age of the child we are attempting to contact, I believe the presence of the Holy Word may enhance his ability to communicate."

"Yes, please," said Mary. "Please try anything that may help."

He placed the Bible beside the candle and led her to a chair. As she sat, the muscles tightened around her belly. Furtively, Mary slipped her hand onto her abdomen. She had felt, or imagined she felt, a few other contractions during the ride home, but the slight jouncing of the buggy made it difficult to be sure. Anyway, she had not had a baby in nine years, and at her age this one was bound to take some time.

"Now, all is ready," Professor Gregg declared, as Nathan entered and was ushered to his place. Mary found herself opposite Horace, Nathan opposite Maria, and for a moment she puzzled what that meant in terms of positive and negative personalities. Horace still looked disgruntled, holding himself aloof from Maria in particular, and a flash of annoyance crossed Mary's mind. That was no way to behave toward his aunt, and Horace, of all people, should know better than to bring a hostile attitude to a seance. Mary concentrated on the globe of ruby light, determined to make up for any negative influence her son might create.

"Friends, spread your hands on the table," the professor intoned, and everyone obeyed. "We are here tonight to summon the spirit of Robert, beloved by all those at this table. Though it has been many years since his untimely death, his memory has never been forgotten in this house. Robert, can you hear us? Will you come?"

A little sigh emerged from Mrs. Gregg, entranced and slumped in her chair. Maria, too, had leaned back, eyes closed, as if willing the spirit to appear. Oh please, Mary prayed, as the professor again coaxed Robert to join them. She moved her hands to the leather cover of the Bible and longed with all her heart.

"Mama?"

The voice was so tiny, Mary was almost not sure she had heard.

"Mama?"

She gazed eagerly through the dark to Mrs. Gregg. The medium's body had straightened, plump and sturdy as a healthy young child. Her eyes sparkled in wonder, and a rosy glow colored her cheeks.

"Robert, is it you?" Mary breathed.

"Yes, Mama. I am your own dear son."

Mary clasped her hands to her breast. "Oh, Robert, I hope it is not hard for you to be here."

"No, Mama. I have come to say I love you and Papa, too."

"Oh, speak to him, Nathan." Mary clutched her husband's arm, too happy to think what to say next.

"How are you, Robert?" Nathan asked.

"I am well, Papa. How good it is to see you!"

"Can you tell us how it was you died? We never knew."

"My heart stopped, Papa. It was too little and could not beat anymore. But you and Mama must know I did not suffer because it was so quick."

Mary held back a sniffle. "Oh, darling, that is just what I needed to hear. But where are you now? Who takes care of you? Is there anything you need?"

"No, Mama, I am fine. Here in Summerland is a little nursery for children like me where kind ladies feed us and rock us till the day our own mothers may come. Mama, watch how strong I have grown!"

Mary glanced around the room, not knowing what to expect, then downward as the table began to move beneath her fingertips. Slowly it rose an inch, two inches, floating above the floor so smoothly and evenly that the candle flame was not disturbed.

"Robert, do not strain yourself," she urged, and slowly the table settled back to the floor.

"I must go now, Mama. It is my nap time."

"Yes, darling, yes, you rest. I shall love you always. Goodbye!"

Happy tears rimmed Mary's eyes, and she wiped them away with her hand. How foolish to be crying when her prayers had been answered. Mrs. Gregg was reviving from her trance, and the professor's face had grown even pinker at the success of his Bible experiment. But Maria had slumped further into her chair, and now a tremble ran through her arms. It grew more pronounced, a painful heave that started at her shoulders and buckled her forward, then shuddered downward as her chest caved over the table. Mary drew a startled breath. Nathan had begun to rise, Professor Gregg to push back his chair. They both sat again, while Mrs. Gregg and Horace stopped in their seats, motionless.

"Shhh." The professor put a finger to his lips, alertly studying Maria as she slowly lifted her head. Her body seemed to have grown larger, huskier, somehow menacing in the dark. Her eyelids rolled open, and she fixed Mary with a glassy stare. A raw, guttural voice rumbled from her throat.

"You want Robert, missus? I'm here."

For one second Mary stared blankly. Then she reeled back, gasping in shock.

"Yes'm, you know me all right. You the one betrayed me. You the one let them take me away!"

The deep voice rang out in anger, and Maria lunged across the table toward her. Mary screamed and struggled clumsily from her chair. Nathan jumped up beside her, enfolding her in his arms.

"What is it? Mary!"

"The slave! It's the slave! Robert Rivers!" She cowered against him, too frightened to look.

"That's impossible! Horace! Get more light!" Nathan set her aside and angrily snatched the red globe from the candle. The room brightened, but not enough to vanquish the enveloping dark. "What are you up to? What kind of trick is this?" Nathan demanded, and to Mary's bewilderment he lifted the candle and threw the table to the floor. He searched the revealed space with the light, as if expecting to find something hidden there. Horace had scurried out of the room, and Mary heard him stumbling around in the blackness of the kitchen, while Mrs. Gregg, lips pursed, stared at Maria who had backed toward the wall, shifting like a cornered animal as Nathan advanced toward her.

"Wait! Wait!" Professor Gregg dashed between them, frantically waving his arms. "What slave? Tell me what is going on!"

"As escaped slave," began Nathan, "who once—"

"I want my freedom!" The voice bellowed from deep in Maria's chest, and she grew to a taller height, fists raised to fight. "I lost my freedom here, and I want it back!"

"And you shall have it!" Professor Gregg cried jubilantly. He turned to Nathan. "Don't you see what has happened? It is a ghost, an unhappy spirit condemned to haunt this house because of some long-ago misfortune done here. It has taken possession of Maria. Her female sensitivity has provided a channel for the tormented soul to manifest itself. No, no," he gestured hurriedly as Horace, white-faced, appeared in the doorway, carrying an oil lamp. "Take the light away or the ghost may be disturbed. We must elicit its story and relieve its burden, so it may pass on to the other world."

Mary felt her knees failing, and unable to speak, she motioned

Nathan to lower her into a chair. His own arms shook as he helped her be seated, and he clasped her hand tightly as if to assure himself he held flesh and blood. Professor Gregg took a step closer to Maria, palms forward in a placating gesture.

"Robert Rivers, is that your name?" he asked, his voice quivering with excitement.

"Robert Rivers," Maria rumbled. "Just one more river to cross."

"Tell us your story, Robert, spare no details, and we shall try to set you free."

I am losing my mind, thought Mary. A helpless inertia overwhelmed her; she felt as if she had stepped into a nightmare. Out of Maria's throat came the slave's voice, mournfully recounting an episode Mary had not thought of in years. Snatches of the story penetrated her ears: cornbread, the fruit cellar, a pearl necklace. Yes, I am going insane, her mind agreed, for the room around her had grown blurred, revolving slowly in the dark, furniture swimming past her eyes. The air flowed like water, and in the center stood Maria, a luminous white swirl, pearls cascading through her hair. Broader and broader grew her shoulders, taller her height. Her skin itself was darkening, surpassing even the shadows of the room. Mary's sight began to fail, and she dared not turn her head to be sure Nathan still stood behind her. Only the disembodied touch of his hand in hers gave her any link to reality at all.

"But I could not help you," she protested. "I tried! I did try!"

"But they took me." The slave's voice descended into a pit of grief. "I was so close!"

"Robert," asked Professor Gregg, "what happened after you were returned to Kentucky?"

"Never got there. Next night, goin' back, they lodge me in jail. I got my shirt into a rope and hanged myself."

Mary buried her face, sobbing.

"That's enough!" Nathan pushed past the professor and savagely gripped Maria's arms. "Stop it, Maria! Stop this charade! Who put you up to this?"

"Nathan, no!" Mary struggled up, horrified. "Don't hurt her. She doesn't know what she is saying. Let her be, Nathan! Let her finish or who knows what this spirit might do to me!"

She pulled at his arms, and Nathan, his face desperate, turned from Mary to his sister and back again.

"Let her finish, Nathan. Please!"

A long breath went out of Nathan's body. Horace still stood open-mouthed by the doorway, while Mrs. Gregg stroked her chin and studied Maria.

"Please," Mary repeated, and Nathan stepped back. Professor Gregg straightened his frock coat, and once again inserted himself before Maria whose head had tipped onto her right shoulder at a grotesque angle. She seemed barely alive.

"Robert," said the professor firmly. "Why have you come back here? What do you want?"

Maria's head lifted slowly. "I want to get to Canada where I can be free."

"Then go, with our blessing. No one here will hinder you. Go, and take away forever your presence from this house." Professor Gregg lifted the Bible from the floor where it had fallen and raised it in benediction.

For a few seconds longer Robert Rivers stood before them, then Maria fainted in a heap on the floor. Nathan carried her to the sofa, and Mary quickly joined him. Together they patted Maria's cheeks and chafed her wrists, calling her name until consciousness returned. She came groggily to a sitting position.

"Oh, what happened?" she asked weakly. "Why is the table overturned? How did I get here on the sofa?"

"You are a sensitive!" Mary exclaimed. "Oh, Maria, at first I was so frightened, but you have lifted a shadow from this house I did not even know existed. Didn't she, Mrs. Gregg?"

She turned to the medium, who had approached behind them.

Mrs. Gregg nodded sagely. "Indeed, it was remarkable. I would say, Maria, that you are definitely one of us."

Mary sat on the sofa and put a comforting arm around her sister-in-law, while Nathan began to restore the room. Professor Gregg paced the floor in jerky, ecstatic movements, declaring his intention to write up the case for the scientific journals. When Maria was sufficiently rested, Nathan ordered Horace to drive her and the Spiritualists home. Mary sat alone in the parlor while Nathan saw them to the buggy. She felt tremulous from head to foot, overjoyed, shaken, breathless, relieved. She could barely believe her eyes and ears. She could hardly think straight at all, and the baby, as if it too had been charged by the commotion, contorted in a violent movement against her ribs.

"Ow!" A real contraction hurt her, yet still she sat, head spinning, until another, harder clench made her mind clear. She could not have helped the slave any more than she did, and though she would have given her own life, she could not have saved little Robert or Clara. But here was a new baby, ready to be born, and the spirits must pass on and leave the living. Here and now, she had a baby to birth, a husband and son to care for, a house to tend. She looked around the parlor, nodding in recognition, welcoming the next contraction with its attendant pain. Nathan's footsteps were returning, and she pushed herself up to meet him.

"Fetch the doctor," she whispered. "It's time."

Nine

Mrs. Gregg settled into the stagecoach and waved goodbye to Horace, who had driven them to the stop. Professor Gregg sat opposite, penning into the notebook on his knees more ideas for his article, entitled "A Case Study of Spiritualism in Livonia, Michigan: The Spontaneous Demonstration of Sensitivity by Miss Maria K." Mrs. Gregg pressed her lips and waved a final time to Horace as the stagecoach started to move. She and her husband were the only passengers, and after making herself comfortable she peeked into her traveling basket at the luncheon Maria had prepared for them. An aroma of hot beef and vegetable pie rose to her nostrils, and she breathed in luxuriously. An hour along the road would be a good time to tuck in.

She glanced out the window, a pleasant view though there was little to see. Flat farmland between stretches of timber, tidy houses and barns, an occasional sawmill or store. Livonia was not much of a place, but out-of-town engagements were useful for polishing and expanding the repertoire. Not that the local residents were necessarily more easily hoodwinked than city folk. Native intelligence might crop up any-where, and Nathan Kingsley, for one, had not been taken in. He had suggested to her so politely and carefully that a brief, unadorned visit from little Robert would be sufficient that she might even have dis-pensed with the table lifting. But Amanda Gregg had her professional pride. Let no one say she did not give value for money. And the people of Livonia had been generous, opening wallets and loosening purse strings to drop dollars into the coffer. Still, even well-to-do farmers tended to be frugal, and in a country town a medium was unlikely to receive a windfall like the one hundred dollars a wealthy widower had pressed on her after one of her better performances in Detroit. Nevertheless, Livonia had provided an adequate income for the month's work, and since they had lived off the community's hospitality as well, they had incurred little by way of expenses. The balance sheet for their Spiritualist foundation was safely in black ink.

The real advantage of working out of town was that any slip-ups while practicing new material were unlikely to become known outside the immediate area. Neighbor would tell neighbor, shocked and scandalized, but since Livonia produced no newspaper, no permanent record of any failure would appear. So if Horace's horn trick had flopped or been exposed, word would not reach her major clients in Detroit. And one did have to keep enhancing the repertoire. The Spiritualist business was getting more competitive all the time, and some of her colleagues now used gutta-percha hands fitted on metal extension rods to reach across the darkness and effect an invisible "spirit touch." Another new trick was a floating guitar fitted with a hidden music box that seemed to strum itself in midair. That devious Kate Fox had even produced a silent "full form" spirit manifestation, which, of course, was merely Kate swathed in a cloud of white gauze celestially enhanced with luminous paint.

I'm getting too old for this, Mrs. Gregg thought wearily, feeling the strain in the small of her back. Did anyone think it was easy lifting a table on your knees? Though she thanked heaven they had opted for that method of levitation, rather than the mechanical jack, the night of Mary Kingsley's seance. It would have been tough work bluffing her way out of that one had the jack been present when Nathan overturned the table.

The warmth of the pie in the luncheon basket had radiated onto her lap, and Mrs. Gregg opened the lid for another whiff. Maybe just a bit off the crust to ease her appetite. She broke off a fluted edge and mmm'd as the buttery pastry melted in her mouth. Her husband was still scribbling in his tiny, cramped script, and every so often he lifted his head and tapped his finger to his brow in serious thought. She began to anticipate the gesture: scribble, scribble, scribble, pause and look up, finger to forehead, tap, tap, tap. Then a minute later: scribble, scribble, scribble, pause and look up, finger to forehead, tap, tap, tap. . . .

"It was nervous hysteria, that's *all*," she said emphatically, interrupting the next round of taps before they stretched her nerves to exasperation. "A flighty young girl got carried away by her imagination and dredged up an old tale."

A stubborn twitch of resistance jerked his mustache, and he lifted his notebook to his chest as if to protect the open pages from her glance. "I disagree. I believe it was a genuine spirit presence speaking through Maria."

"It was *Maria* speaking through Maria. She was emotional. She was overwrought. An unwanted suitor had pressed her at the dance, and she feared her father meant to marry her off against her will."

"Which is precisely why her extreme state of sensitivity would make her a magnet for an unhappy spirit," he countered. "The accuracy of the slave's story is beyond all doubt."

"Well, of course it is. The story was true. Maria had only to repeat what she knew of it."

"She was only two years old when the episode occurred. It is impossible a child of such tender years would understand, let alone recall, what transpired."

"She would have heard it talked about for months afterward," scoffed Mrs. Gregg. "Who knows how often the tale was repeated and spread about town? Maria simply stored it in her impressionable mind, and out it came when circumstances were ripe."

Professor Gregg shook his head. "There were far too many details in her rendition for it to be other than the slave himself speaking. Mr. and Mrs. Kingsley corroborated every fact."

Mrs. Gregg threw up her hands. "There were hardly any details at all, but for a cornbread and some pearls. Almost twenty years later, who remembers more than a faint outline of the events? So whatever Maria said happened, they naturally agreed. Besides, you know full well the biggest advantage a pretty young sensitive has up her sleeve is the fact that no one can conceive such a charming creature would lie."

Professor Gregg puffed indignantly at the word. "Then how did Maria acquire the slave's voice, answer me that? How could an educated young white girl, living far from the plantation South, come to sound like an impoverished, illiterate black man?"

"The same way I can sound like a two-year-old boy or Ben Franklin. Maria was acting, quite well, if I must admit. But there was *no slave present*. Do you understand?"

She fixed him with a piercing glance, but her husband only clutched his treasured notebook closer to his chest and gave her an offended look.

"Oh, go on, write it," she conceded, waving impatiently at the book. "The publicity never hurts. But stop tapping your forehead. It drives me crazy!"

She hunched back in her seat, and after a few seconds, still eyeing her, he cautiously lowered the book. Scribble, scribble, scribble, pause and look up, finger to forehead. . . .

"Stop it!"

Mrs. Gregg broke off another crust of pie to settle her nerves, then unwrapped a fork and dug up a hearty bite. Country fare was plainer than in Detroit where in the finer homes she had dined on pheasant and roast duck. But Maria and Mary Kingsley had both been good cooks, and seconds and thirds were always urged upon her. However, with a new baby daughter to nurse, Mrs. Kingsley could hardly serve guests, and in the two days since the seance, Maria had stayed in bed in a fainting condition, as Henry Houghton discovered when he came to pay court. Airy vapors and a tendency to become spiritually possessed might well scare off a man in search of a sensible, down-to-earth wife, and once Henry thought better of the engagement, Maria would no doubt make a speedy recovery. Although Mrs. Gregg had seen women and even a few men who, once bitten by the medium bug, became gradually more self-deluded and convinced of their powers until they truly believed the spirits spoke through them. And there were a few cases she herself had witnessed and could not entirely explain. She shrugged. It was mere coincidence, a lucky guess, a stab in the dark. Dead was dead, and you could not bring them back, though for a moment her memory brushed the cheek of the little boy she herself had lost so many years ago.

"If you like, I will read over your draft and add anything you may have forgotten," she said to her husband, more kindly.

His cheeks glowed gratefully. "That would be most helpful. We must make every effort to record this incident in a thoroughly scientific manner."

Mrs. Gregg finished her half of the pie, wiped her fingers, and peeked inside the basket. Apples, a wedge of cheese, and cinnamon buns still awaited, plus a flask of autumn cider. She should have asked Horace to spike it for her with a little whiskey from his Grandfather's cupboard. There was a young man who would do anything for money, and she did not begrudge him his share. She had even thought of suggesting that Horace return with them to Detroit. They could use a permanent accomplice, and though Horace was still a clumsy amateur, with proper training he might make the grade. But Nathan Kingsley would never allow it, and Horace himself had been shaken by Maria's spiritual adventure. It had taken some persuading on her part to make him see there were no ghosts in his house after all. Better to let Horace stay on the farm and pursue his own devices where he could not do too great a harm. Mrs. Gregg chuckled. Twice-dead skunks! What a crooked mind that one had!

Well, back to the city. Another day, another seance. The world was full of people muddling through life, loving and grieving, laughing and dying, and the unanswerable "why" of it would forever be the biggest mystery of all. The only thing to do was to keep up one's strength to play your part upon the stage. Mrs. Gregg reached into the basket and extracted a sticky cinnamon bun.

Book Three

1887–1888

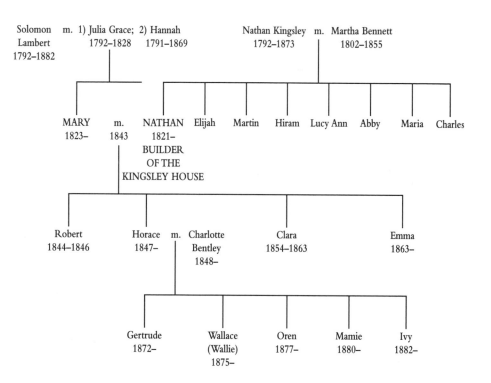

Solomon Lambert 1792–1882   m. 1) Julia Grace; 2) Hannah   Nathan Kingsley   m.   Martha Bennett
1792–1828   1791–1869   1792–1873   1802–1855

MARY 1823–   m. 1843   NATHAN 1821– BUILDER OF THE KINGSLEY HOUSE   Elijah   Martin   Hiram   Lucy Ann   Abby   Maria   Charles

Robert 1844–1846   Horace 1847–   m.   Charlotte Bentley 1848–   Clara 1854–1863   Emma 1863–

Gertrude 1872–   Wallace (Wallie) 1875–   Oren 1877–   Mamie 1880–   Ivy 1882–

One

"More tea, ladies?"

Emma Kingsley lifted the china teapot in a questioning gesture, pitching her voice a little high to override the merry conversation in the parlor of the Kingsley House. A twitter of requests answered her: "With cream and sugar, please." "Half a cup, dear." "May I have another of your delicious molasses cookies?" Happily and efficiently, Emma obliged her guests. She loved this time of year, the last few days before Christmas, when soft, fresh snow frosted the world like a sugar cake, and hearts were glad and hands were busy preparing for the holiday. Ten ladies had come for her sewing party to put the finishing touches on cloth dolls, knit scarves, embroidered handkerchiefs, and other homemade gifts to be bestowed on Christmas morn, and it gave Emma a sense of completion to be helping the holiday along in this way. Only one matter nagged at her content. . . .

"Now do tell us about your brother's new baby," said Emma's mother Mary to Hattie Millard, and Emma willingly returned her attention to the conversation. "Your grandfather Samuel would be so pleased at the great number of his descendants."

Hattie laughed. "We do seem to have multiplied. Of course, Grandfather started it with ten children, of which my father was the fifth. Then he and Mother had eight before she died. So when you add up all my brothers and sisters and aunts and uncles and all our offspring . . ." Hattie began counting off her family on her fingers until Elizabeth Stringer interrupted, "I declare you Millards will overrun the township!" and the ladies burst into fresh laughter.

"Well, it is important for a family to carry on," said Mary. She and several other ladies were sorting petals for dried-flower sachets, and a subtle scent of lavender and roses permeated the room. "After all, when our fathers settled here, this land was untamed wilderness—wolves and bears prowled right outside our door!—and only by hard work and perseverance did they build a community of which we could be proud. And for whom do we toil if not for our children? We want their lives to be better than ours have been."

Emma gave an inward sigh. She knew what was coming. "Why, when I was young," Mary would begin, and up the stories would bubble like soup boiling over a pot. The bitter winters huddled around the kitchen stove, the only heat in the house. Water hauled from the well, bucket by bucket, cranking on the heavy rope. Spinning, weaving, and stitching every garment by hand. Emma smiled to herself. She did not begrudge her mother's memories, and certainly life was far easier nowadays with extra stoves for the parlor and living room, a water pump at the kitchen sink, a reaper and thresher to ease Pa's work in the field. It was only that Emma had heard the same refrain quite frequently this past week, ever since Pa had brought home a large crate from Stringer's General Store.

"A sewing machine! Oh, Nathan!" Mary opened the box in wonder. "How does it work? Can we afford it? I have wanted one for so long!"

"It was to be your Christmas gift," said Nathan, grinning, "but when I pictured how your face would look, I could not wait to give it to you." He nudged Emma, inviting her to share his pleasure, and she squeezed his arm.

Now the marvelous machine held the place of honor at the party, and as Mary proudly began stitching the flower sachets, she broke into fresh raptures of gratitude for modern conveniences. To spare herself another rendition, Emma beckoned her fifteen-year-old niece Gertrude to the kitchen to help her brew more tea.

"So what does my favorite niece want for Christmas?" Emma asked as she set the kettle on the stove.

"A beau." Gertrude blushed.

Emma's eyebrows arched. "Any particular beau?"

"Maybe." Gertrude covered her lips to hide a coy smile. Then her face sobered. "Aunt Emma, do you think I am plain?"

"Plain?" Emma turned, caught off guard and not knowing quite how to answer. The truth? "Well, let me see," she said, gaining time. "You have your father Horace's deep brown eyes and nut-brown hair. You have your mother Charlotte's fine skin and noble forehead. You are just the right height for a young lady, neither too short nor too tall, and you have a kind disposition and a gentle heart." Emma smiled and said with confidence, "No, Gertrude, I do not see how anyone could consider you plain."

"Oh, thank you, Emma. You are so good to me." Gertrude hugged her and turned to spoon tea into the pot.

Emma sliced a fruitcake and arranged it on a plate. The description she had given of Gertrude could almost apply to herself. Twenty-four years of age. Autumn brown hair. Hazel eyes. A firm mouth and chin. Medium height. Patient, sensible, forthright. Plain? Emma shrugged. Beauty was not meant for everyone, and those who did not possess it must be content to develop their inner virtues. She finished arranging the fruitcake as Pa came in the back door.

"How is your party going? Never mind, I can hear," he said, as a crescendo of talk and laughter billowed from the parlor. He rubbed the small of his back and stretched, a familiar motion to unkink his spine. "Hello, Gertrude. I have just cut some willow branches to make Christmas whistles for your brothers and sisters. Are the boys feeling any better?" He set four lengths of green willow on the kitchen table while Gertrude reported no improvement in her brothers' colds. "Emma, tell your mother I am going to pick up our new hired hand."

"Not without your scarf and hat, you aren't." Emma took them from the peg rack on the wall, wrapped the muffler around her father's neck, and clapped the hat on his head of thick gray hair. "There, now you may go." She shooed him out the door.

"You're getting a new farmhand?" Gertrude asked.

Emma nodded and crossed her fingers. "I hope this one works out. It is hard to find a steady man, and Pa does need the help. Your parents are fortunate to have five strong children. I know Wallie and Oren are already a big help doing the chores, and soon the little girls will learn their share of household tasks."

"Papa says five children make five times the trouble."

"Five times the joy." Emma shook her head in exasperation. "I shall have a word with my brother Horace about that. Now before we take in these treats, you must tell me about this mystery beau. 'Fess up, Gertrude. Who is he?"

Gertrude's cheeks crimsoned. "You promise not to tell anyone?"

"Cross my heart."

"R. Z. Millard."

"R. Z.?" Emma's eyebrows shot up. "Hattie's younger brother? Oh, I don't know about him, Gertrude."

"Why not?" Gertrude looked hurt.

"Isn't he the boy who ran away from home when he was only eleven?"

"Yes, because his widowed father was to remarry, and R. Z. did not like the new wife. But that was six years ago. He apprenticed himself to a paperhanger to learn wallpapering and house painting, and now he earns his living at it."

"But what does the R. Z. stand for?" Emma let out a doubtful breath. "I don't think I have ever heard anyone say."

"It does not stand for anything," said Gertrude. "He says his parents could not fix on any name they both liked, so all he got was a pair of initials."

"Well, I suppose that is not his fault," Emma shook her head, considering, "but all the same, fifteen is too young to be thinking of beaus, Gertrude. You must wait until you are older." She smoothed her niece's collar where it had curled up at the back of her dress.

"But if I wait too long," Gertrude fussed with Emma's collar, fondly imitating her aunt's protective motion, "I shall wind up like you, Emma, a mother hen with no chicks of her own."

Laughing, Gertrude picked up the plate of fruitcake and sashayed toward the parlor. Emma lingered, feeling the buffet of the words pass through her. Her niece's comment, she knew, was not meant to be unkind. It was simply true. Emma sighed. Well, it did give her pleasure to fuss over people, to look after Ma and Pa, to dote on Horace's three girls and two boys, to visit sick neighbors and organize sewing parties and put her little extra money in the town's poor fund. I am *not* unhappy, she insisted. I am quite content with my single state, if only everyone would stop telling me I should prefer it otherwise. Her conscience skipped to the unanswered letter on her bureau, and she pushed away rising doubts. It was a miracle the subject of her terminal maidenhood had not arisen so far this afternoon, the ladies dropping none-too-subtle hints as to which men in town might still be eligible. If she did not return to the party soon, the talk might well land on that very topic in her absence. Emma lifted the teapot and sallied back to the parlor.

Too late.

"Emma, dear," said Elizabeth Stringer, "we were just saying that the new year shall be a leap year when a woman may propose to the gentleman of her choice. Now, who would you choose if you wished to avail yourself of that privilege?"

Emma resumed her seat and smiled as cheerfully as possible. Though Mrs. Stringer's tone was playful, it was clear from the circle of expectant faces that they hoped to cajole from her an answer. Why was everyone so anxious to see her wed? Was a single woman of twenty-four such an affront to the natural order that it was an aberration all must endeavor to correct? Or did they merely want her happiness, equating their version of felicity with hers?

"At present, I should not choose anyone at all," she replied. "I am not yet acquainted with any gentleman I think suitable for me." She caught her mother's eye and saw Mary purse her lips.

"Do you mean that no man hereabouts is rich or handsome enough?" Hattie Millard looked a bit reproachful. "Really, Emma, while it is right to be mindful of a husband's prospects, we cannot all afford to set our sights too high."

"Nor shall I, when it comes to wealth or beauty." Emma plied her crochet hook on a half-finished doily. "What constitutes suitableness for me is nobility of soul. Find me a man filled with unselfish love and industrious habits, an honest man who does right by everyone he meets, a man who thinks me quite as perfect as I think him, and gladly will I make a match. But I doubt such a mortal exists."

"But what about—?"

Oh dear, Emma thought, as her helpful guests broke into a cacophony of male names, serving up each with a summary of favorable attributes like a garnished joint on a platter. She must change the subject quickly or find herself affianced to every green youth and toothless widower within ten miles.

"But mightn't a woman nowadays prefer to remain unwed and perhaps pursue a career? Look at you, Mrs. Stringer." Emma gestured generously toward the storekeeper's wife. "You are the town postmaster as well as a full partner in your husband's business. I have often heard him say you are indispensable to his success. And look at Helga Witt, who single-handedly manages the cheese factory and five employees since her husband's death. And in Detroit there are women who support themselves by dressmaking, music lessons, running bakeries or hotels."

"Speaking of cheese . . . ," Mary looked up from stitching another sachet. Her brow furrowed in a troubled expression. "Several times lately our cheeses from Mrs. Witt have not been quite as good as previously.

They tasted, I don't know, thinner somehow. When I ventured to say so, she became most indignant and declared I was imagining it."

"Why, now that you mention it, Mary . . ."

Emma sat back, a smile playing on her lips. Sometimes she watched flocks of starlings approach over the fields. They came like a pulsating black cloud across an ocean of empty sky, then flowed into a river as the lead birds suddenly changed direction and the whole flock lengthened and streamed after them in a flickering ebony current. Emma could never quite predict when or why the starlings would turn, but instinctively every last bird followed. In the same way, the women's conversation had now changed course midflight as they swooped into a discussion on the merits of Livonia's five cheese factories.

"I'm sure I did not mean to offend Helga Witt," said Mary. "After all, hers is the nearest factory, and we count on her to buy our milk." The other neighbors nodded. Many farmers in Livonia sold their surplus milk to the cheese factories, and it provided welcome extra income. "But, oh dear," Mary concluded, "she is a foreigner and so gruff sometimes that I find it difficult to deal with her."

Winter dusk had fallen by the time the ladies packed their sewing kits and prepared to depart. Emma waved them out the door in a chatter of thank-you's and goodbye kisses. Gertrude joined the exodus, saying she must help her mother tend her sick brothers. As the last guests trickled away, a wagon bearing two men grew out of the twilight, and snatches of male laughter and the lively hum of a harmonica reached Emma's ears.

"Pa and the new man," said Emma, beckoning her mother to come see.

"They will be hungry," said Mary. "Put on the soup and potatoes, Emma, and I will collect the teacups from the parlor."

Emma went to the kitchen and added more wood to the stove. In a few minutes Pa and the hired hand arrived at the back door.

"Mary, Emma," said Pa. "This is Joseph McEachran."

The man had already removed his hat, and he nodded to each of the women with a friendly, "Pleased to meet you, Mrs. Kingsley, Miss Kingsley." He was pleasant-looking, of average height and build, sandy-haired, blue-eyed, his narrow cheeks softened by a wide ginger mustache. His clothes were poor, but his face looked willing to smile, to greet each new situation with optimism and goodwill, and as he twirled his hat in his hands, Emma noted with distinct satisfaction that his fingernails were clean. At least this one knew how to bathe.

"Ma-keach-ran." Mary pronounced the syllables carefully. "I don't believe I have heard that name before."

" 'Tis Scots, ma'am. My family were farmers in Argyle Shire." A slight burr rolled off his tongue.

"Joe is an actor," said Nathan, as they sat down to the table. "He is rehearsing with the Livonia Players in . . . what was that play called?"

"*The Truest Heart,*" said Joe. "We plan to perform it at Town Hall in January."

"Oh, I like plays," said Mary, dishing out bowls of hearty soup. "Remember when we saw *The Cheerful Liar* last year, Nathan?"

"Joe plays checkers and chess and all your favorite card games, too, Mary," added Nathan. "And wait until you hear him on the harmonica."

"Perhaps after supper you could play for us, Mr. McEachran," said Mary, "and I will show you my new sewing machine. Why, do you know that when our fathers settled this territory it was a vast wilderness— wolves and bears right outside our door!—and now we are blessed with so many modern conveniences, it takes my breath away."

Emma sighed to herself. Really, Ma and Pa oughtn't to be so trusting. Even though Mr. McEachran had come with a good recommendation from Henry Houghton, one never knew quite what to expect in a hired hand. Some were lazy, some got drunk, and some were rough, blunt characters with no proper upbringing. Still, she had to admit Joe McEachran had made a favorable first impression. It was his eyes, she decided, bright blue eyes that held a twinkle of humor and intelligence, or maybe it was honesty. He seemed to deserve a better station in life, but there was in him no hint of complaint. Well, so long as he proved a help to Pa—and took an interest in her mother's prattle—she would make him welcome.

Later, after Scottish airs on the harmonica and two games of check-ers—did Mr. McEachran deliberately let Pa win? Emma wondered— they went to bed. The hired man was to have the small bedroom off the living room, and thanking Mary for the tidy lodging, he bid them good-night. Emma extinguished the lamps and followed her parents up the stairs. As she changed into her nightgown, her glance fell on the letter on her bureau. She took it to read again by the candle beside her bed, then thinking she had the answer, she found a pencil and paper and began to write.

> *Sir,*
>
> *Unused to writing gentlemen as I am, I am resolved to delay my reply to you no longer. Your suggestion that my company is indispensable to you is flattering, yet how can you arrive at this conclusion on*

*such short acquaintance? We are but barely introduced, and while I
do not deny that I esteem you, I cannot help but wonder at your
haste in wishing to secure me as your lifelong companion—*

Emma struck out the paragraph, crumpled the paper, and dumped it in
the top drawer of her bureau alongside half a dozen other wads.

"You still have not answered Mr. Stewart," said Mary softly. She stood
at her daughter's bedroom door, her braid of gray hair trailing over the
shoulder of her flannel nightgown.

"No. I simply cannot think what to do." Emma sat down on her bed
with a sigh, and Mary came to join her. The candlelight illuminated the
gentle wrinkles that creased her mother's face.

"What does your heart tell you?"

"Nothing at all."

Mary put an arm around her shoulder. "Well," she said reasonably,
"Mr. Stewart, though a widower and somewhat older, is still in the
prime of life. He is kind and agreeable to look upon, if not entirely
handsome. He has developed a profitable lumber business by dint of
much hard work and steadfast principles." She gave her daughter a teasing smile. "Are these not the very qualities befitting a husband you
named to the ladies this afternoon?"

"Yes, I did and still . . ." Helplessly, Emma shook her head. "At least
you and Pa do not pressure me to wed."

"Nor ever shall." Mary's face saddened. "We saw that happen to your
Aunt Maria. Your Grandfather Kingsley was determined she must have a
husband and tried to effect a match with Henry Houghton. Henry is a
fine man, but it went against all Maria's desires, and though Grandfather
relented and said she might live single under his roof as long as she
pleased, yet she went into a decline and died only six months after you
were born. No, Emma, do not rush to marry until you have found the
right man, and when you do, hold him tight and thank the Lord for giving you such a blessing. A good man is more than a fortune. I was lucky
mine came to me."

She kissed Emma's head and rose to go.

"But Mr. Stewart does seem a good man," said Emma.

"Yes."

"And I might grow to care for him."

"You might."

"Then what more should I want?"

"I think," said Mary, "that you want to fall in love."

"At my age? I'm afraid that is hardly sensible."

Mary smiled. "On the contrary, Emma. No matter what our age, sometimes falling in love is the most sensible thing we can do."

She waved goodnight and slipped away, and Emma got into bed. It had been a full day, and she realized she was tired. Mentally, she listed the tasks left to complete, glad to have something safe and comfortable to occupy her mind. Two doilies to crochet to finish the set for Gertrude's mother, Charlotte. Gingerbread cookies to bake and hang on the tree. Silver to polish for the grand dinner she planned for Christmas Day. I would be good at running a business, Emma thought. Don't I organize and manage a dozen different enterprises every day? I sell the milk to the cheese factories and keep track of prices in the Detroit market when we send in our produce by train. Perhaps I should go to the city and earn my living as an independent woman.

For a minute the idea bloomed with promise, then just as quickly faded. Yes, no doubt she could. But everyone and everything she loved was here, Ma and Pa, her nieces and nephews, the farm that would someday be hers. Emma looked around her cozy room. For all Ma talked of modern improvements, for every change of wallpaper or rugs or furniture that marked the passing years, still their house seemed to her to hold onto its past, preserving echoes of long-ago laughter, muted voices and silent tears, invisible footprints on the stairs. It was almost as if the house had a soul, some conscious element built into its walls, embracing its rooms. When she stood outside, Emma felt the same sensation swelling in the fields, in the land beneath her feet, and she was filled with reverence for this special gift entrusted to her care. How could anyone forsake a place that spoke so deeply to your heart?

Emma blew out the candle and closed her eyes. Tomorrow was Christmas Eve, perhaps the most perfect day of the year. She put every thought out of her head and let herself be lulled to sleep by the night sounds—the creak of the windowpane, the distant hoot of an owl, her own breathing slow and quiet as a whisper, the sweet, low note of a harmonica drifting up the stairs.

Two

The morning after her Aunt Emma's sewing party, Gertrude Kingsley awoke with a sore throat. Bother, she thought, the boys have given me their cold. She got out of bed, shivering, threw on her dressing gown, and tiptoed past her sisters, Mamie, seven, and Ivy, five, still asleep in their double bed. The door to her brothers' room was halfway open, and pausing to peek inside she saw her mother sitting on a chair between the boys' beds. Charlotte raised her finger to her lips.

"What is it, Mama?" Gertrude slipped quietly into the room. "Are Wallie and Oren feeling worse?"

"No, no, just a little restless." Charlotte gave a furtive twitch of a smile, as if she were afraid to let any expression of happiness remain on her face too long. Her hands played nervously with the buttons on her nightgown. "They were tossing in their sleep so I came to soothe them."

"They seem peaceful now." Gertrude studied the sleeping boys. Younger brothers were often a nuisance, and when it came to inventing mischief to annoy their three sisters, Wallie and Oren, twelve and ten, were a prime pair. But deep in sleep their faces had taken on a deceptively angelic look, and Gertrude felt a tug of love for her younger siblings. "They look fine, Mama," she repeated. "Why don't you go back to bed and keep warm?"

"No, no, I will stay here so they don't awaken your father." Charlotte shooed her toward the door. "Go along and start the stove like a good girl."

"Yes, Mama."

Yawning, Gertrude made her way downstairs. Outside, the eastern sky had begun to lighten, but the winter sun still hid below the horizon and the interior of the house was enveloped in the leftover grayness of night. Let it be bright and sunny today, Gertrude wished. Her friend Loretta Baxter had invited her on a sleigh ride, and there was a chance R. Z. might be among the party. She pictured him offering his hand to assist her into the sleigh. "Why, thank you, R. Z.," she would say with a flashing smile, dazzling him by her effortless gaiety. R. Z. was on the short side, which made it all the easier to catch the admiring reflection she imagined in his cinnamon brown eyes.

Gertrude sighed away the daydream, kindled the kitchen stove, then went to light the stove in the living room. Their house sat across the road from her grandparents' home, on forty acres that Grandpa Nathan had ceded to her father Horace on his marriage. But since Horace veered between farming and practicing carpentry for his living, many of the acres went to grass and weed. They kept a few cows, pigs, and chickens, but in a haphazard way, and the crops they did plant seemed to grow more in spite of than because of her father's occasional bursts of farming. For Horace, the land was an adversary to be wrestled into submission, and he cursed it roundly when it failed to yield the bounty he felt was his due.

"No man can make a decent living off this useless soil!" he would shout at Charlotte, as if it were somehow her fault. "What good are forty acres if nothing grows? A fine inheritance this is!"

"Perhaps if you plowed more often," Charlotte offered timidly, "or planted winter rye to enrich the soil as your father does."

"Plowing is the boys' job. They've no one but themselves to blame if it isn't done properly."

"But they are small yet, Horace, and plowing is hard work. Couldn't you—"

"No, damn it! Do you think I have all day to spend breaking my back in a field? I will sell the damn land and stick to carpentry."

"But your last two customers refuse to pay because they say the work was not well done."

"Damn fools! I'll have the constable haul them before the justice if I'm not satisfied in full. Whose side do you take in these matters, woman? Do I need to teach you a wife's place?"

"No, Horace. Yes, Horace." Charlotte's voice trailed off in acquiescence as her husband ranted at the injustice of his circumstances.

Gertrude finished stoking the stove and climbed back upstairs. Mama still sat in the boys' room. Mamie and Ivy dreamed beneath their covers. Sleepyheads, thought Gertrude, for her next task was to trudge out to the barn to milk the cows. She donned long flannel underwear, a flannel petticoat, her red wool dress, thick worsted stockings, her worn leather boots. She braided her long brown hair and fetched her coat, hat, mittens, and scarf. She waved to her mother as she descended, hoping Charlotte would have hot bacon and eggs sizzling in a skillet by the time she returned. As she crunched through the snow to the barn, a glimmer of pale yellow sun peeped above the horizon and the gray sky lightened imperceptibly with the promise of blue. Hooray, a fine day for our sleigh ride! Gertrude cheered as she pulled up a stool to the first of their four cows. Coughing, she pulled off her mittens, rubbed her hands to heat them, and began to work the teats.

Ssspit, ssspit, ssspit. Long jets of white milk foamed noisily into the metal pail. In the cold air, the scent rose faint and sweet to Gertrude's nose. Milk was the one truly profitable commodity their household produced, and when delivered to Helga Witt at the cheese factory, it could be exchanged for cheese, cash, or some of each. Horace always preferred hard coin.

"Papa likes money," Gertrude told the cows, and they turned their heads and regarded her with enormous chocolate eyes. "There never seems to be enough to please him. Perhaps it hurts his pride that we have not done better."

She mused over the idea. Her mother's family, the Bentleys, were well-to-do and held respectable positions in education and town government. Whenever Gertrude's family was invited to a Bentley event, a wedding or a party, she sensed her relatives' polite disdain that Charlotte had married beneath her. Why had she? Gertrude shrugged, unable to divine an answer, and moved on to the next cow. Then another thought struck her.

"Why is it," she asked the animals, "that I, with the rather doubtful example of Mama and Papa's marriage before me, have every expectation of marrying in bliss, while Emma, who daily witnesses her parents' happy union, shies away from matrimony like a skittish mare? Or does Emma choose her single state precisely because she fears she can never duplicate Grandma and Grandpa's success?" Gertrude sent a squirt of milk into the mouth of the old barn cat who had come to meow against her leg. "At least I know very well I can do better than what I see here at home."

She coughed and pulled her stool to the third cow. The warmth of the udder helped keep her fingers from stiffening, and every so often the cow mooed encouragingly as she relieved it of its burden. By the time she finished the fourth beast, she had a day's supply for the family plus two full cans for the cheese factory. She petted the cat, put on her mittens, and returned to the kitchen.

"Milk done?" Her father looked up without smiling from a plate of fried eggs, bacon, cornbread, and potatoes. His brown mustache slanted down sharply to the corners of his mouth, and Gertrude murmured obediently, "Yes, Papa." Sometimes her father could be charming, when he was pleased by good luck, when he wanted to beguile someone to his way of thinking. Then the lines around his eyes would crinkle nicely, and his smile shone white and fine. But it was a side he saw little need to show his wife and children.

"Run wake up your sisters," Mama urged, tending the skillet. "Their food will grow cold."

"Yes, Mama." Reluctantly, Gertrude headed up the stairs, her empty stomach grumbling at the appetizing smells she was leaving behind. At the top step a fit of coughing stopped her, and she thumped her chest a few times before continuing to her room.

"Wake up, lazyheads!" She pushed and prodded at Mamie and Ivy, cozy lumps beneath their quilt. "Breakfast is ready, and I will eat your share if you don't come quickly." Ivy did not stir, and only a troubled murmur came from Mamie's lips. "Sweethearts?" Gertrude bent beside them, puzzled. She shook Mamie gently, and the little girl's eyelids fluttered open.

"Gertie, I don't feel good," she mumbled, her cheeks flushed.

"Oh no." Gertrude put her hand to Mamie's forehead, then her neck, half knowing what she would find. "A fever. Swollen glands." She turned to Ivy, who sat up weakly, and repeated the process. "You, too. Lie back down, girls. Cover up."

She tucked the quilt around them and went to to her brothers' room. Wallie and Oren were awake, propped listlessly against their pillows. Both boys seemed paler than yesterday, and Wallie's mop of towheaded hair hung limply on his feverish forehead. Oren's usually plump cheeks had sunk in to small hollows.

"Well, I hope you two are satisfied," she scolded, more in worry than anger. "You rascals have given your colds to the girls. If you keep this up the whole family will be sick tomorrow for Christmas."

The boys cracked weak grins. "Don't blame us, Gert," said Oren. "It is all Timmy Baxter's fault."

"Timmy? What does he have to do with it?"

"He was the first one at school to get sick," Wallie filled in. "He gave his cold to Susie Houghton and then to Oren and me. When school starts again in January, I'm going to punch him in the nose for ruining my holiday."

"Are you sick, too, Gert?" Oren asked. "I heard you coughing on the stairs."

"No, I am not sick. I was just out of breath, running up to fetch the girls, that's all." Gertrude wagged a finger at them. "Don't think for a minute you can give your cold to me."

She went down to the kitchen and reported to her mother, who hurriedly wiped her hands on her apron. "I must go see to the girls. Can you finish your own breakfast, Gertrude?"

"Yes, Mama." Gladly, Gertrude took over the skillet. At last! She heaped a plate with sizzling bacon, fat-fried eggs, and cornbread, pushed the skillet to the side of the stove, sat down opposite her father, and began to eat.

"How many cans of milk, girl?" Horace asked.

"Two, Papa."

"Full to the top?"

"Yes, Papa."

"H'mmm."

Her father weighed the information, but Gertrude's appetite had taken over and she paid little heed. Though her sore throat made it hard to swallow, the food revived her energy. No silly cold was going to keep her from this afternoon's sleigh ride and the chance to see R. Z. Maybe he would sit beside her and grin in that special way that showed the dimple in his right cheek. Maybe she'd find an excuse to lean against him as the sleigh went around a bend. She rose from the table, took her empty plate to the sink, and mounted the stairs. Charlotte looked up anxiously from the girls' bedside as she entered.

"It's all the same," she said, "sore throats, fever, coughing. It must be a congestion of the chest. They should try to eat, though Ivy says she is not hungry. Gertrude, I will need your help today. Can you make some warm milk and bread and bring it up in bowls?"

"What about your breakfast, Mama? I left it for you in the pan."

"No, no, I'll eat later." Charlotte's harried smile twitched across her face and disappeared as quickly as it had come. "Now go make the milk and bread."

All the rest of the morning Gertrude fetched and carried, tucked and soothed. Wallie had begun to make small gasping noises, and she rubbed his back to ease him. Just before noon, glancing out the window, she saw her father drive off toward the cheese factory with three milk cans in the wagon. That's strange, she thought, before a whimper from Ivy called her back. The children drifted into uneasy sleep, and Charlotte flitted between their beds like a moth called to a flame each time one coughed or wheezed. Gertrude felt her own strength ebbing. Her forehead was hot, her throat scratchy and swollen. Bother that Timmy Baxter, she thought. When I see his sister Loretta at the sleigh ride, I shall tell her the mischief he has caused. How disappointed Emma will be if we are too sick to attend her Christmas dinner. She fusses over it so, it would be a shame to have the table empty.

"Gertrude," Charlotte tucked a frayed wisp of graying brown hair back into her bun, "we are out of cough syrup. Can you go to Stringer's Store for another bottle? Tell Mrs. Stringer I will settle accounts with her as soon as I am able."

"Yes, Mama." Gertrude hesitated. Her mother's complexion was drained and worn, and her five-foot height, which Gertrude already topped by an inch, made her want to slip a protective arm around her mother. "Mama, I was to go on a sleigh ride this afternoon with some of my friends. But if you need me . . ."

"Thank you, darling." Charlotte patted her daughter's cheek, and a wistful trace of memory crossed her eyes. "No, go to Stringer's for me, then run along with the young people. I remember what it was like to have fun."

Gertrude pulled on her coat. "I am going to get more medicine for you," she informed Wallie, who opened his eyes as she passed his door. "Nasty, icky medicine to serve you right."

Weakly, Wallie stuck out his tongue.

The day had turned sunny, the top layer of snow melting and glistening in the warm rays. Up ahead at the crossroads was the big maple tree her brothers loved to climb in summer and next to it stood Stringer's Store. She saw Mr. Stringer on his way out, a package under his arm, and he gave her a cheerful wave. From her house to the store was only a quarter mile, but by the time Gertrude arrived, she felt inexplicably winded, and she thumped her chest and coughed before entering. Elizabeth Stringer stood behind the counter, selling a paper of pins to Hattie Millard.

"Hello, Gertrude," they said together. "You look a bit flushed," Mrs. Stringer added.

"Do I? It must be because I walked so quickly." Gertrude dismissed the comment with a bright smile. Several other customers milled about the store, while the usual cluster of old men sat chewing tobacco or smoking pipes around the potbellied stove.

"Hear tell there's a lot of sickness going around," one of them declared. "The youngest Baxter boy is took quite poorly, and Henry Houghton's girl's got a fever."

"My neighbor's young'uns, too," confirmed another. "It's the cold air spreads the germs. Keep indoors, you won't get sick."

"Then what are you doing out?" demanded a third.

"Gettin' away from my old missus. She's a plague all by herself!"

The men hooted with laughter while the women began touting their favorite winter remedies. Gertrude eased away from the crowd. She had begun to feel a little faint, and in the corner, when no one was watching, she put her palm to her forehead. Bother! It was hotter than ever, and her throat seemed to be closing up, cutting off her supply of air. It's the heat from the stove, the smoke from the pipes, she told herself, and she walked briskly back toward the counter. Best to get the cough syrup quickly and head home so she could rest a little before the sleigh ride.

"Afternoon, ladies, gentlemen." Palmer Chilson, the town constable, entered and removed his hat and was greeted by Mrs. Stringer and the customers.

"Have you come to buy your wife those amber earrings for Christmas?" Mrs. Stringer tapped the glass case on the counter where the jewelry and hair ornaments were artfully displayed. "She's had her eye on them all month, you know."

"I wish it was such a good errand that brought me," said Chilson ruefully, and the buzz in the store quieted. The constable was responsible for apprehending and bringing before the justice of the peace those few citizens who misbehaved or broke the law, but he was not an unkind man nor ever misused his office, and most people regarded him as a neighbor and friend. His jowly face saddened, and he sighed. "Guess you maybe know there's been some sickness among the children."

"We just said that little Baxter boy is poorly," piped the old men, all taking credit for the news.

"Timmy Baxter died this morning," said Chilson. "Seems we got an epidemic of diphtheria."

"Oh no!" Elizabeth Stringer's face dropped, and a murmur of exclamations ran through the customers. Gertrude backed against a wall. She had heard of the disease, how it could invade a community, killing children by the dozens. She had felt weak before, and now her body threatened to slip away from her, like clothes dropping off a hanger into a heap on the floor. She propped herself against the wall and heard Constable Chilson's voice, fending off questions from the crowd.

"Ten cases so far that we know of . . . only Timmy dead, but the others are pretty sick, too . . . Justice Allen has issued a quarantine to keep the contagion from spreading . . . I'm riding around now to post the signs . . . No, Dr. Shaw says medicine won't help . . . once it gets in the heart, they're sometimes gone in twenty-four hours. . . ."

A fresh flurry of talk and commotion broke out, as the mothers in the store hurried away home to their children while those remaining tried to recall who else in the community had seemed ill lately. Slowly, her head spinning, Gertrude felt her way toward the door. A cough wracked her chest and she stopped, feeling utter silence as every gaze in the room turned on her.

"Gertrude," said Mrs. Stringer, "didn't you say yesterday at Emma's that your brothers were sick abed?"

"Um . . . well . . . yes." Gertrude forced a smile, still edging her way out. "But they are much better now . . . that is why I came . . . to buy peppermints for them . . . but I must get home . . . Mama needs me. . . ."

"Gertrude?" Mrs. Stringer's voice sounded fuzzy, as if she spoke through a muffler, and the faces around her began to blur.

"I'm fine," she said. "Fine." She walked out the door and paused on the porch, steadying herself with one hand on the railing. Anxious murmurs rose behind her, and to prove that she meant exactly what she said, because nothing was going to keep her from her sleigh ride with R. Z., Gertrude let go of the rail, stepped boldly off the porch, and fainted into the snow.

Three

"There, Mr. McEachran, tell me what you think."

Mary pushed a plate containing two slices of yellow cheese toward the hired man, and Emma sighed. Here it was the afternoon of Christmas Eve, and her mother was still agitating over the sharp words she'd had with Helga Witt at the cheese factory nearly a week before. On the one hand, Emma sympathized with Mary's troubled conscience; it wasn't like Ma to quarrel with anyone. On the other hand, it hardly seemed fair to thrust the burden of judging on poor Mr. McEachran when he'd been in their home barely twenty-four hours.

"Taste them each," Mary urged, "then give me your true opinion."

"Shouldn't I close my eyes, to be absolutely fair?" asked Joe.

"Yes, yes do. Close your eyes and I'll mix them up. Then we shall see who is imagining things."

Joe lowered his lids while Mary switched the plate this way and that to confuse him. It was good of him to play along, thought Emma. At her mother's insistence, she had sampled both cheeses several times herself, but though at first she thought she detected a difference, the more she chewed, the more they tasted the same. Both were creamy yellow in color and of a fairly solid texture, though Joe had opined, to Mary's delight, that the cheddar on the left had a translucent tinge. Emma spooned out dough for the batch of gingerbread cookies she was baking, while across the kitchen table Nathan whittled a set of wood farm animals as Christmas presents for Mamie and Ivy. Pa's palate had also been put to the cheddar trial and found woefully wanting in discrimination.

"All right, taste them," said Mary.

Joe felt for the plate, encountered the two slices of cheese, and lifted the first one to his mouth. He looked to Emma a bit comical, chewing with his eyes closed, his ginger mustache ruminating up and down, but it was obvious from his thoughtful expression that he took her mother's complaint seriously and meant to render an accurate opinion. He and Nathan had labored all morning outside, tending the animals, chopping wood, repairing cracks in the well. It was an auspicious start to his employment, for Emma, contriving frequent excuses to drop in on the men, had kept a sharp eye to ensure Mr. McEachran earned his wages. She found him hard at work even when Nathan was absent, and thanking her for the hot coffee she brought, he went straight back to his chores without stopping to chat. Joe was chewing the second slice of cheddar now, and the change of expression on his face registered a clear decision.

"This one," he said, opening his eyes. "I am sure 'tis better. The taste is heartier, richer, while this one . . . ," he pointed to the first, translucent slice . . .

". . . is thin!" declared Mary triumphantly. "Did I not tell you, Nathan?" She rapped her husband on the arm with her forefinger. "How dare Helga Witt say it was all in my head?"

"Ma," Emma interrupted, "I thought of having Mamie and Ivy over this afternoon to read them stories. It will keep them amused and relieve Charlotte a bit while she cares for Wallie and Oren." She rose as she spoke, and Mr. McEachran automatically pushed back his chair and stood as she left the table. Emma went to the living-room window and glanced across the road to Horace's house. If dinner were over at her brother's, Mamie and Ivy might already be outside playing in the snow.

"What—?"

A small knot of people clustered on Horace's porch, and though she could not at first tell who they were, Emma sucked in her breath with an instant feeling that something was wrong. The figures moved in sharp, sudden jerks of urgency and distress, and as she began to make out their identities—Charlotte, Elizabeth Stringer, Constable Chilson carrying someone in his arms—the act of recognition only quickened her concern. Her glance shot to Mrs. Stringer's buggy and the constable's horse tethered to the rail, then back to the trio on the porch. Chilson was carrying his burden inside, and Charlotte followed, leaving Mrs. Stringer twisting her hands. Emma darted to the kitchen.

"Something is wrong at Horace's, an accident, someone hurt—" She waved her arms as she spoke, then whirled back through the house while her startled family flew up behind her. Outside, the sudden whiteness of sparkling snow blinded her momentarily, and as her frantic mind worked in backward flashes to identify the injured person—a young woman, a hem of red dress, dangling brown braids—she shaped her throat to call.

"Mrs. Stringer! Mrs. Stringer!" Emma ran through the snow, skirt flapping wildly about her ankles.

The storekeeper turned her head and hurried down from the porch. She caught Emma by both shoulders. "No, Emma, you can't go in! It's diphtheria! Gertrude collapsed outside the store. And the little girls are sick, too, Charlotte says. Oh, your poor family!"

Constable Chilson reemerged from the house and pulled the door tight behind him. Emma shrugged out of Mrs. Stringer's grasp.

"Let me in! What has happened?" She tried to duck around Chilson but found her way blocked by his broad chest and outstretched arms.

"I'm sorry, Miss Kingsley. This house is quarantined. Only the family may enter."

"But I *am* family! I must tend them. The children need me!"

"They have their mother." Chilson shook his head, sympathetic but unrelenting. "Now stand back, Miss. I must put up a quarantine sign." He nodded toward his saddlebag, and turning to follow his gaze, Emma saw her parents and Joe McEachran hurrying near, Pa and the hired man supporting Mary between them.

"What is it? Who is hurt?" Ashen-faced, Nathan appealed to the constable, and Mrs. Stringer stepped forward again to recount Gertrude's visit to the store. "Charlotte says she came to get cough syrup for the boys. I thought she looked unwell, but she said no, she felt fine, and now Dr. Shaw says all the children have diphtheria, and poor little Timmy Baxter is dead!"

Mary began to weep, shaky tears of fright, and Nathan laced her into his arms. "Where is Horace?" he demanded.

"Gone to the cheese factory," Mrs. Stringer answered.

"Then I *must* go in," said Emma. "Charlotte cannot manage this alone. Charlotte, I'm coming!" She pushed forward again, but this time Palmer Chilson placed himself squarely in the doorway and crossed his arms.

"Miss Kingsley, Justice Allen has ordered a quarantine of every house where diphtheria is present. If I let you go in, you cannot come out again or you risk taking the infection back to your parents' home and bringing sickness on them and everyone else you encounter. Is that what you want to do?"

Emma glanced to her mother and father, Joe McEachran silent beside them.

"No," she whispered. "But Charlotte . . . she might need help."

"I'll find Horace for you," Chilson offered, "as soon as I put up the sign." He moved a step away from the door and eyed Emma, as if testing to see whether she would disobey him and enter.

"No, I will not go in," she conceded, "but let me just look. . . ." She stepped to the living-room window and peered inside. The room was empty; Charlotte was no doubt tending Gertrude in her bedroom upstairs.

Mrs. Stringer bid a sad farewell and drove away in her buggy. Constable Chilson remounted the porch, carrying hammer, nails, and a red-lettered wood board. Mary had joined Emma, calling and tapping futilely at the downstairs windows, and as the first blows of the hammer rang against the house, the two women instinctively turned into each other's arms. Emma's heart flinched with each thud on the nails.

"Now go home, keep watch, and pray for the best," said Chilson. He clasped Nathan's shoulder. "It may well pass and no harm done." He swung onto his horse and galloped away toward the cheese factory.

"It seems there is nothing more we can do," said Nathan heavily, yet still they stood there, unconvinced and unwilling to depart, their eyes trapped on the forbidding red sign. The beautiful brightness of the winter day, the cardinals in the trees, the azure sky, seemed to mock them, and a dazed sensation passed over Emma as if she might be caught in a dream. She blinked, hoping, until her parents' faces confirmed it was no use.

"You go home." Gently, Emma urged them away. They had all rushed out without coats or shawls, and Mary was shivering. "I'll stay a minute, to call up to Charlotte and see if there is anything she needs." The renewed sense of purpose put energy in her steps, and she walked around to the rear of the house. If Charlotte were in the girls' room, it might be possible to catch her glance as she passed by the window. Emma shaded her eyes from the sun and called toward the pane.

"Charlotte! Charlotte!"

She waved her arms, then paused to await a response. Joe McEachran walked up beside her. "You should'na stay out long, Miss. 'Tis colder than it seems."

Emma nodded. She had barely felt the temperature in her initial panic, but now the chill was seeping through her plaid dress. She shivered, and before she realized his intention the hired man stripped off his jacket and draped it across her shoulders.

"I'll help you call," he offered, and his voice, a resonant tenor, carried upward in a shout. "Mrs. Kingsley! Come to the window!"

They waited, and a moment later the window clattered open. Charlotte's head thrust out, her face stunned, a wild despair in her eyes.

"Emma!" she cried, strident and frantic. "Emma! What shall I do? All my children are dying!"

"No! Charlotte, no! Listen to me! Tell me what you need! I can ride for the doctor or fetch medicine."

Charlotte shook her head, too distracted to hear. "All afternoon the boys have grown worse. Wallie can hardly find breath. He gasps and heaves until he is white. Oh, we are lost, Emma! I must go to him!" She slammed down the window and disappeared.

Emma stared, dumbfounded.

"Miss."

A hand touched her arm, and she turned, recalling Mr. McEachran. His blue eyes regarded her with patience and concern. "Here comes the constable with your brother. Things will go better now, see?"

He nodded along the road, and Emma spotted the hefty outline of Palmer Chilson on his horse followed by Horace's slouched figure on his wagon. She chafed impatiently until they neared, then ran gratefully to meet them.

"Horace," she began, "oh, Horace—" The words died on her lips at the turbulent look on her brother's face. A sudden conviction that something else terrible had happened gripped her stomach.

"What?" she demanded of Chilson, fists clenched at her sides.

"I am sorry indeed, Miss Kingsley, that such a bad day should come to your family." The constable threw an angry look over his shoulder at Horace. "Your brother is under arrest. He has been caught selling watered milk at Helga Witt's cheese factory."

For an instant, though she had never done so in her life before, Emma thought she must faint.

"Arrested?" It was the only word she could muster.

"He and Mrs. Witt were in the heat of an argument when I arrived," said Chilson. "I'm sorry, Miss Kingsley. I know the the state your family is in, but I must do my duty and Mrs. Witt says she will press charges. I have brought your brother home on his pledge to appear before Justice Allen when the matter is called."

"That damn fool of a foreign woman doesn't know her business!" Horace slapped his horse forward. "My milk's never watered! I'll blacken her name for this charge."

"Horace!" Emma grabbed onto the harness, pleading. "The children are sick. Diphtheria!"

"That, too," he snarled, and throwing the reins at her, he jumped down and bolted for the house.

Palmer Chilson shook his head in muted anger, tipped his hat to Emma, and rode away. Emma felt Joe McEachran beside her, once again placing his jacket over her shoulders. It must have fallen off, unnoticed, when she ran toward the wagon.

"I'll take the horse to the barn, Miss," he said quietly. "You go home now."

"No." She said the word out of instinct more than for any real reason to stay. Yet she did need to stay, to be close, and she sought for a purpose to justify remaining. She stared at the house, shut out by its walls, by the cruel red sign. "Cough syrup. Gertrude went to the store to buy some and returned without it. That might be the very help the children need."

She set off at a quick pace down the road, and though Mr. McEachran called after her that they could take Horace's wagon, she shook her head, not stopping. The walking warmed her, then she realized with regret that she had taken off wearing his jacket, leaving him in his shirt in the cold. But when she glanced backward the hired man was calmly leading Horace's horse away to the barn. Still walking, Emma slung her arms into the jacket sleeves so at least she would not lose it this time.

She reached Stringer's, panting but not out of breath, and hurried inside. The store was empty except for Mrs. Stringer, tidying her displays at the counter. When Emma explained her errand, the storekeeper nodded and reached a bottle from a shelf.

"Everyone left when we brought Gertrude home," Mrs. Stringer said, indicating the vacant store. "Some ran to spread the news, others to look after their own. How this disease came here, where Timmy Baxter caught it, no one seems to know."

"Will this do any good?" Emma studied the slim brown bottle in her hand, then gestured toward the shelf of medicines and tinctures in assorted vials and jars. "Is there anything else you know of, Mrs. Stringer, anything that might drive out the disease?"

"I don't know, Emma." The storekeeper searched through the labels. "I have Dr. Foote's Ague Tablets for chill and fever, Hostetter's Stomach Bitters, Herbena Tonic for catarrh. Dr. Shaw says there is no relief but to wait and pray, but at least these could do no harm."

"Let me take them," Emma pleaded, and Mrs. Stringer pressed the bottles into her hands. With a backward thank-you, Emma hurried out the door. As she neared Horace's again, Joe McEachran reappeared from the barn and verged toward her path. Now she was out of breath, but she ran anyway. Medicine, that was it. The very feel of the bottles, hard and sure in her hands, gave her a surge of hope. It was Christmas Eve, after all, the whole world beautiful and bright, a season when miracles surely could occur. She must have faith and never waver, she must believe with all her heart. She raced to the rear of the house and shouted up to the girls' window.

"Charlotte! I have medicines! Come down and I will set them at the door!"

She strained to see a movement, and it startled her when the window at the boys' room flew up instead. Charlotte's face, shocked and drained of color, stared out wild-eyed, and in her arms she clasped upright a limp body with dangling arms and a bent towhead.

"Dead, Emma!" Charlotte's voice wailed like a banshee, and she clutched the swaying body, its head lolling against her breast. "My boy Wallie, dead!"

Tears of grief and terror sprang to Emma's eyes. The medicine bottles dropped into the snow.

"No, Charlotte, it can't be!" she cried, but her sister-in-law had disappeared from the window and only the rise and fall of heartbroken sobs came from within.

"I am going in."

Emma's feet were in motion before the words left her mouth, and she strode forward in a blindness of spirit, her heart pounding in loud thumps of disbelief. Her arms swung out as she rounded the corner of the house, and a hand around her wrist jerked her to a sudden stop.

"You canna go in." Joe McEachran spoke each word slowly and clearly, looking on her in sorrow, and in her shock and outrage that he should detain her, Emma swung at his jaw with her free fist. He ducked, she swung again, and the force of her effort propelled her into his arms.

"Let me go!" She twisted so violently that her elbow thudded into his ribs, and she heard the "oof" of breath knocked from him. But as she broke free, her foot tripped his ankle, and down they fell into the snow. As she tried to crawl away, Joe's arm clutched her waist, and they wrestled, Emma kicking and fighting, oblivious of the wet snow plastering her face and leaking down her neck, Joe stiff and struggling to hold without hurting her.

"You canna go in, Miss," he panted. "You'll expose yourself and bring it back on your parents, too. I have seen the diphtheria. I lost my three sisters to it. There is *nothing* you can do."

The finality of the word stabbed through Emma, and all her strength vanished. For a moment she lay staring up at the bright blue sky. Then a sob broke from her chest, and she curled over in the snow and began to cry. Joe McEachran's arms went gently around her, saying nothing, letting her weep, only trying to keep her warm. In a part of her mind she thought, he must be so cold himself by now, I still have his jacket, but the crying kept on a long time more until it was spent. Slowly, Emma sat up, wet to the skin from tears and snow, and poor Joe looking no better.

"I'm sorry," she said.

"So am I, Miss." Joe stood, collected the medicine bottles, and walked to the porch where he left them beside the door. He returned to her side and held out his hand. "Come, let me take you home."

Four

I dinna belong here. I should go away.

Joe McEachran looked around the Christmas table at the Kingsley house. They had done their best to make it seem a holiday, set greens on the mantel, piled presents beneath the tree, stuffed a turkey and surrounded it with roast potatoes, carrots, buttermilk biscuits, and gravy. They smiled and tried to make conversation. For a while hope and courage would buoy them, and they convinced themselves all would be well. Then the brightness passed, the room echoed with absences, and they fell silent and forlorn. Their torn state of mind was reflected in their dress, black mourning ornamented with a sprig of red-berried holly pinned to the women's dresses as a Christmas brooch.

"For though we grieve for Wallie, it does not seem right to fix our minds only on death on the day of our Lord's birth," said Mrs. Kingsley, clutching at one of the bright moments. "We must keep faith for the other children. . . ." She clenched her hands, tears in her eyes, unable to say more. She had been pretty once, thought Joe, and was pretty still in the way of an older woman whose face holds a lingering imprint of how she had looked in youth. Beside her, Nathan Kingsley resembled a spar of granite, weathered but strong. He had said little, comforting his wife when she grew distressed and methodically pacing to the window to stare across at his son's house.

I am too new here, thought Joe, an intruder. The poor people canna cry and grieve and pray as they might without a stranger in their midst.

But where would he go? Hired work was scarce this time of year, and with at least fifteen children in Livonia now stricken with diphtheria and houses quarantined throughout the town, neither he nor anyone else could move freely for fear of spreading the disease. Besides, it would leave Nathan Kingsley short-handed, for even on Christmas Day the stables must be cleaned, the cows milked, the livestock fed. And though as yet he owed the family no devotion or allegiance, might walk away to some other unsuspecting town, it was not in Joe to desert. If a man dinna face trouble where it found him, he must spend his life running away.

"I fear we are not giving you a very happy Christmas, Mr. McEachran." Mary's lips quivered in an apologetic smile.

"Please, Mrs. Kingsley, I would'na have you act merry on my account."

"Are you still rehearsing your play? When the children are well again, perhaps we could come see your performance."

"I've been practicing my part at night, by the lamp in my room," said Joe. "I hope I've not disturbed you upstairs?"

"No, not at all. I have forgotten . . . what play is it again?"

The three Kingsleys leaned forward, the invitation to speak, to divert them for a while, clear on their faces.

"*The Truest Heart,*" said Joe. " 'Tis a romantic comedy, the story of a beautiful young heiress pursued by a greedy villain for her fortune and her land and the hero who loves her for her true worth." He paused, not wanting to misgauge their eagerness and speak of frivolous matter if they were not of a mind to hear. But their expressions urged him to go on.

"What part do you play?" asked Nathan.

"Why, I am the hero, of course." He made the dashing gesture he meant to employ at the end of Act 3, and they laughed, the first unforced gaiety in the house that day. An idea roused him. "I have a copy of the script in my room, if you would like to see it."

"Yes, yes." They nodded gladly. "We'll clear away the dinner," said Nathan, "and perhaps you could read to us a little."

They stood and suddenly became enthusiastic, putting away food, carrying dishes to the sink. They resettled in the parlor, and Joe fetched his script.

"There is a scene here," he flipped the pages, "that calls for two actors, the hero—me—and the rich heiress he strives to protect. If you would read the female role, Miss Kingsley, I know my part." He handed her the script.

"But I . . . I have never acted before." Emma hesitated at the out-thrust sheaf.

"Dinna worry. Only read your lines as if they were a story."

"Yes, go on, dear." Mary shooed her into the center of the room toward Joe. She took Nathan's hand and sat him beside her on the sofa. "Pa and I will be the audience."

"We'll start here," Joe whispered to Emma and pointed to the line.

She gave him a game smile, and he made a debonair turn and began to speak. Haltingly at first, then with quick confidence Emma read out her lines, even venturing to act a little as he drew her into the scene. She had a straightforward manner that was a shade too forceful for the demure heroine the script intended, but Joe smiled encouragingly and beckoned her with silent cues to move this way or that. As they parried lines, exchanged longing glances, and yearned for the happiness of a perfect ending, he relished the familiar pleasure of a play coming to life.

"Oh, sir, you are my hero, she flings herself into his arms!" Already a step toward him, Emma tried too late to halt and toppled into his embrace. They grappled backward to extract themselves, Emma murmuring in a fluster, "Wait, that isn't right." Cheeks pink, she ducked her face behind the script and searched for the culprit line.

" 'Tis the stage direction," Joe explained, feeling foolish not to have forewarned her, though Mary and Nathan laughed and clapped enthusiastically. "You did very well, Miss Kingsley."

"Did I?" She blushed deeper at the praise. "I did find it fun."

"Read some more," Mary begged. "Do you know, I quite believed you were that character, Mr. McEachran. It was most convincing. How did you learn to act? Is it hard?"

"People tell me I have a natural ability for it, Mrs. Kingsley." He gave a modest shrug. "I know some say 'tis a frivolous pastime, but to become another person, to live a different life for an hour on a stage, lets you imagine things outside your own experience. 'Tis called 'getting into character,' but I think it more likely that the character gets into you."

Emma nodded, wondering. "I felt that also. It carries you away and inspires emotions that are . . . well, perhaps a trifle strong for ordinary life." Self-consciously, she smoothed her hair.

"You must take a part, too, Mrs. Kingsley," Joe offered.

"Who, me? Oh no—"

But Nathan pushed her forward, laughing, while Joe located the part of an interfering old aunt. Mary performed it with flair, tripping once or twice over unfamiliar lines, but embellishing her part with a tapping foot and a rapping finger well suited to the character's disposition.

"You dinna tell me you were all actors here!" Joe exclaimed, when the scene ended. "Come, Mr. Kingsley, I have just the role for you."

Eagerly, he offered Nathan the script. Nathan put up his hands in a regretful gesture of refusal.

"I cannot read, Joe," he said quietly. "I had a little tutor once, but she left us and I lost the heart for learning."

Joe's spirits sank. Not yet knowing their history, thrust among them when their feelings were vulnerable and exposed, he had feared an inadvertent blunder and here it was. Adeptly, Emma smoothed over the awkward moment.

"Pa, you must sit and be the audience in any case. I can play a man's part. Give Ma my role, Mr. McEachran, and let me be the greedy suitor."

They acted for an hour more, forgetting themselves, forgetting the sickness in the house across the road. When they reached the end, they laughed heartily, and it seemed to Joe the respite had done them good.

"I know!" cried Emma. She gestured to the tree where the Christmas gifts waited. "Let's take the presents over to the children. We can pass them through the door. After all, they may be feeling better, and it is Christmas Day. The toys are sure to cheer them."

A grimace crossed Nathan's face. "Perhaps it would be best if you went, Emma, and Joe with you. I was over early this morning to speak to Horace about his trouble, and it did not go well."

The mood in the room shifted again, a quarter turn toward gloom. So far, the Kingsleys had said nothing in Joe's presence about their son's arrest, but he had marked Nathan's departure to Horace's house after milking that morning, and his silent return. Now the shame of the incident thrust itself back upon them, and Mary murmured despairingly, "How could he? How could he?"

"I'll help you carry the presents, Miss," Joe offered. It seemed a good moment to leave Nathan and Mary alone. He did not know yet what to make of Horace, whether sheer greed or some financial need had driven his act, but although the charge of selling watered milk was not a serious crime, Joe had sensed in his brief meeting with Emma's brother a meanness of spirit that made dishonesty and petty dealings all too likable to his nature.

Emma arranged the gifts in one basket, cookies and sweets in another, and they donned their coats and set off across the road. The day was mild for December, snow melting in puddles to reveal a few bare patches of brown grass. For a minute or two they did not speak, and Joe felt an awkward space between them now they were alone. As if she felt it, too, Emma bent her head and busied herself tucking the dolls and carved animals more securely in place.

"I never asked, Mr. McEachran," she said finally, "if you have other family in Livonia. Yesterday, you mentioned three sisters. . . ." She faltered, then strove for a ray of hope. "Did you have diphtheria, too? And you survived."

"No, Miss." He was sorry to see her face fall, but it was not in him to lie. "We were children in Scotland then, and somehow it missed me. But there were other children who had it and recovered, so might your brother's bairns, too."

The corners of her mouth lifted gratefully, and Joe did not tell her what he remembered most of all. In their cramped, thatched cottage his sisters' painful gasping for breath had seemed to torture the very air. Forgotten in the crisis, he huddled against the wall and stared as his parents and the local doctor, a shabby, well-meaning old man, crowded around the bed. While his mother cried to God for mercy, the doctor tried to prop the little girls so they could catch a breath. On a tray sat all the wishful brews and concoctions that had failed. Joe heard the doctor offer one last suggestion, and his father's grim "Aye." Then a blade shone and a gurgling noise sounded as the old man slit deep into each girl's throat and pried open their windpipes with fishhooks. It had not worked.

"And your parents?" Emma asked, shaking him from the memory. "Do they live in Scotland still?"

"No. 'Tis only me left, Miss. My parents were tenants on another man's land, and when they died I saw little future in it."

"But was it not hard to leave your birthplace?" She glanced around the sweep of acres that belonged to her father and brother, and he saw in her face a love that even fierce adversity could not beat down.

"Aye, it was hard. I miss the smell of heather on the hills, the cold blue lochs, the spring mist in the valleys and glens." He gestured around him. " 'Tis a winding place, Scotland, not flat and straight as you have here."

They had reached Horace's house, and as they mounted the porch steps the ominous red sign confronted them like a bully that must be faced down. For a moment he saw Emma's jaw work, then she lifted her fist and knocked loudly. After a minute the door opened a crack, and Charlotte's face peered out. She seemed more composed than yesterday, but wan and exhausted.

"Charlotte, how are the children?" Emma pressed forward, but her sister-in-law raised a warning hand.

"The same, Emma. I am giving them the medicine you brought, but do not come in. Stay away."

"Perhaps if you boiled pans of hot water to set in their rooms," said Emma. "The steam may make the air easier to breathe."

"Yes, yes, I will try that." Charlotte's face gave a sad perk of hope, then fell again. "Horace is in the barn, Emma, making Wallie's coffin. Do not go there," she added hastily as Emma turned, "there may still be some contagion. But tell your father we shall need his help to dig the grave, the ground frozen as it is."

"I will." Emma pushed the baskets of toys and sweets through the door into Charlotte's hands. "We brought these over to cheer the children."

For a moment no more words came from Charlotte as she stared at the gifts. Then with difficulty she spoke. "Wallie's last words were to give his toys to his brother Oren." She burst into tears and closed the door.

Emma stood staring at the shut panel, and when Joe gently took her elbow to lead her away, she raised a hand and quickly wiped her eye. In silence they recrossed the road to her house.

It was a listless evening. Darkness fell. Joe played checkers with Nathan, their minds not on the game. The women read and sewed. At any other Christmas there would have been songs and music, sleigh rides, snowball fights, parties and storytelling, dances, jokes. Maybe in some homes, Joe thought, there still were. He pondered bringing out his harmonica, but the mood was not right. The whole day seemed artificial, trapping them in expectations that could not be met, and they were all relieved when the hour finally drew late enough to bring Christmas to an end and bid one another goodnight.

Joe went to his room, sat on his bed, and pulled off his shoes and socks.

"Mr. McEachran."

Emma stood in his doorway, holding an oil lamp, the living room dark behind her. She exhaled a breath after his name, as if it had taken her some resolve to approach, and Joe stood and waited respectfully, though a little embarrassed that she should see him in his bare feet.

"Mr. McEachran, I wish to apologize for my distraught behavior yesterday in front of Horace's house when I tripped you into the snow. And I never thanked you for the loan of your jacket. It was kind of you to show concern for my well being."

"No, Miss, 'tis I who am sorry for laying hands on you as I did. I dinna mean to. My only thought was to keep you from harm."

"I am sorry to have provoked it," said Emma. "I'm afraid I lost control."

" 'Tis not to be wondered at, Miss. I am sorry your family has encountered such misfortune."

They both stopped, a little sheepish, at the growing litany of apologies. At least Emma seemed not to have noticed his bare toes. A soft glow from the lamp fell around her, making her appear like a luminous figure in a painting, and Joe thought how she had inherited neither her mother's prettiness nor her father's chiseled lines, but was separate from each of them, her face marked by thoughtfulness and a down-to-earth turn of mind.

Emma gave a slight nod, as if to recall her purpose in coming. "I also thank you for your help today, trying to entertain us and put a good face on the holiday. It hardly seems fair you should be drawn into our sorrow when you have only just entered our home. What you must think of our character, after Horace's wicked behavior, it pains me to contemplate." She winced.

"Dinna feel badly, Miss. 'Tis a difficult time for all. No doubt I have been in your way, being a newcomer and underfoot."

"But we want you to feel welcome." Emma reached a hand toward his sleeve in protest, then quickly withdrew it as she realized the impropriety of her motion. She glanced around his small, neat room. "Is there anything else you need to be comfortable?"

" 'Tis not that, Miss. No, my room is fine. I only meant that a hired man canna help but be an outsider. 'Tis the nature of the job." He gestured toward the rest of the house. "No matter how hard I labor here, 'tis yours, not mine. No matter how long I stay, though you may count me a friend, I can never be family. 'Tis no injustice, for you have worked to earn this farm, and so may I to gain mine. Some fellows say 'tis better to be free to come and go as the wind, and a hired hand can do that, sure. But what I like best about America is that any man who has a mind to can sink his hands and feet and heart into it and build up something that makes him proud. Look!" He stooped and dug under his mattress and brought out a drawstring leather pouch. A slither of coins sounded as he displayed the bag in his palm. "I am saving to buy land, maybe even here in Livonia, for it seems a good place with good people. I dinna claim to start with something grand, only a stake of my own where I can work to my soul's content."

He stopped, surprised he had let the dream spill so freely from his mouth, not knowing whether by now she was vexed, insulted, offended, or amazed at the comparisons he had dared to make between his station and hers. But for some reason, he wanted her to understand that he meant to be better than he now stood before her, meant to raise himself in the world.

"Why, that is exactly how I should feel were I in your position!" Emma exclaimed. "Yes, I do see what you mean. I am so glad you have come, Mr. McEachran, for now I know we can rely on you to work diligently, and we shall pay you fairly in return. And don't you think it is work that keeps us happy, that gives us purpose and content? Surely there can be no greater satisfaction than to tend to all the honest chores that make a well-run home."

They gazed eagerly at each other, eyes shining, as if they had hatched a marvelous plan. If her face had such a light in it all the time, thought Joe . . . and as if Emma's mind had followed a parallel track about him, they both flushed.

"Well," said Joe, recalling his place, "here we stand spouting big dreams when we'd best get to bed or we'll not be up with the cock."

"Yes, yes." Emma laughed, embarrassed, withdrawing a step. "Well, I do thank you, Mr. McEachran. Goodnight."

"Goodnight, Miss Kingsley. Merry Christmas."

She turned away with the lamp, and Joe sat down on his bed. He was not a religious man, but sometimes he felt unexpected moments of grace, and now his spirits lifted for no clear reason he could name. Perhaps there had been some blessing in this day after all. Perhaps tomorrow the bairns would be better, the crisis passed, and life could resume its ordinary way. He gazed out the window at the starry night sky. Though only a few hours remained, it was still Christmas. He took his harmonica from the shelf and put it to his lips, playing soft, low notes for a silent night.

Five

Someone, thought Gertrude, is wailing. The sound seemed close yet far away, as if it traveled through water to reach her. *Orrrennn!* The lament curved up, up, up, like a giant wave in a picture she had once seen of the ocean, then it curled and tumbled over, its crested shape collapsing into a flood of foam. She imagined it flattening, subsiding into a tranquil gleam of gray water. Then the next wave climbed upward, towering into an agony it could not sustain, plunging into a grief-stricken descent. It rushed up the shore of her consciousness carrying her brother's name. *Orrrennn!*

Maybe *I* am underwater, Gertrude thought, and the idea soothed her a little for it seemed to explain why her hearing was impaired and why her limbs lay so heavy and useless in her bed and why no speech issued from her throat when she opened her mouth. Above all, it explained why so little air went in and out of her lungs. Surely it was amazing she could still breathe at all.

The next time Gertrude awoke, the noises were dreamlike but clearer. They came through the wall of her brothers' bedroom next door, and since she still could not move or speak she played a silly guessing game to amuse herself and pass away this strange time. She heard footsteps . . . Mama's . . . walking around a bed . . . a blanket drawn back . . . soft, heavy sounds . . . a body shifting on a mattress . . . no, being turned. Gertrude sucked in a small breath. She could see it now, each sound vivid as a word communicating a piece of the picture. There was Mama, disheveled, her dress stained with spilled medicine, her hair undone, her pale, ghostlike fingers undoing the buttons on Oren's nightgown. She slipped the garment gently over his head, and there lay

Oren naked, his thin body with fever-tousled hair frail as an angel on the white sheet.

So Oren is dead, too, Gertrude thought, without surprise, for everything seemed unreal in this airless world. She did remember Wallie had died Christmas Eve, the same day she had been carried home from Stringer's Store, and yesterday she had regained her senses long enough to understand it was Christmas. Late in the afternoon Mama had appeared with a basket of presents from Emma and had passed out to Mamie and Ivy the dolls stitched by Grandma and the willow whistles and toy animals Grandpa had carved. For Gertrude there was a fringed lavender shawl crocheted by Emma and a pair of white gloves Grandma had adorned with fancy beadwork.

A cough drew her attention, and her eyes traveled to the double bed where her sisters drifted in and out of consciousness under their quilt. Poor little ones, Gertrude thought, we are all going to die. The new gloves and shawl were folded by her feet, and she wished she could reach them and put them on for she wanted to look beautiful on her deathbed. But her limbs would not move, and it took all her effort simply to let the thin stream of breath she possessed pass silently in and out through her lips.

"Hush little baby, do not cry . . ."

The wavering song came from her brothers' room, and Gertrude saw in her mind the melancholy motions as Mama turned Oren's body to dress him in his Sunday suit for burial. Oren would not like that, being called a baby, for, though small for his age and chubby, he had always been fast and clever and brave. Besides, Mama was getting the lyrics wrong.

> You'll be in heaven by and by
> Take your mother's heart with you
> It's forever broke in two.

A heavy tread mounted the stair.

"Charlotte!"

Papa's voice cut into the trembling song, and Gertrude shuddered at its sudden loudness. Fully conscious now, she heard each word hard and resonant as a bell.

"Charlotte, is the boy ready?"

"No, go away. You shall not have him."

"He cannot stay in the house. Let me take him out to lie beside his brother while I build the coffin."

"No. My boys shall not go like this, no service, no prayers, no farewells from their little playmates, no funeral feast."

"They've given no service to any of the dead children, only buried them quick to end the contagion. Get off your knees, woman!"

"Our Father, who art in heaven—"

"What good will that do? If your prayers could not save him when he was alive, there's no salvation in them now."

"Hallowed be thy name—"

"God isn't listening, woman. He never was. He enjoys suffering."

"Horace, no! Don't speak blasphemy! Not with our girls still in danger."

"Why not? Were you not yourself about to say, 'Thy kingdom come, thy will be done.'? This is *his* doing, *his* curse."

"This is *your* doing! It is God's judgment on us, Horace, for your wickedness. To cheat our neighbors and ruin our good name! No one will ever buy milk from us again!"

"I told you not to speak of that! Go back to your useless praying then. I've done with that forever."

A rough shove and a stumbling sound penetrated the wall, and choking gasps clawed up Gertrude's throat. Her lungs heaved with the search for air. It felt as if someone were pressing a pillow over her face, but though she pushed and struggled no one came to help her. As she slipped away again, a faint song reached her ears.

> *Such a good sweet boy you've been*
> *Too soon your time is at an end*
> *Now my three girls I must save*
> *Never let them know the grave.*

The next thing that happened, Gertrude took to be a real dream. She saw her bedroom window slide open and standing below in the snow were her grandparents and Emma. Grandma was weeping in Grandpa's arms and—this was most strange—Grandpa, too, was crying. She could not ever before remember seeing tears on his cheeks.

"The ground is ready," Grandpa called in a choked voice, though to whom Gertrude was unsure. "Joe has stayed all day beside the fire in the cemetery, digging down each layer of earth as it warms."

"It should have been us," Grandma cried, clutching her husband's hand. "We are old, we should not mind. Let us be taken instead, and we would count it a blessing."

Emma said nothing, only stared in white-faced grief. Poor Emma, thought Gertrude. Who will you fuss over when we are gone? Why don't you marry and have children of your own? Emma, what are you afraid of? You will be the only one left who can carry on the family to the next generation. The images drifted away, and Gertrude tossed and turned, trying to bring them back. A cold hand pressed on her forehead, and a voice hissed in her ear.

"Shhh, shhh. Lie quiet and he will not find you."

Gertrude's eyelids flew open. She saw first a flickering candle, felt its heat on her cheeks like a small orange sun, then above it her mother's shadowy face staring down at her, warning finger to her lips. An uncanny light shone in Mama's eyes. Behind her loomed blackness. For the first time, Gertrude felt afraid.

Who? Who won't get me? she tried to ask, but no sound came. The room felt stuffy, and as her vision adjusted to the darkness, she saw the door was closed and a large bureau had been pushed against it, barricading them in the room. It felt like the middle of the night. Gertrude peered across to her sisters' bed where Mamie and Ivy were asleep.

"I will not let him in. I will not let him take you," whispered Mama. "Shhh, darling, shhh. Go back to sleep." She brushed Gertrude's hair and receded with the candle. Unsure if she were dreaming again, Gertrude watched her mother set the taper on a table, ease herself into the center of Mamie and Ivy's bed, and gather a daughter into each arm.

"Go away. You shall not have them. You may not enter this room. I am here to drive you away."

The chant intoned and repeated from the girls' bed, and Gertrude grew muddled, listening. But Mama, she thought, you must fall asleep sometime. . . . Gertrude yawned and slumbered. How much time passed, she could not tell. Once she heard Papa swearing and pounding on the door. Twice, bitter shrieks jolted her awake, the bedroom door opened, and she imagined the sound of a bundle laid outside in the hall. Then the door closed, and the bureau scraped heavily into place. Gertrude was jostled uncomfortably toward the edge of her bed. *A fine way to treat a dying person,* she harrumphed to herself. Why couldn't Mama go sleep in her own bed? Her mother's arms tightened around her, and her voice whispered fiercely in Gertrude's ear.

"Shhh, darling, shhh. Do not fret. Tonight the year is ended. Mamie and Ivy are gone. My four dear ones are dead. Four coffins in the barn. I will *not* let him have you! You, my first and now my last. I will give you my breath."

A warm air filled Gertrude's throat, and she felt the brush of her mother's lips on hers. Poor Mama, she thought, I never guessed how much you loved us. If I had lived and married R. Z., I would have given you grandchildren to love, too. Tell Emma I said she must get married. What is a woman without children? What good is life if you do not pass the gift on?

Hours later, for one clear moment, Gertrude awoke. The candle guttered on the table. Her mother lay in exhausted sleep at her side. Gertrude put her arm around her. That's all right, Mama. You rest. Outside the window it was snowing, great white flakes patting in friendly insistence on the panes. A round silver moon shone through the window, and she imagined she heard a midnight bell ring. I wish I had gone on that sleigh ride with R. Z., Gertrude thought, as her eyelids closed. How foolish of me to die without ever having been kissed.

Six

Sometimes, thought Joe, there was reason to be grateful for the cold. It kept the carrots and turnips in the cellar crisp and unspoiled all winter long. It kept the metal cans of milk in the barn chilled and fit to drink. Across the road at Horace Kingsley's house it preserved the bodies in four pine coffins laid side by side in the barn.

Joe turned away from the living-room window. It was New Year's Day 1888, and he was the first in the house to awaken. He walked through the kitchen and out the back door into deep, new-fallen snow. In the barn, he took a clean pail, lifted the milking stool from its nail on the wall, and hunched up to the first cow. Today, midmorning, the four bairns were to be buried, and he prayed that overnight it had not become five. Yesterday when he and Emma had made their daily pilgrimage across the road to call for news, Horace Kingsley had not opened to their shouts. Emma had walked round and round the house, tapping at the windows and calling plaintively, until finally the front door opened and her brother stormed out. A three day's stubble shadowed his chin and a faint vapor of whiskey emanated from his rumpled clothes.

"Go away, Emma!" he snarled. "You only make it worse."

"But what about Gertrude?" Emma pleaded. "Is Charlotte still with her? Is she still alive?"

"How would I know? The madwoman will not open the door."

"But she has been in there six days, Horace. She must come out, at least to eat, or she will lose her own strength."

"She says she has everything she needs. There is no reasoning with the daft creature. Does she think she can stop death by barricading the door? He may as well take the girl and have done with it! What a curse this life is!" Horace stalked back inside and slammed the door.

Joe had thought for sure then that Emma must cry. All week, as first Oren, then Mamie and Ivy were carried out in their father's arms, Emma had ached from a distance in dry-eyed despair. Now the tears loomed so large in her eyes they pooled like a lake ready to overflow a dam. But somehow she blinked them back.

"If Charlotte is still shut in the girls' room, Gertrude must be alive," she said, pressing her fist into her palm. "When Mamie and Ivy died, she opened the door and laid them in the hall. Gertrude must be alive or the door would open."

She turned to him, desperate for confirmation of her logic, and Joe nodded encouragement. What more could he do? This last week of the year had surely been one of the grimmest in his memory. Even an outsider could not fail to be moved by the misfortune the disease had brought to families throughout the town. Though the Kingsleys had suffered one of the hardest tolls, the Galbraith family, he had heard, had also lost four children, and here and there it was one or two, with the total now approaching twenty children dead. To get accurate news was difficult, for the quarantine remained in effect, and even Stringer's Store, the blacksmith shop, and other places of business were mostly deserted. Only when a buggy or wagon passed on the road and he or Nathan shouted to the driver from a safe distance might they gain a word of how the other families fared.

And there were snips of good news. Henry Houghton's daughter was recovering, and Gertrude's friend, Loretta Baxter, whose brother Timmy had been the first to succumb, was on the mend. Mary Kingsley clasped her hands in gratitude each time such news trickled in, and Joe wondered in admiration that she could feel joy for another while her own grandchildren lay dying. That had made it all the sadder to spend his afternoons at the cemetery, shifting the fire to warm the soil, digging off layer after layer of thawed earth, thinking each time the job was done, only to walk over to Horace's house with Emma and learn the plot must be made wider.

Joe moved his stool to the next udder. Nathan Kingsley tended his animals well, and the six cows produced generously. At present, however, the bountiful flow was no blessing. Two days after Christmas, he and Emma had tried to deliver their surplus milk to the cheese factory and been refused by Helga Witt.

"You expect I should buy milk from your dishonest family?" Blunt, red-faced, Mrs. Witt stared disdainfully at the metal cans.

"Dishonest?" Emma's face registered shock, then she drew herself taller with indignant pride. "It is true my brother has behaved shamefully, and for that I am sure he must pay. But my parents have never in their lives cheated anyone, and I guarantee our milk is good."

"*Nein,* not for me." Helga Witt crossed her arms defiantly.

"Then we shall take our milk elsewhere," said Emma loftily.

"*Ja,* you do that. Just you try."

"Well," said Emma angrily as they drove away, "Helga Witt may be the closest and most convenient, but she is certainly not the only cheese factory in town."

But when they drove to the next two establishments they were again met with short refusals, and at the fourth the scowling owner suspiciously sniffed, inspected, and tasted their milk, then offered half the usual price. For a moment Emma stood perfectly still, though Joe could almost feel the quiver of outrage traveling up her spine. Then in a movement so swift and sure it caught him by surprise, she upended the can and dashed a cascade of foaming milk over the man's shoes. While he ranted and danced his way out of the puddle, Emma marched to the wagon and Joe quickly followed and drove them away. Only then did he venture to speak.

" 'Twas well done, Miss."

"Was it?" She gnawed her lower lip. "I fear I may only have made matters worse. When word of this spreads . . ."

Joe shook his head. "I should have spoken up myself, but you beat me to it and in a much more dramatic fashion." He offered her a smile, and she returned it, letting the rueful humor relax her worried expression. "It came better from you anyway," said Joe.

"Because it is my family honor at stake," she agreed, "whereas you are an outsider. Please do not be offended, Mr. McEachran." Her hazel eyes searched his for understanding. "It is only that what you said Christmas night on that subject has stayed on my mind."

"I dinna mean it to trouble you."

"No. But it has caused me to think that perhaps I . . ." She shook her head, as if some idea still eluded her, and fell silent the rest of the way home.

Joe finished the milking and transferred the still warm liquid from his pail to the last empty can. He fastened the lid and gazed down at it, rub–

bing his chin. When he and Emma had returned from their fruitless circuit of the cheese factories, Nathan murmured they would get by without the money until some appeasement with the owners could be found. Meanwhile the milk cans accumulated in the barn in shiny metal rows of disgrace.

Joe stepped outside and scanned the winter sky. He could feel the sun, knew it had crested the horizon, though it remained invisible behind a smooth blanket of gray cloud. The cheese factory would not be open today, but the Witt house was on the same property, and Helga Witt would surely be awake tending to her livestock. Joe set off along the road, glancing right and left to the scattered farms as he passed. Land of my own, someday soon, he promised himself. All of Livonia's thirty-six square miles had long ago been claimed and parceled into plots, and for years the population had held steady at some sixteen hundred souls. But farms still came up for sale as people died or moved away or sold off part of their land.

He reached Helga Witt's house and spotted her instantly, hauling slop pails toward the pigpen. He walked up, introduced himself, and offered to carry the buckets.

"*Nein, danke.* I know who you are. You came with Miss Kingsley." Helga Witt eyed him suspiciously and kept on walking. She was a stout, beefy woman, her blond hair, the same color as her cheese, scraped back from her forehead in a severe knot, tiny purple veins like miniature spider webs weaving their tracery on her red cheeks. Joe took off his hat and walked beside her.

"I suppose you have heard the sorrow the Kingsleys have suffered this past week."

"*Ja,* the three children dead. But that does not change—"

"Four," said Joe. " 'Tis four now."

Helga Witt clucked her tongue. "*Ach,* I am sorry. But their father, he is a crook, and no one should make excuses for him."

"I dinna come to," said Joe. "I hardly know the man, yet I canna have a good feeling toward him. 'Tis an unchristian thought, but it will not leave my head."

"Huh! Why should it, when it is true?" Helga Witt strode on, walking in long strides like a man. "You are new with them, so let me tell you. He is bad, Horace Kingsley. He takes no pride in his work. If he can skimp on any job, so he does. But not me. I make good cheese, like my husband, like my father in Germany, and I give fair price to every farmer who brings his milk." She stopped and turned to face Joe, deep anger in her eyes and the tight set of her mouth. "He might have ruined my business, that one. Who would buy my cheese if the quality was not good? How many times already, not knowing, did I send a bad wheel to the market in Detroit? He thinks he can cheat me because I am a woman who runs her business alone, *ja*? He thinks I have no backbone like that unhappy wife of his."

Joe nodded. "This week has near to crushed her spirit. I fear the poor woman's mind is touched."

"*Ja?*"

They had reached the pigpen, both of them breathing heavily from the cold, and though the hogs snuffled forward, snorting and grunting, Helga Witt paused. Regret and concern mingled in her question, and though he had not meant to, Joe found himself relating what he knew of Charlotte Kingsley's disturbed behavior.

"*Ja*, I am sorry for her," Helga said. "She is a sad one, and who would not be with such a husband? He treats her like the dirt, the *scheiss,* stuck to his boots. But every bad person has a family who suffers when they do wrong, and if we let all the bad people go for pity of the others, what then?" She dumped the slops into the pen and shook her head in renewed anger. "*Nein,* I will not drop my charges. Maybe this time he learns a lesson."

"Aye, you are right, and I dinna ask you to excuse Horace Kingsley." Joe turned his hat in his hand. "I am only trying to find some fairness in it to his parents. Even good people can have a bad son, and though I am new here, as you say, I would wager my land money that Nathan Kingsley had no knowledge of his son's doings nor ever sold you but the best milk himself."

"*Ja*." Helga shrugged grudgingly. "It is sure they did not know, or his wife Mary would not be the one to tell me my cheese tasted poor. I can feel, here, when a person is honest even as when they are not so." She thumped her chest above her heart.

"Then what I ask is that if you canna see your way to buy Nathan Kingsley's milk yourself, at least dinna blacken his name with the other cheese factories and the people in town."

Joe stopped turning his hat. It had been a gamble to come, and if Helga Witt denied him, it might cause the Kingsleys' reputation still more harm. If Nathan found out, it might also cost Joe his place. And what would Emma say? What right had he to interfere in her family's business, to think of her at all?

For a long minute Helga Witt stood silent, an empty bucket in each hand. Joe's glance skimmed past her, taking in the snowy fields, the fenced pastures, the huge barn, the business she ran alone. His gaze returned to meet hers.

"*Ja,* I will not be unfair," she said. She studied Joe. "You are here without telling them?"

"Aye."

"You are a foreigner like me?"

"From Scotland."

Helga fixed small blue eyes on him, and Joe looked back, patient and unflinching. "Tell Mary Kingsley I am sorry about the four children," she said. "*Ja,* I will buy their milk if they come. But the justice must hear my charges against Horace, and from him I will buy no milk again. He is a scoundrel to all of them, and I bet this won't be the last evil he does."

Joe donned his hat. "Thank you, Mrs. Witt. I am sure the Kingsleys will be glad to do business here again. 'Tis the new year today, and I hope it will bring a prosperous twelvemonth for us all."

She nodded and walked away toward the barn. Joe headed back along the road. Nathan, Mary, and Emma were at the breakfast table when he arrived, already dressed in black for the children's burial, and he did not mention his visit to Helga Witt. On such a morning, milk was a trivial thing.

They spoke little, and when the meal was done Joe changed into his one black suit and went with Nathan to the barn. They hitched one horse to the buggy, the other to the work wagon.

"I'll bring Mary and Emma, and we'll meet at the cemetery," said Nathan.

Joe mounted the wagon seat, flicked the reins, and directed the horse across the road. The sky had lightened to a wispy gray, as if only a thin veil of gauze held back the emerging blue of the upper atmosphere. A single track of footprints in the fresh snow led away from Horace's house to the barn, and Joe drove the wagon alongside them to the open door. In the pale light, Horace stood silent before the four coffins laid side by side on the ground. He did not turn when Joe walked up beside him.

"I have come with the wagon," Joe said.

Horace nodded and said nothing. He was neatly dressed in a stiff white shirt and black suit, his rich brown hair slicked into place, his chin clean shaven and mustache trimmed. Though his hair showed no strands of gray, his face today looked far older and grimmer than a man of forty.

"Is there any change for Gertrude?" Joe asked when Horace still did not speak. Even before the question was off his lips he prayed for a safe answer.

"She seems better."

Horace stared down at the coffins, brooding and grinding his teeth, and Joe followed his gaze. He had taken in a first impression of the plain pine caskets on entering, but it had not seemed decent to look at them too hard. Now he felt his attention caught by the pale yellow shapes, for although they were of simple design, neither were they the rough-hewn boxes he had expected must be crafted in haste and grief. They ranged in size from the largest for Wallie, then Oren, then Mamie, to little Ivy's, not much longer than a cradle. Each was of true proportions, finely measured and shaped, the seams of the planks so closely fitted as to be almost invisible. Horace spoke again, and it took a second for Joe to catch up to his words.

"The girl sat up this morning and had sense in her eyes. But she has no voice and last night, overnight, her hair turned white."

A finger of hope plucked at Joe's sleeve, and he wished Emma were here to receive the news. "The fever is gone, then? Gertrude can breathe?"

"So my wife says, through the door."

Horace continued to stare at the coffins, and Joe looked down again. The boards had been carefully selected to match color and grain, and where a knothole or imperfection traveled the pine, it was positioned to make the flaw a mark of beauty rather than a scar. The wood had been sanded to satin smoothness, and every nail was new, spaced at equal distance along the joints and securely fastening the lid. Where the nails had been driven in, not one dent remained. Every last blow of the hammer had been sanded away until the four coffins rested in perfect peace.

"My wife will not come to the burial," said Horace, and Joe looked up, though Horace still stared down. "She is afraid to leave the girl. She says she has blown her life into her, and she will not let it escape. Who can tell what the crazy woman means?" He gave a bitter laugh, and now he did look up, so suddenly and piercingly, that Joe started.

"Do you believe in hell, McEachran?"

Joe gave a wary shrug. " 'Tis written in the Bible."

"So is heaven, but a man would be a fool to believe in that."

Joe said nothing, and suddenly Horace's foot shot out and kicked the nearest coffin, Mamie's, making a thick, dull thud. Joe blanched.

"You've dug the graves wide and deep?" Horace asked.

"Aye."

"Then let us load these coffins and bury them where no eye will ever see them again." Horace gave a last hard stare down at the smooth, yellow boxes, each one simple and perfect beyond earthly design. "And let no man say my work is not well done."

Seven

"Gertrude? Are you awake?"

Emma tapped hesitantly at the bedroom door, then pushed it open and peeked inside. Propped against a cloud of pillows, Gertrude mouthed the word "Emma" and held out weak arms for a hug.

"Oh, my darling!" Emma flew in and embraced her, happy tears trickling down her cheeks. "Dear girl, you are thin as a needle! Are you eating? Are you warm? No, no, don't try to talk, only nod your head."

She tidied the blankets, plumped the pillows, and anxiously studied her niece. Gertrude's long braids, freshly plaited and tied with blue bows, had turned from glossy brown to ghostly white, but a tinge of returning color marked her cheeks and her eyes shone with renewed light. Draped around the shoulders of her nightgown was the lavender shawl Emma had crocheted for her Christmas present. Gertrude held up a fringed corner.

"Pretty," she mouthed and smiled. "Thank you." She took a paper and pencil from the table and wrote *Tell me all the news.*

Emma pulled a chair close to the bed. "Well," she began, "your father—" Her mind, running ahead, halted. Gertrude had been carried home unconscious from Stringer's Store just before Constable Chilson brought Horace from the cheese factory, arrested. She might have no inkling yet of her father's misdeed, and if so, she should be spared as long as possible while she recuperated. Emma shelved the news she had been about to relate, that the hearing before Justice Allen had taken place that morning and Horace was fined a hundred fifty dollars, a stiff sum. The payment would pinch the family for months to come. At least Helga Witt had stated plainly, for the town record and for all present to hear, that she held no other Kingsley accountable and trusted to buy their milk in future. Afterward, in her blunt way, she had consoled Mary on the dead grandchildren.

"Well, your father is out looking for work," Emma supplied instead, "and your mother, now that I am here to mind you, has gone to visit the graveyard."

Gertrude nodded sadly and gazed to Mamie and Ivy's empty bed. Emma's thoughts traveled to Charlotte, and she pictured her in the cemetery with foreboding. During her vigil, Charlotte had grown almost as wasted as her daughter, a twig in a black mourning dress, and though Emma had brought over roast chicken, bread pudding, glazed carrots, and jelly cake to put flesh back on both their bones, Charlotte's recovery seemed the less certain of the two. She behaved normally enough now, though even more quiet and listless than usual. But it was the faint, vacant look in her eyes that Emma mistrusted. It was as if Charlotte, waging her solitary siege in the bedroom against death, had gazed into some other place, had perhaps for a time even entered it, and though she was pulled safely back from its border, that place now owned a corner of her imagination and tantalized her to return.

Gertrude scribbled again on the paper. *Grandma and Grandpa, are they very sad?*

"Yes. Pa says the one blessing to being old is that each year brings him and Ma closer to the ones who have gone before. Every night, while the children were ill, I heard them praying together to be taken instead. What is it?" Emma stopped in alarm as Gertrude's jaw dropped and a breathy gasp escaped her throat. "No, no, you must not be sick again! Oh, how could I be so thoughtless to tell you that!" Emma jumped up, frantically feeling her niece's forehead, until Gertrude pushed away her hand and vigorously shook her head. She snatched up her writing tools.

Emma! I saw that! Grandpa and Grandma praying, or calling outside my window to someone to spare us and take them. How could that be?

"I don't know. Are you sure, Gertrude? It must have been a dream, an illusion." They searched each other's eyes, doubtful of a conclusion.

After a minute, Gertrude wrote again. *We missed your Christmas dinner.*

Emma sighed. "I wonder how we made it through that day, except that Mr. McEachran read to us from his play to keep our minds off our grief." She described the play for Gertrude, not mentioning how she had thrown herself into Joe's embrace when she misspoke her cue. Bad enough to have landed in his arms that first time when they toppled into the snow at Horace's. But twice? What was the matter with her? She patted her niece's hand. "If you are well enough, I will take you to see him act when the troupe performs."

Yes! Fun! Gertrude jotted. *He is a nice man then? He will stay?*

"Yes. He will stay." She said no more, until Gertrude nudged her and mouthed, "My friends?"

Mentally, Emma searched the sad roll call of the nineteen children who had died. "Most are well," she hedged, anxious to spare her niece more distress. Why was it the children made victims? Why had none of the medicines or prayers or vigils been of effect? Or had they? Had those who survived received some gleam of assistance more than the rest? No one knew, and though there was some comfort the diphtheria had not spread further, the loss still came hard to a small town. "Oh, Loretta Baxter is much better, and her mother told me in Stringer's that she sends you her love."

And R. Z.? Gertrude wrote. *Have you seen him?*

"Yes," said Emma good-humoredly. "I met him in Stringer's also, buying a new brush for a painting job, and he asked after you."

"He did?" If Gertrude could have made a sound, the words she shaped would have been an excited squeal. Then her face fell, and she wrote furiously on the paper. *But Emma! Look at me! Skinny as a plucked chicken! My hair white as a sheet! I can't speak even a word. What will R. Z. think when he sees me? How can I ever be pretty again? Why would he want to marry me now?*

"Marry you?" Emma laughed. "What a ninny you are, Gertrude, to be thinking of beaus when you nearly died and left us! But at least I am assured that with such frivolous romantic thoughts in your head you are truly on the mend. Now snuggle up and nap and I will sit with you until your mother returns. Really, Gertrude, what a flirt you are!" She bent to kiss the girl's forehead, and Gertrude grabbed her in her thin arms and squeezed her in a bear hug.

Emma waited until Gertrude slept, then at the sound of Charlotte returning, she slipped downstairs. Charlotte stared at her, seeing but not acknowledging her presence, and Emma quietly left. Constable Chilson had ridden by that morning to remove the quarantine sign, and with the fateful red message gone, her brother's house looked normal again. A stranger driving by would never guess what had so recently transpired within its walls. She gazed at her own house and all the other normal-looking homes dotting the winter landscape, and an ache tugged at her heart. Why must we be so vulnerable? she thought. Who knows what hurt may at any minute descend upon our lives? Yet joy might befall us also. . . . She crossed her arms and rubbed the sleeves of her coat to keep warm. The day was bright and windless but bone-cold, and if she did not move soon, her toes would freeze in her shoes.

Town Hall was a ten-minute walk, a square red-brick building just past Stringer's Store. When not in use for civic meetings or elections, its one main room might be rented for lectures, dances, or social events. It had a stage at one end, and when Emma entered, Joe McEachran and several other people stood upon it, conferring over a script. She took a seat on a bench, and when the discussion ended, Joe jumped down and came to her.

"Is everything all right, Miss? Your father gave me the afternoon off to rehearse, but if some matter has arisen—"

"No, everything is fine." Emma smiled. "I only felt the need for a little diversion. Would your friends mind if I sat a while and watched?" She nodded inquiringly toward the stage where the other actors awaited Joe's return.

"Not at all," he said. "Please stay. We are nearly done."

He returned to the cast, and they started a scene. Emma recognized a few of the players. Polly Noble Mason, once Horace's schoolteacher, acted the role of the meddlesome aunt, which Mary had read on Christmas Day. Old Silas Joslin, bald as an egg and peering through thick spectacles, did a comical turn as a nearsighted parson. She did not recognize the young woman who played the heroine, a coquettish blond girl who had no trouble flinging herself into Joe's arms on cue. Emma shifted in her seat, nettled at the sight, still more annoyed to admit the feeling. This is not at all like me, she protested. But she had known where she wanted to be this afternoon, whom she wanted to be with. Joe's presence beside her these past two weeks—walking across the road to Horace's, sitting at the dinner table, riding in the wagon to deliver their milk—had come to feel comfortable and right. And when each day ended, with its grief for the children, the dishonor inflicted by Horace, what soothed her tired mind to rest was the memory of those brief sweet seconds when Joe had held her in his arms. Was this how love started? If she let it, would it grow?

On stage the scene had ended, and the players began to gather their belongings and bid each other farewell. Emma stood and cleared her thoughts. She had all but forgotten Mr. Stewart and his proposal during her family's troubles, and he had made no further attempt to contact her. Perhaps he feared the diphtheria or, having heard of Horace's crime, was even now regretting his offer to align himself with such a disreputable family. Either way, their mutual behavior had told Emma what her answer must be. She had posted it that morning, a brief missive acknowledging Mr. Stewart's fine qualities but politely declining his suit.

Joe strode up beside her.

"How did we do?" He grinned, still animated from his stint on stage, and Emma thought that if his narrow face and blue eyes always glowed so brightly, she would think him quite handsome.

"It sounds very well. It reminds me of what you said Christmas Day about how the characters get into the actors, and so the play comes to life. Why, Silas Joslin is usually the most humorless man in town, yet I had to stifle a laugh when he peered like a buzzard into his Bible a few minutes ago. And Polly Mason took up the aunt's part with such spirit, and that young lady, the heroine, was so convincing when she flung herself into your arms. . . ."

Emma nodded toward the stage, anxious to catch a hint of Joe's reaction to the blond girl, and was pleasantly surprised to see her departing on the arm of a dark-haired man. The other players were also making their way to the exit, and Silas called to Joe to shut the door when he left. Emma studied the empty stage. She had come here from a simple yearning to be with him, but now they were alone she did not know quite what to say.

"Perhaps there is some magic in a stage itself," she ventured, "that sets free thoughts and emotions we are not accustomed to show. May I walk up there a minute?" She pointed, and Joe gestured for her to proceed. He waited below while she took a few careful steps, testing the floorboards, extending her arms.

"I feel foolish," she confessed.

"No, I dinna think you are. Go on."

Slowly, Emma twirled across the stage, waiting for some spell to enfold her and carry her away. And for a minute, it did. A lightness filled her and she closed her eyes and lifted on her toes, half-expecting to float into the air. But high as her soles arched, gravity tugged at her heels, and reluctantly they returned to the floor. At the solid feel of the boards beneath her shoes she opened her eyes and turned to find Joe watching her.

He gave a rueful smile. "The magic of a play, Miss, is that the lines are already written to make the ending come out right. 'Tis not always so in real life."

"But you made it come out right for us with Helga Witt."

Emma stepped down from the stage, glad to remember and thank him. "This morning at the hearing she told my mother about your speaking on our behalf. I am very grateful."

"I'm happy if it helped. Mrs. Witt dinna mean to be unfair, only angry. She would have made amends herself soon enough."

"Yes, I suppose she would. And for our part, I believe we owe her better than to treat her as a foreigner, an outsider." They regarded each other, and the warmth in Joe's eyes emboldened her to continue. "You see, Mr. McEachran, what I have discovered is that I am an outsider myself."

"You?" He looked puzzled. "I dinna understand. You have family, friends, home."

"Yes, but look how I have spent my twenty-four years. Safe at home with my parents. Fussing, as Gertrude would tell me, over my nieces and nephews, children who are not mine. Do-gooding for sick or elderly neighbors, bringing soup or gossip to amuse them on a lonely afternoon. I believed myself indispensable to everyone's well-being, but in fact I am only an onlooker to other people's lives."

"Nay, I am sure they—" Joe began, but Emma cut him short.

"It's true. Now the four little ones are gone, and someday soon Gertrude will marry and leave home. My parents will pass on. Then what will I have that is mine? The farm—but with whom will I share it? What son or daughter will carry on after me as a family ought? All these past sad days when we stood outside Horace's house I have felt like a beggar in the snow. I had no claim to enter, no matter how deep my love and grief. Hard as Charlotte's fate is now, I envied her being there, being *inside.* I suppose you think I am terrible, Mr. McEachran, to be thinking of myself and my own selfish needs when others have suffered so much."

"Nay, lass, do not be hard on yourself. 'Tis only natural when a tragedy has befallen to ask how it will affect us. 'Tis the way we survive." He tipped his head in quiet sympathy, and Emma nodded, grateful for his understanding.

"I suppose the other thing I ask myself is if I have not been a dreadful coward."

"A coward?" He startled at the word and stepped toward her, shaking his head in denial. "That is the last name anyone could call you. I saw you ready to barge into your brother's house to care for the sick bairns. You knocked me flat when I tried to stop you. I saw the way you held up your head and dashed milk on that factory man's shoes. 'Twas as bravely done as any man."

His eyes reflected admiration, and Emma longed to accept his compliment. But she shook her head.

"I was brave about all the easy things and a coward about the hard ones. I watched as joy or sorrow came to those around me, and I joined their celebrations and rushed to comfort their distress. But I never took chances with my own life, never plumbed my heart to the bottom, never risked my own happiness." She nodded toward the stage. "It is as if I have spent my whole life in the audience, applauding while others fearlessly took a real part. Now *I* want a turn in the play."

She bit her lip. Why could she not speak plainly? She knew what she wanted to say. That she cared for him, liked him, admired him. That she wanted to be near him, because without him she felt alone. That she wanted to give him her heart—a foolish, romantic notion, though Gertrude would no doubt approve—if only he felt the same.

Emma looked into Joe's eyes, and they seemed to say he understood and wished he could reply. But she was his employer's daughter, he the hired hand, and she knew that whatever his feelings for her, he could not speak until his own prospects were certain, his plans for land and a farm secure.

She released them from the moment. "Perhaps we should head home. It's growing late, and supper will soon be on the table."

Joe nodded, though the tender look did not leave his face. Unhurried, they made their way out the door. Twilight had fallen, a pale lavender sky banked by a low line of charcoal clouds, and they paused on the porch to gaze over the peaceful scene of houses and fields. They stood but an inch apart, and though they could not hold hands or even share a touch, Emma felt Joe's closeness like a warmth around her, and she knew this was the way it should be.

" 'Tis a new year," he said softly, "with much to look forward to."

"Aye, I mean yes," she corrected, and they laughed together. A leap year, her mind added, recalling the old custom that allowed a woman to propose to the man of her choice. Would she dare be so bold? Perhaps, but meanwhile there was no need to hurry for almost a full twelvemonth lay ahead. That would give them time to better know and understand one another, to learn if they were truly compatible and held fast to common goals. Plenty of time to be sensible, for hadn't her mother said, that night of her Christmas sewing party, that falling in love was the most sensible thing a person could do? Joe began to whistle, a low, sweet note, and Emma smiled in the darkness as they began the gentle walk home.

Book Four

1904

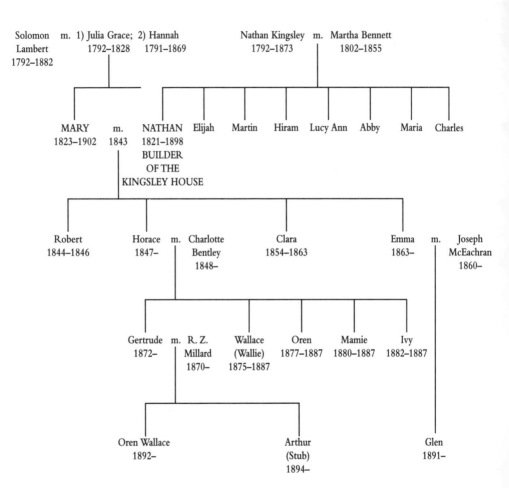

Solomon   m. 1) Julia Grace; 2) Hannah   Nathan Kingsley   m.   Martha Bennett
Lambert   1792–1828   1791–1869   1792–1873   1802–1855
1792–1882

        MARY   m.   NATHAN   Elijah   Martin   Hiram   Lucy Ann   Abby   Maria   Charles
      1823–1902   1843   1821–1898
                          BUILDER
                          OF THE
                          KINGSLEY HOUSE

    Robert   Horace   m.   Charlotte   Clara   Emma   m.   Joseph
  1844–1846   1847–   Bentley   1854–1863   1863–   McEachran
                                   1848–   1860–

            Gertrude   m.   R. Z.   Wallace   Oren   Mamie   Ivy
            1872–   Millard   (Wallie)   1877–1887   1880–1887   1882–1887
                            1870–   1875–1887

        Oren Wallace   Arthur   Glen
        1892–   (Stub)   1891–
                                       1894–

One

Geography is everything, thought twelve-year-old Oren Wallace Millard, as he surveyed his domain from high in the branches of the big maple tree that stood at the crossroads of Livonia Center. Hadn't Hannibal made history by crossing the Alps with his elephants in 218 B.C.? Didn't William the Conqueror gain the crown of England by luring his enemy down from the ridge at Hastings in 1066? Why, there might not even be a United States of America if George Washington and his brave men hadn't rowed across the icy Delaware River that fateful Christmas Night in 1776.

Oren smiled to himself, well content with his facts. All year the teacher had drilled his sixth-grade class in geography and history—not to mention reading, writing, and arithmetic—and having only yesterday passed his final examination and been promoted to grade seven, Oren was spending his first full day of summer vacation atop his command post in the maple tree, reconnoitering the lay of the land. On the branch below sat his ten-year-old brother, Arthur, better known as Stub.

"Where's Glen? When's he coming?" Stub grumbled, taking a dried pea from his pocket and cocking it into his slingshot. Oren frowned at the weapon. That past Christmas, Stub had received a Daisy BB rifle for a present, and one bitter March day when the laundry froze on the line, he used the gun to shoot holes through their father's long underwear. Pa had confiscated the rifle until further notice, but that didn't stop Stub from concocting makeshift artillery from whatever materials came to hand. Oren watched dubiously as Stub stretched the rubber band taut and fired the pea upward. It ricocheted off a branch, and the boys ducked and yelped as the hard little missile zinged back between them and pattered through the leaves to the ground below.

"Cut that out!" Oren rubbed his head where he had bumped it on a branch trying to avoid the pea. "Glen will get here soon as he's able. He's probably helping Uncle Joe with the chores. Now be quiet and let me think. I'm working on our summer plan."

Stub muttered beneath his breath and subsided. Oren resumed his scrutiny of the geography of Livonia Center. The maple tree stood on the northeast corner of the crossroads and right next to it, going east, was Stringer's Store, Town Hall, and then Oren's own house that his father R. Z. had rented for his mother Gertrude when they married. Oren already understood quite clearly that obtaining a house was absolutely the first thing a man must do before taking a wife. Because when he looked north from the crossroads, he spied first the house Grandpa Horace had built for Grandma Charlotte when they got wed, and then, across the road, the Kingsley House that Great-grandpa Nathan had built for Great-grandma Mary all the way back in 1843. So that just proved that getting a wife put a man to a lot of hard work and trouble, and why should a fellow do all that for a girl?

"Any sign of Glen yet?" Stub tugged on Oren's trousers, and Oren kicked his foot to get free.

"No. Now let me think, I told you. Who's the leader here anyway?"

"You are," Stub allowed grudgingly, though his eyebrows knit in a hint of rebellion.

Oren ignored him and peered through the leaves. The June day was blue and sunny, and a gentle breeze stirred the maple boughs in leafy green eddies. Where was Glen anyway? Oren scanned the Kingsley property, the barn, the shed, the greenhouse Uncle Joe had built. Now there was a man who got his house the smart way, by marrying a woman who already had one, though once when Oren had ventured to say something of the sort to Ma, she had near to washed out his mouth with soap.

"That is *not* how it happened." Gertrude shook a stern finger under her son's nose. "If you are going to tell stories, tell true ones, or people will think you are the boy who cried 'wolf.' Now listen carefully and I will set you straight."

Then Ma told him—he knew this part already—the tale of the diphtheria epidemic and how he was named, in reverse order, for Wallie and Oren, her two brothers who had died. But this time she added a new part that made his ears, which stuck out a little, prick to attention. Uncle Joe and Aunt Emma had spent that year falling in love, said Ma, but Joe being the hired man, he could not rightfully ask for Emma's hand for the very reason people might think it was really her property he coveted. So Emma, on the last day of 1888, boldly took a woman's leap-year privilege and asked Joe to marry her.

"Joe said yes, and they wed and had your cousin Glen," Gertrude concluded. "Joe put all his land money he'd saved into the Kingsley farm and was as kind to your great-grandparents in their old age as if he had been their natural son."

Oren sighed, the maple leaves brushing his face as they stirred again in the breeze. He hadn't meant to be rude about Uncle Joe, who was always good to him and Stub and let them run around the farm like a second home. Still, it was telling that although Joe's name was McEachran, everyone in Livonia continued to call his residence the Kingsley House and perhaps always would. Oren remembered, though faintly, how Great-grandpa Nathan used to sit on his back porch in his last days, gazing over his eighty acres as the evening sun went down. The memory put him in mind of geography again, and he sent his glance southward from the crossroads, past the blacksmith shop and the school to the cemetery where his great-grandparents were buried. Oren had figured from the dates on their tombstones that Nathan had lived to age seventy-seven in 1898 and Mary to seventy-nine in 1902, truly advanced years. He was beginning to think he would be old himself by the time Glen arrived. Stub was fitting another pea into his slingshot, and to avoid another misfire by his younger brother, Oren took command.

"All right," he said. "Glen must be slow with his chores today or maybe he's had another weak spell. If we go over and help him, the sooner he'll be done. Climb down."

The two boys shimmied and scrambled their way down the trunk, ignoring the snags when their clothes caught on the bark, the sap and dirt that collected on their hands. The maple had been their headquarters ever since the momentous day two years before when they finally managed to boost and haul each other into the first notch and gazed upward in awe. A welcoming green canopy spread around and above them, sunshine dappling through its leaves in a kaleidoscope pattern of dancing lemon light, thick branches forking into a network of strategic perches to spy out every corner of the land. In no time they'd become nimble as monkeys running through it and soon coaxed Glen to join them. Being at the crossroads right next to Stringer's Store, the maple was the best place in town to catch wind of all the local doings, and from this lookout Oren often dispatched Stub and Glen on vital secret missions. Though Glen was actually a year older than Oren, he was frail, and without any word or resentment between them, Glen had ceded, and Oren automatically accepted command.

"We are the Three Musketeers!" Oren cried, and they raised imaginary swords and cheered, "All for one and one for all!"

Now Oren and Stub trotted up the road, a pair of hardy, dark-haired boys, their skin already tanned, arms and legs adorned with bruises, scrapes, and mosquito bites from their outdoor escapades. Oren scratched at his ears and frowned.

"I wonder should we stop by Grandma Charlotte's," he said, his conscience needling. He would prefer not to. Grandma Charlotte had some strange ways of acting, and increasingly she confused him and Stub for her two diphtheria boys, Wallie and Oren, which, he complained to Ma, was what came of naming him after dead people.

"It is only because you and Stub are now the same ages as my brothers when they died," Ma replied. "There is nothing wrong with your grandma except that she is forgetful."

But Oren suspected the problem went deeper than that. Some of the kids at school said Grandma Charlotte was cuckoo. "Your grandma belongs in Eloise!" they shouted, which was the short name for the Eloise Infirmary, Sanatorium and Hospital in the neighboring town of Nankin, the place where the crazy people were kept. To silence the taunters, he and Stub had put up their dukes and dared anyone to repeat it. Meanwhile, Ma had instructed him and Stub to check on Grandma whenever they passed, especially because Grandpa Horace was away so much, doing whatever it was he did in Detroit. Oren was just as glad to have Grandpa Horace absent. When he, Stub, and Glen were little, Horace had frightened them with tales of bogeymen, and once he scared Glen sleepless by saying a moaning black ghost haunted the Kingsley House. Aunt Emma said she had never heard such nonsense, but Grandpa Horace only gave a wicked laugh. Now there was a mean old man.

"We better stop and see Grandma," he told Stub, who groaned in reply, but as they approached the house, voices came from inside. Oren put a finger to his lips, and they tiptoed under the living-room window.

"Now see, Charlotte, how easy this will make it for you? No more worries about repairs or upkeep, taxes or legal matters. That will all be my problem. I'll take you on a trip into Detroit, we'll sign the paper, and you'll get some money. Then wouldn't you like lunch in a nice hotel restaurant?"

It was Grandpa Horace's voice, and the two boys exchanged quizzical glances.

"He must have come home last night," Oren whispered.

"Does that mean we don't have to go in?" Stub whispered back.

Oren scratched his ears and considered. Grandma Charlotte was speaking, but her voice was so feeble he could not make out the reply. She talked like that a lot of the time, half to herself, as if she were holding a conversation with a person who wasn't there. But if Grandpa were home, at least someone was taking care of her, so with a nod Oren motioned his brother on toward the Kingsley House. As they reached the back porch, a familiar aroma wafted out to greet them, and a smile split their faces.

"Cornbread!" they exulted.

"Come in, boys. I hear you out there," called Aunt Emma, laughing. "The cornbread is hot out of the pan, and the butter's melting into it like sunshine. Come in and meet someone."

They elbowed their way through the door, then stopped short. At the kitchen table sat their cousin Glen, and across from him sat, of all things, a girl. She looked about their age, and she stared shyly at them through round blue eyes fringed by tawny lashes. Long blond ringlets, the color of spun gold, hung over the shoulders of her frilly white dress.

"This is Miss Ethel Pearl Allen," said Aunt Emma, nudging Oren and Stub forward to seats at the table. "She and her mother are related by marriage to old Mr. Allen who used to be justice of the peace. They're visiting Livonia for the summer, and I persuaded Mrs. Allen to let Ethel stay with us this afternoon while she sets up her house. Glen and I are going to help Ethel meet some of the children in the neighborhood."

Oren stretched his mouth in a smile while his brain groaned at this complication to his summer plan. Summer was for exploring the woods, jumping in haystacks, eating licorice and taffy before dinner, swimming naked in the pond. It was *not* about dolls and tea parties and other sissy stuff. Besides, Aunt Emma was getting this all wrong. Oren's head cleared, and his face brightened. Yes, that was it, Emma had got this wrong, for though he loved his aunt, she did have a way of always organizing things, and even now she was tucking napkins under his and Stub's chins and insisting Glen drink more buttermilk and brushing crumbs from the table. So it was only natural, meeting newcomers in town, that his helpful aunt would want to fix them up with company. Except that what Miss Ethel Pearl Allen obviously needed, nice as she might otherwise be, was *girl* company, and once Aunt Emma realized this, which would no doubt be shortly, she would set about obtaining more appropriate friends for Ethel and leave the Three Musketeers to their merry ways. In the meantime Oren could afford to be polite.

"Where do you live?" he asked her, between bites of cornbread.

"In Detroit." Ethel sipped her buttermilk, blue eyes peeping at him over the rim of the glass.

"How old are you?"

"Thirteen."

"Oh well, I guess you finished seventh grade this year, like Glen."

Ethel looked down at her plate. "No. I didn't start school until I was eight. Mama thought I was too delicate."

She spoke softly, as if embarrassed, and Oren sought for a suitable reply. He was used to Glen being sickly, but gee whiz, Ethel wouldn't graduate eighth grade until she was sixteen, and all the time she had to be three years older than everyone else in her class. Hard luck!

"That's okay," he said heartily to encourage her. "I bet you're real smart anyway."

She smiled gratefully, and Oren smiled back. Then he began to feel stupid, grinning at a girl, and it dawned on him he was the only one contributing to this conversation. Aunt Emma was at the sink washing dishes, Stub was stuffing his mouth with cornbread, and Glen . . . Oren frowned as he looked at his cousin. What on earth was the matter with Glen? He looked like a goony bird, a moony cow, a sappy face. From his sandy hair to his sky-blue eyes to the scant dusting of freckles across his nose he was glowing brighter than one of Mr. Edison's incandescent light bulbs. He looked as if he'd seen an angel float into his kitchen. Now why would Glen behave like that?

"Well, listen here," Oren said a little brusquely to Ethel, trying to get his summer plan back on track. "What sorts of things do you like to do?" Once he knew her interests, he could pair her up with some like-minded girls.

"I like to read and play the piano," said Ethel. "When I grow up I want to be a music teacher."

"H'mmm." Oren put on his thinking cap to recall other musically inclined girls and was about to name two when Aunt Emma returned to the table.

"Why don't you young gentlemen take Ethel on a nice walk around the farm and the neighborhood," she said, collecting their plates. "Take her to the creek where Joe is clearing brush and to the barn to see the animals and over to Stringer's Store." Emma smiled at Ethel. "I know your mother worries about your health, dear, but once you have spent a summer in our fresh country air, you'll have a skip in your step and roses in your cheeks. Look at the wonders it does for my Glen."

She gestured fondly to her son, and Glen beamed back eagerly at his mother and Ethel.

"But—" Oren opened his mouth to protest, but Emma had turned back to the sink. Stub was scowling. Ethel bit her lip. Her expression seemed to say that her mother would not approve of her traipsing around with boys, but she was too polite to say so to Emma.

"You got any brothers or sisters?" Oren asked in a last-ditch effort to fob her off on someone, anyone else.

"No." She hung her head. "I am an only child."

Oren heaved a long, inward sigh. His first day of summer—ruined!—stuck with a girl. And not just any girl, but a delicate city girl at that. Why did Aunt Emma always have to go arranging things that nobody wanted arranged? Consarn it! Oren loosed a silent oath, at least he assumed he was swearing, for that was the word he heard most often from the crotchety old men at Stringer's when something provoked them to an uproar. He watched helplessly as Glen, his face still aglow, came around the table to pull out Ethel's chair. She stood and thanked him, and Oren took a full look at her white dress. It had a high neck, long sleeves, dainty frills, a wide blue sash and bow. Glossy pearl buttons dotted the bodice and cuffs, and when Ethel stepped away from the table Oren glimpsed white hose and black patent leather shoes. An idea began to form in his head.

"That's a real pretty dress," he said.

"Thank you," replied Ethel. "My mama made it. She is very good at sewing and fancy work."

Oren nodded. "Well, come along with us. There's a place or two we can show you. But I'm the leader so you have to do what I say."

Ethel nodded obediently, and with a chorus of thank-you's to Emma, Oren beckoned his troop out the door. It wasn't that he meant to be unkind, he told himself, only to show everyone how impractical Aunt Emma's scheme was. He led them toward Stringer's, repassing Grandma Charlotte's house on the way, though not as closely this time to avoid any encounter with Grandpa Horace. Their house was quiet, and Oren racked his brain to recall the bit of conversation he and Stub had overheard earlier. Something about legal matters in Detroit. He'd mention it to Ma if he remembered. Meanwhile, he had a more important task at hand. He quickened his step, and when he glanced back he noted with satisfaction that Ethel had fallen a dozen paces to the rear. Glen dropped back beside her.

"We gotta ditch her," Stub hissed in Oren's ear. He pulled his slingshot from his hind pocket and surreptitiously mimed a shot at Ethel as she bent to pick a burr from her hose.

"I know, I know. Leave it to me," Oren whispered back, though already he was less sure of his plan. Sometimes on their adventures Glen grew short-winded. Then Oren would invent some pretext to call a halt and pretend not to notice while Glen caught his breath. But this was different, he reminded himself stoutly, this was a girl. Her very presence might spell doom for the Three Musketeers. Besides, once Ethel saw what he intended she would thank them for their hospitality, politely decline, and ask to go home.

He and Stub reached the maple tree, Ethel and Glen trailing behind. Oren watched as she paused to admire a butterfly and cup her hands to smell the blooms on a wild rose bush growing beside the road. Glen dawdled happily beside her. Finally, they reached the tree.

"Everybody ready?" asked Oren brightly, and Glen and Ethel nodded. "Right then, up we go."

He pointed into the lofty branches. Stub snickered behind his hand. Slowly, Ethel's head tilted upward, and as her glance traveled up the solid trunk her jaw dropped lower and lower. For a long minute she stared helplessly into the tree while its green leaves swished and swayed in the breeze. Then to Oren's utter shame a tear gathered on her lashes and trickled out the corner of her eye.

"If you don't like me, just say so," she whispered.

"Not like you?" Glen turned, astonished. He had followed Ethel's gaze into the maple and hadn't seen the tear fall. "Why, of course we like you fine! Is it too high for you? Haven't you ever climbed a tree before? Are you worried about your dress? Here, let me help you."

Before Oren could say a word, Glen dropped on all fours, offering himself to Ethel like a footstool. "Step on my back, Ethel. Oren, Stub, get in the first notch and draw her up—careful! so she doesn't spoil her dress."

It was Oren's turn to drop his jaw. Glen had braced himself and was ordering Stub into the tree. Ethel, one hand steady against the trunk, was preparing to step on Glen's back. Who was the leader here anyway?

"That won't work," Oren scoffed. "That won't get her high enough. Here, this is what I had in mind." He strode forward, shifting his shoulders as if he were pushing his way through a crowd. "Glen, you and Stub get in the tree. Ethel, put your foot in my hands and I'll boost you."

Glen scrambled to obey, and Stub, after Oren silenced him with a threatening look, reluctantly followed. Oren gauged the distance to the first branch, bent his knees, and laced his fingers. Ethel took a deep breath, placed her hands on his shoulders, and slipped her dainty black shoe into his hands.

"Oomph!" cried Oren, and hoisted upward. Instantly a flurry of white dress and petticoats engulfed his face. "I can't see! I can't see!" he cried, as Ethel pitched forward. "Let go my shoulders! Stub! Glen! Somebody catch her!" Oren staggered, blinded and suffocated by ruffles. He felt Ethel's hands leave his shoulders, only to clasp in a death grip around his head.

"Oh! Oh!" she cried in little ladylike gasps.

"This way! This way!" Stub and Glen shouted, but unable to see which way "this way" meant, Oren teetered like a blindfolded juggler trying to balance a swaying stack of teacups. His knees began to buckle, and amidst the boys' cries and Ethel's delicate shrieks, he heard a chorus of guffaws from the porch of Stringer's Store. Oren's face flamed red beneath the petticoats. If the other boys heard about this, he would never live it down!

"Arms UP!" he shouted, and finally he felt Ethel throw herself upright and her body straighten as Glen called, "We got her! It's okay! We got her!" The shoe disappeared from Oren's hands, the petticoat whooshed off his face, and he blinked his eyes to see the trio safe in the tree. Stub looked disgruntled. Glen was grinning. But it was Ethel's face that made Oren's heart stop. She was radiant, her blue eyes shining so brilliantly it seemed they had diamonds in them. Oren jumped, caught the lowest branch, and swung up to join them.

"I'm in a tree," Ethel whispered breathlessly. "I'm in a tree!" She clutched the trunk and gazed around her in wonder.

"Would you like to go higher?" Glen held out his hand.

"Watch your step." Oren quickly offered his arm. "It's tricky here."

"Thank you." Ethel accepted first one, then the other, and carefully picked her way up two more notches. They had reached a spot where several sturdy limbs branched out from the trunk like spokes on a wheel, and Glen took out a clean pocket handkerchief, spread it across one branch, and invited Ethel to sit down. The three boys found places around her.

"Do you like it?" Glen asked, beaming.

"It's beautiful," said Ethel. She added solemnly, "This is the bravest thing I have ever done."

Oren said nothing. He was wishing his ma made him carry a clean pocket handkerchief the way Glen's ma did.

"I thought we were going to ditch her," Stub hissed in his ear.

Oren grimaced. He couldn't figure quite how this had happened—a girl in their tree. Not only that, somehow she had managed it without a smudge or tear on that frilly white dress, while he and his comrades collected nicks and scratches from every shimmy up and down. Well, of course, we do, Oren told himself, we are hardy veterans, the Three Musketeers, used to blood and danger. Which made him think that maybe, just for today, or until she found proper girlfriends, Ethel could be their apprentice, like D'Artagnan, a little clumsy and awkward, needing to be taken under their wing. It might be kind of fun to show the ropes to someone new, which, as leader, would naturally be his job.

"So what do you think of it?" he asked, remembering too late that Glen had already posed a very similar question. But Ethel's reply, when it came after a pause, made him think he had asked something quite different after all.

"It isn't sad up here like it is down there," she whispered, her gaze drifting toward the ground. "We're safe and hidden, and no one can take us away. All the cares of the world are far, far below." She lifted her head, and for a moment Oren caught a look of desperate longing in her round blue eyes. "Maybe," she said, "I won't ever want to come down."

Two

Horace Kingsley woke at seven-thirty in the morning, donned a maroon dressing gown over his nightshirt, and stretched his arms. Sunlight flooded through the bedroom window, promising a fine day. He had instructed Charlotte to have his breakfast ready at eight, which gave him time to wash, shave, dress, and visit the outhouse. Horace parted the curtain and rolled his eyes at the primitive sight. The hotels he frequented in Detroit had private bathrooms with indoor plumbing, hot running water, scented towels beside the sink. But here in Livonia? Horace shook his head at the backwardness of the locals who seemed woefully content to trudge outside in all weather, closet themselves in a ramshackle wood box, and piss into a noxious hole. Well, he would be done with all that soon enough.

He stepped into the hall and peeked into Gertrude's old room to be sure Charlotte had arisen. A faint clatter of pots from downstairs confirmed it. "I take up too much space," he always told her on his visits. "You'll be more comfortable in the girl's bed." Obediently Charlotte trotted away, not that anything would have passed between husband and wife if she had stayed. That had ended years ago, and a gentleman like himself had no trouble securing female companionship in the city.

Horace glanced from Gertrude's room to the silent bedroom next door. Since that distant year when the four children had died, Charlotte had maintained the boys' room, and the little girls' beds, exactly as they had left them. Even those long-ago Christmas presents were still neatly and forlornly displayed on each child's pillow. At first the sight had torn at Horace, then it enraged and sickened him. But he forbore flinging away the trinkets while Gertrude was still sick, and by the time, months later, that her voice finally crept back and her hair, like spring earth, warmed again to its rich brown hue, he told himself he did not give a damn anymore.

He returned to his bedroom, poured water from a jug into the washbasin, and began his shave. His appearance, at age fifty-seven, pleased him, for his figure was still lean and hard and no sign of thinning was imminent in his nut-brown hair. In Detroit the ladies called him dapper, amusing, and a fine dresser. He was fond of whiskey and the latest entertainments and plays, and he gave a scoffing laugh to think how proud Emma was of the local drama club productions in which Joe still acted. Amateur stuff! Why had he ever stayed in this backward town so long?

Horace completed his toilet, dressed, and made the repugnant trip to the outhouse, returning as Charlotte was scraping the eggs onto his plate. Whatever looks his wife had once possessed had deserted her, leaving only an impression of pale nothingness. She wore a pink print dress faded from many washings, and her gray hair was pinned into a soft knot and trimmed, somewhat ludicrously, with a little pink bow. Emma had dared tell him he should give Charlotte money to buy new clothes.

"You like your dresses well enough, eh, Charlotte?" he had asked her. "You wouldn't want any more to wash and iron, would you?"

"Yes, Horace. No, Horace," she agreed.

There! Who was he to force new clothes on the woman when her old garments suited her just fine?

At least she could still cook. She brought him a heaping plate, and he sat down at the kitchen table and spread his napkin in his lap. That was the way it was done in the city, not tucked into your collar like a child's bib.

"Breakfast looks good," he said.

A hopeful smile perked across Charlotte's lips. "I have made everything just as you like it, the eggs soft and the bacon crisp."

"Yes, well sit down and eat." He motioned her to a chair, not wanting her to hover beside his plate. Besides, he was feeling generous. "Now, Charlotte, you remember that business we discussed yesterday?"

"Yesterday?"

"I told you about a paper we must sign."

A blank look stole over Charlotte's face, and she tipped her head from side to side as if trying to corner an idea that slid loose in her brain. It reminded Horace of those dime-store toys in which children tilted and tapped a miniature metal maze to coax a tiny ball into the center hole.

"A paper?" asked Charlotte.

"Yes. So you don't have to worry about the house anymore."

Her expression grew more puzzled, and Horace's teeth set on edge. Think, woman, think—but not too much. Somewhere in that vacant mind was the glimmer of cooperation he required, and it would not do for him to be impatient. If he lost his temper, raised his voice, whatever sense his addled wife still possessed would scatter like dry leaves before a storm.

"Good morning, Mama!" Gertrude's voice called at the kitchen door as she swung it open. "Is Papa . . . ? Oh yes, you are here. Oren said you'd come."

She smiled, but Horace detected the slight cooling in her tone, the curve of disapproval in the upward turn of her mouth. Gertrude wore a brown plaid skirt and a beige blouse, and her figure had gained a little fullness to suit her thirty-two years. But grown woman though she might be, let her not forget who was the head of this house.

"Well, daughter," he said amicably, matching her false welcome. "It has been a while. How are the boys?"

"Yes," Charlotte interrupted, "why are they not up yet, Gertrude? Run fetch them for breakfast like a good girl, and I will fry more bacon."

"No, Mama." Gently, Gertrude stayed her mother's hand as she moved to add meat to the pan. She cast an apologetic look at Horace and covered Charlotte's blunder with a bright laugh. "The boys have eaten already and gone out to play. It seems they have a new friend they are anxious to meet up with—a girl." Gertrude took a seat at the table and helped herself to a piece of toast. "Emma has met a Mrs. Julius Allen, who is staying in Livonia this summer with her daughter Ethel. The boys and Glen spent all yesterday entertaining her, and what a sweet child she is! Shy, though. She barely says a word. Emma has invited Mrs. Allen for tea on Saturday, so I shall meet her then."

Horace grunted. So Emma was up to her usual busybody ways, arranging teas and introducing people. Didn't she have enough to keep her occupied, fawning over that sickly boy of hers and pestering Joe to fix this and build that? Women were meddlesome by nature, and Emma was the worst, thinking she had some right as his sister to confront him about new clothes for Charlotte or his speculations in the city. Gertrude was less forward, relying on subtle complaints and a chilly cast of eye when she was unhappy with his behavior. At least his son-in-law R. Z. and Emma's husband Joe knew better than to interfere in his affairs.

They steered clear of him, as he did of them. You could trust a man to know when his opinions were not wanted.

Horace rose and walked out to the front porch, leaving the women chatting in the kitchen. The weather had been dry this spring, and a thin film of dust from the brownish front yard had settled on the porch railing. Horace nudged with his shoe at a loose board underfoot. Charlotte did not put much effort into maintaining the place, and it continued to deteriorate during his absences. He noted the peeling paint on the clapboard walls, the impudent yellow dandelions standing high in the scraggly grass. The barn, too, was looking shabby, and as for his forty acres . . .

Horace shook his head. Why had the misguided fools who first settled this territory not recognized at once the poor quality of the soil? His own father had often admitted it to be too sandy for prosperous farming, yet he plugged away at tending it until his last days. What an exercise in futility! Horace swept the flat landscape with a disdainful glance. All that pride in the land, and what did it profit a man in the end? You died and the land went on as if you had never set foot upon it, never made a mark at all. It swallowed your body in the grave the same way it swallowed your soul while you lived, and not a penny to show for your labor. Anyone could see the real future in this new century was in the cities, where a man could put his talents to any number of lucrative enterprises.

A satisfied smile settled on Horace's face. He had dabbled in the city for years, and it was time to abandon any last pretense of caring about his godforsaken farm. Real estate, construction, banking, investments— a whole metropolis was rising skyward, and Horace prided himself on being a wheeler-dealer, one of that sharp new class of men with an eye for opportunity and the finesse to wrap up a smart deal. If a few fools lost money in the process, that was only part of the game. He himself had taken considerable risks to bring his various projects to fruition, and only a bit of bad luck lately had lightened his wallet and sidetracked his plans. But he'd get there, oh yes. Horace Kingsley was never down for long.

A movement across the road caught his eye, and he saw Joe McEachran crossing from the barn toward the greenhouse with his dog. Horace squinted at his sister's house. That farm should have been his— not that he wanted it for its own sake. It was a matter of principle. Everyone knew it was a woman's duty to marry a man who could amply provide for her, and if Emma had done that, instead of abasing herself with the hired hand, she would have taken off to her new husband's home on her wedding night and left Horace clear claim to their father's land. Instead, she had contrived to feed the old man a misguided notion of fairness, as Horace learned when, three months before his death, Nathan had summoned him, Emma, and Joe to the living room of the Kingsley House.

"Your mother and I have decided it's time to settle our property between you," said Nathan, as Mary patted his hand. Their white hair matched almost exactly, and Nathan's stooped back brought him closer to his wife's height. "You, Horace, already have the forty acres I deeded to you on your marriage. This farm, then, should pass to Emma and Joe, who have worked it faithfully these ten years. But they have here eighty acres, and to even the difference is not easily done since we are on opposite sides of the road. So Emma has suggested I bequeath you the back twenty, beyond the creek—"

"—and Joe and I will buy it back from you at a fair price," Emma concluded. "I'm sure you will agree, Horace, that is a sound solution, and since your interests do not tend to farming, the land would only lie idle anyway."

She spread her hands at the neat outcome, and his parents beamed, proud of this generous legacy. At the time it had seemed a reasonable proposition. Yes, why not? He was short of cash just then, and the quick money would fill a hole in his pocket. But he scowled, looking back, at the way the whole transaction had been plotted without him. Now there sat Emma's house across the road, freshly painted a crisp white, an intricate new railing set between the six porch pillars, beds of red roses blooming exuberantly beneath the windows. The barn, greenhouse, and other outbuildings looked prosperous and tidy. Land values had risen in the past six years, and if Horace had those twenty acres now he could turn a fast profit on them. If he had the whole farm . . .

"Are you back for long, Papa?" Gertrude appeared beside him, and Horace shelved his budding designs and resumed a genial pose.

"I may be, daughter. Your mother has been well, I take it?"

"Yes, though last month she tried by herself to replace a broken window and cut her hand quite badly."

A hint of accusation tinged Gertrude's voice, and Horace bristled. "I thought I could trust you and R. Z. to help her with those chores when I am away."

"We try, Papa. I planted the vegetable garden for her and had the boys clean out the barn this spring. But you are away almost all the time, and we do have our own household to run. As it is, Mama keeps only one cow and a few chickens to supply eggs. All the land has gone to brush. This farm is too much for her to handle alone."

"Especially in her state of mind." Horace frowned. "She has grown worse since the last time I visited, and this confusion about the boys is a bad sign. How long have you let this go on?"

"Let what go on? Mama is fine, only a little forgetful, that's all. It is perfectly common for a person to mix up names on occasion. Don't I sometimes call Oren, Stub, and Stub, Oren, when I am in a hurry?"

"But you know the difference."

"So does Mama. I'm sure of it."

Gertrude shook her shoulders, nettled, and he shrugged. Anyone could see Charlotte was daft, but if Gertrude chose to ignore it . . .

"Papa," she continued, "I do not mean to criticize, but when you come so rarely, people in town begin to talk—"

"Talk?" Horace's face darkened. He could just imagine the whispers and gossip of these small-town minds, spreading an evil reputation about him, just as they had tried to do over that long-ago milk incident. No doubt they were now trumpeting lies that he neglected his wife. He would not be surprised to learn it was Emma leading the tongue cluck- ing. If they only knew the truth, that it was Charlotte who neglected him. The woman was incapable of fulfilling the position a wife of his should maintain.

"My business in Detroit is far too important to jaunt back and forth at my leisure," he lectured Gertrude indignantly. "Would you have me uproot your mother and take her with me, away from her home and family, to spend all day in a strange hotel while I am occupied else- where? No, daughter, what I am thinking is that it is high time she came to live with you."

"With me?" Gertrude's mouth opened. "Papa, that is hardly possible. Our house is small, and the boys run through it like a whirlwind. Mama would never have any peace and quiet."

She let out a worried puff of breath, brooding over the idea, and Horace smugly stroked his mustache. Gertrude's house was indeed cramped, and though she had spoken only of the boys, he knew full well it was her husband's wishes she must consider. He could picture R. Z.'s reaction, all right. What man wanted his lunatic mother-in-law wander- ing from room to room? Not to mention that R. Z. was a confirmed tightwad who would not welcome the expense of another mouth to feed.

"Besides," Gertrude shrugged uncomfortably, as if her blouse had too much starch, "R. Z. is talking of us moving to Detroit as well. Work has been scarce—it seems no one is decorating or painting their house at present—and he is concerned at our expenses."

"Well, I suppose your mother is all right here for the time being," Horace conceded, and a look of relief passed over Gertrude's face. Huh, he thought. Before others rebuked him for his behavior toward his wife, let them examine their own charity. "I may spend more time here this summer anyway. How would those boys of yours like to earn a little pocket money? There are some odd jobs I have a mind to set them."

"I'm sure they could do whatever you need, Papa." Gertrude perked at the news. "Your being here more regularly will be good for Mama, too."

She smiled, hopeful again, and Horace waved broadly as his daughter headed home. Then he hooked his thumbs in his vest pockets, surveyed his property, and mused. Slap on a coat of paint. Weed the lawn and mend the fence. Pull down the old pigsty. Plant a rosebush or two. The interior of the house was tolerable enough; the barn would do as is. No need to go overboard. The door creaked behind him, and Charlotte emerged.

"Well, Charlotte," he said warmly. "Remember I promised you a trip to Detroit? I'm thinking we may as well go today."

"Today?" Charlotte blinked.

"Yes. We can take the train and be there by ten-thirty. We'll stop at a notary office to sign that paper I mentioned. Then I'll take you to lunch in a restaurant, and afterward we'll have a nice promenade along the riverfront. You can see the boats and visit the stores. We'll be back here in time for you to cook dinner. And Charlotte, I may visit you more often this summer. You'd like that, wouldn't you?"

"No, Horace."

He started, and on seeing his sudden movement, Charlotte, too, gave a jerk. Her forehead wrinkled, and he watched her face cloud as she tried to backtrack through their conversation and discover how she had arrived at that answer. When no light dawned, she stared dumbly at him. Horace's jaw worked. It took a full minute before he could warp his expression into a smile.

"Now, Charlotte," he gestured to her faded pink frock, "if we're going to the city, hadn't you better put on your fancy dress? You want to look nice, don't you? And we'll have to hurry to catch the train." He took his gold watch from his vest pocket and studied it, shaking his head, while from the corner of his eye he assessed his wife. What had he ever expected of a woman like that? How unjust that in the prime of his life he should be yoked to such a pathetic, washed-out creature. Look at her! Charlotte's lips made tiny puckers of confusion, and her hands patted like little paws over her dress, checking buttons and bodice. Not a brain left in her head to untangle the complications he had thrown at her.

"Yes, Horace." The words blurted from her throat, and she heaved a sigh of relief to have found the correct response at last.

"Run along then and get ready." Horace nodded toward the door, and with a last puzzled shake to clear her head, Charlotte hurried away. Horace stretched and looked out on the land before him, and his smile shone white and fine.

Three

"Shhh!"

Creeping like burglars in the broad light of day, Oren, Stub, and Glen sneaked across the front lawn of the Kingsley House on Saturday afternoon. They tiptoed to a position beneath the parlor window and hunkered down amidst the rosebushes.

"Ouch," said Stub.

"Ouch, ouch," said Glen.

"Quiet," said Oren. "Listen."

They strained their ears to catch the conversation passing through the open window. One voice, at least, presented no difficulty.

"I cannot think what some merchants allow to pass for quality these days. Seams trimmed so narrow they are certain to fray. Buttons affixed with three flimsy stitches. Crooked hems and pockets set askew. That is why I make all Ethel's and my clothes myself. If you do not dress like a person of quality, you surely will not be mistaken for one."

The Three Musketeers looked at each other and shuddered. Mrs. Julius Allen had a voice as sharp and swift as a rapier. It gleamed with the delight of thrusting into a subject and skewering it to her satisfaction. From their post high in the maple tree they had spied her arriving by buggy for Emma's tea party, Ethel seated demurely by her side. The situation was ripe for further investigation.

"Boost me up," Oren whispered, pointing toward the sill.

Stub and Glen each grabbed one of his legs and shoved, hoisted, and manhandled him upward. Oren clutched the windowsill and peeped over the ledge.

Emma, his ma, and Mrs. Allen sat around a small table set with teapot, cups, plates of iced cakes, and strawberry tarts. Ethel, too, had a chair at the table, but she sat so quietly she hardly seemed to be present at all. Oren watched her politely nibble a cookie and smile a thank-you as Emma poured her more milk. She wore a yellow dress, and her blond ringlets were adorned by a blue velvet bow that matched the color of her eyes. Oren sighed as he gazed on her, until a grunt from Stub reminded him he was supposed to be spying on the enemy. For that was exactly what Mrs. Julius Allen had become. The morning following that first day with Ethel, he had rounded up Stub and Glen, marched to the house where Ethel and her mother were lodged, and confidently knocked on the door.

"Hi! Can Ethel come out to play?"

"What? My daughter play with boys?" Mrs. Allen's hand went to her throat in genteel shock, and she raised herself so that her figure seemed to loom above the three boys on her doorstep. A pile of stiff brown hair sat atop her head, and her corseted bosom pressed forward against its stays like a battering ram. Her squarish face showed a marked predisposition to frown.

"Um, sure," said Oren, "why, yesterday we—" He stopped. Ethel stood behind her mother, eyes horrified, fingers clapped over her mouth, vigorously shaking her head. "Ahem," Oren corrected. "Yesterday my Aunt Emma introduced us and said we should be gentlemen and look after Ethel as she is a visitor to our town." He pulled off his cap and nudged Stub and Glen to do likewise.

"Well," said Mrs. Allen, appearing somewhat mollified. "That is a courteous notion and not one I would have expected to encounter in a country town. But young ladies do not associate with boys except on formal occasions, and Ethel is far too delicate to be outside in any case. Good day."

The door closed in their faces, and Oren's hopes fell so far they nearly hit the ground. When he turned to his comrades, Glen, too, looked crestfallen, though Stub merely shrugged.

"This is serious," Oren informed them. "How are we supposed to play with Ethel if she can't come out?"

"She'll be cooped up all summer," said Glen. "She won't have any fun."

Maybe there's some way we can convince her ma." Oren raised his fist to knock. "I'll try again."

"No, don't." Worriedly, Glen caught his hand. "She might get mad and order us to stay away forever."

"Who cares? Who wants a girl?" said Stub. "C'mon, let's go put stuff on the railroad tracks for the trains to squash."

Oren and Glen ignored him.

"Mrs. Allen has as good as made Ethel a prisoner," Oren declared.

"But what can we do?" asked Glen.

"We must rescue her!" vowed Oren, for already an image was taking shape in his mind: Ethel, transformed into a fairy-tale princess, had been carried off by—yes, that was it!—a fearsome dragon. When he confided the news to his comrades, Stub's face twitched with renewed interest, and Glen's pale cheeks flushed so dark you could barely see his freckles.

"To the rescue!" he cried.

But how to rescue fair Ethel, that was the question, for in the days following their unsuccessful assault on Mrs. Allen's front door, the dragon had kept her captive close by her side when they ventured out at all. Only once, when they visited Stringer's Store and Ethel remained on the porch gazing wistfully toward the maple tree, were the boys able to shimmy down to the lower branches, call "pssst," and wave a surreptitious hello. Otherwise the Three Musketeers were reduced to snooping around Mrs. Allen's lodging in a futile siege on the dragon's lair. Now even that activity was to be curtailed, for Grandpa Horace had conscripted Oren and Stub to paint his house, and starting Monday they would spend most of each day up to their elbows in whitewash. Peeping in at Aunt Emma's tea party, Oren racked his head for a plan.

"What are they doing?" hissed Glen, and Oren motioned his comrades to lower him back to the rose bed.

"Ethel is eating a sugar cookie," he reported.

"How does she look?" demanded Glen.

"Trapped," said Oren glumly.

"What about the dragon?" Stub interrupted. The idea of Mrs. Allen as a loathsome reptile was the one aspect of the situation he relished, and twice already Oren had had to stop his younger brother from launching a slingshot attack on Mrs. Allen's behind.

"Breathing fire," Oren responded, and as if to confirm his assessment, the voice of Mrs. Julius Allen lanced through the air. But this time Oren thought he detected some other meaning beneath the indignant words, like a hurt that you tried to hide even from yourself.

"When people do not behave like quality, they wound not only themselves but those who ought to mean the most to them. It is why we have standards, rules for civilized behavior, and those who violate them do not deserve to be received in decent society until they come to their senses."

Oren stretched, trying to catch either Emma's or his mother's reply, but neither had the razor pitch to match Mrs. Allen. A moment later their espionage was interrupted by a joyful barking as Uncle Joe's spaniel Scout bounded toward them. They scrambled out of the flower bed to avoid being discovered, just as Joe rounded the corner of the house. He eyed them with an amused glance.

"Are you boys eavesdropping on the ladies' tea party?"

"We weren't exactly listening, Pa," said Glen.

"We were . . . resting," said Oren, "against the side of the house."

"Smelling the roses, I suppose," said Joe.

"Yes, that's it," they chimed.

Joe laughed. "And I'm a monkey's uncle. What could possibly be so interesting about a ladies' tea party anyway? Dinna you know there are times a man is wise to make himself scarce?" He rubbed Scout's head as the spaniel returned to his side. "Tell you what, I've an errand to keep you boys out of mischief a while. I was down clearing dead wood by the creek this morning, and I've left my hatchet by the trunk of that old sycamore tree. Take Scout and go fetch it for me, and I'll see Emma saves you each a piece of cake."

"Cake!" cheered Stub. "Let's go!"

He set off across the fields, and Oren and Glen reluctantly followed. Uncle Joe planted corn, wheat, and potatoes, and had five acres in apple, cherry, and peach trees. In the greenhouse he started early tomatoes, and when they were ripe he let the boys pick a whole one apiece and eat it warm with a sprinkle of salt, dripping juice through their fingers. In the garden grew peppers, cucumbers, cabbage, carrots, turnips, parsnips, and herbs. Six cows, two horses, four pigs, and a coop full of chickens constituted the animal population, not forgetting Scout. Back by the creek, the property was still woodland, providing firewood for the stoves, rabbits and pheasants for the table. Altogether, Oren thought, a farm was a much more interesting place than an ordinary house like his, which sat on a postage-stamp plot and gave a fellow no space to roam.

They reached the creek, which flowed west to east between grassy banks. After a good rain, the water hurried along like a traveler anxious to reach his destination, but this summer being dry, the stream had slowed and shallowed. Still, there was cool mud at the bottom, and after locating Uncle Joe's hatchet, Glen and Stub kicked off their shoes and socks and plopped along the creek bed looking for frogs. Oren sat back against the sycamore tree to think, his eyes following the lazy movement of the water. If you followed it eastward, the creek gradually widened and met up with the northern branch of the Rouge River. If you kept on, that river led you all the way to Detroit. Oren shook his head, amazed. There you had it—geography again. Wasn't it remarkable that this unobtrusive little stream, hidden among the trees on his aunt and uncle's land, flowed like a magical pathway right to the very city where Ethel lived?

Glen and Stub began jumping off the low bank into the water to see how big a splash they could make, while Scout barked happily at the commotion. Oren only half heard. Miss Ethel Pearl Allen. He liked her middle name best, because that was what she was, a beautiful white pearl, softly luminous and wondrous to behold. A pearl guarded by a fierce dragon, Mother of Pearl, and the thought of Mrs. Allen made Oren shudder. She could probably stop a snarling dog in its tracks and send it away whimpering with its tail curled between its legs. He bet Mr. Julius Allen was glad to escape her for the summer. Come to think of it, no one, including Ethel, had yet mentioned her father. Would he come to visit them, or was he too busy to leave the city? And here was another mystery: if Mrs. Allen cared so much for quality, why had she chosen rented lodgings in Livonia for her summer residence? Rich people from Detroit vacationed in places like the Grand Hotel on Mackinaw Island or traveled by lake boat to stupendous Niagara Falls, places Ma had read to them about in the society pages of the Detroit newspaper. On the other hand, no one had ever exactly said that Mrs. Allen was rich, though she tried to dress that way. Today at the tea party she wore a pale purple dress trimmed in black lace and an enormous hat topped with three tall black feathers. Oren had never seen Ma or Aunt Emma in anything quite so fine. But Mrs. Allen said she made all her clothes herself, and wouldn't a rich lady have her own seamstress?

"Hey, Oren, we found a bullfrog! Let's see how far he'll jump!" Stub, a short way along the creek, hoisted in his hands a muddy greenish object with long, dangling legs.

"In a minute!" Oren called. "I'm thinking." He scratched his back against the sycamore tree, then scratched his ears for good measure. An idea was coming about rescuing Ethel; he could feel it sprouting like a seedling about to break ground. He stood and hurried toward his comrades.

"Music!"

They scrunched their faces. "What?"

"Music. Ethel wants to be a piano teacher. And you," Oren pointed at Glen, "have a piano in your parlor." He rubbed his hands in excitement. Aunt Emma had bought the piano some years ago so she and Glen could take lessons together, but it was Uncle Joe who had become most adept at what he called "plunking out a tune." Whenever the play Joe was in contained musical numbers, he would practice the songs for them, and at Christmas Aunt Emma invited all the neighbors over for cocoa and a carol sing.

"Can you play anything?" he asked Glen.

"Not much. Ma never makes me practice."

"Good. We just tell your ma you want to take up the piano again, ask if Ethel can be your teacher, and your ma will arrange it with Mrs. Allen."

A dawning light spread over Glen's face, and he nodded eagerly.

"Music lessons?" Stub interrupted. "What are we supposed to do while Glen's having music lessons? Do we have to sit there and listen? Not me!"

He spit on the ground, and Oren felt a flash of annoyance. This was no time for Stub to go sticking jam in the works. He surveyed his younger brother in disgust. Water dripped from Stub's bare feet, his soggy pants were rolled up to his knees, and dabs of mud splattered his shirt from the fat, squiggling frog in his hands.

"It won't kill you," said Oren. "Look, Stub, once Ethel comes to Glen's house they'll practice for a little bit, then we can all go off exploring. Aunt Emma already said what Ethel needs is fresh air and sunshine."

"No," said Stub. "I ain't listening to any music lessons."

"Yes, you are."

"Says who?"

"Says me and I'm the leader."

"Who wants a leader who's gooey on girls?"

"I'm *not* gooey on girls."

"Or-en li-kes gir-ls, Or-en li-kes gir-ls."

"Why, you—!"

"Wait!" Glen leaped bravely between them. Stub had dropped the frog and raised his dukes; Oren reluctantly lowered his. Glen bruised easily, and in his present position he'd be pummeled. "We don't want to fight over Ethel," said Glen. "Our job is to rescue her from the dragon, and if I have to sit beside her for half an hour on the piano bench, learning about clefs and tempos . . ." His face grew dreamy. "Sit beside her on the piano bench," he murmured.

Oren straightened and reassumed an air of command. "I'm the leader, and I say Glen's right. Our first duty is to rescue Ethel. We have to move quick before the dragon takes off with her. Glen, Stub, get your shoes on, and Stub, leave that frog alone!"

Glen fetched the hatchet, and at a brisk pace they marched back toward the house, Scout frisking along beside them. Stub still grumbled mutiny, and when they reached the back door and Oren tried to brush his brother's shirt and trousers, Stub slapped away his hands.

"You stay behind Glen and me so Mrs. Allen can't see how dirty you are," warned Oren. "Glen, you go first. You're the one who has to do the asking."

Glen set down the hatchet, inhaled a deep swallow of air, and led the way through the kitchen to the parlor. The women looked up at their approach, and Oren's heart lifted right into his throat to see the smile Ethel bestowed on them. Then a panting sound behind him distracted his attention. Oh no, Stub had let Scout follow them in. A wet dog in the parlor was sure to count against them with Mrs. Allen. He tried to shoo the spaniel out, but there was no time. Emma had risen and come to usher them forward.

"Hello, boys. Where have you been? Mrs. Allen, you remember my son Glen whom you met that first day at Stringer's, and these are Gertrude's boys, Oren and Arthur." Emma patted their heads, and Oren cringed in embarrassment. But any indignity was worth it to save Ethel.

"Yes, I have met your sons, Mrs. Millard," said Mrs. Allen, eyeing them with a look that said they must be guilty of something. Gertrude gave a nervous laugh and automatically began the "boys will be boys" speech Oren had heard her resort to on a number of occasions when he and Stub had been hauled up for wrongdoing. He tried to look like he deserved his mother's description as "really good at heart," but for some worrisome reason, Stub was wickedly grinning. Scout, at least, had sat nicely on his haunches, swishing his tail and alertly surveying the interesting parlor scene. Oren nudged Glen forward.

"We're sorry to interrupt your tea party, Ma," he said, as Oren had rehearsed him on their way to the house, "but we . . . I have had an idea."

"What is it?" Emma beamed and turned to Mrs. Allen. "Didn't I tell you my Glen was a clever boy?"

"It's about our piano. I've been thinking I ought to practice more, and since Ethel is going to be a music teacher, we . . . I was wondering—"

"—how you'd like a great fat frog!" yelled Stub.

His arms flashed from his pocket, and with a loud "Crooooaaak," a huge greenish-brown blob flew from his hands, arced through the air, and splooshed like a mud pie among the cups on the tea table. Shrieks, pandemonium, and disaster broke loose. Mrs. Allen fell back in her chair, Ma and Emma rushed to assist her, Scout, barking furiously, ears flapping like kites, bounded madly onto the table in pursuit of the muddy prey, which hopped and flopped among the saucers. Glen dashed after the dog, crying, "No, Scout, don't eat him!" Gertrude collared Stub and began boxing his ears, squashed cakes and tarts littered the parlor, and all Oren could do was grab Ethel by the hand and rush her out the door. She had shrieked at the first commotion and was now wide-eyed and breathing heavily. Oren hurried her out of sight around the corner of the house.

"Oh!" said Ethel. "My!"

"Are you all right? Did the tea spill on your dress?" Oren checked her over anxiously, relieved to see the yellow frills as clean and spotless as ever.

"I'm fine, though it did scare me a minute." Ethel regarded him with eyes as wide and blue as the June sky. "Why did Stub do that? Won't he get in trouble?"

A heavy sigh emerged from Oren's chest. He could still hear from the parlor window the subsiding sounds of the tragedy. Trouble! They'd be lucky if Pa didn't tan their hides to smithereens when Ma told him, and they'd be grounded and sent to bed without supper, too. His wonderful plan for rescuing Ethel—dashed to pieces by that terror Stub. Then the worst thought of all struck. If he were grounded, he'd never get to see Ethel at all. What misery!

"We only wanted to have you come play," he said morosely. "I bet your ma won't even let you speak to us now."

"Probably not." Ethel's face grew downcast. "I did have a nice time that other day, Oren, when you helped me climb your tree and took me to visit your house."

"But why won't your ma let you come out at all? Why shouldn't you have some fun?" He kicked at the ground.

"Mama doesn't want me to get hurt."

"But we'd look after you. We'd help you climb the fences and make a seat for you by the creek. If there was a puddle in the road, I'd spread my shirt over it for you to walk on."

"Thank you, Oren," she said, and though the future was the bleakest he could imagine, her smile warmed him right down to his toes. "That's very kind. But I think it's not that kind of hurt Mama is trying to protect me from."

She looked away, and the dragon's voice, still rapier sharp but frantic, stabbed through the air. "Ethel! Ethel! Where are you?"

"I have to go."

"All right, but she can't keep you locked up forever. I'll find a way to set you free."

Wistfully, Ethel put a finger to her lips in a pledge of silence. Then she walked calmly back around the house, and Oren's pearl was gone.

Four

Gertrude tied the ribbons of her straw bonnet under her chin and stepped back to appraise her reflection in the bedroom mirror. True, they were only going to Emma's to spend the afternoon picking cherries, but she felt a need to look presentable. Ever since the tea party—terrible, awful day!—Gertrude had suffered from a nagging conscience. Part of it was Stub's dreadful behavior, of course. Two weeks had elapsed since the incident, and she still felt an urge to strangle him every time it rose to mind. But there was more to her lingering sense of guilt, and it stemmed from Mrs. Allen's emphatic pronouncements on the subject of quality. Somehow, Gertrude felt, it was precisely that attribute which her family lacked.

But what gave a person quality? She turned left and right, watching her plain blue skirt swish before the mirror. Was it the clothes you wore, the sweep of your hem, the cut of the cloth? Certainly, Mrs. Allen's dresses were the latest fashion, though not necessarily the most expensive fabrics, and her workmanship was unimpeachable. Gertrude reproached herself for her own sewing skills. She was a hasty seamstress, willing to let a quick stitch pass for finished as long as it was out of sight. Mrs. Allen's stitches were probably perfect right down to her underwear. Gertrude fingered the simple buttons on her print blouse. Maybe quality was something extra that went on after the basic design was complete, like the black lace on Mrs. Allen's mauve dress or the three proud feathers on her hat. But such trimmings were hardly practical when you spent your days at stove, sink, and laundry tub, trying to keep a husband and two rambunctious boys clean and fed.

Gertrude sighed and started downstairs. No doubt her house also lacked quality, despite the fine wallpapering done by R. Z. But the rooms were small, the furnishings worn, and no matter how often she swept and tidied, the floors bore a constant trail of seasonal debris, from spring mud to autumn leaves, as her family traipsed in and out. Whatever level of comfort Mrs. Allen enjoyed at her residence in Detroit, you could be sure there was no chewing gum stuck to the sofa or finger-prints on the wall, especially with such a dainty, well-mannered child as Ethel.

Gertrude's sigh following this last reflection was enormous. Oh, that devil Stub! R. Z. had taken a birch rod to their younger son's behind, and though Oren had been spared a whipping, for Gertrude believed his account that Stub had plotted the catastrophe alone, both boys had been grounded the past two weeks with the exception of going to paint their grandparents' house. Would the punishment do any good? Would Stub ever learn? Was it asking too much that for just one hour, in the presence of company, he not bring the house crashing down upon their heads?

She reached the front door and found her husband and sons waiting on the porch. The boys were scuffling and swiping at each other, their pent-up energy seeking release after their two weeks' confinement. R. Z. chewed on a toothpick and leaned against the porch rail. There was another example of lack of quality, thought Gertrude, instantly ashamed of her disloyal thought. She loved her husband and knew he loved her, but to be a paperhanger and painter, no matter how skilled, was hardly as impressive as to be a doctor or banker or judge. Well, you should have thought of that before you married him, she chided herself, for R. Z. never pretended to be other than what he was. Besides, who was she? Royalty? R. Z. was honest, hard working, and still boyishly handsome, especially when his smile revealed that elusive dimple in his right cheek. But she had not guessed before their wedding that he would be so tight with money, or that he would snore so loudly, or that he would pick his teeth on the front porch. She wondered what Mr. Julius Allen's occupation was, for Mrs. Allen had not mentioned her husband during the tea party.

"Ready?" asked R. Z.

Gertrude eyed the old striped shirt and work trousers her husband wore. "Couldn't you wear something a little better?"

"To pick cherries?" He gave her a puzzled look. "We'll only get juice stains on our clothes."

"I suppose you're right." Gertrude let out a final sigh. "Let's get along then. I want to stop by Mama's on the way."

They cut through their dusty backyard, passed behind Town Hall, and waved to Elizabeth Stringer and her son, John, unloading a delivery of bread at the back door of their store. Maybe quality, thought Gertrude, was being able to afford store-bought goods, instead of making do with homemade. She made a mental list of the items she regularly purchased, hoping to find a respectable tally of quality therein. Shoes, socks, soap, lamp oil, butter, cheese, flour, sugar, coffee, tea. When she could squeeze a little extra from her weekly budget, she bought tinned baked beans or condensed tomato soup, the newest foods to reach Stringer's shelves, but R. Z. complained at the expense and said her home-cooked meals and the vegetables she canned from their garden tasted far better than anything in a tin. He would be pleased at this afternoon's harvest, for as each basket of cherries came from the tree, she and Emma would pit, sugar, boil, and preserve them in wax-sealed glass jars for storage in the fruit cellar until needed. For their help, Emma always sent them home with a generous supply, while the bulk went for sale at Stringer's Store.

They had reached her parents' house, and while R. Z. walked around the outside examining the boys' paint job, Gertrude called at the door. Charlotte came to answer, a dust cloth in her hand.

"Hello, Mama. Are you busy? We're on our way to Emma's to pick cherries, and I thought you might like to come sit in the orchard a while."

"Oh, I cannot, Gertrude. I have far too many chores."

"Chores?" Gertrude peered into the living room. "Is Papa here?"

"No, he is back in the city, but he left me a list."

Charlotte beckoned her inside to a pad on the living room table. A line ran down the center of the paper, forming two columns headed "Charlotte" and "Boys." Under the first column were penciled tasks such as "dust furniture, beat rugs, wash windows, sweep floors." The second column listed "paint house, weed yard, mend fence," and other outdoor work. Gertrude gazed around the living room. Her mother's house usually wore a dejected look, but today it did seem cleaner than usual and a general sense of improvement pervaded the air.

"I do my list every day," said Charlotte, "and Horace is very pleased."

"Well, I'm sure you don't have to do the whole list every day," said Gertrude.

Charlotte seemed not to heed her. "Have you seen how nicely Wallie and Oren have done their painting job?"

"Oren and Stub, Mama."

"It is a pleasure to have such good, helpful boys."

Charlotte smiled and began dusting a small desk, and Gertrude's conscience nagged again. She knew the comments that circulated in town concerning her mother's state of mind. The tones ranged from sympathetic to snide. There is nothing wrong with my mama, Gertrude huffed in an imaginary reply. She gets along quite nicely, thank you, and if she mixes up the boys' names on occasion, where is the harm? Besides, it surely was *not* quality to discuss private family matters in public, and since Mama rarely went out anyway, the townspeople had no call to make remarks. Charlotte plied her cloth, humming, and Gertrude pushed away her discontent. At least her father was taking an interest in Mama and the house again, and that would stop another item of gossip, the way Horace Kingsley shamefully neglected his wife and property.

Charlotte opened the desk drawer, lifted out a brown envelope, and handed it to Gertrude. "See what your father gave me?" she said proudly.

Gertrude opened the envelope, and her mouth dropped. "Mama, where did this money come from?"

"Horace gave it to me, that day we went to Detroit."

"What is it for?"

"It is for me, all for me, Horace said so."

"You mean it is household money, to buy the things you need?"

"Horace said I may do whatever I like with it. It is all mine."

Gertrude spread the bills and counted. "Mama, this is two hundred dollars. That is a lot of money to keep in the house. Have you told anyone else you have it in this desk?"

"No, Gertrude."

"Well, don't mention it and don't show it to anyone."

"All right."

"Next time Papa comes you must ask him about putting it in a bank."

She handed back the money, and Charlotte returned the envelope to the drawer and resumed dusting. Gertrude knit her brow. Papa always claimed his business was doing well in Detroit, though in truth, no one ever inquired too closely these days what that business was. At various times he had boasted vaguely of construction projects, an insurance fund, and building stocks, a far cry from the carpentry work he had done of old. Perhaps her father's sojourns in the city had finally raised him to a better position in the world, for two hundred dollars was not a sum to be argued with. Gertrude began to feel a little hopeful.

"Well, I'm glad you are happy, Mama," she said. "I'll bring you some cherry preserves."

She emerged from the house, and R. Z. joined her. His mouth was pressed into a thin line.

"What is your father up to, Gert? He's having the boys paint right over the old, flaking paint. A job like that will never last."

"I don't know." Gertrude gazed back at the house as they walked away. The freshly painted parts looked such an improvement over the dingy walls remaining that she had not bothered to give the work a closer glance. "Perhaps he is in some hurry to have it done. Or maybe the boys are being lazy?" Her eye glinted suspiciously at Stub as he and Oren ran ahead.

"They know better than that. Haven't I always taught them that any surface, indoors or out, must be clean and well prepared before paint or paper goes on? Oren says he tries to scrape off the worst of the old coat before he lays on the new, but your father tells him not to bother."

"I don't know," Gertrude repeated. "Perhaps if you spoke to Papa about it, he would hire you to do a proper job."

"Not likely."

His tone made Gertrude feel unhappy again. She wished her husband and her parents enjoyed more cordial relations. Shortly after her marriage, she had urged R. Z. to work alongside her father on a house being built for a new family in town. The partnership had caused friction from the start and ended in a disagreement over working methods. R. Z. had kept his distance from Horace ever since, and though he tried to please Gertrude by making conversation with Charlotte, her mother's tendency to wander and repeat herself often left him annoyed. And perhaps it wasn't fair to expect her husband to embrace her family. When he ran away from his own home at the age of eleven, his father and new stepmother made no effort to call him back, and after apprenticing with an elderly paperhanger, R. Z. at sixteen had gone into business for himself. Having done without family connections for so long, it was hardly surprising that he saw no need of them.

"Besides," he often said, "if we don't interfere in your parents' affairs, they won't interfere in ours."

They crossed the road, and Emma hailed them from the orchard. She wore a red apron over her checked dress and carried a large metal pan on her hip.

"Joe and Glen are already up in the trees," she said, giving Oren and Stub a pat as they raced past her. "Mind you don't eat so many cherries you make yourselves sick!"

She offered Gertrude and R. Z. a sample from her pan, and Gertrude determined to put aside her cares and enjoy the afternoon. It was the kind of July day that stole into your senses, leaving you no will to resist. First came the sun, golden and generous, warm as a honey drop melting down your throat. Then came the scent of dark red cherries, their fruity aroma teasing the air. A bee buzzed in and out of earshot, dancing its way across the flowers. Joe, R. Z., and the boys shouted to one another and laughed, their voices breaking clear from the green leaves that hid them, as if the trees had taken to speech. The dog Scout slept with his muzzle draped over a favorite bone. Emma had brought her cooking pots from the house, and as the men brought down each pail of cherries, the women plied the stoner to separate pit from pulp and collect the fruit for cooking. While the men continued picking, Gertrude and Emma took the fruit to the house to sugar and boil.

In the kitchen, Gertrude donned a spare apron and stirred the bubbling pot while Emma heated wax for the seals. They drank lemonade while they worked and talked about their boys. It was an unspoken agreement between the two women that they might boast and bemoan at length every aspect of their sons' behavior, though Gertrude found it was most often Emma who did the boasting while the bemoaning fell to her.

"Have you seen Mrs. Allen?" she asked. "Despite all the apologies we made that day, I don't know how I shall hold up my head if I encounter her."

"No, I have not caught a glimpse of her or Ethel," replied Emma. "Mrs. Stringer did mention that they come to the store for groceries and to collect their mail."

"Perhaps Mrs. Allen thinks no one in Livonia good enough to associate with her," said Gertrude. "Perhaps we are deficient in quality." She accented the word with regret.

"I daresay we are," Emma replied. "But truly, Gertrude, every time I think back to that fat, muddy frog flopping among the teacups, and Scout crashing over the table, and Stub diving under a chair to escape your wrath . . ." She began to chuckle, and Gertrude found herself joining in.

"Did you see the look on Mrs. Allen's face?"

"It's a miracle the frog wasn't squashed flat!"

"And that strawberry tart stuck to her behind as she stormed out the door?"

They began to laugh, recalling the scene in detail and imitating Mrs. Allen's panicked cries and gestures. The more they laughed, the sillier it seemed.

"She will tell everyone in Detroit never to set foot in Livonia again!" hooted Gertrude.

"We'll be written up in the society pages as the worst hostesses in town!" Emma raised a tragic hand to her forehead.

"We'll be banned from polite society!"

"Stricken from every guest list!"

They sat down at the kitchen table and held their sides, gasping and giggling. Gertrude wheezed and stamped her foot.

"Emma, Emma, no more," she cried. "I'm getting the hiccups."

But Emma was rocking so hard she knocked a pot of cherries off the table, and a cascade of red fruit sloshed across the floor. For an instant both women stopped entirely, then they looked at each other and doubled over in fresh shrieks.

"What on earth—?" Joe stepped into the kitchen, carrying a pail of cherries.

R. Z. followed, cautiously sidestepping the slushy mess on the floor. He glanced from Emma to Gertrude. "You're making more racket than the boys."

"We . . . teacups . . . frog," panted Emma.

Gertrude dabbed at her eyes, drew two deep breaths, and was overcome by another spell of giggles.

R. Z. twirled his finger at his temple. "Women," he said to Joe. The men raised their eyebrows in mutual agreement, deposited the cherry pails, and retreated out the back door.

"Oh, my ribs ache," moaned Emma.

Gertrude sighed. "Now look at the mess we have to clean up. This only proves how dreadful we are to make sport at the expense of poor Mrs. Allen."

"We have no quality," Emma agreed.

They fetched a mop and sponge and began to wipe cherries and juice from the floor. Emma still let out an occasional chuckle, but an empty feeling had begun to creep into Gertrude, filling the space where all the laughter had been.

"We may have to leave Livonia," she blurted suddenly, and the minute the words were out, she knew how heavily the thought had weighed on her mind. Perhaps it had been at the bottom of her discontent all along. "I have been meaning to tell you, but it's not decided yet, and we've said nothing to the boys. Please don't tell them."

Emma, on her knees, stopped sponging. She sat back on her heels and shook her head as if she hadn't quite heard. "Leave? But why, Gertrude? What's wrong? Aren't you happy here?"

"Yes, but R. Z. thinks he will do better in the city."

"Does he need more work? Surely there must be some new houses being built or old ones that need redoing? And what about that hotel they plan to erect in Plymouth? They'll want someone to paint and paper all the rooms."

"Yes, they might. But R. Z. says he needs steady work to support us instead of chasing after every job."

"But this is our *home.*" Emma got to her feet and gripped Gertrude's hands. "It is not a place you can leave."

Gertrude's shoulders slumped, and for a minute the women regarded each other in silent despair.

"I know," she whispered. "Sometimes the thought of living in the city seems exciting and full of possibilities. Other times, it makes me feel like a timid child. We know no one there, Emma, and how can we be sure R. Z. will do any better? And what about Oren and Stub? They are so happy playing with Glen and running about as if they owned the whole world."

"Maybe it won't happen," Emma coaxed. "Maybe your situation will improve. If only there were something Joe and I could do." She threw her arms around Gertrude, tears starting to her eyes. "I can't bear the thought of your leaving. You are my best friend."

"You, too," said Gertrude, and she began to cry.

The back door opened.

"We've brought another bucket," said Joe. "Uh-oh, what's wrong?"

"Nothing!" Gertrude and Emma cried together.

"Go away!" Gertrude waved angrily at her husband.

"Yes, leave us alone!" Emma blubbered to Joe. She and Gertrude fell sobbing back into each other's arms.

The men exchanged glances, shrugged, and headed for the back door. R. Z. twirled his finger to his temple.

"Women," he said.

Five

Never fear, Princess Ethel! I have come to your rescue! Sir Oren lifted his mighty sword—make that a mighty jewel-studded sword—and his valiant shield—make that a valiant shield with a silver cross on a blue background—and as Princess Ethel clasped her hands toward him, the enraged dragon reared back on its haunches and blasted fire toward the stalwart—make that handsome and stalwart—knight. . . .

"Wallie? Wallie? Oh, there you are. Would you like some cookies?"

The fantasy vanished in a puff of dragon smoke, and Oren, blinking, glanced first at his paintbrush held mightily aloft, then down the ladder to see Grandma Charlotte appearing around the corner of the house. She carried a plate of cookies and a glass of lemonade, and when she squinted up to see him against the noon sun her face took on the curious, crinkled look of a little gray mouse.

"Yes, Grandma, thank you." Oren wiped his sword—make that paintbrush—on the edge of his bucket and climbed down to meet her. He almost matched her in height, and while he had shot up a good three inches this past year, he also had the feeling that Grandma Charlotte was gradually shrinking, like a dewdrop drying in the sun. What if she kept on shrinking until she evaporated right out of the world? What if he looked one day and she was gone?

"Come sit in the shade," said Charlotte. "My goodness, I think this is the hottest day of summer yet."

Oren followed her to a shady spot beneath a tree. He wore old trousers and a paint-splattered shirt with rolled-up sleeves, and his forearms were sticky with white dribbles that had trickled from his upraised brush. More speckles of paint dotted his face and hair. He drank thirstily from the glass, alternating gulps of sweet, cold lemonade with bites of dark molasses cookie.

"I wish Horace would paint the second story himself," said Charlotte. She cast a fretting look at the tall stepladder propped against the house. "I don't like you teetering up there, Wallie."

"I don't teeter, Grandma. I make sure the ladder is firmly set on the ground as Pa has taught me."

Charlotte smiled. "What a good boy you are, to do your chores so well. Doesn't our house look nice?"

Oren nodded. His grandparents' house was much improved since he and Stub had begun working on it three weeks before. Yet Oren was not entirely satisfied. There were too many patches near the beginning of the job where he and Stub, at Grandpa Horace's insistence, had slapped the new paint over the old, flaking coat, and though at a casual glance no one would notice, still Oren knew in his heart it was not right. At least for the remainder of the job he had thought to borrow his father's metal scraper and chip away the worst patches.

"I expect Horace will come any day now to see us," Charlotte predicted. "I am anxious to show him how I have dusted and cleaned."

Oren took a long drink, not sure what to answer. At first, working outside, he had paid little attention to his grandmother's bustling about the rooms. But after a week or so he had begun to observe her activities more closely.

"Didn't Grandma just wash that tablecloth yesterday?" he'd ask Stub as Charlotte came out to hang the damp linen on the clothesline. "Didn't she beat that same rug only a few days ago?"

To which Stub, who within an hour of starting to paint looked like he'd been dipped in whitewash from head to toe, would reply, "I guess so," or "Maybe," or most often "I dunno."

But the inside of the house did look better also. It had shaken off the listless, unfresh air that had always made the boys reluctant to go in. Grandma seemed livelier, too, though Oren had given up any hope of her ever understanding that he was not her dead son Wallie. No matter how many times he called her "Grandma," the word bounced off her like a harmless rubber ball. No matter how loudly and repeatedly Stub called him "Oren" in her presence, she refused to take the hint. She also continued to believe that Stub was her second dead son, Oren, causing him, the *real* Oren, to start and stop each time it was Stub whom Grandma meant to summon. Nor did it seem to disturb Charlotte that her imagined sons did not live under her roof. She waved them off fondly when their day's work was complete, and today, when Stub had been excused from painting with an itchy case of poison ivy, Grandma did not even notice he was gone. She simply welcomed them whenever they appeared, and what she thought of their absences, Oren could not tell. Of course, there was one way to convince her of his true identity: tell her the real Wallie was dead. But not for all the licorice and peppermint in Stringer's Store would he be the one to do that.

"Oh look, here comes Horace now."

Charlotte stood and pointed along the road. Oren jumped up beside her. Grandma had been expecting Grandpa every day for two weeks, and he had assumed this was another of her misunderstandings. Now he squinted at the approaching buggy and saw she was right. Grandpa Horace drove, and another man sat beside him. They wore city suits and bowler hats, and Oren guessed they had come by train and hired the buggy at the livery station. He glanced nervously at the house. The extra time he'd spent scraping plus a few days' rain the previous week had slowed the job, and Grandpa was sure to be displeased. Oren tapped his grandma's arm, remembering another matter he and Stub had debated at length.

"Grandma, do you think you could ask Grandpa to pay us? We haven't had any money since the last time he came, and then it was only a dollar apiece."

"Oh dear." Charlotte's face crinkled in worry, her little mouse look. "Are you sure? Horace does not like me to ask him about money. I don't like to make him cross." She plucked at her fingers, first one hand, then the other, as if they were paws. "I know! I will pay you myself. I have two—" She stopped. "Oh dear, what did Gertrude say about that?"

"Never mind, Grandma," said Oren. The buggy was rapidly approaching, and he was anxious to have her appear normal in front of the stranger. He smiled at her, and she let out a little breath and relaxed. They walked to the front lawn and waited while Horace dismounted and tied the horse's reins to the hitching post. As he led the stranger up the walk, he glanced toward the unfinished paint job, and his glare made Oren flinch. But when he turned to introduce the newcomer, he parted his lips in a broad smile.

"Charlotte, this is Mr. John Quincy from Detroit," said Horace. "Mr. Quincy is in manufacturing, and his firm plans to expand hereabouts. I am showing him the local real estate."

"Pleased to meet you, Mrs. Kingsley." Mr. Quincy doffed his hat. He was a cheerful young man of medium build and sported a blond handlebar mustache. "I hope we have not come upon you at an inopportune time?"

"Oh, I have been expecting Horace daily," said Charlotte brightly. "Would you like some cookies and lemonade? Such a hot day it is!"

"That would be most agreeable, ma'am, if it is not too much trouble."

"Oh no, not at all. Horace, I have cleaned the house exactly as you asked me."

Horace beamed. "My wife is an excellent housekeeper," he said to Mr. Quincy. "You go ahead to the kitchen, Charlotte, and prepare the refreshments."

Charlotte pattered away, and Mr. Quincy turned to Oren. "You are the painter, I see," he said in a friendly way, and Oren spoke up as Ma would have wanted.

"I am Oren Millard, sir."

"My grandson," Horace supplied. "I had expected he would have the job done by now, but the boy is very thorough, and to do a job well you must do it right, I always say. Come, let me show you the inside. I believe you'll be pleased at the sensible layout of the rooms."

Mr. Quincy gave Oren a parting wave, and the two men proceeded up the walk. Oren scratched his ears, perplexed. No visitors ever came to his grandparents' house. He waited until the men were inside, then he hurried after them and pretended to clean his paintbrush in the jar of turpentine he had left on the porch. Grandma Charlotte had most of the windows open to catch whatever flimsy breeze stirred, so he had no difficulty overhearing snatches of conversation as they moved from room to room. Grandpa Horace did most of the talking.

"The parlor is a fine size, as you see . . . warm in winter . . . yes, all the furniture included . . . only wants a little modern plumbing . . . thank you, Charlotte . . . did you ever taste such delicious cookies, sir? . . . Charlotte, show Mr. Quincy your kitchen . . ."

The voices moved to the rear of the house, and Oren jumped over the porch railing and ran around to plaster himself beside the back door.

". . . this is my stove . . . here is my table . . . I have a lot of pots and pans . . ."

"Thank you, Charlotte . . . rest on the porch while I show Mr. Quincy upstairs . . ."

Oren raced around the house and scrambled up the ladder.

". . . three snug bedrooms . . . one for the boys, one for the girls . . .

take you out to see the land . . . forty acres, easy to sell off parcels if you've a mind . . . fine town to raise a family . . ."

The footsteps receded and sounded a descent on the stairs. Oren slid down the ladder and dashed to the front porch where Grandma Charlotte sat obediently in a chair. He was whistling and cleaning his paintbrush when the men emerged.

"Charlotte," said Horace, and Grandma stood. "I am taking Mr. Quincy to see the lay of the town. I'll be back for supper."

"Thank you for your hospitality, ma'am." Mr. Quincy made a short bow and set his bowler hat atop his head. "Keep up the good work, Oren."

"Yes, sir."

The two men returned to the buggy, and Horace flicked the reins and drove them away.

"Why did Mr. Quincy want to see your house, Grandma?" Oren asked.

"To see how well kept it is." Charlotte smiled proudly, her cheeks warm with the praise the two men had bestowed on her. "An excellent housekeeper, delicious cookies—did you hear how Horace spoke of me, Wallie?"

"Yes, Grandma." He dipped a rag in the turpentine and began scrubbing the paint from his knuckles. Maybe grown-ups liked to show off their houses to each other the way he, Stub, and Glen had prided themselves on introducing Ethel to their territory. Yet a vague discontent lingered. "Grandma, I have to go home for lunch."

"All right, Wallie. Such a good boy you are."

Charlotte waved him away, smiling affectionately. Oren gave an uncomfortable grin and departed. Sometimes being around his grandmother felt like wearing scratchy long underwear. No matter how you moved—or tried not to move—it prickled against your skin and made you want to peel it away. Some of the kids at school said craziness was inherited and if anybody in your family went cuckoo, you would, too. But when Oren checked back through his relatives, living and dead, he encountered no one else who behaved like Grandma Charlotte.

He cut along his usual path, behind Stringer's Store and Town Hall, and when he reached his house, Pa, Ma, and Stub were eating lunch at the kitchen table. Stub was daubed all over his face and bare arms with pink calamine lotion.

"Come eat," said Ma, filling a plate for him.

"Grandpa Horace is selling his house," Oren announced. He stopped, surprised at the words, for he didn't remember exactly thinking them as he crossed the field. Now he was sure of it. "He's selling the house, he brought a Mr. Quincy to see it, I don't think Grandma understands." He ran his sentences together in sudden agitation, seeing, but ignoring the plate of bread, sausage, and pickled beets Ma placed before him. He hopped from foot to foot. "Grandpa's selling the house!"

"Hold on, Oren." Pa raised his eyebrows and motioned with his fork for him to take his chair. "Where would you get that idea?"

In a rush, Oren related what he'd observed of Mr. Quincy's visit, half distracted by Stub who squirmed in his seat, looking eager to interrupt.

"Papa wouldn't sell the house," said Gertrude sensibly. She refilled Stub's glass of milk. "He knows Mama is content there. If he said he would show Mr. Quincy the local real estate, he only meant he is introducing him to town, as Emma tried to do for Mrs. Allen."

"No, Ma, that's *not* what he's doing." Oren stopped to recall the exact words Grandpa Horace had spoken, and Stub snatched the chance to break in.

"Did you get our money? Did you ask him?"

"No, I forgot. There wasn't a chance."

"Aw, Oren! We're never going to get paid! We're working all summer for nothing! This isn't fair!"

"Horace still hasn't paid you?" Pa glowered. "Gert, what's going on? It's bad enough to order a job half done, but I won't have him cheating the boys of their wages. Oren, sit down. How many days is it now you've spent painting?"

"Three weeks, Pa. But Grandpa Horace is selling the house! Why won't you listen to me? I'm not making this up!"

"We are listening," said Ma, "but I'm sure you misunderstood. I'll ask Mama next time I go over."

"But it won't do any good to ask her. She's too loony to understand!"

"Oren! For shame!" Ma's hand slammed down so hard the plates rattled, and Stub's milk sloshed over the rim of his glass. Her face flushed with an anger Oren had never seen. "There is *nothing* wrong with my mama. Don't you *ever* speak of her like that again. Don't you *ever* use that word or I will wash out your mouth with soap and strap your behind!"

"Sit!" commanded Pa, his pointing fork leaving no room for doubt. He shook his head, muttering under his breath, "The last thing I need for business is for our own sons to spread talk like that. Now, Oren, one last time. What makes you think the house is for sale?"

Shaken, Oren assumed his chair. Never had Ma burst out at him like that. Never had she threatened to strap him. Her words stung his ears and hurt his head, and when he tried to recall what Grandpa Horace had said, all he could remember was something about the size of the parlor and how warm it was in winter.

"All right, that's enough." Pa silenced him with a motion of his hand. "Eat your lunch, Oren. Gert, sort it out with your mother when you have time."

Glumly, Oren swallowed his food. No one said much more, and when the meal was done, Ma yanked away the dishes, two high, red spots still burning on her cheeks. Oren slunk out with Stub to their tower in the maple tree, Stub nagging all the way about the money Grandpa Horace owed them. "Shut up and go ask him yourself!" retorted Oren, which effectively clamped Stub's mouth. They climbed into the branches, and after a while Glen appeared and joined them, panting from the heat. Stub pulled an old wad of taffy from his pocket and began chewing.

"So what are we going to do today?" he demanded. "C'mon, let's go shoot marbles or wade in the creek and catch frogs." At the mention of frogs, Oren and Glen glared at him, but Stub only made a bulldog face, stubbornly unrepentant. "C'mon! All you want to do anymore is sit here waiting for Ethel to show up at Stringer's. This is no fun!"

"Well, you don't have to stay," said Oren.

"Well, maybe I won't." Stub hunched against the trunk and crossed his arms in defiance, muttering and sending veiled, scathing glances from his brother to his cousin.

"It's been three days," Glen sighed. "They must need something at the store by now."

Oren nodded. Waiting for the dragon to appear with Ethel was a long and tiresome business. Meanwhile, here it was mid-July already, and what had become of his grand summer plan? Yet every time he resolved to quit his surveillance, the idea that he might miss Ethel while he was chasing rabbits or blazing trails through the woods glued him more firmly to the maple tree. He glanced at Glen, stretched out on his stomach along a thick branch, arms and legs dangling aimlessly. His freckled face was flushed from the heat, and every so often his breathing sputtered and he coughed it back to life. Glen seemed content to lie here in peace, and Oren wondered if it was partly a relief to be spared their usual exertions. Maybe for Glen's sake they ought to do more quiet things, like play checkers or read books in the town library. He resolved to be more heedful of his frail, good-natured cousin.

They waited a half hour longer, Stub's complaints growing in crankiness and volume, when Glen suddenly stiffened and peered through the leaves.

"They're coming! It's Ethel!" he squeaked, his face shining like a beacon. "There! They've just passed the cemetery!"

Oren and Stub clambered to Glen's branch to see a buggy clipping toward the crossroads.

"The dragon!" Stub gloated. He slurped on the wad of taffy, drawing up a good mouthful of spit and edging out along the limb.

"No, Stub!" Oren whacked him, and Stub scrambled away to another branch, blowing raspberries. Oren let him go. An idea was forming in his head. "I got it!" He snapped his fingers. "I know how we can get Ethel away from the dragon!"

"What? How?" Glen turned eagerly to Oren, and even Stub crept back at the hint of a plan.

"Geography." Oren pointed southward. "What is just beyond the cemetery?"

"The Minkley house," said Glen.

"And what is in the Minkley house?"

"The books. The library."

"That's it," said Oren.

His comrades shook their heads, and Oren smiled, not about to reveal prematurely such a magnificent plan. "We need to get Ethel's attention, get her alone on the porch, then I'll explain." He motioned them to silence, and they hunkered down, intent on their mission. The buggy bearing the dragon and Princess Ethel had reached the crossroads and was about to turn in front of the maple tree.

"Don't let the dragon see you!" commanded Oren, and they flattened themselves against the branches like leeches. "Get Ethel's attention!" he ordered, and they burst from the leaves, waving madly and spitting out so many "Psssts!" that the tree seemed home to a horde of hissing cats. This pantomime was repeated half a dozen times as the buggy neared, and the only thing that kept them from falling out of the tree in disgrace was that Ethel, sitting quiet and obedient while her mother's mouth moved in a constant lecture, was nevertheless shooting furtive glances toward the maple, and at the first sight of the Three Musketeers hanging like monkeys from its limbs, her blue eyes flew wide open and she gave a quick nod to indicate she understood. Oren beckoned his troops back to cover, relieved. What a smart girl!

They waited, hidden, until dragon and princess arrived at the store and disappeared inside. A few minutes later, Ethel casually appeared on the porch and wandered over to the railing. In a flash the boys were down the trunk and barreling across the short stretch of grass.

"Ethel!" they cried, breathless, and she put a finger to her lips and whispered, "Shhh! What is it?"

"I have found a way to free you," Oren declared. "You must get to the library in the Minkley house, just before the cemetery." He pointed back along the route she had come, and as Ethel turned her head to follow his direction, her long blond ringlets brushed like silk across the back of Oren's hand. He exhaled a deep sigh.

"The library? But why?" she asked.

"So we can meet you there. You tell your Ma you want to go to the library, and she'll have to say yes because it's education. We'll hide out in the cemetery and wait for you. Then we can go off exploring, and no one will know."

"But Mama never lets me go anywhere alone."

"Say you want to stay and read a while in the parlor like Mrs. Minkley lets us do. Once your ma sees how safe it is, she'll leave you there for the afternoon."

Ethel cast another glance southward and bit her lip.

"You can do it," Oren urged, and Glen, nodding so vehemently his cheeks flushed again, said, "Please, Ethel!"

"All right. I'll try tomorrow afternoon." Her face grew brave, then wistful as she glanced at the maple tree. "Is it as nice as ever up there, all cool and gentle and green?"

Oren nodded. He could feel the longing in her, as if she yearned for some place where no hurt could ever come. "What is it, Ethel? Are you sad about something? If it's a secret, you can trust us. We won't tell." He crossed his heart, and Glen and Stub quickly did the same.

Ethel lowered her eyes, silent a long minute. "Mama thinks I don't know," she whispered. "She doesn't tell me anything, and I'm not allowed to ask. But sometimes I overhear her talking, or people say things they think I won't understand. But I do. I knew it even before we left Detroit. I heard them fighting through the bedroom walls. My papa has had a scandal with another woman, and if he doesn't come back soon our reputation will be ruined."

"What's a scandal?" asked Stub, but Oren and Glen elbowed him in the ribs and said, "Shhh!"

"Go on," Oren urged.

Ethel bowed her head. "Yesterday a lawyer came to our house. Mama sent me to my room, but I opened the door. The lawyer said if Papa does not come to his senses, there must be a divorce. After he left, Mama cried. She has written Papa another letter, but he sends us no replies. What shall we do? He has abandoned us! He does not love us anymore!"

Ethel's cheeks crimsoned in shame, and she ran away into the store. The three boys stood aghast. A divorce! That was almost the worst that could happen to a family, even more disastrous, thought Oren, than having a loony grandma. He shook his head, and Glen puffed out an astounded breath, and even Stub gaped in open-mouthed shock. No decent people ever got a divorce.

"Come, Ethel, don't dawdle." The rapier voice slit the blue air, and a simultaneous chill shuddered down the spines of the Three Musketeers.

"To the tree!" cried Oren hoarsely, and they dashed pell-mell to their sanctuary, stepping on each other in their haste to climb aloft and avoid the imagined scorch of dragon's breath at their heels. They hugged the leafy branches until the clip-clop of a horse's hooves sounded below, then they peeked down to spy the buggy driving by. Mrs. Allen looked fierce as ever, and Oren wondered at the strange idea that the dragon had really cried. He turned his eyes to Princess Ethel. Calm, poised, her cheeks returned to alabaster pale, she rode away in silence, a prisoner once more.

Six

Charlotte liked windows, had always liked them, she thought, large clear panes of sturdy glass. She liked the way they let slanting rectangles of whitened sunlight pattern the rug and creep across the floor, marking the minutes and hours as surely as any clock. She liked the way tormented raindrops splashed against the glass in a thunderstorm and the way the wind-blown autumn leaves, red, gold, and orange, brushed past the panes in a last caress before dying to the ground. She liked the snow that drifted on the sills in winter and, oh yes, once—in autumn this was—a speckled brown spider had spun her web outside right across one of the living-room windows. Charlotte had watched in fascination as the busy weaver slung gossamer lines from corner to corner, anchoring them to the window frame. Then round and round the fat little stitcher went, plunking down concentric threads as neatly as a sewing machine. The work took a full hour, and the web nearly filled the pane. No sooner was it complete than a moth flew smack into the center, and oh! you should have seen what happened then. Miss Arachne shot from the corner, twirled that moth in sticky thread, and spun a gauzy white cocoon around him so fast he was trussed for dinner before he knew what hit him. Charlotte had watched the scene repeated with dozens of hapless insects as the weeks passed, until one November day the spider was gone. The vacant web remained for nearly a month afterward, fraying until only loose fragments clung to the corners. All that drama Charlotte had seen in one window—but that was not all.

If she looked across the road from her windows she saw Emma's house, a well-contented place. She liked those six Greek pillars spaced across the porch, the symmetry and balance of the design, the rosebushes strung like a red garland around the walls. Sometimes she saw Emma sweeping the porch or setting out on errands, or she saw Emma's husband, the nice man with the ginger mustache, whose name she could not recall, going to and fro with his dog. If she looked out the parlor window to the south, she saw the crossroads and the big maple tree where Wallie and Oren liked to hide. Upstairs, she could gaze from the bedroom windows to glimpse the rooftops of other houses, the smithy, Stringer's Store, Town Hall. Some of these buildings could not be seen from downstairs because trees or other obstacles blocked the view, and it seemed to Charlotte both wondrous and ominous that on one level you could see nothing, while on another level all was revealed. If her house did not have windows, those other places might not even exist, and sometimes she spent hours going from room to room, upstairs and down, looking out each pane in turn to make sure everything was real. Of course, she did not have so much time for that now, not since Horace had instructed her to clean the house every day.

"I'll be bringing people here, important people," he had told her. "I'm showing them the town, and you must show them what a good housekeeper you are."

"Yes, Horace," she replied, and in the weeks since that young Mr. Quincy had come, Horace had brought perhaps half a dozen other gentlemen and ladies to admire their home. Charlotte's thoughts stopped, snagged like a careless kite in a tree, and she frowned. How many weeks had it been? Was this still July or might the month now be August? She blinked, looked at her hands. One held a soapy sponge, the other a damp cloth, and the drip, drip, drip of water on her shoes recalled her to her task. That's right, she was on her porch, washing the windows, and she liked them even more now they were so clean. One morning when she was outside soaping the windows she had had a fine idea.

Windows were the eyes of a house. They opened, they closed, they let you see. If her house had no windows, and she were inside, she would feel blind. But what if she stood outside her house and looked *in?* What would she see? Excited, she had put down her sponge, and cupping her hands to her temples to shield out the sun's reflection, she pressed her face to the pane and peered inside. Was that really her living room? Was that what people saw? How strange! How odd! It had such a thought-less look, as if the ill-assorted pieces of furniture, the shabby rugs, the knickknacks and pictures on the mantel and walls had been assembled by imps picking through a secondhand shop. She walked along the porch to the parlor window and stared inside. The impression was somewhat better here, the furnishings a little nicer, but who had hung that ugly painting on the wall? Charlotte stepped off the porch and walked around the house, stretching on tiptoe toward the other panes. Most were too high off the ground to see into. She went looking for the ladder, but Wallie and Oren had finished painting and moved on to the next task Horace had assigned them, weeding the lawn, and Charlotte wandered through the barn in vain, unable to discover where the ladder was stored. She returned to the house and began jumping up and down on the grass, trying to gain enough height to peek inside. She was getting a little breathless, when Gertrude's voice startled her from behind.

"Mama! What are you doing?" Her face registered dismay. "I saw you jumping as I was going to Stringer's. What is going on?"

"I am looking in." Charlotte tipped her head, wondering why Gertrude seemed so upset.

"Well, you mustn't do that. What if someone saw?" Gertrude glanced anxiously over her shoulder and hustled Charlotte back to the porch. Charlotte smiled, accepting the move in good humor. How big her daughter had grown! No doubt she would be attracting a husband soon. Already there was that short fellow who kept hanging around her. "Mama," Gertrude continued, her face still clouded, "Oren has got an idea in his head that Papa means to sell the house. Can there be any truth to this? He says Papa keeps bringing people to see it."

"Oh yes," agreed Charlotte. "There was that young Mr. Quincy. . . . I don't recall the names of the others. Horace likes to show off what a good housekeeper I am, then he takes them to see the town."

"They've come to see Livonia?"

"Yes, the whole town. They are Horace's business associates, and after I serve them refreshments, they go on a tour. Mr. Quincy is going to expand his manufacturing business here."

Charlotte nodded, proud of how much she had remembered, and Gertrude's expression slowly cleared.

"Papa must be doing well in the city then. If he is bringing these people to start new businesses in Livonia, that will mean new stores and houses to be built, more work for R. Z. I'll hurry home to tell him."

Drip, drip. Charlotte stared at her wet shoes. Where was she? Her mind had snagged again, and she saw flashes of many windows, the panes of tall skyscrapers glittering in the sun. That was the day Horace had taken her to the notary's office in Detroit, and last week—was it last week?—he had guided her to the city yet again. Another paper to sign. She was getting very good at signing important documents, she informed the notary. Her writing on that first paper had been so feeble and threadlike she hardly recognized her own name. This time the script was stronger and more pleasing to the eye. But now the thought of those two signatures worried her. What did they mean? She stooped and peered through the living-room window, even though Gertrude had told her not to do that anymore. She saw the desk and knew the envelope containing her two hundred dollars was safe in the top drawer. But what had become of those papers? There were important legal records about the house. Charlotte stared at the desk, and it began to frighten her.

"Hello, Grandma."

The sound startled her, and the kite in her mind broke free and floated away. She turned to see Wallie, Oren, and their cousin Glen, waving to her as they walked along the road on their way to the maple tree. That Glen was a polite boy. He had the same coloring as his father, the ginger-mustache man whose name she couldn't recall. It was a pity Glen was so frail, not hardy like her two boys.

"Hello, my dears," she called and waved.

That pretty angel was with them again, too, her long blond ringlets shining around her head, her sweet face composed in a gentle smile. She never said anything, she was that shy, but sometimes she laughed or giggled, and Charlotte hadn't known angels could do that. She was delighted, of course, that her boys had found this divine companion. Certainly no harm could come to them with an angel by their side. She appeared almost every afternoon, and Charlotte watched them climb the maple tree, shoot marbles on Emma's porch, play tag and blind man's bluff, throw sticks for the spaniel that belonged to Glen's father, the nice man. Sometimes the boys turned a rope so the angel could skip over it in graceful little steps. Charlotte hadn't known angels could do that either, and it made her proud to see her boys and Glen behave in such a gentlemanly fashion. The angel always disappeared before suppertime, and in the long, lazy summer evenings Charlotte heard the shouts of the boys as they continued their play past twilight and into the fringes of the dark.

Charlotte's hands began to feel cold, and she looked at them, puzzled. How very strange! They had grown as white and puckered as if she had plunged them in water for hours, and when she peered into her bucket only a puddle in the bottom remained. Yet she had washed only those few windows that fronted on the porch. Perhaps it was later than she realized. She glanced toward Emma's house and saw the sun westering. Somehow evening had sneaked up on her, spreading shadows over the land. She went inside, ate some bread and butter, and tidied her kitchen for the morrow. When night came she walked through her house and shut any windows still open, like closing her eyes before she went to sleep.

Seven

There is a sucker born every minute.

Horace Kingsley aimed a broad smile at the young couple sitting across the table in the lawyer's office in the town of Nankin. The pair beamed in return. She was plump and bubbly, her brown hair springing out from her bonnet in a profusion of corkscrew curls. He was big-boned and earnest, dressed in his Sunday suit. They thought Horace smiled at them in camaraderie, wishing them good luck and fair fortune as they embarked on newly married life in their first home. They thought he shared their shining optimism that they could turn forty pitiful acres into the best darn farm in all Livonia. In fact, they thought the whole world smiled on them at this auspicious moment, when in truth they sat there in perfect exemplification of P. T. Barnum's famous maxim.

Suckers!

Not that Horace hadn't given them a fair price. Twelve hundred dollars for the house and land, all furniture and farm equipment included, was a noble gesture. No, what made the pair so ludicrous was their blind faith in outdated dreams. Just eighteen miles away in Detroit, the future of this country was being built—factories, businesses, transportation, stores—while here in Livonia the peasants clung to their cherished dirt. You'll end up grubbing to make ends meet, Horace thought, forcing yet another smile at the young husband. You'll owe the bank for twenty years for worthless land, ruin your health with back-breaking labor, dull your hopes and blunt your dreams while smarter men move on. She'll grow fat, coarse, and complaining, a passel of obnoxious children clinging to her skirts, and you'll wonder how you ever took your pleasure on her. But since that's your choice—hurry up and sign.

"Now," said the lawyer, a short, rosy man, "if all parties understand and agree to the terms of sale, you sign here and here."

He offered his pen to the newlyweds and Horace in turn. Charlotte's signature was already on the deed of sale. His wife, he had explained, suffered from poor health, so to facilitate matters he would arrange to have a notary witness her signature at home. Instead he had taken her again to Detroit, where Charlotte had been most cooperative. Now everything was tidy and legal: the quitclaim in which Charlotte turned her interest in the property over to him, the deed of sale, and finally . . . the lawyer handed Horace a check. Ahhh! It was made out in both his and Charlotte's names, but once she signed the money over to him, the business would be complete. Minus the two hundred he had paid her for the quitclaim, he counted a neat profit of one thousand dollars. Best of all, he was done forever with the wretched land.

The newlyweds stood and hugged each other. They were from Nankin, which bordered Livonia on the south, and for their convenience, Horace had suggested a Nankin attorney prepare the deed of sale. He had not advertised the property in Livonia itself, to forestall the news creeping back to Gertrude or Emma along the local grapevine. Not that they had any say in the matter—a man's home was his castle to do with as he pleased, and the only way they could challenge the sale would be to admit Charlotte was incompetent and not responsible for what she signed. How would they like that trumpeted around town? Besides, if you looked at it properly, Horace had been most generous to his wife. He could have let her sign away her interests and never paid her a dime. Now she had two hundred dollars, more than sufficient to meet her needs in the place to which she was going.

"Mrs. Kingsley and I will vacate the house by the end of August," he informed the new owners, and smiling a blessing on two more of life's easy marks, he left.

Outside, a polished blue sky and beneficent sunshine added to Horace's genial mood. He had come from Detroit that morning, rented a horse and buggy at the livery stable near the train station, and driven straight to the attorney's office. His next destination was not far, and mounting the buggy he set the horse off at a trot along the dirt road. In the city, shiny new automobiles were becoming a regular sight. Horace meant to have one of those soon, meant to have a lot of things he desired while he was still in the prime of life. He sucked his teeth and shook his head in regret. In the past he had been too quick to take whatever fate offered, had set his sights low instead of waiting for a better choice to come along. So it had been with Charlotte. She was pretty enough as a girl, and he had been eager to bed her. He even tried to talk her into it without promising marriage in return. But she trembled and protested while he contrived every which way to get his fingers into her bodice and up her skirt, plying sweet words in her ears, until frustration got the better of him and he proposed. Besides, he had believed her family, the Bentleys, had enough importance in town to push him ahead. When he looked back, he saw how shortsighted his goals had been. Not only were there prettier girls than Charlotte, but the Bentleys were merely big fish pompously paddling in a small pond. If he had had a more accurate scope of the world when he was twenty-two, he would have stuck to relieving himself and held off for a better wife.

He drove two miles to an expansive complex of red-brick buildings, surrounded by a wrought-iron fence. Clipped green lawn, shade trees, and scattered park benches greeted the eye. Here and there a figure in white crossed the grounds, or an elderly soul nodded off on a bench. The place had a well-ordered but remote look, as if the fence marked the boundary of a sovereign territory that declined communication with the outside world. The sign beside the open gate read: Eloise Infirmary, Sanatorium and Hospital.

An eerie sensation passed over Horace, and for a moment the horse balked and would not enter. "Gee-up," he ordered, shaking off his unease. "Gee-up, you dumb beast." He snapped the reins, and the horse jerked the buggy through the gate, and though nothing changed in the clear summer day, Horace felt strangely as if he had been swallowed. He drove to the central building and entered the double door. Inside was a high-ceilinged hallway, its gray walls impressively lined with electric light sconces. A woman in a nurse's uniform pointed him to a flight of polished stone stairs. On the second floor he found the office he sought: a frosted glass door stenciled SUPERINTENDENT. Horace knocked.

"Answer that, Susan," boomed a male voice. The handle clicked, the door swung inward, and half hidden behind it stood a young woman of twenty or so with lowered eyes. She closed the door after Horace, returned quickly to a corner, and resumed scrubbing the floor on her knees. A second young woman in a navy blue skirt and prim white blouse sat at a typist's desk to the right, file cabinets and bookshelves lining the wall behind her. The center of the office was dominated by a carved mahogany desk set before a wide window. A tall, florid man of handsome features and bushy, sandy eyebrows occupied the leather chair. He rose and heartily extended his hand.

"Mr. Kingsley, right on time. I am Dr. Henry Thornton. I have your letter explaining your wife's unfortunate condition." He lifted a paper from atop a stack on his desk and offered Horace a comfortable chair. "Susan, bring us coffee."

The housemaid rose and ducked out of the room. A comely girl, thought Horace, noting her oval face and excellent figure. The typist, by contrast, was flat-chested and wore a miffed expression, which eased when the maid departed.

"Your wife presents a most interesting case to add to my collection," said Dr. Thornton. "Please give me the particulars. Miss Prescott, take notes." He nodded toward the secretary, who flipped open a stenographer's pad and prepared to write.

Horace settled back in his chair, pleased at the cordial reception. The place was clean, wholesome, no sign of lunatics wandering the halls. He remembered occasional articles in the local papers about the growth of the massive hospital and asylum complex. It was a noble project aimed at gathering all the county's burdens in one convenient and self-sufficient location. The buildings housed orphans, paupers, tuberculosis patients, the feeble-minded and idiots, the civil and criminally insane. The grounds contained a farm that raised cattle, a slaughterhouse, bakery, laundry, and even a cemetery, affording decent burial for those who had nowhere else to die. The name Eloise commemorated the little daughter of the chairman of the board. Some citizens of Nankin decried the location of an asylum in their town. Lunatics and ax murderers would break loose, they claimed, and terrorize the countryside. The idiots would send up a constant din and howl inside the fenced grounds. But nothing untoward had ever happened. Indeed, the inhabitants, when seen outside at all, were peaceful and quiet.

Susan returned with the coffee, and as she handed Horace his cup, she spilled a little onto the saucer. The secretary impaled her with an icy look. Seemed a bit hard on the poor maid, thought Horace, sparing another glance at the girl's figure and willing to be lenient. He smiled at her mumbled apology to show he had taken no offense.

"Well, Doctor," he said, "as my letter explained, my wife suffers from delusions concerning our grandsons, and now I find the problem has grown."

"In what way?" Dr. Thornton steepled his hands and leaned forward intently, and Horace nodded to emphasize his concern. The business about their dead sons had been coming on gradually for years, but two weeks ago he had discovered that Charlotte believed the boys were keeping company with an angel.

"See, Horace, there she is," she said, pointing out the living-room window. "Wallie and Oren have a dear friend from heaven. They will always be safe now." She proceeded to tell him how the angel skipped rope and played marbles and even climbed the maple tree.

He related this new development, and the doctor's bushy eyebrows rose appreciatively. You could always trust another man to understand. Women were unstable enough even in their normal state, and Horace felt a surge of gratitude at being able to unburden himself to a fellow male. Not that he was complaining. No, his only concern was for his wife, and now he recalled another worrisome incident.

"She tries to do things by herself when I am not there. Earlier this spring she attempted to replace a broken window and nearly caused herself a serious injury."

Horace shook his head, grieving over the accident, and speculating where such irrationality might lead. If Charlotte didn't understand that broken glass was dangerous, what might she do with matches? Kitchen knives? No, she would never intentionally hurt herself or anyone else, but he feared for her safety, it dogged him every minute he had to spend away in Detroit. The doctor's eyes flashed with insight, and he jabbed his finger repeatedly toward the secretary's pad, emphasizing the importance of recording these valuable observations. Miss Prescott wrote furiously.

"I only want the best for her," Horace declared. She was alone so much of the time. It was impossible to take her with him to Detroit. The unfamiliar surroundings, unsympathetic strangers. He had thought of moving her to his married daughter's home, but her house was small, their income tight, his son-in-law, a lowly paperhanger and painter, struggling to find business. They might have to uproot and move them-selves. And—Horace's face lit as the idea dawned on him, and the thought became so momentous that for several seconds he could not begin to speak—wouldn't forcing Charlotte to live with the very boys she believed to be her dead sons only intensify her delusions? It might destroy whatever remained of her sanity and push her over the brink into total madness! The doctor's eyes positively lit with admiration as he proclaimed the astuteness of this observation.

"It is a tragedy," Horace declared. "A mind lost and wandering in the mists! I cannot tell you how I have suffered to witness the decline of a once-loving wife and mother."

"She has ceased to fulfill her matrimonial duties toward you?" the doctor asked.

"Years since," Horace conceded sadly, "and I would not for the world insist."

Dr. Thornton dipped his head in deep respect. "Mr. Kingsley, you are to be commended for your forbearance. Take comfort in the knowledge that you are not alone. The emotional, indeed, hysterical nature of females makes them especially prone to mental instability, and a great number of our inmates are wives who cannot or will not fulfill their obligations as nature intended and society demands. Many husbands like yourself have been deprived of their due rights by a deficient woman."

Horace sighed heavily. So much he had had to bear! Why had this happened to him? Was there any way he could have foreseen Charlotte would prove defective? No, he was blameless, and whatever Charlotte had done to bring this upon herself, he must endeavor to secure the best possible situation for the poor woman.

"My wife must have expert care and medical treatment," he proclaimed. "I will send money with her—two hundred dollars—to purchase whatever comforts she desires."

"That is most magnanimous." Dr. Thornton's face gleamed. "May I suggest, however, that you deposit the funds in my safekeeping. The strain of managing such an amount may be too taxing for your wife, and should the other ladies learn of her personal wealth, they may be jealous."

"Is it too much, do you think?" worried Horace. He had several times wondered, since Charlotte signed the quitclaim, if his generosity had not been out of bounds.

"No, no, not at all," Dr. Thornton replied. "And rest assured your wife will be in excellent hands. We are a thoroughly modern and humane institution. Come, look." He beckoned Horace to the window behind his desk. It gave a wide view of more red-brick buildings, spaced over many acres of well-tended grounds. The doctor swept his hand, bristling with sandy hairs and decorated with a gold signet ring, toward one of the more distant structures. "That is where we house the violently insane, and it is the only building with barred windows. Our other patients have pleasant accommodations and free use of the grounds. The days are long gone, Mr. Kingsley, when we confined poor idiots and unbalanced women together with raging madmen and criminals. We use straitjackets and other healthful restraints only in cases of extreme necessity and employ punishments only when patients misbehave. And you have said, have you not, that your wife is docile?"

"She is meek as a lamb," Horace averred.

"Then she will do very well here. In fact, we may put her to work immediately at some wholesome occupation, perhaps in our sewing room or at housekeeping chores such as Susan here performs." He gestured toward the maid, and Horace's jaw dropped. The doctor gave a booming laugh. "You see," he said, taking amusement in Horace's surprise, "did I not tell you we are a modern facility? You never guessed a female inmate was in this very room. Susan, come here!"

Dr. Thornton crooked his finger, and the girl tensed over her scrub brush. She curled herself upward, shoulders hunched, and approached the desk. Miss Prescott pursed her lips in distaste.

"Stand straight, Susan. Now here is a fine example, Mr. Kingsley, of what humane institutional care can accomplish. At the age of seventeen this girl developed an unnatural affection for an older woman, a family relation who, to my mind, should have been prosecuted for enticing an innocent young female down this reprehensible path. Fortunately, Susan's parents became alerted to the deviant behavior, and after only four years of treatment she is nearly cured of her shameful and aberrant feelings. Is that not correct, Susan?"

"Yes, Dr. Thornton." A bare whisper came from the girl's lowered head.

"Stand straight, Susan. What did you say?" In a jovial mood, the doctor cupped his hand under her chin and brought her flaming face up to view.

"Yes, Doctor."

"Very good, Susan. Continue your work." He released her jaw, and she ducked her head and hurried back to her scrubbing. "We make every effort to retrain our female inmates in the skills every true woman ought to know. Susan is becoming so adept at her tasks, I may find it difficult to let her go."

He laughed, and Horace nodded approval. To think he had found that young woman attractive when all the time such vile thoughts lurked in so tempting a form. How fortunate that her caring parents had acted promptly to stamp out the deviant tendencies before they could take root.

250

"My wife has become very good at cleaning of late," Horace offered. "I am sure you can put her to good use."

"Perhaps you would like to inspect the circumstances in which she will be housed?" Dr. Thornton checked his watch. "I rarely visit the patients myself, but I am due to leave shortly for an appointment in town and I can show you on the way. Miss Prescott, bring me the commitment form. If you would care to sign this now, Mr. Kingsley, Miss Prescott can type in the information later. It will save you another trip to my office."

"Most agreeable," said Horace, penning his name.

Dr. Thornton led the way downstairs and out a side door. Horace carried himself along with justifiable pride. Nothing but the best for Charlotte, he told himself, pleased at the deferential attitude shown toward the doctor by the attendants they passed. They crossed the lawn and entered another building, its halls lined with small rooms. Each room was painted white and contained a metal frame bed, a chair, and chest of drawers. Sunlight trickled in the windows. Horace looked around, content. Clean, tidy, and after all, how much space did one person really need? At the end of the corridor was a large room lined with stations of sewing machines operated by women of all ages. The machines gave out a steady whirr and clatter, and only a few of those sewing looked up— hopeful or frightened—at the men's approach. Most of them appeared much like Charlotte, blank-faced and unprotesting.

"One of our workrooms," said Dr. Thornton proudly. "These women are sewing clothes for our less-able residents. They are always well supervised," he nodded toward a heavyset woman at a desk, "and when their day's work is done, they may rest at leisure in their rooms or visit the sitting room to read or socialize. Continue your good work, ladies!" he called.

"Most impressive," said Horace.

As they headed toward the exit, a strange sound from a hallway opposite echoed to Horace's ear. Dr. Thornton, hearing it also, beckoned him that way. In an empty wing a boy of about seven thrashed on the floor of a large cage. He was made of skin and bones, and a wild expression possessed his face. Foam dripped from his contorted mouth.

"An orphan," said Dr. Thornton. "He was bitten by a wild dog and contracted rabies."

The child groveled on his belly, his clothes fouled by the smell of excrement. Incoherent noises came from between his teeth.

Horace wrinkled his nose and backed away. "Why is he here with the women? I shouldn't like my wife exposed to this sort of thing."

"Nor I," the doctor confessed. "But he cannot be housed with the healthy orphans, and when we tried to place him among the idiots his behavior frightened them and they set up a howl. The women don't mind, however, and some of them sit by him in their free time and sing him lullabies. He will die in a matter of days, so do not be concerned that your wife will see him." He gestured to leave. "You'll bring her in yourself?"

"Yes, I'm sure that is the best way."

They passed out of the building and walked back to where the buggy was hitched. The ripple of doubt that had passed through Horace on first entering the gate was long gone. A comfortable place, a homey place, that's what it was. Why, even the lunatics were charitable to each other, the daft women soothing that rabid boy with meaningless songs. He gave a last glance at the attractive red-brick buildings. Here Charlotte would find only peace, quiet, and relaxation to fill her mind.

"A lovely day," said the doctor, drawing in a lungful of summer air. He offered his palm to Horace in a parting handshake. "I am glad we could be of assistance to you, Mr. Kingsley."

"It is I who owe thanks to you," Horace affirmed. "You have taken a great load off my mind." He mounted the buggy, tipped his hat, and drove the horse toward the gate, basking in his own praise.

Yes, a fine day for a fine fellow. Everything is going my way!

Eight

Something was wrong.

Charlotte stared out the upstairs window toward the giant maple tree at the crossroads, her brow creased in troubled lines. She had been tidying the boys' bedroom this sunny afternoon—never a difficult task since they always kept it so neat—just dusting a little along the windowsills, when she noticed a woman stalking toward the tree. The woman made an imposing figure, although her size seemed no more than average. No, it was her bearing, the upper half of her body pitched forward as if leading a charge into battle. Charlotte could almost feel the quiver of purpose that gripped her, from the three indignant plumes atop her fashionable hat down to the hem of her stylish mauve dress. She advanced on the tree in high temper, and Charlotte held her breath. Wallie, Oren, Glen, and the angel had scurried into the maple's sheltering green leaves only a few minutes before. The woman in the feather hat shook a furious finger toward the branches.

Charlotte pulled the dust cloth through her fingers, first one hand and then the other. Oh dear, something was wrong, and there was so little she could do. That was the way life was: things happened all around you, they poked and pushed you this way and that, but you never quite got a grasp on them, never saw them fully until it was too late. Life swirled around you like a game of blind man's bluff, taunting you with cries and laughter, but every time you got close to understanding, to identifying what it all meant, whoosh!, it slipped through your fingers, leaving only an empty thrill of hope or fear or despair. You never got to clutch it in your hands. You never really knew what it meant.

The mauve-dress woman showed no sign of retreating. Charlotte could almost see her jaw barking open and shut. Oh dear, oh dear. What could she do? They didn't like her to come out of the house. She wished Horace were here. He would deal with that angry woman. He was good at taking care of things. On his last visit, a few days before, she had signed yet another paper, a check, and Horace said the business was now all done. Meanwhile, the house looked so nice, all painted and spruced up, and she had her two hundred dollars safe in the desk drawer.

Wait—there came the children and the angel down from the tree. The feather-hat woman grabbed the angel's hand, and though the angel made no resistance, she wiped her cheeks as if she were crying. Oh, poor angel! Now that horrible woman was shaking her finger and berating the three boys, who stood before her in poses of mixed shame and defiance. How dare that dreadful person scold her children?

A burst of anguish exploded in Charlotte's chest, and she whirled and hurried down the stairs, the dust cloth fluttering in her hand like a long white ghost. She flew through the living room, out the front door, and down the porch steps. She stopped. Where was she going? An urgent impulse turned her toward the crossroads where she sighted her boys and Glen beneath the maple tree. She saw a woman in a buggy, a golden-haired figure beside her . . . the angel . . . she was stealing the boys' angel! Charlotte hurried forward, unused to running, her breath coming in hard little puffs, the dust cloth wafting in her hand. She thought she was going fast, but the buggy turned down the road and was gone before she reached the corner.

"We've lost her!" moaned Glen. "Oh, Ethel!"

"The dragon has struck!" cried Wallie, fist raised. "This is war, men!"

Oren scrunched his face into a horrible leer, bared his teeth, pulled a slingshot from his pocket, and vowed to shoot the dragon dead.

Charlotte stopped, puzzled. The three boys were unaware she had come up behind them, and for several minutes longer their talk ran on in this vein, full of curses, bravado, and death threats to the dragon. Charlotte became confused. What dragon? She had not seen a dragon. She looked carefully about her, front and back, in case she had missed something.

"Grandma?"

The sound of Wallie's voice recalled her, and Charlotte pulled the dust cloth through her fingers, waiting obediently for someone to tell her what had happened. Just like blind man's bluff, it had slipped through her grasp once again.

"Grandma, what are you doing here?" Wallie tore his glance from the vanishing buggy. Charlotte stared blankly. What was she doing here? He was supposed to tell her that. He looked angry, ashamed, and dejected. He looked like her little boy who wanted to cry at something precious he had lost, and she thought she should hug him, except big boys didn't liked to be hugged in front of their friends. Already, manfully, Wallie was straightening himself. "Grandma, I'll take you home. Glen, you better go tell your ma what's happened before Mrs. Allen lights into her. Stub, you—"

"No." Oren pouted. "I ain't having nothing to do with any more girls. They're stinkers—all of 'em!"

"Stub, I'm the leader, and I said—"

"No!"

He stuck out his tongue and ran away, and Charlotte shook her head. What was she to do about her younger son? He had no call to be rude to his older brother, especially when Wallie was trying so hard to figure out what should be done. Wallie sighed and let Oren go.

"Come on, Grandma." He took her arm. "You know Ma doesn't like you to be wandering outside."

He led her back toward the house, and Charlotte trotted along. It was so much easier when people told you what to do.

"Come inside and have some buttermilk and cookies, Wallie," she said. "You're all flushed."

"Thank you, Grandma. I need to sit down quiet and work out a plan."

They went to the kitchen, and while Charlotte poured milk and set out a plate of cinnamon jumbles, Wallie paced and muttered to himself about the Three Musketeers and a princess named Ethel. Charlotte hadn't realized Livonia was such an interesting place to attract royal visitors. She must watch carefully from her windows to see if she could spot the princess, who could probably be identified by her crown. Wallie had begun to eat, still muttering, when suddenly Charlotte had an idea.

"You should ransom her," she said, for it sounded as if Princess Ethel were being held captive against her will.

"No, Grandma, I don't think that would work."

"Yes, it will." Charlotte nodded vigorously. The excitement of running to the crossroads was still with her, and she felt confident she had the solution. "Here, I'll show you, Wallie." She took his hand and led him to the desk in the living room. The money was hers, Horace had said she could do as she liked with it, and when she spread the bills across the desk she felt proud to see her son's eyes go so round. What a nice surprise she had given him!

"Grandma, this is one-twenty, one-forty . . . two hundred dollars! Where did you get it?"

Charlotte smiled and explained. Such a handsome, serious boy he was. A strong jaw and straight nose. Long lashes fringing deep brown eyes. Never mind that his ears stuck out a little. "I signed the paper at the notary office, Horace gave me the money, then we went for lunch in a fancy restaurant. I have signed a lot of papers lately, a deed and a check for twelve hundred dollars." The words popped out proudly, and she paused, listening to the sound of them.

Wallie's face drained white. "A deed, Grandma? What kind of deed?" He began asking her questions. What was the first paper? Did the second one say deed of sale? Was Grandpa Horace still bringing people to see the house? She tried to answer as best she could, but it was hard to remember exactly. No, there weren't any more people coming to see the house. The last visitors had been a jolly, newlywed couple from Nankin. They had liked her cookies even more than Mr. Quincy had.

"Does Ma know about this?" Wallie interrupted.

"Of course, I do. I just told you."

"No, I mean," he chewed his lip, searching, "does my ma, Gertrude, does she know?"

"She told me not to tell anyone. Oh dear, that was the money I wasn't supposed to mention—"

A creak of buggy wheels sounded outside, and Wallie dashed to the window. "It's Grandpa Horace!"

Charlotte let out a cry. Horace had told her not to tell about the papers, Gertrude told her not to tell about the money, now they would both be angry with her! She turned to Wallie in dismay, but already her smart boy had taken control. He scooped the bills together, stashed them in the envelope, and slammed the desk drawer.

"Grandma," he whispered urgently. "I don't know for sure what those papers mean, but I think Grandpa is selling your house. Don't tell him I've been here! Don't tell anyone anything! Something is wrong, and I have to tell Ma!"

The sound of Horace's footsteps neared on the walk, and with a last gesture of finger to lips, Wallie darted for the back door. Charlotte stood, heart pounding, her brains in a muddle, a creeping sense of fear running along her nerves. So many secrets! So many things she was forbidden to tell! But people were telling and swirling and taunting all around her. Blind man's bluff!

"Charlotte! There you are."

Horace came into the living room. He was dressed in a handsome black suit, and his tone was jovial. Charlotte relaxed a little. She wouldn't have to think now. Horace would tell her what to do. And he did. He had important news. Tomorrow she was going on a trip, and she must collect her dresses, shoes, as many personal belongings as she liked. He would get the old trunk from the attic for her to pack them in. It was a nice place where she was going, with even less to worry about than she did here. She could sit and sew and chat all day with other women while someone cooked her meals and cleaned for her—imagine that! She asked if it was like the fancy hotel they had visited in Detroit, and Horace said that was very clever of her to make the comparison, and yes, indeed it was. He fetched the trunk to their bedroom and told her to pack.

Charlotte folded her dresses on the bed. A sense of excitement prickled the back of her neck, but she took her time, wanting the job done neatly. Should she pack the clothes in the trunk first or her shoes? What about nightgowns? Horace hadn't said anything about them. Personal belongings . . . she scanned the bedroom, then her mind traveled through the other rooms of the house. What were her personal belongings? Her pots and pans? No, Horace had said someone would cook for her. Her hairbrush and comb? She added them to the trunk. The colored seashell soaps Gertrude had given her one year for her birthday and she had thought too pretty to use? Yes, she would take those and her jewelry, although it was strange about her jewelry, for pieces of it had mysteriously disappeared over the years and she could not imagine where she had lost them. She was thinking she should ask Horace how long they would be away when voices rose downstairs.

"You can't do this, Papa! Tell him, R. Z.! Tell him, Emma! This is her home. Where will she go?"

"What business is it of yours? I offered to let you take her. You didn't want her."

"But I didn't know you meant this! R. Z.!"

"What do you want me to do, Gert? She's signed a quitclaim on everything, a deed of sale, a check. How could she sign three times without meaning to?"

"Because he tricked her! Look! Look on the quitclaim how feeble her signature is! She can't have meant to sign away everything she owns! Oh, why didn't I listen to Oren?"

Charlotte moved to the bedroom door and cautiously peeked around it. She could see no one, but the voices came clearly from her living room, and she edged down the stairs just far enough to glimpse inside without revealing herself. My, what a commotion! She could not remember the last time so many people had been in her house. Gertrude, Emma and her husband, that nice ginger-mustache man. Gertrude was pleading with another man, that short fellow who was always hanging around her. Charlotte ducked back as the ginger-mustache man angrily broke in.

" 'Tis not right, Kingsley. I dinna care if all the laws in the state be on your side. What is it you need, money for more shady dealings in Detroit? You can take what Emma and I have saved, but leave the poor woman her home."

"Too late. It's sold."

"Then she'll stay with us." Emma's voice rang out. "This is despicable, Horace! To turn her out with nothing but the clothes on her back!"

"She got her money."

"What good is money? It's a home she needs!"

Oh dear, they were all angry now, yelling and shouting at Horace and each other. Charlotte sat on the stairs and clapped her hands to her ears, but the voices crashed through, jangling her nerves like cymbals clashing. This was probably her fault. All those secrets . . . she must have told the wrong one.

"Eloise? What do you mean she is going to Eloise?"

The voice was Emma's, shocked, and for a moment the quiet in the living room was so intense that Charlotte, huddled on the stairs, felt a curious fear that everyone must have died. She pictured them lying lifeless in various poses on the rug, and she experimented in her mind, arranging them this way and that until the scene looked right. Then suddenly they all sprang alive again, Horace's voice snarling above the rest.

"It's done, I tell you! I have the commitment papers right here, and your moral sentiments don't mean a damn. You ought to thank me for relieving you of the burden. She's crazy, a lunatic, the doctor agrees completely. All these years, you've denied it. At least now she'll get proper help."

"Help? Papa, it's an insane asylum! They tie people up, they let them howl and beat their heads on walls. How could you?"

"Quiet, girl! You know nothing about it. It's a modern, humane facility. As long as she behaves, she'll be treated fine."

"R. Z., please!"

"All right. All right, Gert, we'll find room for her somehow."

A weeping sound came from the living room, and Charlotte leaned forward again, peeping. Oh dear, Gertrude was crying, the short man trying to comfort her. Emma seemed to want to speak, but it was taking a great effort. She kept clenching her fists and working her jaw before any words came out.

"I swear, Horace, though we are brother and sister, I wish I may never speak to you again. I don't believe any of these papers are legal, and I will find a lawyer who can dispute them in court."

"Just you try." Horace cocked his thumbs in his vest pockets. "I should have had your miserable farm, too, if it weren't for this freeloader coming along to steal it. Everyone knows he only married you for your land."

Horace swept his hand disdainfully at the ginger-mustache man, and, so fast that Charlotte could hardly believe it, that nice man's fist shot out and punched Horace in the face. He crashed backward into a table and fell to the floor as the short fellow whisked Gertrude aside. Then all was pandemonium, Emma crying, "No, Joe, no!" and Horace bellowing, "I'll sue you for this! I have my rights! The woman's crazy, and I'll have her locked up for life!"

Charlotte clambered up the stairs, stumbling on her skirt and struggling to the bedroom door. Once inside, she slammed it shut, and as if she had thrown a blanket over the noise downstairs, it quieted to a muffled din.

She understood now.

It was all clear.

She could feel the answers coming into her hands.

Horace had lied.

Cheated.

Condemned her.

Now she was crazy.

A lunatic.

A madwoman.

Charlotte closed her fingers on her palms, and this time nothing escaped her grasp.

Blind man's bluff.

The game was near an end.

She turned. The air in the bedroom had taken on an exceptional clarity, bright and polished as a window, clear and hard as glass. She could see everything—past, present, future—as if she looked out of every pane in her house all at the same time.

"Charlotte!"

She walked downstairs. Horace sat in a chair in the living room, an overturned table and broken lamp on the floor. He bent forward, pinching his nose in his hands. Blood ran through his fingers and dripped onto his pants. Everyone else was gone.

"Don't stand there, woman! Get me a cloth!"

"Yes, Horace."

Calmly she went to the kitchen cupboard, found cotton dressings, and brought one to him. Horace pressed it to his nose and cursed. Splatters of bright red splotched his face and white shirt.

"If that fool McEachran has broken my nose, I'll have the law on him. What are you staring at? Get me a whiskey!"

"Yes, Horace."

She brought him the drink and watched while he gulped it down and wiped his nose.

"I'm going to clean up," he growled. "Get me some dinner."

"Yes, Horace."

In the kitchen she fried potatoes in the skillet, boiled green beans and salted ham. She did not feel hungry herself, so she sat at the table and watched him eat. His nose had stopped bleeding, but it was red and ugly-looking, and he drank more whiskey after dinner. The light began to fade from the sky, a warm, peach-colored sunset suffusing the horizon. It was almost the last day of August. Summer was at an end.

"I take up too much room in the bed," Horace grumbled. "You sleep in the girl's room. Tomorrow I'll take you on that trip I promised."

"Yes, Horace." She followed him up the stairs and watched as he closed the trunk that held her belongings. He rubbed his head and groaned. "Would you like another whiskey, Horace?"

"Yes, a good idea. I'll sue that damn McEachran."

She brought him a glass and the bottle, and he poured himself a full shot. Charlotte went to Gertrude's room and sat on the bed. Outside the window the sunset had intensified to a vivid shade of orange; gradually it faded to ash gray. She watched the color deepen until velvety blackness enveloped the land and crept into the room, hovering around her as she sat beside the lamp. From her bedroom came the regular sound of Horace breathing. Charlotte stood and shook out her skirt. She carried the lamp downstairs to the kitchen and opened the cupboard where she kept her dust cloths. All this time, cleaning her house for someone else. She picked out the cloths, set them in the skillet, which she had washed carefully after dinner, then located her wood rolling pin. All those cookies she had baked. She carried everything back upstairs.

Horace lay on his back, breathing deeply. Charlotte set the lamp on the bedside table. The window was open, and her husband had covered himself with only a sheet, the August nights still being warm. He stirred when Charlotte peeled it back, then subsided into deeper slumber. She stared at him. His linen nightshirt had rumpled up around his thighs, exposing bony knees and white legs covered with coarse, dark hair. His toes were long and thin. Charlotte lifted the hem of the nightshirt and stared underneath. That was long and thin, too, and it lay curled in its thatch bush like a pale, wrinkled slug. To think she had once fancied that, had enjoyed it, something decent women were not supposed to do. But that was what had started it between her and Horace, so many years ago. He had been handsome and charming and coaxing, contriving places to find her alone, using his hands to touch her in ways that made her heart pound. She knew it was sinful, and she had done the right thing and fought her urges until he married her. For what? Charlotte stared at her husband's privates, then she shrugged and let the nightshirt drop.

Horace muttered, and she stepped back, but he did not awaken. The whiskey smell lingered in his mustache, and in the lamplight his face with its blooming red nose looked stupid and sore. His left eyelid was puffy also, and Charlotte guessed with satisfaction that the nice ginger-mustache man had landed more than one blow. She remembered his name now, Joe McEachran, Emma's husband, who used to be the hired man. There were a lot more things she could remember this very moment if she tried. She could feel them waiting around her, no longer swirling or taunting but stopped obediently on the periphery of the game. She had only to reach out her hand and draw them in. Blind man's bluff. She could win. But to do so she would have to grasp all the other memories, the sad, heartbreaking ones, and though she knew they were there, she could not bear to embrace them.

Carefully, Charlotte tied together her dust cloths, testing each knot with a tug until she had four strong, ample lengths. Horace grunted as she worked around his wrists and ankles, but his eyelids did not open. When she was done Charlotte stood back to inspect her handiwork, and she recalled the spider that one autumn had spun a web across her window, deftly wrapping the moth in her sticky net. Charlotte smiled, pleased as she surveyed her husband, his arms and legs securely roped to the four posts of their bed. Only one decision remained to be made, for after this all would be over and she must be crazy forever.

Did she want Horace to see what was coming, or didn't she? She decided she did.

"Horace," she whispered. "Oh, Horace." She lifted the rolling pin in her left hand, the cast-iron skillet in her right. She hefted them to get the best grip. "Horace," she cooed. "Time to wake up!"

Horace's eyelids blinked open. Charlotte raised her arms and grinned. For one startled instant, he jerked against his bonds, but the dust cloths held tight. As the rolling pin and skillet rained down joyful blows, Horace began to scream.

Nine

Big boys don't cry.

But what else could you do when you were twelve years old and the world was falling apart and there was nothing in your power to stop it?

Oren hugged his arms around the trunk of the maple tree, pressed his cheek against the bark, and squeezed his eyes tight. He had climbed as high as he could possibly go, to the very top where the slender limbs swayed precariously beneath his weight. Oren didn't care. So many bad things had happened since yesterday, let the tree split in two and crash to the ground with him in its leaves. That was how he felt.

But the tree didn't split, and after a while he opened his eyes. The huge green leaves hovered around him like friendly, patting hands, imploring him to tell them his cares. A few sparrows twittered, and from below came occasional laughter or the sound of a buggy arriving at Stringer's Store. Oren sighed. Where to begin?

He crawled around the branches to scan north to his grandparents' house. How could he face the kids next week when he returned to school? "Your grandma's gone to Eloise! She's in the loony bin!" they'd taunt. No use putting up his dukes this time. Even Ma couldn't deny any longer that Grandma Charlotte was crazy. If Aunt Emma and Uncle Joe had not heard Grandpa Horace's terrified cries through the open window and rushed to free him, Grandma Charlotte might have laid claim to becoming a murderess as well. Grandpa Horace was said to be black and blue all over and had several broken ribs. Secretly, Oren was glad about the beating. Served him right, the mean old man.

Of course, Oren was not supposed to know any of this had happened.

All the frantic to-ings and fro-ings in the night, the hurried conversations behind closed doors, were off-limits to him and Stub.

"Stay in your bedroom and don't come out," Pa had ordered. But they did come out and spy and eavesdrop and piece together the disaster while the grown-ups were too distracted to notice. Now Grandma Charlotte had been carted away to be locked up forever with the mad people, Grandpa Horace was confined to his bed, and Ma sat home weeping, fighting with Pa, berating herself, sobbing at the kitchen table.

Oren parted the maple leaves to get a glimpse of Aunt Emma's house. He wished he were there now, sitting in the sunny kitchen, drinking buttermilk and eating cornbread, everything safe and calm. But when he and Stub had trudged over midmorning, Uncle Joe met them with the news that Glen had fallen into one of his weak spells.

"Best you let him rest today, boys. 'Twas a bad night for everyone." Joe grimaced, his mustache drooping on his normally cheerful face. "Run along and play and dinna make any trouble."

So Oren and Stub had wandered here and there, kicking stones in the dirt, punching each other in the arm, until they reached the railroad tracks. Stub, in a devilish mood, lay down on the metal rails.

"Get up, Stub," Oren said crossly, but Stub only grinned, closed his eyes, and folded his arms across his chest in a death pose. "Get up, Stub," Oren repeated, and he kept on repeating it until a train sounded and his pleas and anger grew suddenly frantic. "Get up, Stub, get up!" he yelled. He grabbed his brother's legs and tried to pull him off the tracks, but Stub clung to the rails with both hands, laughing. Only at the last minute, the train whistle shrieking in their ears, did Stub jump clear, dancing a jig as the engine hurtled past.

"I'll kill you, Stub!" Oren cried in a fury. "I hope the next train does run you over!"

Then he ran away and took refuge here in his leafy sanctuary, feeling ready to burst with tears. He wanted to be left alone for the rest of his life.

Except for Ethel.

Oren sniffed and gave his nose a backhanded swipe. So much had happened in the past twenty-four hours he'd had almost no time to think of his princess. Yet she was there in his heart, a soft, warm spot that glowed like a light cupped between his hands. He did not know how Mrs. Allen had discovered their secret meetings. They must have grown too carefree, strolling about in the sunshine, playing at games, until someone casually mentioned their passage to Ethel's ma. Or maybe the dragon just got suspicious, jealous at having her treasure escape her claws for even an hour. However it had happened, Oren would not soon forget the wrath Mrs. Allen had vented upon him yesterday beneath this very tree.

Deceitful! Dishonest! Impertinent boy!

Go ahead, tell my ma, get me a whipping, he had thought, his heart turned to steel in his chest. Anything is worth it for Ethel.

But so far Mrs. Allen had not followed up on her threats to see the boys punished, and once the news about Grandma Charlotte rippled through town, no doubt she would shun any contact whatever with his disgraced family.

Oren blinked back the wetness in his eyes. A part of him wanted to bawl so badly he thought he would spray out tears like a fountain. Then another, stronger part of him fought its way up his chest. No! He would not be defeated! Let all the terrors of the world stand before him, he would not quail. He was the leader, the champion, the knight in shining armor, and he must never abandon his quest.

He slid down the tree, scraping his bare shins, and marched along the road to the house where Ethel was staying. It was a good mile distant, but he covered it in long strides, never flagging. He would march straight to the door, demand to see Ethel, and . . . and . . . well, he didn't really know what else, but he kept on marching, his determination altered not one whit.

As he neared the house he saw Ethel sitting on the porch swing. She spotted him the same instant and stood quickly, a finger to her lips. Oren checked his march. Ethel was tipping her head to the left, away from the house, signaling him . . . to where? He scratched his ear, scanned the territory, and shook his head at her. Ethel sidled to the edge of the porch, tucked her right finger beneath her left elbow, and pointed. Ah! Oren ducked behind a tree, skirted a hedge, and made for the lilac bush she had indicated. Ethel nonchalantly descended the porch steps, glanced back over her shoulder, and wandered aimlessly in his direction. She stepped around the bush and let out a pent-up breath.

"Oh, Oren, I've been sitting and wishing and hoping all day that you'd come! Sometimes if you wish hard enough, you can make things come true."

"I would have tried to see you sooner, but my grandma got . . . uh . . . sick. Maybe you heard?" He winced, hoping the news hadn't spread this far.

Ethel shook her head. "No, I didn't know. I hope she'll feel better soon." She stared forlornly at her black patent leather shoes. "My papa has not come to his senses, Oren, and it is sure my parents must have a divorce. Mama is in there talking to the lawyer now. Do you know what 'adultery' means?"

"No."

"Me either. But if I keep listening, I guess I'll figure it out."

"They never tell us anything," said Oren bitterly. "They don't listen when we try to tell them. They say 'Little pitchers have big ears' and send us to our rooms. It's not fair!"

Ethel sighed, and Oren pulled out his clean pocket handkerchief—he always carried one now—and spread it beside the lilac bush so Ethel could sit without getting grass stains on her lacy pink dress. He sat down beside her.

"Why did you wish to see me, Ethel?"

"To say goodbye. We are leaving Livonia."

Oren's heart sank. The whole earth might as well open and swallow him, that was how awful he felt.

"But you can't go." It was a feeble protest. He had known from the beginning that Mrs. Allen meant to stay only for the summer, and now summer was at an end. "Can't you tell your ma you want to stay and live here? You could go to our school."

"I'd like that," said Ethel wistfully, "but we have to go back to the city. Mama is going to try to support us doing sewing and fancy work for the ladies. I don't think we have much money. Do you know what 'squandered' means?"

He shook his head, too distressed to care much about vocabulary. "When are you leaving?"

"This afternoon, on the train."

That was it—the end of the world. He would die this very minute.

"I'll never see you again, Ethel."

"I know. What else can we do?"

"Run away. Let's run away right now. We'll hide in the woods and live off the land." Oren smacked his fist into his palm. "We'll get Glen, soon as he's feeling better, and Stub, if he promises to behave, and we'll build a fort and cook on campfires—"

Quietly, Ethel shook her head. "I can't leave my mama, Oren. I am all she has."

Oren's shoulders slumped. For a long minute they sat in silence. A bee hummed somewhere above them, and the sweet scent of lilacs teased the air. The day was as beautiful as the last day of August could be, simmering in golden blue perfection, the grass lush and green. Overhead, the sky stretched wide as an ocean, and all around the earth sang with colors and shimmered with light. Oren wished he could wrap up the day like a treasure with him and Ethel inside it forever.

"My pa says we will move to Detroit soon," he said. "Maybe I can find you in the city. But I don't want to go, Ethel. I want to stay here and have it always be summer, and you, me, Stub, and Glen will play. I don't want anything to change. I don't want to grow up."

The tears were spilling now, dribbling down his cheeks in rivulets while he sniffed in vain to hold them back. Ethel put her arm around his shoulder, and they hugged each other for comfort.

"I wished for you today, and you came," she whispered. "Maybe if I keep on wishing, you'll come again."

"Ethel!" The dragon's voice sliced the air and drove them apart, its rapier blade sharpened to a gleaming point. "Ethel! Where are you?"

"Coming, Mama!" Ethel jumped up and waved around the bush. She smiled, motioning Oren to stay down out of sight. "I'm just picking some lilacs."

"Very well, but come back on the porch in five minutes. You are much too delicate to be out in this hot sun."

Mrs. Allen's shoes clacked away, and Oren heard the door close. He stood and plucked a spray of purple flowers off the lilac bush.

"Take this, so she'll believe you."

"Thank you, Oren. Say goodbye to Glen and Stub for me. Thank you for the best summer of my life."

She started to go, but impulsively Oren caught her wrist. Then he did something so amazing, so incredible, so heroic, he knew he would never in his life experience anything quite like it again. He threw his arms around Miss Ethel Pearl Allen, and with all his might he kissed a girl. Princess Ethel was so startled, she barely had time to resist. The next instant it was over, and with a last longing look in her wide blue eyes she ran away toward the house.

Oren stayed looking after her. He stood taller in his shoes. The dragon has you for now, he thought, his chin lifting to the challenge, but she can't keep you forever. Someday, somewhere, Ethel, I will find you again and set you free.

He turned and marched away toward the crossroads, to the maple tree, to his solitary citadel among the leaves.

Book Five

1925-1926

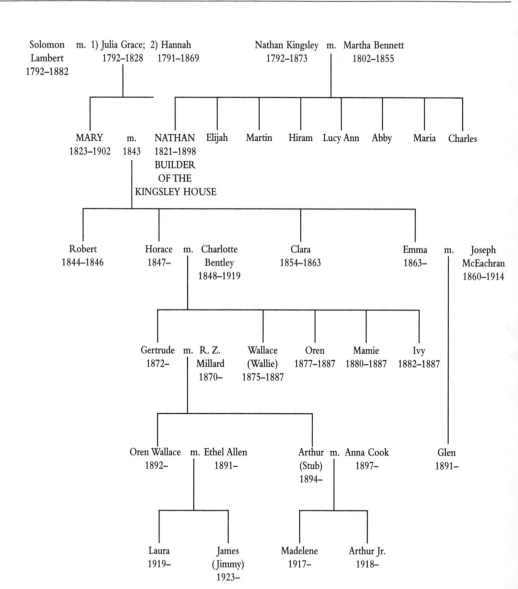

Solomon Lambert 1792–1882 m. 1) Julia Grace; 1792–1828 2) Hannah 1791–1869

Nathan Kingsley 1792–1873 m. Martha Bennett 1802–1855

MARY 1823–1902 m. 1843 NATHAN 1821–1898 BUILDER OF THE KINGSLEY HOUSE — Elijah — Martin — Hiram — Lucy Ann — Abby — Maria — Charles

Robert 1844–1846

Horace 1847– m. Charlotte Bentley 1848–1919

Clara 1854–1863

Emma 1863– m. Joseph McEachran 1860–1914

Gertrude 1872– m. R. Z. Millard 1870–

Wallace (Wallie) 1875–1887

Oren 1877–1887

Mamie 1880–1887

Ivy 1882–1887

Oren Wallace 1892– m. Ethel Allen 1891–

Arthur (Stub) 1894– m. Anna Cook 1897–

Glen 1891–

Laura 1919–

James (Jimmy) 1923–

Madelene 1917–

Arthur Jr. 1918–

One

"Well, lass, it's been a long day's work. What are my chances for a cup of cider to wet my throat?"

"Joe?"

Emma turned from the kitchen sink, her hands soapy from the dishwater, her heart stopped between beats. He stood before her, dressed in rumpled work clothes, a twinkle in his blue eyes, lips parted in a grin beneath his ginger mustache. Pulling a handkerchief from his pocket, he mopped the sweat that dampened his brow.

"So do I get my cider or not?" he teased. "After all the haying I've done today, I think I've earned it."

"Joe?" Emma's heart still did not beat, and wonder tinged her voice. "Joe, is that you?"

"Of course it is."

"But you . . . you're not supposed to be here."

He chuckled and held out his arms. "Well, I'm back."

She stepped into his embrace, and his arms wrapped around her, a touch so real she closed her eyes to savor it. She pressed her head against his chest, felt the solidity of his flesh, smelled the fragrant scent of sun-warmed hay that clung to his clothes. Then Emma's heart beat, and she awoke.

For a minute, lying in her bed in the cool dawn light, Emma stared at the ceiling without moving. Slowly, she turned her head to the empty pillow beside her. It had been eleven years this month since Joe died, and though on occasion she still dreamed of him, the scenes were always vague and without sense, as if she were surrounded by the distorted reflections in a carnival hall of mirrors. But this—she closed her eyes and sought again the feel of his hug. Yes, there it was, warm and real as in her dream, and she tried to draw the touch into her, impressing it not only into her memory but onto the very texture of her skin. Don't leave me, she begged, don't leave me. But already the force of the dream was receding, slipping away in the morning sun, and clinging to the last faint sensation of Joe's arms around her, Emma began to cry.

After a while, she wiped her eyes, first with her hands, then with the bed sheet, feeling clumsy and bereft. Stop it, she ordered, stop it. Do you want Glen to see you like this?

The thought of her son got her out of bed and to the mirror where a teary, reddened face greeted her. She poured cold water from a pitcher into a basin and splashed it on her cheeks. Then she went to her wardrobe, donned a pleated brown dress, brushed and pinned her ash gray hair. But the dream kept pulling at her, impeding her progress toward the day, and finally she sat down on the bed to consider what it meant. Surely, having come to her today of all days, it must mean something.

She replayed the vision in her mind's eye, taking care to let it unfold at its proper pace. The overall impression of reality had faded, but the shapes, colors, and sounds were still clear. She saw her face, heard her voice, and knew the time was the present, herself a rather stoic-looking widow of sixty-two years. Joe looked and sounded the same age as at his death, fifty-four, although his appearance had changed so little since his late thirties that it had become a source of amusement to their neighbors.

"Look at him! Hardly a wrinkle on his brow and not a speck of gray in his hair," Elizabeth Stringer used to declare. "Is that fair to us ladies, who must resort to ever more cosmetics to stay the march of time? Look your age, sir!"

"I'll do my best to oblige you," Joe replied, winking, and the next day he presented himself at the store, wobbling on a cane, sporting a fake white beard, his face lined with grease pencil and his hair silvered with powder from the makeup supplies of the Livonia Players. It had caused such a fit of laughter among the customers that the town board, holding a budget meeting in Town Hall next door, came rushing over to investigate the uproar.

Emma stood and hugged herself, an old sadness following the happy memory. Why was it then that Joe, seeming so fit and healthy, had so abruptly and unexpectedly died? He had simply walked in from the field one September day, exhaled a heavy breath, and gently thumped his chest.

"You look flushed," she had said.

" 'Tis only the heat, lass. Dinna worry."

Then he frowned, pressed his hand to his heart, let out a gasp, and buckled to the floor. By the time Emma, with a cry, had swooped to her knees and lifted his head, he was gone.

She shook herself and walked to the bedroom window. The sun was fully up now, its buttercup yellow light illuminating the panes. Emma parted the curtain to stand in its warmth. She wanted that hug back, wanted it the way a weary traveler longs to sink into a welcoming chair. But already the exact feel of it was gone, and she must be content with the knowledge that it had happened, that she had felt it as surely as the press of her hand against her lips.

But why had Joe come to her? Even in the dream, they both knew he had died. She'd been about to say it, "You're dead," but instinctively amended it to "You're not supposed to be here," as if pronouncing the word might drive him away.

"Well, I'm back," he said, and the strength of his reply filled her with a sudden conviction that even now, unseen, he was beside her in this room. Not a ghost—she was far too practical to believe in that, and Joe himself would have been bemused by the idea. Not an angel—they had never been regular churchgoers or given much thought to the hereafter when there was so much work to be done here on earth. But she felt his presence near her, and clearly the dream was a message, from his soul or spirit or whatever one liked to call it, to let her know that he still watched over her and Glen. He had come to give her courage, today of all days.

A cough sounded from her son's bedroom, and she went into the hallway and rapped on his door.

"Glen, are you all right?"

"Yes, it's . . . nothing . . . I'll be up . . . in a minute."

More coughs punctuated the sentence, and as Emma pushed open the door he hastily tucked his handkerchief beneath his pillow and propped himself against the headboard, smiling to greet her. Her heart sank. He must be coughing up blood again.

"Stay in bed," she urged. "It's early yet. I'll wake Lillian, and we'll call you when breakfast is ready."

She mustered a smile. Glen seemed to have grown thinner overnight, his pajamas hanging loosely on his slight frame, as if he were lost inside them. She glanced over the bedroom, the smaller of the two on the second floor, the room that had been hers as a child. The walls were papered in ivory traced with a pale blue vine pattern and hung with Glen's watercolors, tranquil landscapes or harbor scenes he copied from photographs in magazines. The furniture was oak, white curtains freshened the windows, and altogether the room had a pleasant, reassuring aspect. But perhaps her bedroom, facing east to the rising sun, might possess a healthier influence? And perhaps he should eat more or dress more warmly or give up entirely his clerking job at the clothing store in Plymouth, from which he had taken a leave to fight off this latest bout of illness. She would ask the doctor this morning. The solution was probably so very simple, they would laugh and shake their heads that it hadn't occurred to them before.

Emma's glance returned to her son, and the dream of Joe brushed the corner of her mind. Glen's hair was almost the same color as his father's, sandy with a bright touch of copper that took on a burnished look in the sun. His sky blue eyes were Joe's, too, and his fair, freckled skin. But where her husband had claimed a wry, narrow face, her son's was rounder, an innocent choir-boy visage, and as Glen had never grown very tall, he always gave the impression of being younger than his years. Now, thinned by illness, he looked more like a sick child than a grown man of thirty-four.

"Porridge?" she asked. "Would you like porridge with maple syrup for breakfast?"

"Yes, thank you."

He smiled again, cheering her, and she went downstairs. From the first-floor bedroom came the surly sounds of Lillian dressing, a skirt rustling angrily, a drawer roughly closed, as if the girl were frustrated, on awakening, to discover her situation had not magically improved over the night before. Emma felt her own anger rising. No, she vowed, I will not tolerate your unhappiness, not today. But a minute later, when the hired girl emerged and came to the kitchen, a tight smile was screwed onto her mouth. All right, thought Emma, summoning a matching expression onto her face, if that's the mood you choose today. It is not my fault that life has treated you unfairly. Or should I say fairly, since you have only yourself to blame for your fate.

"Glen is a little weak this morning," she said, forcing a pleasant tone. "I'll start the coffee and make him porridge while you milk the cow and fetch the eggs. Would you like toast and sausage?"

"Yes, thank you." Lillian's voice seemed to grate on the words, though she nodded civilly. She skirted past Emma and went out the back door.

Emma filled the kettle and set it on the stove. Should she speak to the girl? Adopt a motherly approach? Lillian was twenty-four, the same age Emma had been when she met Joe, and she remembered the none-too-subtle pressures she had felt to correct her single state. Even in this modern century, opinions had not changed that much, and a woman still unmarried beyond a certain age aroused murmurs of consolation and pitying remarks. Perhaps Emma's example would hearten the girl that true love was worth the wait, though for Lillian it might prove harder to find. She was not pretty, her small blue eyes close set under scrawny brows, her cheeks fleshy, her figure well endowed but thick at the waist. Recently, she had bobbed her brown hair in the new short style, and though Emma agreed it was "chic" and "sophisticated," secretly she thought the blunt cut only emphasized Lillian's wide jaw. Yet despite her lack of physical beauty, Lillian might still have found a kind, caring husband—if only she had remained chaste.

Emma tsked aloud as she laid sausage in the skillet and stirred porridge into a saucepot. Two years ago, determined to secure a beau, Lillian had thrown herself at a disreputable young man. He accepted her favors and nimbly skipped town when her condition began to show. At least that was the story Emma had from Elizabeth Stringer, who knew the girl's family in Nankin. The baby had been given away at birth; Lillian remained at home in disgrace.

"I could give her room, board, and a little spending money in exchange for housekeeping," Emma had offered. "The change of scene might provide her an opportunity to start afresh."

So it was arranged, and Lillian Hobbs came to live at the Kingsley House. At first she had been grateful and eager to please, and Emma found her help unexpectedly welcome. It was nice to come in from hanging laundry and find the kitchen mopped and scrubbed. It was easier to do the ironing when the dishes fell to someone else. Lillian was not always as adept at her chores as Emma would have liked, but to have them done adequately, to have them done at all, was a blessing, especially on those days her fingers ached with rheumatism or the tiredness crept up her spine and pinched at the base of her neck.

But within six months Lillian's gratitude had ceded to a sense of boredom and oppression, then impatience with her lot. She grumbled at her work, spoke boldly of becoming a secretary or a salesgirl in a shop, yet made no effort to change her place. Her tongue grew sharp, her temper petulant; she seemed to take pleasure in self-disdain. It was almost, thought Emma, as if she liked her unhappiness too much to let it go. When she did meet an eligible male, she fastened on him with alacrity, fussing with his tie, laughing too loudly at his jokes. The men backed away, sensing something hard-edged in her pursuit, or perhaps they'd heard of her past, though Emma had never breathed a word, even to her son. Their rejections only angered Lillian the more, and lately, as if in desperation to snare any man at all, she had begun making advances toward Glen. At that, Emma almost sent her packing, but Glen seemed oblivious to her intentions, and Lillian, frustrated, had backed off to circle before making her next move.

"Over my dead body," Emma muttered aloud. "If you wanted a husband as fine as my Glen, you should have kept your knees shut."

She winced at her language. How could she have spoken so crudely? It was all this brash new talk the young people used nowadays, the cigarette smoking, the short skirts, the flapper girls pouting their carmine lips. She didn't approve of any of it, she wore her own dresses halfway down her shins, and she would sooner cut off her nose than her hair. Emma had not set out to become old-fashioned, but somewhere along the way it had inevitably happened. Would it have been different, would she have kept some spark of exuberance and youth, if Joe were still alive?

She turned the sausage in the skillet, sliced bread for toast, and stirred Glen's porridge to ensure there were no lumps. That was the kind of detail, small but not insignificant, that Lillian would overlook. Emma spooned the porridge into a bowl and was drizzling on maple syrup when the hired girl returned carrying a jug of milk and a basket of eggs.

"The sausage is almost ready," Emma said. "You can fry the eggs while I take Glen's breakfast up to him."

"Breakfast in bed?" Lillian raised her eyebrows. "My, what a luxury."

"He isn't well, Lillian." Emma's nerves tightened. "You know he must rest. You ought to have a little more compassion if you ever expect to become a wife and mother."

"Oh!" Lillian let out an indignant breath, and Emma's chest heaved in preparation for the long-simmering fight. Yes, let's have it out now, she thought. The strain of waiting for Glen's hospital appointment today has been almost more than I can bear. Go ahead and try me. I can get another hired girl, or Glen and I will go back to doing for ourselves. It was better, just the two of us, before you came.

But instead of retorting, Lillian smoothed her lips into a guileless smile.

"Yes, we must do everything for Glen's comfort," she cooed. "We only want what's best for him."

"Good morning."

Glen stepped into the kitchen, and Emma turned. Lillian, facing the doorway, smiled warmly at his entrance. She must have seen him coming—Emma shelved her irritation, preoccupied with her son's appearance. He was dressed in a blue suit, white shirt, and red bow tie, and he looked livelier than he had on awakening. The fever that troubled him most evenings was always gone come dawn.

"I was going to bring breakfast up to you," she said.

"It's all right. I don't want to cause you extra work."

"Oh, it's never work to take care of you, Glen," Lillian chimed. She picked up the porridge bowl and set it before him as if she had just finished preparing it. "Would you like more syrup?"

"I'll make your toast," said Emma.

"I've brought you fresh milk," said Lillian.

"Thank you, but I wish you wouldn't fuss over me." Glen smiled at both of them and clasped Emma's hand as it rested on the table. "I'm sure everything will be fine."

He released her hand and began to eat. Lillian sat down beside him, and Emma found herself left to fry the eggs. All right then, she thought, and she made sure to give Lillian the two with the smallest yolks. It was childish, she knew, but she couldn't seem to help it. All her pent-up emotions had tied in a knot in her stomach, and this tiny act of revenge was her sole release.

She sat and ate, half her mind tuned to Lillian's chatter, the other half seeking escape from the girl's ingratiating voice. Everyone was coming from Detroit on Sunday for a picnic—Gert and R. Z., Oren, Stub, and their families—and Emma mentally walked over the farm, tracing the paths they might take on their ramble, imagining the children's laughter as they surprised rabbits in the overgrown fields. She had tried hard to keep the land tilled and sown after Joe's death, but Glen hadn't the strength to be a farmer and using hired hands had proven inefficient and more costly than she could afford. The last six or seven years she had let the fields go entirely, keeping only a single cow, her vegetable garden and the orchard, and running a small business in chickens and eggs. It was not the way she wanted it. She wanted acres of golden wheat undulating in the breeze, rows of tall green corn shooting toward the sky. She wanted brown-eyed cows grazing in the pasture, a sturdy horse in the barn, spring piglets squealing in the pen. She wanted Joe back alive and Glen well. She wanted the richness of what had been.

"I'll clean up." She stood abruptly, interrupting Lillian as she coaxed Glen to eat just one more bite of porridge. About to sputter, Lillian quickly recovered and began collecting dishes.

"Let me do that, Emma. You and Glen don't want to be late to the hospital."

She bustled about the kitchen, and Emma glanced to her son. He smiled at her, always that quiet smile that accepted whatever came without tremor or protest. Was it better to know, or not to know, thought Emma, and a sudden irrational desire seized her to forget the appointment, grab her son, and run away to some sunny place where they could laugh and enjoy themselves in stubborn ignorance. Surely it was just the same old weakness of the chest that had plagued him since he was a child? It might heal itself again, as it usually had over the years, giving him long respites when he breathed and laughed as easily as any other young man. But never before had the fever run so high, drenching him with night sweats. Never before had he spit up blood when he coughed.

"I'll bring the car around to the front," said Glen, rising, and Emma was forced back to the reality that lay ahead.

"I'll get my purse and meet you," she replied.

The Model T was idling beside the walk when she came out, and she got into the passenger seat. Glen drove the short distance south to the crossroads, then turned east past Stringer's Store. John Stringer waved from the porch. Since his mother Elizabeth's death the previous autumn, he had modernized the store with new display shelves that carried more kinds of tinned and packaged foods than people had dreamed of a decade before. But so much else had disappeared over the years: the shoes and bolts of cloth, the ladies' jewelry and children's toys, the shaving razors and suspenders, the paint, rope, and chicken wire. Nowadays if people wanted such items they got in their car and drove to a dry-goods shop, a jeweler's, or a hardware store. And when they came to buy their groceries at Stringer's, they did not stay to talk. They got in their cars and drove somewhere else.

"Everything is changing," said Emma, and Glen gave a gentle laugh, as if he had read her unspoken train of thought.

"Hardly anything changes here."

"Yes, it does. What about that article in the newspaper last week that

278

said a real estate company has purchased land on the south side of town to build—what did they call it?—a subdivision."

"Rosedale Gardens," supplied Glen.

"Well, it will change everything. Houses side by side on little plots, people living here but driving off each day in all directions to work somewhere else. They call them commuters and say we will become a suburb of Detroit, whatever that means."

"It means we will get sewers and utility lines and have indoor plumbing and electric lights. They may even pave the roads," Glen teased. "Besides, I'm already a commuter. Don't I drive to my job at the clothing store in Plymouth?"

"That's only four miles, right next door," countered Emma. "And I admit having utilities and indoor plumbing will be pleasant for us all. But it won't *feel* the same. The town will get crowded, people and cars crisscrossing everywhere and getting in each other's way. That's why my grandfather, your great-grandfather Kingsley who died before you were born, came here from New York State almost a hundred years ago. 'Too much pushing and shoving,' he used to say. 'Who wants a neighbor you see more than twice a year?' "

Glen chuckled, and Emma settled into a grumbly silence. She stared at the scenery as they passed. Shingled farmhouses, herds of dairy cows, red barns, ripening fields of corn. In fact, Livonia's population had not grown in forty years, and the town still had no library building, high school, or bank. Except for the few cars they passed on the road, the tractors and steam combines in the fields, the landscape would have been familiar to her grandfather's eyes. I am foolish, thought Emma. Glen's right. In a hundred years, almost nothing has changed here at all. Why did I prattle on like that? Because I'm afraid of what is coming, she answered herself, and I want to hold tight all that is safe and ordinary in our lives.

They drove the rest of the way in relative silence. The hospital was in Detroit, and as they neared the city the traffic increased and the houses drew closer together until they crossed an invisible boundary into a busy metropolis of skyscrapers, factories, and stores. A stream of people passed on the sidewalks, and Emma's eye fell on a smart young businessman carrying a briefcase in one hand and a newspaper tucked under his arm. What if Glen had come to the city? What if she and Joe, instead of keeping him on the farm after he finished eighth grade, had sent him to the high school in Plymouth? He might have gone on to college, in Detroit or Ann Arbor, for his marks had always been the highest in his class. What would his life be like now? Would he be a newspaper reporter, a banker, an architect? Would he have met and married some nice girl? Might he have escaped his illness, tricked it into taking the left fork in the road, while he turned right? She saw the hospital ahead, and again the urge seized her to grab her son and run away.

"Here we are."

Glen parked the car, a note of contentment, almost of gladness in his voice. He wants to know, thought Emma, and putting aside any last hope of escape, she accepted his offered arm as they mounted the hospital stairs. Whatever effort it cost her, she would match her son's bravery, and as they proceeded through the morning—the examinations and X-rays, the consultations and nodding of heads—she held to her pledge. It was almost, she thought, like one of Joe's plays where everyone had memorized their part. Dr. Ash was kindly and sympathetic. Glen received the diagnosis with his usual calm. Emma asked all her questions about food and switching Glen to her bedroom, pointless though she now knew them to be. There was no simple remedy, no easy cure. *Tuberculosis.* She held the word in her mouth like a smooth, round stone, weighing it on her tongue, knowing that eventually she must swallow it down.

"I'll be all right," said Glen firmly. "But what about my family? The people with whom I worked? It worries me that I may have infected them."

"Then you may set your mind at rest," said Dr. Ash. He was a tall, bespectacled, silver-haired man, and his white coat, craning neck, and long limbs reminded Emma of a stork. He opened each new topic slowly, as if offering it for their approval. Then warming to his subject, his sentences would gather speed and his gestures grow more enthusiastic, his arms flapping like wings. "Long-term, close contact is required before the infection can be transmitted, and even your mother here, though she should be examined, appears to have avoided the disease. But you, Glen, must enter a sanatorium as soon as possible. I can recommend an excellent facility in Silver City, New Mexico. Several of the patients I've sent there have made a complete recovery and returned to their normal lives."

"New Mexico?" Emma shook her head, unsure if she had heard him right. All week she had lived in dread of the diagnosis and had heard it without a cry. She welcomed the prescription of a sanatorium; at least the illness was not so far advanced that nothing could be done. But New Mexico? "Why so far away? Surely Glen could receive treatment somewhere closer to home?" She clutched her son's hand as if he might be bundled off that instant, her clasp the only link to keep him here.

"Because a dry climate is the most effective way to counteract the moisture in his lungs. Silver City is surrounded by mountains," Dr. Ash raised his arms as if to summon up invisible peaks, "and the sanatorium sits at an elevation of six thousand feet. It is renowned for the purity of the air. Of course, you may accompany your son, Mrs. McEachran. The sanatorium has cottages for patients and their families, and a well-supervised regimen of diet, rest, and medical care."

"New Mexico," Emma said again. The words seemed to increase the size and weight of the stone on her tongue, and she turned to Glen, expecting his face to mirror her doubts. Instead, he wore an expression of growing interest, as if he had been presented with an unlooked-for gift.

"Imagine the scenery," he said softly. "Imagine the painting I could do there." His eyes glowed as if he were picturing the landscape that moment in his head, and for an instant he looked so much like Joe that Emma nearly spoke the name aloud.

"Oh no." Emphatically, Dr. Ash shook his head. "You must have almost no activity of any kind, at least not at first. When the lesions in the lungs start to heal they form a tissue more delicate than a cobweb. Any quickness of breath or exercise may cause it to break. You must let the tissue grow stronger and wall in the germs until the lesions are entirely filled. Then we will have a complete cure."

Dr. Ash launched into a lecture on the importance of a positive attitude and cooperation with the sanatorium's regime, but though she tried to listen, Emma's mind would not obey. Her thoughts buzzed from her dream of Joe to Glen and back to New Mexico again. It sounded so foreign, distant, exotic, yet a tremble of hope ran through her. A complete cure, Glen better forever, happy, healthy—then a cold fact clutched her, and her hopes sank. *The cost.* Travel to New Mexico, months at a sanatorium, the loss of Glen's job and her egg business, no more income from any source.

"Well," said Dr. Ash heartily, "if you agree, I'll contact Silver City immediately to arrange for Glen's admission." He peered at them over his spectacles, craning his head eagerly from one to the other.

"Yes, we certainly must consider it," Emma hedged. "We'll need some time to plan."

"It should not be delayed," Dr. Ash declared. "The sooner he begins the treatment, the sooner he will be cured."

"Yes, we understand." She glanced to her son. He seemed half in a daydream, an eager, faraway expression drawing warm color onto his hollow cheeks. "Glen, why don't you go ahead to the car? I'd like to use the restroom before we leave."

They stood, and Dr. Ash escorted Glen to the door while Emma dawdled, rummaging in her purse. When her son was gone, she spoke.

"How much will it cost?"

"H'mmm." Dr. Ash furrowed his brow, as if he, too, had suddenly recalled this practical matter. His elbows stuck out at wide angles like bent white wings. "It's not inexpensive, that's true, Mrs. McEachran. The fee at the sanatorium covers lodging, food, and medical care, but you'll also have travel and personal expenses, and there may be other, unanticipated costs. I should estimate . . ." He named a sum and paused. "I can see by your face that is a worrisome amount."

"Yes." Emma's voice sounded faint to her ears. She cleared her throat. "Doctor, you mustn't think I don't love my son or would ever skimp on anything his health requires—" Her tone rose to a pleading note, and Dr. Ash's white sleeves flew into movement.

"Oh no, no, no," he said. "I understand completely."

"Then couldn't we try a sanatorium closer to home? Or perhaps I could convert our house into Glen's own private sanatorium, following the exact regimen and diet he would have in New Mexico? I assure you I would watch over him day and night to fulfill his every need."

Dr. Ash brought his fluttering arms back to his sides. He let out a breath and his manner slowed, a signal to Emma that he was preparing to offer a new idea for consideration. She leaned forward, as if shortening the distance between them by a few inches would bring the hopeful news that much sooner.

"Some patients do stay in our climate and recover with good care," he agreed. "But the X-ray showed your son's tuberculosis is in an advanced state. I didn't say so in his presence because, as I explained, a positive attitude is of the utmost importance. Mrs. McEachran, are you all right?"

"Yes. No." She sank into a chair, and he hurried awkwardly toward her. She motioned him to silence, shaking her head. Now was not the time to lose her fortitude. She must get the question out before her courage failed.

"Will he die?"

In the few seconds that the doctor paused to answer, Emma felt the heavy, round stone in her mouth move to the back of her throat.

"I don't know." Dr. Ash sighed. "Each case runs its own course. I have seen genuine recoveries made even when the end seemed near, and I assure you Glen's case is by no means at that extreme. The scars on his X-ray show he has suffered bouts of the disease before, and his body has fought it off without any medical assistance at all. What's more, he has an excellent attitude and that may well be the single most important factor in his cure. But I believe the warm, dry climate in Silver City is his best chance, and that cannot be duplicated here. Perhaps you have family who could help you with the expense? I'll communicate personally with the sanatorium to do whatever we can to assist you. Why, I have seen . . ." The white sleeves began to flap again as Dr. Ash, his enthusiasm taking wing, began to recount joyful cases of success.

Gently, Emma interrupted. "Please contact Silver City. Make whatever arrangements are required."

She sat back quietly in her chair. The stone was in the pit of her stomach now. It had slipped down as she finished speaking, all in an instant, almost of its own accord. Too late she had felt it going, leaving her no chance to cough it back up or even to gag. Now it lay deep inside her, waiting to be digested. It was not as painful as she had expected, but foreign, strange, and she felt belated surprise that she had swallowed it and still lived. *New Mexico*. She saw again the shine in Glen's eyes, the moment of uncanny resemblance to Joe, and the dream of her husband touched her skin. She glanced around the room, aching to feel his presence near.

Dr. Ash went to the door of his office and began regaling his secretary with instructions to notify Silver City that Mrs. Joseph McEachran and her son Glen would be arriving as soon as they could make ready. Emma half-listened, her mind already occupied with the logistics of the trip.

We'll have to close the house, she thought, sell the chickens, do something about Lillian, arrange to forward the mail. Maybe the Andersons across the street could keep the cow. Gather the fruit from the orchard, ask John to sell it for us at the store. Pack our trunks, collect the necessary funds. She halted on the last word, then her mind went briskly forward. No, she did not have the money, and she could not ask her few relatives to help. Gert and R. Z. were always struggling. Oren and Stub had wives and young children to support. Horace she had not seen or heard from in years. But she did have something of value, and perhaps this is what she had been saving it for.

Emma closed her eyes and sent her mind out of the hospital, past the skyscrapers and out of the city, back over the houses and fields to the crossroads at Livonia Center, back to her eighty acres of land.

Two

"She'll be comin' round the mountain when she comes! She'll be comin' round the mountain when she comes! She'll be . . ."

"Oren, Laura, could you keep it down just a little?"

Ethel Millard made a lowering motion with her hand, then smiled indulgently at her husband and daughter as their car bumped comfortably along the dirt road toward Emma's house. She nestled baby Jimmy more snugly on her lap. Despite the singing, the chubby two-year-old had fallen asleep, lulled as always by the steady motion of the car. Contentedly, Ethel stroked his cheek and gazed out the window at the passing farmland. They couldn't have asked for better weather for their Sunday picnic, a perfect Indian summer day. She turned to check on six-year-old Laura, piping another verse in the backseat. Behind her, out the rear window, Ethel glimpsed her father-in-law R. Z.'s car, and an equal distance beyond that, bringing up the rear of their little caravan, came Stub and his family. All three cars were black model Ts, of course, since both Oren and Stub were employees of the Ford Motor Company.

"Daddy," said Laura, interrupting the song, "a lady would look funny driving six white horses in red pajamas."

"Horses wearing red pajamas would look pretty funny," Oren agreed, and there was a moment of confused silence before Laura's brow unfurrowed and she answered roundly, "No, Daddy! Not *horses* in red pajamas. The *lady.* You know what I mean!"

Oren chuckled, and Ethel smiled to herself. Tonight, when they got home after dark, Laura would pretend to be sound asleep in the backseat, a ruse to compel her father into carrying her upstairs to bed. "Oh, what a lump of lead! What a sack of potatoes!" Oren would groan, staggering up the stairs and winking sideways to his wife while Laura, draped across his arms like a motion-picture heroine, slumped as though lifeless.

Oren pointed as the Kingsley House came into view. "Almost there." His voice rang cheerfully, and Ethel knew it was more than the prospect of an afternoon in the country that inspired him. It was what they had left behind—her mother—the only member of the family not to join the outing. Mama disapproved of the country, or rather she disapproved of subjecting herself to it. She did not mind, for example, riding in the car to view pastoral scenes, as long as the drive could be accomplished between luncheon and dinner with no need to disembark from the vehicle and set foot on the ground along the way. But to tramp through fields and woods, sit on blankets beside a creek, eat-out-of-doors like gypsies, was not to be contemplated, and Mama had watched tight-lipped from the window, as Ethel quietly, disobediently, took the children away from her iron-willed domain. That Oren had tolerated Mama living with them since the day of their marriage ten years before never ceased to amaze her. In her teenage years, she had assumed her mother would prove too great an obstacle for any man to marry her at all. But Oren had persisted, courting her for five long years until they could afford to marry and Mama grew amenable to the idea. And although Mama ruled their household by day, at night, when they retired to their room, Oren firmly shut the door.

"No dragons allowed in here," he whispered in Ethel's ear, unpinning her coils of blond hair and drawing her to bed.

The three cars pulled up to the house, and Emma, Glen, and Lillian waved and hurried down from the porch. Laura hopped out of the backseat. Oren came around to Ethel's door to help her alight carrying the baby.

"Gert! R. Z.! Oren! Stub!" Emma moved from one to the other, dispensing welcoming hugs. Patiently, Ethel awaited her turn. Glen edged through the group toward her, Lillian close at his side. He clasped Ethel's free hand, and she felt as always the special warmth of his smile. It was never more than a simple curve of his lips, yet it seemed to radiate from some inner source until it touched and lightened every feature of his face, like a flower opening in the morning sun.

"I ordered some new duet music, and it came yesterday in the mail," he said. "Shall we practice it later?"

"Yes, I'd like that," she replied. "Did you get the piano tuned?"

"Yes, even that plunking key is fixed."

"Glen plays so beautifully, don't you think, Mrs. Millard?"

Lillian wedged between them. She wore a pink dress cut rather low in the neckline and a smile that sharpened in defense of her territory.

"No, I play passably." Glen laughed, his tone firm in correction. "Ethel is our true musician."

"I only meant to compliment you," Lillian pouted.

Gertrude bustled boxes from their car, handing them to her husband. "We've brought a lemon custard and a chocolate cake," she informed Emma. "Don't crush the cake, R. Z."

"I'm not crushing it. It's fine, see?"

"Well, I just don't want it to get battered."

"It's not battered, Gert. You're the one tipping the custard. Watch out there."

"Let me take it," said Emma. "I have the hampers all organized. I've made fried chicken, deviled eggs, cornbread. . . ."

The party moved toward the house, Stub and his wife Anna shepherding their two children. Ethel followed Oren and Laura, the baby dozing on her shoulder. She was grateful for Oren's relations and liked being among them. Without them, she would have no family at all. She hadn't seen or heard from her father since that summer he had left them, and not a word of him, not so much as his name, had passed Mama's grim lips in all those years. In fact, sometime after the divorce, Mama must have taken her sewing scissors to their photograph album, for when Ethel opened it months later she discovered the pictures had been systematically mutilated, her father's face and figure cut out of every portrait, every scene, leaving mother and daughter to face the world alone.

"My camera," she said aloud, remembering. "I left it in the car."

"I'll get it for you." Glen turned back, returning a moment later with the black leather case. "I'll carry it. You have your hands full with Jimmy. Will you immortalize our picnic today?"

"Yes," cooed Lillian, close as ever at Glen's side. "Could you take a picture of us together, Mrs. Millard?"

"I'll try," said Ethel, feeling strangely unwilling. "Before I take a photograph, I like to compose each setting in my head." She nuzzled Jimmy, who had yawned himself awake. "Let's go in and join the others."

They entered the parlor, and Emma ushered her to a rocking chair. Ethel sat, bouncing her son on her knee, while Oren's family caught up on recent news. R. Z. had secured a job to paint and wallpaper a hotel lobby; Gertrude fretted that at his age, fifty-five, he ought to at least hire a boy to fetch and carry while he worked. Stub had taken his son, seven-year-old Arthur Junior, to see Ty Cobb play baseball; Anna proudly patted the boy's head while their daughter, eight-year-old Madelene, waited hopefully to be mentioned. Oren talked about work. Henry Ford was gradually moving his operations from Detroit to his huge new plant at the mouth of the Rouge River and opening a string of small, water-powered factories along the Rouge Valley. Oren hoped his own transfer, when it came in the spring, would include a promotion from his job as a tool-and-die maker to a fore-man's role.

Stub scoffed at the idea. "Why would you want to do that, Oren? The best work is on the production line, putting together the cars, not boss-ing other men to do their work."

"It's better pay, an advancement," countered Oren, but Stub shook his head and laughed it off.

Ethel listened, content not to speak. One of the advantages of being an in-law, she had discovered, was that you weren't expected to be too prominent at family gatherings. On the contrary, it would be rude if you did thrust yourself forward, for much as your relations by marriage might like you and enjoy your company, it was really themselves they wished to talk about on such occasions. Aside from a kindly, "And how are you, Ethel dear? Are your piano students progressing?" she would not be troubled to converse much this afternoon. Which was just as well, since Jimmy, who was cutting new molars, was apt to be drooly and cranky, requiring extra care. But for the moment, fresh from his nap, he was amiable, and Ethel's mind traveled elsewhere. Her eye fell on her camera, and she began to compose portraits of her in-laws in her head. At first, the images presented themselves in formal groupings; then, like a shadowy double exposure, a second set of images began to appear.

She saw Gertrude and R. Z., seated on the picnic blanket with a wicker hamper between them, a long-married couple, proper in their Sunday clothes. Over the years, their expressions had grown to look alike, a little tired but persevering, a little wishful for better circum-stances but not complaining at their lot. Then the picture changed, the hamper opened, the food emerged, and Ethel imagined their voices as they tugged over the plates. "Don't crush the cake, R. Z." "It's fine, Gert. Mind the deviled eggs." "I am minding the eggs. But your sleeve is in the custard." "Well, it wouldn't be if you weren't waving fried chicken under my nose." "Me? You're the one——" They scolded each other in mildly exasperated voices, hardly realizing it had become their normal conversational tone.

Ethel framed a mental photograph of Stub's family, posing them side by side in a grassy field. Her sister-in-law Anna was a perky blond woman with a tongue quick enough to match Stub's every jibe and jest. Both Arthur Junior and Madelene had inherited their parents' lively nature. But somehow it was the boy who always took center stage. As Ethel studied the family portrait, the figures rearranged themselves into a different pose. Stub and Anna stepped behind their son to form a fond trio, while Madelene, left aside, jumped and waved to catch her parents' eyes. Did they know they did that, Ethel wondered, favoring the boy so blatantly over the girl? She would be sure to center the real photograph on Madelene when the shutter clicked.

The next shot—Emma, Glen, Lillian—ought to be easy. Ethel pictured them on the front porch of the Kingsley House, Emma and Glen standing before the front door. Emma's arm rested around her son's waist while Lillian appeared to one side, framed between two of the white porch pillars. Instead of her low-cut pink dress, she wore the starched white apron and cap of an old-fashioned servant girl. Not quite fair, thought Ethel, and an opposite image asserted itself. Now it was Lillian with her arm about Glen, Emma shunted off-center between the pillars. The scene made Ethel glance across the room to where Lillian hovered at Glen's elbow. Ethel could almost feel the hired girl's fingers itching to snare him. Didn't Emma see her son's peril? But Emma, offering peppermints to the children, seemed in her own way distracted. Though she kept up a bright chatter, her face pulled in lines of worry and her shoulders drooped with an unexplained weight. What was going on here?

Disturbed, Ethel brought a last picture into focus—herself, Oren, Laura, Jimmy. A fine young family, just beginning to be prosperous. Both children had Oren's dark hair, her wide blue eyes, and cheerful dispositions. She put her arms around them, Oren laced his arms around her, and the picture held. Yet she felt troubled. Was there some hidden image she couldn't foresee, waiting to emerge?

"Let's gather our picnic and go out to the woods," said Emma. "We'll stop to see the chickens on the way, children."

Ethel stood, setting Jimmy down beside her to walk. It took several more minutes for the expedition to be organized to Emma's satisfaction, then the party headed out the door. While the children clustered around the chicken coop, feeding corn to the hens, Ethel glanced toward the crossroads. A smile stole over her lips at the sight of the big maple tree, its uppermost leaves beginning to tinge from summer green to autumn gold.

"Remember?" Glen's voice sounded beside her, his note gently teasing.

"How could I forget? I look for the maple every time we come. As soon as Laura gets a little older, I'll boost her into its branches myself. Every young girl should climb a tree at least once in her life."

They laughed together, then a third laugh pushed between them.

"Laura in a tree? Oh, she's much too pretty to be a tomboy, Mrs. Millard. And Jimmy is such a dear." Lillian patted the toddler's head as he clung to Ethel's hand. "Would you like me to help you watch him today? I do love little children."

"Well, he's a bit—" Ethel stopped. A bit shy around strangers, she had been about to say, but Lillian had already trapped the boy's hand. Jimmy quickly stuffed his other hand into his mother's palm and edged closer to her.

"Here we go. Come along, Glen," said Lillian.

They strolled after the others across the field, Lillian bubbling about how nice it was to have the family together, how sweetly the children were dressed, how she and Glen had been looking forward all week to their visit. Glen had positioned himself beside Ethel, putting maximum distance, she noted, between himself and Lillian.

"How did you and Mr. Millard meet?" Lillian probed. "I'm sure it must have been very romantic."

Ethel shrugged. "We knew each other one summer as children when my mother and I visited Livonia. Then, years later, we met again at a social evening in Detroit." She tried to make it sound ordinary, unwilling to share her personal story with the girl. She hoped Glen would not offer any of the details, which were preserved in a letter Oren had written to him later that same night.

> *Dear Glen,*
>
> *The most wonderful thing has happened! Stub and I were at a dance at the Statler Ballroom when across the room I saw the most beautiful girl in the world. I said to Stub, "There is the girl I'm going to marry," and when I crossed the floor to introduce myself, who do*

you think it was? Ethel! It was Ethel! Glen, I am smitten! I am madly, hopelessly in love!

All for one and one for all!

Oren

Ethel pressed her lips to keep the smile off her mouth. Glen had presented her with the letter on her wedding day.

"And how is your dear mother?" pursued Lillian. "I hope she's well?"

"Mama's fine. She prefers the city, that's all."

"It must be such a help having your mother live with you and assist with your household. Her wisdom and experience are surely a great support. When I marry I should think it an honor for, say, my mother-in-law to share our home."

Ethel forced a smile. How transparent. How pushy. It was one thing to let a man know you liked him but to make such presumptions. . . . Lillian shot a riveting smile along the line to Glen, and Ethel could almost feel the girl's body arch and purr like a cat in heat. A word came to mind, not a nice word, but apt. *Hussy.*

They reached a shady spot by the creek, spread their blankets, opened the hampers. Emma's lunch was delicious, and Stub had brought bottles of beer for the men. Ethel watched the children at play, contributing an occasional remark as a good in-law should. Oren stretched full-length on a blanket and laced his hands behind his head, gazing at the leafy branches above them.

"I love coming here," he sighed. "It's the best place on earth."

"What makes you say that?" asked Emma. She was seated on the blanket next to theirs, and once or twice during the meal Ethel had caught again that worried tug of muscles across her face, as if she wrestled with some unpleasant turn of mind. Now a light came alive in her eyes, as if Oren's words had touched a glad spot within her.

"I don't know exactly," he replied. "Part of it's all the great memories, of course, from when Stub and I were kids and your house was our second home. But it just feels right to be here, like something slips into place each time we arrive, and when we leave it always feels like, well, like we shouldn't be going."

"Maybe you should move back to Livonia and take up farming," mocked Stub, "instead of aiming to be a plant boss." He ducked, laughing, as Oren threw a twig at him.

"I'm afraid it would take too much work to turn this back into a profitable farm," said Emma. A rare note of sadness crept into her voice. "I've let it go, the fields, the crops, the barn. Sometimes I feel I've let Joe and my parents down."

"Oh no, Mother."

Glen knelt behind her and wrapped his arms around her shoulders in a hug. Emma reached up and clasped his wrists, drawing his embrace tighter, as if she needed to draw strength from his touch. That is the photograph I want, thought Ethel, and quickly, while the others broke into sympathetic protests aimed at soothing Emma's regrets, she picked up her camera and snapped the image of mother and son. By the time she lowered the lens, Emma had resumed her usual chin-up expression. The party lazed about for another hour, and while the children sailed paper boats in the creek, Ethel fulfilled her role as photographer, posing the formal pictures she knew would please her in-laws when they looked back on the occasion.

"Don't forget me and Glen," chirped Lillian, pressing herself close to his side, swishing her skirt, smiling broadly for the lens. Politely, Ethel complied.

"Now Ethel and I must return to the house to practice our duet," Glen announced. "No, no, Lillian, everyone must stay here while we rehearse so we can surprise you with a grand performance."

"Yes, it would be most embarrassing for the piano teacher to fumble her notes," Ethel agreed. "Oren, will you mind the children?"

Her husband gave a genial assent, and she and Glen walked away. The late afternoon sun was mellow, buttering the grass with warmth, and they took their time crossing the fields. Of all Oren's relatives, it was Glen to whom she had always felt closest—naturally, since they had so much in common. Both shy, only children; both deemed to be of delicate constitution, though Glen's frailness was real, her's mostly her mother's imagination. Both had their creative outlet, she her music, Glen his painting; both knowing they were amateurs rather than artists of true talent. Both tied—there was no other word for it—to mothers who dominated their lives, although Emma did not so much control her son as pair with him, their lives intertwined like a two-part harmony ever since Joe's death. She and Glen had talked over all these matters in perfect understanding, each seeking out the other like a mirror in which to see themselves. So now Ethel felt no hesitation in speaking what was on her mind.

"Lillian has gone quite sweet on you, hasn't she?"

"Yes, although I don't think it's me in particular she wants. Anyone else in the same place would do as well."

"Do you feel anything for her?"

"No."

"I thought it was rather clever the way you wriggled out of her grasp just now."

"I've had to do it a lot lately. I wish she'd leave off. I've tried ignoring her, but she refuses to take the hint. Do you mind if we stop a minute, Ethel? I'm a little winded."

They were halfway toward the house, crossing a field of tall, pale yellow grass, and Glen sat down on his knees and began to cough.

"Oh my goodness, are you all right?" Ethel stooped beside him, her hand on his shoulder, as a spasm of coughing racked him. The coughs had a strange, gurgling sound, as if soap bubbles frothed in his chest. "Glen, are you all right?" Her hand brushed his forehead, and she started at the heat on her fingertips. "You're feverish. Have you been ill all afternoon? You should have been home in bed."

He shook his head, waiting until the cough subsided before he spoke. "No, I'm all right. Well, actually I'm not." He eased himself to a sitting position, and Ethel did likewise, so they were hidden in the tall grass. "We were going to tell everyone later, at the end of the day when the children were out of hearing. But I'd rather tell you now, myself, while we're alone. I have tuberculosis." She gasped, her mouth opening to protest the news, and he clasped her hands, imploring, "Don't be frightened for me, Ethel."

"But are you sure? Have you been to a doctor? What can be done?"

She searched his sky blue eyes. How he could be so calm, faced with such a serious illness, a disease he might well die from? A chill ran over her skin, and though she chided herself for leaping to such a drastic conclusion, still the fear gripped her like a cold wind that had swirled out of nowhere and snatched away the sun's warmth. So this was what had been hurting Emma all afternoon, and in typical fashion she had concealed it to carry out the picnic as planned. But she may lose her only child! Tears started to Ethel's eyes at the enormity of it, and her thoughts flew back to Laura and Jimmy at the creek in an irrational need to picture them safe and well. Glen pressed her hands, murmuring, and explaining about his diagnosis, a sanatorium in New Mexico, their plans to travel to the Southwest. He spoke about the painting he would do, the scenes he imagined, and that slow, radiant smile blossomed on his face as he looked into her eyes.

"Don't be sad, Ethel. I'm not. It's really so much better now that I know."

"Yes, because now we can do something about it." She nodded resolutely, taking her cue from his own attitude. The feel of the sun was returning to her skin, and she looked around, seeking to ground her sensations in what was solid and real. She saw each blade of grass, separate and distinct, pale yellow shafts angled like an army of spears on the march. She heard crickets chirping and the breeze stirring, and she drew a long breath and pulled the smell of farm earth and autumn leaves into her lungs.

"At first we thought we'd close the house, sell the chickens, stop the mail." Glen was speaking again, and she tuned her mind to his voice, following it like a river through this unfamiliar territory. "Mother told Lillian we'd help her find a new position or she could go back to her family in Nankin. But Lillian's been arguing that she should stay here and run things while we're gone, and it does make sense. That way we could come back and pick up where we left off instead of having to start all over again."

"Can you trust her? Will she do a good job?"

"She might." Glen flinched. "You can see how hard she's trying to fit in. The Andersons across the road will help keep an eye on the place, and maybe you and Oren could come sometimes from the city to check up."

"We'd do anything to help. Do you know how long you'll be gone?"

"Six months, at least. I'll write to you, to you and Oren. May I?"

"Of course, and we'll write back. Oh, Glen."

"Don't be sad, Ethel, don't be sad."

He smiled and stroked her hair, and she leaned against him, knowing she ought to be the one comforting him. He lifted his chin above her head, then gave a sudden start and ducked.

"It's Lillian!" He pulled her down beside him. "She's coming after us!"

"Oh dear, how will we explain—? Should we get up?"

"No, stay down."

"Maybe she won't see us."

"She's coming straight our way!"

They whispered frantically, staring at each other in wide-eyed panic, although what they were guilty of, Ethel couldn't say. She unclasped a strand of colored stones from her wrist and tossed it into the grass.

"Quick! We're looking for my bracelet!"

With a conspiratorial glance, they began scrambling on their hands and knees, industriously searching for the lost treasure.

"Oren always said you were a smart girl," Glen whispered, eyes twinkling.

"Glen? What are you doing?"

They looked up in innocent surprise. Lillian peered down at them in suspicion.

"Ethel lost her bracelet."

"It must have slipped off my wrist." She held up her bare arm as evidence. "Could you help us look, Lillian? I'm sure three sets of eyes will find it faster than two."

"Yes, we really need your help," Glen seconded.

"Well. . . ." Lillian got to her hands and knees, shooting lingering glances at the pair of them. Glen and Ethel bent doggedly to their search. A few minutes later, it was Lillian who cried, "I've found it!"

"Oh, thank you!" Ethel hurried to claim her jewelry. "I really must have this clasp fixed. Lillian, you are a marvel!"

"Yes, indeed," said Glen.

Lillian smiled, pleased with the outcome. "What would you do without me?" she teased, wagging her finger at Glen.

"Here come the others." He nodded behind them, and turning, Ethel saw Oren and Emma leading the group as they trooped toward the house laden with blankets and hampers. Laura and Madelene skipped hand in hand while Jimmy clung piggyback to his father's shoulders.

"I thought you two were going to practice a duet," hooted Stub as they approached. "Now I see you only wanted to get out of carrying all these baskets."

"It's my fault."

Ethel began to retell the story of the bracelet but found the tale unnecessary. Her in-laws surrounded her, Gertrude and R. Z. scolding over who had chipped the cake platter, Anna tousling Arthur Junior's towhead, and she fell silently into place and walked along. Lillian had elbowed Glen to one side, claiming him for herself. Oren was entertaining Emma with his memories of the farm. Emma's face wore two looks at once—on the surface an expression of gratitude for Oren's devotion; underneath, an ever-present ache for her son—just like the double images Ethel had pictured in her photographs. How will Emma bear it, she thought, if anything happens to Glen? He is her joy, her life. There's no room even for another woman, although if Lillian has her way . . . Ethel glanced again to the hired girl. She was regaling Glen with loud chatter, tossing her head so her blunt brown hair swung in choppy little jerks. Glen lifted his eyes above the crowd and caught Ethel's gaze. The beautiful smile crept over his lips, as if some inner light fueled its soft glow. Ethel smiled back, feeling helpless, thinking suddenly that she might never see him again.

Three

"Damn!"

Horace Kingsley flinched as the razor nicked his stubbled chin and a bubble of bright red appeared. He grabbed a damp washcloth and pressed it to the cut.

"Ouch!"

He wiped the spot clean, smarting at the sting of the soap lather, then he threw his razor into the sink with a clatter of disgust. This was no way for a man to live.

"Horace? Horace, honey, are you there? I need a drink."

A hand rapped and a voice called plaintively at his door.

"Go away, Ginny," he growled. "Go back to bed. It's only eight o'clock."

"I can't sleep, Horace. Please, I need a drink."

The voice whined like a tinny violin, and to be rid of the sound he took a glass from the sink, poured it half full of whiskey from his flask, went to the door, and thrust out the liquor to the woman who stood in the hall. Peroxide blond curls tumbled about her lined, rouged cheeks, and she gripped a ruffled pink negligee across her sagging breasts.

"Here. Now go away."

"Let me come in, Horace. You liked me well enough last night."

"I have business this morning. Damn it, go away!"

He shut the door, ignoring her last few pleas, until the whining subsided and he heard her shuffle back to her room. Horace shuddered. To think he had spent last night in such company. The woman was fifty if she was a day. And look at this place. He glanced around the seedy hotel room, his lip curled in distaste. Water stains on the ceiling. Cigarette burns in the faded rug. The bed sheets tinged a dirty gray. He kicked the cold radiator, out of heat again on this chilly December morning, two days before Christmas. Well, only a turn of bad luck had brought him here, and once his fortunes were on the mend he would procure more dignified accommodations.

Horace returned to the bathroom and finished his shave. Then he pinned a towel around his shoulders, took a bottle from his shaving kit, and ran water in the sink. Dampening his comb, he stroked it through his hair and mustache until both were thoroughly wet. Then he donned a pair of rubber gloves, opened the bottle, and applied the dark brown dye to his scalp and upper lip. The change, when he finished, was not drastic; Horace never let more than a quarter inch of gray show before touching up his hair. But he always felt a new man afterward. Why, no one would take him for more than sixty, sixty-two at most, and he scrutinized his reflection with pleasure, quite forgetting that he was in his seventy-ninth year.

"Money," he muttered aloud. "All I need is a little money to get back on my feet."

But where to get it? He had been pondering the dilemma for days. Most of his usual sources were tapped out, and although he had several new schemes in the making, he required hard cash to live on until they bore fruit. Moreover, circumstances had forced him to leave a string of debts throughout the city, and he had to look over his shoulder every time he went out to ensure no creditors were on his trail. He was almost thinking it might be best to absent himself from Detroit a while, maybe head to a warmer clime. He had heard that Miami, Florida, was a booming place. Why not? A vigorous man in the prime of life could make his fortune anywhere.

Meanwhile, he wanted money, and when a man was short of friends and opportunities, it was high time his family helped him out. Horace had already given a good deal of thought to this option, and the more he considered it, the better it sounded. What was a family for, after all, but to support each other through thick and thin, and wasn't he the head of the Kingsley family, the patriarch? Of course, there was no point in going to Gertrude and R. Z., though come to think of it, they were the ones in *his* debt. Hadn't he, many times over the years, generously referred his colleagues and acquaintances to R. Z.'s ever-struggling business? "You want the best house painter and paperhanger in Detroit? Call R. Z. Millard. His ad is in the telephone directory." That's what he always said, and this despite the way Gertrude had blamed him for that long-ago business about her mother and shunned him thereafter. But even had he anticipated a warmer welcome, there was probably little money to be had from his daughter. The girl ought to have had more sense than to marry a lowly paperhanger.

Horace went to his closet and began to dress. There was no point either in going to Emma, a hard-minded woman if ever there was one. The way she had contrived with their father to disinherit him all those years ago was proof enough of her shabby treatment of him. Horace gnawed his lip at the thought of his sister's eighty acres. Suburbs like Livonia were becoming prime areas for real estate development, and the land might bring a pretty penny. Didn't he deserve a share? But Emma would never let go her grip on the farm, and that milquetoast son of hers was bound to inherit everything when she was gone.

That left his two grandsons. Horace tied his necktie and buttoned his vest. He knew where Oren and Stub worked, where they lived. He'd thought of doing them the favor of letting them in on his investments a few times before. Oren was the more likely prospect, a sober young husband bent on rising in the world. And what better time to call than two days before Christmas, to wish him a happy holiday? Horace donned his jacket, overcoat, hat, and gloves. He checked out the door to make sure Ginny was in her room, then he walked down the hallway, descended the stairs, and left the hotel.

Outside, on the next street, his automobile was parked. It was a Packard single-six sedan, a true gentleman's car, its rich blue body handsomely finished with black fenders and running gear. The car gleamed a welcome in the winter sun, and Horace let out a pleased "ahhh" at the sight. He had bought the Packard in better days, and he spared no expense, when he was able, on its maintenance. Lately it had grown weathered and somewhat dinged up, but although every nick and scratch grieved him, Horace loved his car nonetheless. In this modern world an automobile was the key to mobility, prosperity, and respect. A man who showed up at his bank, his tailor's, or his business appointments by trolley or on foot was a man of no substance at all. But let his fortunes be ever so low, he was a king if only he had a car.

Horace started the engine and drove to a restaurant for breakfast. It was Saturday, and already the streets were alive with Christmas shoppers heading toward the gaily decorated stores. After a meal of fried eggs and bacon, Horace spent the morning calling on his last few trusted contacts, firming up plans for their newest venture, a private gambling club.

Then he made a quick stop at a candy store and set out for Oren's house.

His grandson's home was a cream-colored, two-story residence on a pleasant, middle-class street. A cluster of children played in the snow on the lawn of the house next door. They were bundled in wool coats, plaid scarves, and colorful mittens, and as they romped and shouted, Horace's heart warmed to the sight. Maybe Oren's little ones—what were their names anyway?—were among the frolicking tots. How glad they would be to see their dear old great-grandpapa! What stories he would tell them as they bounced on his knee! Yes, they had been estranged for far too long, and it was his duty to reunite them this joyous holiday season.

Horace strode up the walk, mounted the porch steps, and knocked confidently on the door. A woman in her sixties answered. Stiff iron-gray hair was piled atop her head, and the frown on her squarish face did not bode well for intruders on her doorstep. She measured him head to toe, as if he were a traveling salesman about to ply her with a bag of cheap merchandise. Horace doffed his hat and put on his best smile.

"Good day, madam. I am Horace Kingsley. May I speak with Oren Millard?"

"He isn't home. You may leave your card."

"No, no." Horace gave a genial laugh. "Perhaps you did not catch my name. I am Horace Kingsley, Oren's grandfather, and I have come to wish him a merry Christmas. Why, there are my dear great-grandchildren, peeking around the door." He reached into his coat pocket and brought out two striped candy canes tied with green bows. The little girl, a wide-eyed creature capped with glossy brunette hair, started forward, while a toddler boy peeped from behind her skirt.

"Back into the house, both of you," the woman ordered, her command slicing down like a hatchet on a chopping block. The children turned tail and scurried out of sight. "Laura and Jimmy have colds and must not be anywhere near this frigid air," she declared. The frown on her mouth deepened. "Horace Kingsley, you say. I don't believe I have ever heard Oren speak of you."

"Oh, I'm not surprised," Horace agreed. "We have been out of touch for quite a while. I am a businessman, you see, and my affairs keep me constantly occupied. I regret I have not had the pleasure of meeting you, Mrs.—?"

"I am Mrs. Allen, mother of Ethel."

She drew herself up taller, pronouncing the words as if they were a royal title. Horace inclined his head.

"Of course, dear lady. Forgive me for not guessing your identity. Well, I am truly sorry to have missed Oren. Will he be at home later this afternoon?"

"I can't say. They have gone to Livonia on family business and may not be back before dark."

"Family business." Horace nodded his understanding. It was obvious he would have to make a good impression on this female watch dog if he were to gain entry on Oren's return. "I have ties in Livonia myself, you know. My sister's farm, the Kingsley House, is at Livonia Center."

"But that is exactly where Oren and Ethel have gone." Mrs. Allen's expression changed to one of surprise. "You are brother to Emma McEachran? Have you not been in touch with your sister either?"

"Regrettably, no." Horace adopted a cautious note. Mrs. Allen's tone seemed to signal that important news was in the offing, and he bowed his head a little sadly to indicate his regret at the lapse in communication.

"Then I'm afraid I must tell you that Emma is at a sanatorium in New Mexico with her son Glen, who is very ill with tuberculosis. They have left their farm in charge of their hired girl, and Oren is keeping track of her."

She seemed pleased to deliver this dire information, and Horace reacted with due shock and gravity.

"How unfortunate! I knew the lad was often sickly, of course, but I had no idea it had come to this." He shook his head in remorse. "It's to be hoped he will make a speedy and complete recovery. Is it known how long they will be away?"

"Six months at the least, Emma said, though I personally expect it to take much longer. It is that strenuous life on the farm that has undermined his delicate constitution. If Glen were my son, I should have removed him to a less rigorous environment long ago."

"H'mmm," agreed Horace. "Well, I certainly mustn't keep you standing here in the cold, madam. Do take this candy for the children, and I will pay my respects to Oren another time."

He bowed his head, donned his hat, and left her with the candy canes. Musing, he walked to the car. Glen ill with tuberculosis? But perhaps it wasn't surprising. Given his weak health, the true surprise was that he had not succumbed to some malady or other long before now. And what were the chances of recovery? If Glen died . . .

Horace's mind sharpened to the possibilities as he drove back to his hotel. Maybe he ought to visit Livonia and survey the situation for himself. The Kingsley House was, after all, his dear old homestead, and with

Emma and Glen so far away, it was only natural he should be concerned about its condition and upkeep during their absence. Why, it was his family duty to take a hand in this matter. But he couldn't show up in Livonia today, not with Oren and his wife already there. Best to think about this a little, make a few plans.

The next afternoon, Christmas Eve, Horace set out in his car. His whiskey flask was tucked in his pocket to ward off the frosty bite of the air. On the passenger seat rested a gaudy box of chocolates—for hadn't Mrs. Allen said the farm was left in the care of a hired girl? He drove merrily along, enjoying the robust purr of the car's engine, the spirit of Christmas in the air. A dusting of new snow overnight had given the world a fresh sparkle, and the bare tree branches etched delicate patterns against a washed blue sky. All in all, a lovely day. Horace could positively feel his luck turning for the better.

The buildings thinned the farther he left the city behind, and soon he was passing shingled farmhouses and open fields. As he neared Livonia Center, a few dark thoughts intruded on his convivial mood. There was Gertrude and R. Z.'s old house and just past it Town Hall where he had been fined for selling perfectly good milk to Helga Witt. A quick calculation of age convinced him she must be dead by now, and he banished the incident with a satisfied "hah." He passed Stringer's Store and turning north at the crossroads he spied his own former house. It had passed through several hands, he'd heard, since he sold it to the naive young couple from Nankin, and was actually looking rather better than he'd left it, despite its added years. But the property had been divided, and two other homes now occupied parts of the forty acres. No doubt the parcels had been sold off as the land proved unproductive for farming. Wasn't that just as Horace had predicted? Hadn't he always told them the soil was no good?

The final justification of his return came when Horace parked in front of Emma's place. Even in winter, when the fields were bare, a prosperous farm declared itself by its sturdy fences, grazing animals, cleared acreage. Emma's land had a ragged, abandoned look. The barn roof sagged, clumps of dead autumn leaves clogged the flower beds, stumps of cornstalks, frozen tomato plants, and rickety beanpoles littered the vegetable garden. The house needed painting, and no one had bothered to wash the porch railing where a number of birds had left their mark. The more Horace studied the scene, the more he rejoiced at the signs of decay. It served Emma right. The last time he'd heard anything from her had been six years before, when, in a disdainful letter forwarded to his then-current address, she had taken it upon herself to inform him that Charlotte had died at Eloise and would be buried beside her dead children in the Livonia Center Cemetery. As if it was any business of his.

Carrying the chocolates, Horace mounted the porch steps, and knocked on the door. A sullen-looking young woman opened it halfway. It was the second time in as many days, Horace reflected, that he'd had to contend with a scowling female on a doorstep. This one wore a shapeless, low-waisted, mustard yellow dress, and although Horace knew the style was considered quite fashionable, paraded by smart young office girls in the city, the present model had a bit too much meat on her bones to achieve the boyishly appealing look the garment intended. She squinted at him through close-pinched blue eyes.

"Good afternoon! Merry Christmas to you!" He held out the box of candy and lifted his hat. "I am Horace Kingsley, brother to Mrs. Emma McEachran, come to pay you my respects."

"They aren't here. They've gone away." The girl spoke dismissively but didn't quite shut the door.

"Yes, I know. Poor Glen, poor Emma." Horace lengthened his face in sympathy. "But it's you I've come to see."

"Me?" She gave a scoffing laugh. "No one ever comes to see me. I'm just supposed to sit here and do nothing while they're off enjoying themselves in New Mexico."

"Exactly why I came." Horace's senses quickened. Off enjoying themselves in New Mexico? So that was how matters stood. What might the girl not reveal in her resentment? He watched her craftily as he spoke, looking for those little clues—that jut of the jaw, that muttered "huh" of agreement—that would tell him he was on the right track. "I heard about your plight, and I knew at once what to expect out here. You see, I used to own that very property across the road," he turned and pointed, "but I sold it years ago. Why, how could anyone go off and expect you to manage a house, a farm, in winter, on your own." He paused to accentuate each grievance and was gratified to see the girl's face take on a correspondingly indignant glow with each additional burden laid upon her. "And this being Christmas, and you left alone."

She grimaced, and for a minute Horace feared he had taken a wrong turn.

"Well, Mr. and Mrs. Millard did invite me to their house for dinner tomorrow," she conceded. "They'll pick me up and drive me home. But who wants to spend all day with them and their spoiled brats and their old mother-in-law and relatives sitting around? They only come out here to inspect and spy on me and write reports to Emma, as if she doesn't already send me enough letters saying 'do this' and 'see to that.' "

She huffed an angry breath, and her cheeks puffed so that her close-set eyes seemed to recede even further into her fleshy face. Horace wondered how long the discontent had been building.

"Exactly why I came," he repeated. "The situation is intolerable. I can tell you plainly, Miss—?"

"Hobbs. Lillian Hobbs."

"—Miss Hobbs, that my sister and I are not on the best terms. She is demanding, unreasonable, unsympathetic, and that is why, although I am a successful businessman in Detroit, I have seldom made the short trip to this, my family home. We had better go inside so I may hear the full extent of the matter."

He placed the candy in her hands and with a gentlemanly gesture of his arm invited her to precede him into the house. The girl led him to the living room, and without further pause began to spout a long list of injustices and complaints. Horace barely had time to remove his coat and seat himself in an armchair before the accusations began.

"She left me an open account at Stringer's to buy whatever I need, then when Mr. Stringer sent her the bills she said it was too much and I'm restricted to ten dollars a week. She left the car, but I'm only allowed to drive it to deliver eggs to her customers. I've a good mind to take off in it and just see how far away I can get. I have to feed the chickens, clean the coop, mind the house—"

"For a pittance in wages, I expect," Horace supplied.

"Wages? I get nothing! Two years I've worked here, and all I'm paid is a little pocket money now and again."

"That is scandalous! I am ashamed to think you have received such treatment at the hands of my family."

"Huh! They couldn't even run this place without me. And did they remember me for Christmas? Oh yes, she mailed me a card with five dollars, but did I get any packages, any gifts?"

Tears welled in her eyes, and Horace gallantly drew his flask from his coat pocket, fetched two glasses from the kitchen, and poured them each a shot.

"You must brace yourself, Miss Hobbs, recover your spirits. A little whiskey will do the trick."

He handed her the glass and she sniffed up her tears. "Isn't this illegal? Where did you get it?"

"Dear miss, a man of my importance need not heed those trifling prohibition laws. Besides, if a gentleman can't offer a restorative drink to a distressed lady, on his own property, in his own house, on Christmas Eve, what is this country coming to?"

Defiantly, he clinked his glass to hers and raised it to his lips. Miss Hobbs jerked up her chin and followed suit, gasping a little as the raw liquor went down her throat.

"Have some chocolates," Horace urged, opening the box.

"This is very kind of you, Mr. Kingsley." She soothed herself with several pieces of candy and several more swallows of whiskey. "You don't know how I've been used here."

"You must tell me the whole story," Horace affirmed. "I am eager to be of service to you."

It was a long tale, two years' worth, and Horace made sure Miss Hobbs's glass was refilled at just the right pace to assist her loquaciousness, never too much to slur her delivery or leave her with a headache from his visit. About halfway through her recitation, he suggested a light repast would sustain them, and she was only too happy to prepare a luncheon of chops, potatoes, carrots, and leftover lemon cake. Emma, she said, did not appreciate her housekeeping and cooking skills, and as for Glen . . . Fresh tears started to her eyes, and Horace patted her shoulder. She loved Glen, she had done everything for him, and what was her reward? He hardly knew she existed, he barely answered her letters with two paragraphs, and she was getting tired, yes damn tired, of being so patient when plenty of other handsome young men would be glad to have her by their side. She had often thought of going to Detroit and becoming a shopgirl or a typist. If she only had a little money to get started or a place to go, she would leave this very minute. That would show them.

"You must write to Emma and demand back wages for your years of devoted service," said Horace.

Miss Hobbs snorted and pushed her empty glass toward him. Her eyes were bleary, and two red spots flamed high on her cheeks. "Emma doesn't have any money. You think you can get rich selling eggs? And Glen was hardly able to work all summer. I don't know how they can even afford to pay for the sanatorium in New Mexico."

Horace tipped a dribble into her glass and pushed it back. His flask was almost empty, and the sun was setting on the short winter day, but his expedition had proven most fruitful. Now it was time to bring his visit to a close.

"What would you say, Miss Hobbs, if I could get you a position in a shop or an office and find you a nice boardinghouse for young ladies?"

"I'd say you were the only person in this whole family who's ever been kind to me, and I'd do anything to thank you!"

"Then I'll look into it immediately." Horace rose. "But you mustn't say a word of my visit to anyone, do you understand?"

"I promise." She nodded her head so that it dropped forward like a doll's.

"Not to Oren, not to anyone. And you must go to the Millards for Christmas tomorrow and be a pleasant guest. Do you agree?"

"I promise." She gave another disjointed nod.

"Very good. I'll be in touch with you as soon as I can."

Miss Hobbs's eyelids were fighting to stay open, and Horace hoped he hadn't overdone the whiskey after all. She looked like the kind who could harden up and get used to it, like Ginny. He let himself out the door and stopped to admire the last traces of sunset, a rosy glow in the twilit sky. Then he cast a final gaze over the Kingsley House and land. How provident that he had come! The situation cried out for him to step in. There were Emma and Glen, thousands of miles away in New Mexico, Glen desperately ill and battling for his life, their funds running low. Here was their family home—Horace's and Emma's, that is—left in the care of a tippling hired girl who couldn't be bothered to clean the bird droppings from the porch railing and who now planned to desert her post. The place would fall into even deeper ruin once she was gone, a sorry greeting for Glen and Emma on their return—if they returned at all. If Glen's health didn't improve, he might have to stay at the sanatorium indefinitely or at least until their money was exhausted, and Emma would never willingly leave her son's side. Or he might—how tragic!—expire of his tuberculosis in faraway New Mexico. Emma wouldn't want the farm then, couldn't manage it on her own. It was a miracle his poor sister had held onto it so valiantly for so long, all that work, all that worry, and her getting on in years.

Fortunately, Horace saw the solution as clearly as if it had been presented to him in a shining light. He would sell the farm for Emma, act as her agent to find a worthy purchaser. If they stayed in New Mexico, they'd need the money. If Glen died and Emma returned, she'd be too devastated to handle the negotiations properly herself and some unscrupulous character would surely take advantage of her. Besides, even if Glen recovered and they both returned, how much happier mother and son would be in some small, quiet lodgings, free of work and care, for just as Mrs. Allen said, Glen must not tax his health again. Yes, the time was right to sell the Kingsley House and farm, and who better to arrange it than Horace, the last true living Kingsley? Once the sale was transacted, he'd magnanimously settle for sixty percent, fifty for his half of the inheritance and ten as his commission for brokering the deal. He wouldn't dream of accepting a penny more.

Horace got into his Packard, tipped his flask to his lips, and drained the last few drops. He must make a few more visits to Livonia, now that he had business interests here. Get the lay of the land, survey the local real estate, assess market values. In fact, maybe he ought to buy out Emma's share, then develop the Kingsley property himself. He could see it all now, the eighty acres sectioned into neat little plots, each with its tidy house and lawn. He'd establish his own real estate company, and there'd be no problem finding investors, not with a sure deal like this. And he'd erect a sign at the crossroads—Livonia, Town of Opportunity—and there'd be jobs, prosperity, new roads, schools, all thanks to his selfless efforts.

Welcome back, Horace, he told himself on behalf of the grateful townspeople. *Welcome back!*

Four

How do you capture the sky?

Paintbrush held softly in his fingertips, Glen paused over his paper and contemplated his last brush stroke. He was attempting, yet again, to render the vista from the porch of their cottage, a sweep of short, rugged mountains that fell away to flat desert valleys, streaked in the colors of an endless sunset. The landscape was even more glorious than he had imagined it would be, and he gazed at it day after day without tiring. As for the climate, he had almost forgotten what rain was. Since their arrival in mid-October, he could count the spells of precipitation on the fingers of one hand. When it did shower, for it was never more than that, the droplets evaporated so quickly in the brilliant sun that it was like watching diamonds vanish under a magician's wand.

Perhaps it was that brilliance which made the sky so elusive to his brush. At this altitude the air itself seemed to be alight, and no matter what mingling of blue, gold, or orange he tried in his watercolors, the effect fell flat to his eyes. Of course, it might be his own lack of talent to blame, for Glen readily conceded he was but an amateur artist. Yet he was almost glad he could not capture the sky; he liked the idea that it was too big for him, that it could not be reduced to a sheet of paper or sized to fit a frame. Often he sensed that the sky here was not only above, but around and below him. He could feel it down in the valleys, where distant hawks circled below his feet. He walked through it every time he stepped outside and the pure blue air touched his skin. When he lay out in his reclining chair, two hours each morning and afternoon as prescribed for his cure, the atmosphere enveloped him, and he surrendered to a rarefied sensation that was almost like floating aloft without wings. To have come from Michigan, so flat, so down to earth, and be thrust up on a mountain was the strangest thing he had ever done, and when he stretched his arm toward the radiant sun he could have sworn it felt that much closer to his hand.

Of course, it might also be his imagination, which had always been lively and—Glen chuckled—was even livelier now that he was dying.

He dipped his brush and tried a streak of pink across his paper. The color blushed into the blue and darkened to rose. He had finished his afternoon rest, then stayed to paint while Emma went for a walk with the lady in the neighboring cottage. Maybe she'd bring back a letter from Ethel in the mail. Ethel had become their main correspondent, reporting every two weeks or so on their visits to the Kingsley House and relating tidbits about Oren's job, the children, the piano recital her students were preparing. She asked about his health and his painting and inquired after Emma's bird-watching, a hobby his mother had taken up to help fill her time. But her last letter had arrived mid-January and it was now almost Valentine's Day. Was she too busy? Had she forgotten him? Ethel always addressed the letters "Dear Emma and Glen," and he replied "Dear Oren and Ethel" as was only proper. But in his heart it was to her alone he wrote, and he mulled over the pairings, Oren and Ethel, Glen and Emma, and he dreamed that it might have been otherwise.

Dreamed, but not wished. Glen put down his paintbrush. No, he wasn't sad, not really, at the way his life had turned out. How could you despair or rail at something once you understood it was foreordained? By that summer of his thirteenth year, when Ethel first came to Livonia, he had begun to suspect how it would be. To experience complete health, to be physically carefree, was like the brass ring on the carousel when the circus came to town. No matter how far he stretched, it never quite met his hand. He tried to ignore his weakness, not be a sissy, keep up with Oren and Stub. He pitched baseballs, pedaled his bike, whooped and hollered when they played cowboys and Indians. Then he paid for his exertions with painful breaths and such a trembling in his knees he'd have to lean nonchalantly against the maple tree or a fence post to keep his legs from buckling. Nothing he did changed this or made it go away. He ate extra helpings of meat and mashed potatoes but failed to gain weight. In secret, he did push-ups and other strengthening exercises, but when he flexed his biceps only two small knots arose on his pale arms. Gradually, he came to accept that being sick was a physical part of him, like his freckles or his smile, and though he still reached for the brass ring, he no longer blamed himself or anyone else when his hand came up empty.

That was why he had known Oren must be the leader, the hero, and it was therefore only right that Oren should get the girl. Glen wanted him to have her, because Ethel deserved the best. But that didn't stop him from falling in love with her all over again when they were grown, and Oren, after meeting her at that dance in Detroit, brought her to Livonia to visit. Sometimes he thought Ethel guessed how he felt, giving him a searching look as if something in his expression might confirm her hunch. But she never pressed to know, and as long as he said nothing, they could remain friends.

Meanwhile, he dreamed of her. In fact, he had a whole repertoire of pleasant fantasies he could call upon at will. Some were fully developed stories in which he rescued her from precarious situations or they accomplished brave adventures like rafting down a jungle river or discovering a lost gold mine. In another private tale he and Ethel were barnstorming stunt pilots dressed in leather jackets, eye goggles, and trailing white silk scarves. Other fantasies were merely scenes in which he painted her portrait or walked beside her in a moonlit city, harmless tableaux scripted with tender conversations about poetry or art. All the feats he could never achieve in real life, all the places he could never visit, all the words he could never say, he celebrated in his dreams. His imaginings were always chaste; the most he dared envision was to hold Ethel's hand or press a gentle kiss upon her lips. But although he would never have whispered a word of his fantasies for anyone else to hear, he felt neither foolish nor embarrassed by them. On the contrary, he felt entitled to them as compensation for what life had denied. That was why he dreamed but never wished. Dreams were fulfilling. Wishes were futile.

A fit of coughing racked him, blurring his eyes with tears, and he hurriedly picked a handkerchief from his pocket and hacked into it. More blood. He must be sure to send the handkerchief to the laundry with his other linen so Emma didn't notice. She was so positive he would be cured, had shaped her mind to it as an article of faith, that lately he had begun cheating on his temperature chart, falsely marking the required thrice-daily readings a notch lower than the truth. As a result, his temperature, which had risen slowly but inexorably since their arrival, now appeared to have fallen, a fact the doctor eyed with puzzlement since the monthly X-rays and auscultations performed on his chest confirmed his deteriorating condition. That, too, he concealed from his mother, although it was unlikely he could maintain the deception much longer. The young man in the cottage behind theirs had died in January, providing Glen a model of how his own end would transpire, and already he was fighting two of the symptoms, mounting fever and a constantly sore throat. Shortly there would follow an inability to take solid food and to rise from bed, as his lungs continued to degenerate into a bubbling, spongy mass. Then perhaps some confusion or delirium in between lengthening patches of sleep, and soon he would be gone. But he would spare Emma as long as possible, and meanwhile, it was beautiful here, peaceful, and he loved the flaming colors, the splendid sunsets, the vast emptiness of blue sky. He wanted to enjoy each day without grief, to have this one extraordinary experience in a life that was so unremarkable.

Two figures appeared on the walk, and Glen quickly added paint to his brush and resumed painting. The neighbor lady waved to him as she and Emma paused at the door of her cottage, and Glen returned a cheery smile. Then Emma came on, smiling. Her face was tanned from their months in the sun, and she wore the yellow print dress she had bought last week in a shop in the city after he convinced her it was not at all too youthful a style. In her hand she carried her birding book and yes, an envelope addressed in Ethel's familiar hand.

"Did you see any new birds?" he asked, not to show too immediate an interest in the mail. He tried a stroke of pale blue on the horizon of his painting, but the effect was still not quite right.

"I think I glimpsed a Mexican junco, but it flew too quickly out of sight. Look, a letter from Oren and Ethel. I was beginning to worry that we hadn't heard from them in a while."

She sat on a chair beside him, opened the envelope, and began to read. "February 8. Dear Emma and Glen. I'm sorry we've been delayed in writing, but some puzzling events have occurred, and we didn't want to alarm you until we uncovered the full circumstances. . . ." Emma's voice trailed, and she scanned anxiously down the page.

"What is it?" Glen sat forward, and Emma picked up reading in mid-paragraph.

". . . had been checking on the house every two weeks and everything seemed fine. But when we visited at the end of January, Lillian did not answer our knock. At first we thought she might be on an errand, but the car was there, so we walked out back to look for her. It was when we passed the chicken coop that we knew something was wrong. The eggs had not been gathered, the hens' feed had run out, and half a dozen of the poor creatures were dead, whether from hunger, the cold, or both, we couldn't tell. We fed the ones remaining, then hurried back to the front door and used the key you left us to enter. The house was ice cold, as if it hadn't been heated in days, but although we searched everywhere we found no clue as to Lillian's whereabouts, no message nor anything out of place.

"We then crossed the road and inquired of the Andersons. Mrs. Anderson recalled seeing Lillian about a week before, but since then the weather had been so bitter cold that no one had ventured out much. We went on to Stringer's, and on checking your account John Stringer said Lillian had last come in on the 17th but said nothing amiss to him. With his help we made further inquiries around town and even located Lillian's parents in Nankin. They hadn't heard from her and apparently cared not to. All this took several days, and finally, having produced no results, we turned to the police. They, too, are baffled, but since no crime has been committed, no theft or damage of your property, no sign that Lillian was the victim of foul play, they assume she has left of her own free will and cannot be considered a missing person. No one in Livonia knows what to make of this, and although I fault Lillian for deserting her place without a word and causing such distress, still I feel uneasy for her and hope she is all right."

Emma paused in her reading and took a deep breath.

"How strange!" said Glen. "If she wanted to leave, why didn't she at least let us know?"

Emma shook her head. "I don't know. But there's more."

She found her place and continued reading.

"Meanwhile, a second strange event has occurred. Since Lillian's disappearance we have been at the house more frequently to be sure all is well. The Anderson boy, Amos, is taking care of the chickens and delivering eggs by bicycle to your customers, so you needn't worry about that. But Mrs. Anderson told us that twice last week she saw men arrive by car and walk along the road, gesturing at your property as if making plans, and yesterday when Oren and I were there, three men appeared. They said they were real estate investors, ready to offer a fair price for your land, which they planned to turn into a subdivision. Oren said there must be some mistake, that the farm was not for sale, but they said, quite adamantly, that your agent was handling the transaction while you and Glen were in New Mexico. Oren demanded to know the agent's name, and they said it was Mr. Horace Kingsley."

Emma gasped and lowered the letter. Glen shook himself, not sure he had heard right. Horace Kingsley? He could barely remember the last time anyone in the family had even spoken that name, and it took a conscious effort to call up a faded mental image of his uncle. Emma had wet her lips, and strengthening her voice she read the rest of Ethel's account.

"So you see, we didn't know what to think. Back at Christmas time, my mother said a man calling himself Horace Kingsley appeared at our house while we were out and left candy canes for Laura and Jimmy. But he never called again, and Oren felt sure you would have advised us if you had made some arrangement with your brother. But perhaps you did write and your letter went astray? And did you know about Lillian? Have you heard from her? All is fine at the house, but please answer by return post and let us know the situation.

"I will save the chitchat for another time and only send our best wishes that Glen's health continues to improve. Love from all, Ethel."

Emma's face had gone white beneath her tan. "Horace," she breathed.

Glen shook his head. "It doesn't make sense. Is there some connection between him and Lillian?"

"Not that I can imagine." Emma rose, the letter clenched in her fist. "Lillian." She spit the word. "I always knew that girl was bad, and I blame myself for ever letting her in the house. I'm glad she has gone and good riddance. But Horace—" She began to pace, and Glen spoke soothingly to calm her.

"It's all right, Mother. There's probably a logical explanation. Perhaps it's the same real estate company that's building Rosedale Gardens, and they're scouting out other locations. They could easily have heard from someone in town that we were away."

"But Horace." Emma gripped the letter tighter, and when Glen stood and tried to guide her to a chair, she brushed free. "You don't understand. Horace is wicked. You don't know half the things he has done. The way he treated poor Charlotte, the time he was arrested for cheating Helga Witt. He used to substitute inferior building materials on carpentry jobs all over town, and I still hear complaints about his shoddy work from the people he shortchanged."

Her pacing grew more agitated, but for the moment Glen said nothing, too absorbed with the information his mother had just revealed. Horace arrested? Who was Helga Witt? What shoddy carpentry jobs? He had a sudden feeling that there was much about his uncle he had never been told. And what did his mother mean by saying she had always known Lillian was bad? Emma was still pacing, her movements jerky and distraught, and Glen set his curiosity aside. The main thing to do now was to reassure her.

"It's all right, Mother, don't fret. Whatever Uncle Horace is up to, he can't sell our farm. His name isn't on the deed, is it? And you've never authorized him to be your agent, have you? So you see, there's nothing to worry about. He can't sell something he doesn't own."

"But you don't know Horace. He cheats, he's underhanded, unscrupulous." Emma let out a breath and rubbed her arms as if to comfort herself while letting Glen's words sink in. "Yes, you're right. He has no title to the property. He'll be found out and caught at some point in his scheme. Still, it worries me. He's capable of such dishonesty, Glen. Could he forge the papers somehow, make it look as if he has rights to our farm? My mind is so upset. . . ."

"Then we must go back."

It cost him an effort to say it, and although his voice was firm, his eyes turned to the desert vista and regret sighed in his heart. He had expected to die here, he was ready, and it couldn't be much longer, a month or six weeks at most. The thought of packing, uprooting, the tiring journey by train back to the frigid Michigan winter, was like having to reshoulder a burden he had cast off, and already it seemed to cut his strength by half.

"But that would interrupt your cure. We can't do that, not when your temperature is falling and the monthly examinations show your chest is stable."

A fond light appeared in Emma's eyes, and she smiled at her son. Feebly, Glen smiled back.

"Yes, my cure," he said uncomfortably, then an idea came to his rescue. "Maybe you should go alone, just to find out what's going on. I'll be fine here until you return." It would also, he reflected, allow his health to take an unexpected turn for the worse during Emma's absence and release him from the deception he had begun. Then his heart squeezed in warning, and he opened his mouth as if to suck back the words. If he worsened or even died while Emma was away, she would blame herself, adding guilt to her grief.

"No, we'd better go together," he corrected, as Emma said simultaneously, "No, we'll both stay here." She shrugged one shoulder as if it twitched and bothered her. "Going back would be a little expensive and probably unnecessary. You're right—Horace can't sell what he doesn't own. I'll write to Oren immediately and set the matter straight. We're not going home until you're completely well."

She kissed his forehead and went into the cottage to fetch stationery and a pen. Glen stared at his unfinished painting. Damn! The oath was so rare that he followed it with a heavy sigh of apology. He had accepted and neatly reconciled everything about his dying, except for acknowledging what it would do to his mother. Emma and Glen. Always close, they had become, after his father's death, a self-sufficient unit, a story unto themselves, and he could not in good conscience abandon her even by dying. Oh yes, his mother was strong, everyone said so, but the source of her strength was him. Now he was deserting her, and the best he could do was go quickly, so she could return to Michigan and protect herself from whatever trouble Horace Kingsley was brewing.

Glen lifted his head and gazed out at the glowing landscape. It was approaching sunset, and the glorious streaks of crimson and orange that fired the sky met the same burn of colors on the desert floor. Yes, now, let this short life be over, he thought, and he clenched his fists, wishing, knowing wishes were for fools.

Five

Spring. Spring at last. What a long, grim winter it had been.

Horace Kingsley gazed in pleasure at the passing countryside as he motored along in his blue Packard. It was a Wednesday afternoon in early April, and the withered earth had finally begun to revive from its imprisonment in the ice and snow. The grass had put out a declaration of fresh green. Tight new buds studded the bare branches of the trees, and although the temperature was still cool, there was a hint of mildness in the air and a promise of warmth from the sun that was pure welcome after the battering storms of winter. The past few months had battered Horace personally as well, felling him with a series of racking colds, draining his finances, thwarting his plans, and as he drove he tried to put to rest the memory of his misfortunes.

First, back in January, there had been that unlucky encounter between the real estate investors and Oren Millard at the Kingsley House. "A complete misunderstanding," Horace had assured his ruffled clients when they confronted him on their return to Detroit. "My grandson wasn't aware that my sister had decided to sell her farm, and he was only being protective." To further soothe them, he had produced a letter, dictated by himself and obligingly penned by a half-drunken Ginny, in which Emma wrote to him from New Mexico describing the expenses of Glen's treatment and begging him, as her trusted brother, to get the best possible price for her land so that her dear son might live and be restored to health. So feeling was the letter that Horace's eyes misted as he read it aloud. But then he had fallen ill and missed the opportunity to push the deal along, and the investors found another property better suited to their plans. Coughing and wheezing, Horace had had to start all over, nudging his connections, introducing himself to likely prospects, extolling the profits to be reaped from real estate development in Livonia, "Town of Opportunity." Spring was approaching, his tongue was getting tired, and his pockets were nearly empty when his luck finally turned. Now he had a buyer almost in the palm of his hand, and he did not intend to let anything spoil the game.

The car engine stopped, a sudden absence of noise, and Horace cursed as he felt the loss of power and the Packard glided silently to the side of the road. His fine automobile had taken to stalling for no apparent reason, and he hadn't the money to hire a mechanic for a repair. He turned the key in the ignition, muttering, "Come on, come on," and after a few tries the engine jumped back to life. Horace's spirits lifted, and he continued on his way. It was especially important that he get to Livonia today because his client was close to accepting his price, and then all that remained was the paperwork to close the sale.

Best of all, this time he would not have to settle for a mere sixty percent of the deal. The inspiration had dawned like a redeeming light after the collapse of his first effort in January, rallying him from the defeat. If Ginny could write a letter as Emma, why couldn't she simply *be* Emma? Properly dressed and sobered up, her peroxide blond hair dyed a mousey brown, she could look the part. It would obviate any need to involve the real Emma—a tricky business he hadn't entirely worked out the first time around. He and Ginny would go to a lawyer and have a power of attorney drawn up making Horace the legal agent for all transactions regarding the Kingsley House. In consequence, he could pocket one hundred percent of the sale. To speed the matter, he would even provide the lawyer with Emma's deed to the property. Lillian had told him just where to find it.

"Ish in 'er desk," she said, tapping her empty glass to indicate a refill. "Top draw'r, livin' room. Saw 'er take it out'n read it jus' before she'n Glen left."

Horace had poured her more whiskey and smiled. True to his promise, he had helped Lillian find a shopgirl position and a room at a boardinghouse in the city, but already she complained that her job was boring, the pay lousy, and the boardinghouse no fun at all. So Horace had introduced Lillian to Ginny, and anyone could see where that would lead. It surely wasn't his fault if some women were immoral by nature.

Horace helped himself to a swig from his flask and turned onto the road that led to Livonia Center. Getting into the house was no problem since Lillian had given him the key when she moved out, and today being a weekday there was little chance of encountering Oren and his family. Probably it would be best to make his entry after dark. In the meantime, it was a lovely day, and after a preliminary reconnaissance of Emma's place he would take that leisurely drive around Livonia he had promised himself back in December. It would be his grand farewell tour, for once the sale was complete and the cash in his hand, Horace's next destination was sunny Florida. This winter had convinced him that a life without snow and cold would suit him just fine.

At the crossroads by Stringer's Store, Horace turned north and slowed the car. He could see the Kingsley House ahead, but what were those cars doing parked out front? He pulled to the side of the road, frowning as he counted a half dozen vehicles. He was pondering this unexpected complication when the sound of bicycle tires crunching on the road behind him caused him to turn his head. A boy of about thirteen was pedaling his way, and Horace hastily rolled down the window and hailed him with a wave.

"Boy! Boy, stop a minute."

The lad braked and halted, tipping the bike so he could brace one foot on the ground.

"Yes, sir?"

"Boy, do you live hereabouts?"

"Right there." He pointed to the house across the street from Emma's, Horace's old home.

"Ah, good. Then perhaps you can tell me who is visiting today at your neighbor's." He nodded toward the Kingsley House. "I understood Mrs. McEachran and her son were away in New Mexico."

"Yes, sir, they were." The boy's round face, topped by a cowlick of blond hair, grew solemn with the duty of imparting momentous news. "But Mr. Glen died, and today is his funeral. They brought his body all the way from New Mexico in a train. He's been laid out in the parlor for people to pay their final respects, and he's to be buried at three o'clock. My ma is baking cakes for the tea after the service, and I just finished delivering Mrs. McEachran's eggs." He pointed to the empty wicker basket affixed to his handlebars, pink-cheeked with pride and responsibility for his role in this event.

"And how is Mrs. McEachran taking her son's death?" Horace inquired.

Gravely, the boy shook his head. "My ma says she is being very brave, but anyone can see her heart is broken because Mr. Glen was all she had and now she's all alone."

Horace nodded. "Well, you get along and help your mother."

"Yes, sir." The boy pedaled on.

Horace leaned back against his seat. Damn! Just when he was so close! Now what? He unscrewed his flask and soothed his frustration with a generous mouthful. If only Glen had had the sense to survive a month longer. Still, the neighbor boy's comments confirmed Horace's original musings on the outcome of the New Mexico sojourn. Glen was dead, and Emma was heartbroken. Most definitely, she wouldn't want the farm now. It was too much work, too much worry. Horace nodded agreement with himself as he gazed over the eighty acres. How fortunate that he had a buyer ready! Once he explained, Emma could not help but be grateful that he had taken this initiative on her behalf. Of course, it meant he would once again have to settle for sixty percent. . . . Horace gnawed his lip. Maybe he could still find some way around that.

He checked his watch. It was two-thirty now, and the cemetery was just down the road. If he reversed direction, he could park out of sight and observe those arriving for the service. In five minutes he was positioned as planned, and soon afterward a procession of cars came along the road from the Kingsley House. More autos appeared from other directions, while some neighbors arrived on foot, walking across the fields. At a distance and with all the mourners dressed in black, it was difficult at first to identify his own family, especially since he had not laid eyes on them in a great many years. But he soon picked out Emma by the deference the others showed her, making way for her to approach the grave site, offering a comforting hug or pat on the arm as she passed. The sight of the pallbearers carrying the casket into the cemetery effected a few more identifications, for it was only logical that R. Z., Oren, and Stub would be among them, and after some squinting Horace made them out. A little more spying revealed Gertrude, flanked by two young women, each tending a pair of small children—Oren's and Stub's families, no doubt. Then the crowd converged around the grave, and Horace saw only a collection of figures in black. It was not a large group, and he shivered as a sudden icy touch prickled the nape of his neck. How many people would come to *his* funeral? Who would stand mourning at his grave? The icy sensation trickled down his spine, and he shuddered like a dog to rid himself of its nasty feel. A man couldn't afford to think like that. Besides, his family would do right by him. Wasn't he about to do a great service for them?

Horace sat back, reassured, and watched until the funeral service ended and the company dispersed toward Emma's house. Surely the best way to begin his approach to his grieving sister was by appearing at the tea to pay his condolences. He smoothed his hair and checked his reflection in the rearview mirror, approving his most recent tonsorial dye job. Then he drove to the Kingsley House.

Everyone was already inside, and seeing no reason to inconvenience them by knocking, Horace let himself in the front door and scanned the scene. A buffet table had been set in the living room, and the guests, plates in hand, mingled and conversed in subdued tones. The crowd had seemed small at the cemetery, but here in the house it caused some pressing of shoulders, affording Horace a degree of anonymity as he edged to the buffet table. Most of his family were in the parlor adjoining, with the exception of Oren's and Stub's wives, who wouldn't recognize him. The neighbor boy's mother had prepared a generous spread of cakes, bread, cheese, cold cuts, and fruits, and Horace heaped his plate. No need to pass up a free meal.

He was finishing his repast and listening to the murmurs of conversation—mostly along the lines of "Glen was such a sweet young man"—when he bumped against an oak desk by the window. His wits snapped to attention. This must be the desk where Emma kept the deed. He set down his plate and glanced around the living room. None of his family had entered, and the two young wives were occupied greeting neighbors. An itchy feeling took possession of Horace's fingers. He sidled his hand behind his back and along the desk until he felt the handle of the top drawer. He slid it open, barely an inch, and it made not a squeak. Horace's heart leapt for joy. Fortune had smiled on him, the way was clear. All he had to do—Horace edged toward the door—was leave now—he squeezed against the wall to allow a stout man to pass—before anyone in the family saw him—Emma turned her head in his direction but he ducked to one side, averting his face—and return after dark when all the people were gone and Emma was asleep. He slipped out the front door and hurried to his car. He almost felt like kicking up his heels. Yes, why trouble Emma at all in her time of sorrow? She'd never even know the deed was missing. Then he could substitute Ginny for his sister, as planned, collect the full one hundred percent of the sale, and be off to Florida where endless sunshine and prosperity awaited him.

Horace got in his car and helped himself to a congratulatory swig from his flask. When he lowered it, a small girl of about six years old, wide blue eyes and brunette hair, was staring at him.

"I know you," she said. Her mouth pursed in a frown. "You're a bad man."

"What?" Horace nearly spluttered out his swallow of whiskey. Who was this impertinent child? She looked familiar, and after a moment he placed her. Oren's daughter—she had come to the door with her grandmother that day before Christmas; he had left her a candy cane. What was her name? Laura.

"Why were you inside my Aunt Emma's house?" she asked.

"Why, to pay my respects to your dear aunt, of course." Horace spread his lips to reveal his fine, white smile. If the child snitched on him, his scheme would be ruined. "What makes you say I am a bad man? Haven't your parents taught you that isn't polite?"

"It is my daddy who says you are bad," the girl replied. "When my grandma told him you came to our house, he said he would never let you inside." She drew back, crossed her arms, and eyed him, as if imitating a disdainful pose by one of her elders.

"Well then, you needn't worry, because I am going away and never coming back. Does that suit you?"

Horace continued smiling, and after a thoughtful moment the child relaxed her stance and nodded.

"Yes."

"Good, then we're settled. Don't bother about me anymore. Run along and enjoy yourself. Eat lots of cake."

He made a genial shooing motion with his hand, and after weighing the alternatives and licking her lips, the girl scampered away. Horace started the car and drove off. *A bad man.* So that was how the family thought of him, that was the tale they passed on to their children. The injustice of it! The untruth! After he had driven all the way out here today to lend his support in their time of tragedy and grief. Did they ever care to hear his side of the story, try to see his point of view?

With a heavy heart, Horace drove to the crossroads and continued southward. The hum of the Packard's engine soothed him and recalled him to his plan. The sun would set in less than two hours, then he could return to Emma's, park out of sight, and wait for the lights to go out. Meanwhile, he was not about to let a rude child's comment spoil his anticipated drive around the town. He always felt better motoring along at the wheel of his car.

In a few miles he came upon a sign that said "Rosedale Gardens." On the tract of land beyond, a crew of workers was leveling an old farm-house, and farther on he spotted more men setting stakes for building lots, marking paths for roads, and digging sewer lines. He got out of his car and had a pleasant chat with the road crew, who described for him the neat rows of modern houses to be erected on the site.

"I'm in real estate myself," Horace told them, cheered by this vision of the future he was bringing to the Kingsley farm. "It's good to see progress coming to this town."

He drove eastward and by chance passed the Brigham house where he had been the unseen helper in that long-ago seance with Professor and Mrs. What's-Their-Names. Horace laughed aloud and had another drink. This was beginning to be fun. He motored here and there, past Silas Joslin's old house—twice-dead skunks, ha!—past homes that had benefited from his excellent carpentry jobs. Yes, those were the good old days. By the time the sun was down, Horace was feeling quite jovial and his whiskey was nearly gone. He had driven a little north of town, and in the glowing sunset, he started back toward Emma's.

Now, once and for all, his fate was going to come out right. He could almost feel the deed to the Kingsley House in his hand. And really, wasn't this how it should have turned out anyway? Shouldn't he have been the one to inherit the house in the first place? Wasn't it only just that all proceeds from the sale belonged to him? Life was not always fair, and people did not always get what they deserved, and often it had been up to him to bravely set matters right. Horace slurped the last of his whiskey and straightened with satisfied pride to think that once again he was single-handedly balancing the cosmic scale of justice. Let Emma betake herself to an old ladies' home or go to live with Gertrude or Oren. After the way his family had treated him, they deserved—fools that they were—this comeuppance at his hand. A bad man, indeed!

He had just driven up the rise to the railroad tracks when the engine stopped and the Packard coasted to a halt. Horace felt the bump as the wheels passed onto the rails. Twilight was gathering, and there were no other cars on the road. He tried the ignition, and the car gave out a reluctant grrrr. Damn. If it wasn't one thing, it was another. Horace sat back to wait a bit, not wanting to drain the battery. A minute later, his eyes blinked open and he shook his head. Had he dozed off? He ran his tongue inside his mouth. It tasted stale with whiskey, and his eyes peered blearily into the growing dark. He tried the ignition again. No luck. Horace's eyelids dropped closed. He dreamed he heard a rumbling noise and some rude character shouting at him, "Move! Move!"

"All right, all right," Horace muttered, rousing himself and fumbling for the key. Outside it was dark, and he half glimpsed a strange man running toward him, frantically waving his arms. The whole car was vibrating, and a wind seemed to be rushing at him from one side. What was that roaring noise anyway?

"Train!" a voice screamed, and with a jerk and a gasp Horace turned toward the roar. A great white light was bearing down upon him, its demon whistle shrieking in his ears. He grabbed the steering wheel and ground the ignition with all his might. He must get to Emma's, must get what was his, must—

The blinding light smashed into him, and Horace screamed. His Packard! His beloved car!

Then Horace and his automobile slammed along the track in a fury of hellish noise, tumbling, crashing into darkness, moving no more.

Six

"They say death always comes in threes," said Gertrude. "This gives me such an ominous feeling."

Emma flinched. They were standing over the fresh dirt of Horace's grave in Livonia Center Cemetery. There had been no memorial service, no other family in attendance, no pretense of mourning. She and Gertrude had shared the cost of a casket and had ordered a small granite headstone. The undertaker had arranged for men to dig the grave and transport Horace to his final resting place.

"But he's *not* to be buried next to my mother," Gertrude decreed. Instead they found a space for him a short distance apart, a not unpleasant spot but far enough away to ensure that Charlotte's eternal rest should in no way be disturbed.

Gertrude strolled over to visit the graves of her mother and her four siblings. Emma remained staring at Horace's grave, as if it could yield the answers she sought. She had barely fallen asleep the night of Glen's funeral when the police officer pounded on her door. Horace killed by a train? Here in Livonia? How? Why? She hastened with the officer to the scene, but it was well after dark and despite the lanterns that had been procured to illuminate the railroad tracks, Emma could not comprehend the scope of the accident. It wasn't until she returned the next morning in daylight that she was able to picture the event and confirm the details given by the police. Horace's Packard had been struck by a sixty-car freight train, which carried the automobile a hundred and fifty feet along the tracks before dropping it into a deep ditch. The man who saw the accident had been out walking his dog at the time. He said that when he shouted, the figure in the car seemed to jerk awake and try to start the engine. Why the driver didn't jump out of the car and save his own life, the witness couldn't say.

Horace's body had already been taken to the morgue, and Emma watched as the police supervised the removal of his automobile from the ditch. The blue Packard was crushed and crumpled, twisted in the middle, one door torn off, the headlights and windshield shattered, the fenders askew. The car looked as if a giant fist had smashed into it, destroying it with a single blow. It was hard to know, the policeman said, whether Horace had died instantly or not until the car landed in the ditch. Emma preferred not to think about that.

But what had Horace been up to that night? Nothing good, she felt sure. The mystery had only deepened when, two days later, Laura piped up with her story of seeing him in Emma's very house.

"Are you sure, Laura?" Ethel had coaxed. "Are you sure you're not mistaken?"

"I'm positive, Mama! He was eating cake in the living room, and I followed him outside."

Meanwhile, the police had located Horace's address, a hotel in Detroit, and Emma and Gertrude had proposed a visit to see what else they could learn. R. Z. forestalled them.

"That's not a respectable neighborhood," he said, frowning. "Oren, Stub, and I will go."

The men returned with the news that the hotelkeeper, a thin, scar-faced man, knew and cared little about his tenants' doings. He had already confiscated Horace's meager belongings as compensation for his overdue bills.

"He let us into Horace's room," said R. Z., "and we found this letter from you, Emma, written from New Mexico, asking him to sell the house on your behalf." He offered her a handwritten sheet.

"But I never wrote this! That's not my writing. It's a forgery!"

"There were a few other papers," R. Z. added, "bits and pieces about cooked-up business schemes that apparently never got off the ground. I've brought them back if you and Gert want to see them."

"We also found Lillian," said Oren.

"Drunk as a skunk and chumming around with a blond floozy," said Stub. "Excuse my language," he added, as Oren jabbed him in the ribs.

"Well, at least I will notify Lillian's family of her whereabouts," said Emma. "It's up to them to contact her, if they wish."

Now Horace was buried, the second time in four days, Emma reflected, that she had stood in the cemetery for a funeral. She felt dis-

jointed, her emotions at odds. Horace's violent end had jarred and confused her at a time when she wanted only to grieve for Glen. She
walked over to her husband's and son's graves and was gazing at the
empty plot between them when Gertrude touched her shoulder.

"Shall we go back and have a cup of tea?"

They walked to the Kingsley House. The day was balmy, crocus and
daffodils in bloom along the road, and after brewing the tea they sat
drinking it on the front porch.

"Remember when you and Joe were married, and you gave me your
bouquet?" said Gertrude. "You said I should be next, and I was."

"That was hardly a difficult prediction. Anyone could see from the
way you flirted with R. Z. that poor young man didn't stand a chance."

"And I suppose you never blew a kiss to Joe when your parents' backs
were turned?"

"How young we were," said Emma. "How happy."

Gertrude sighed. "I'm sorry. I shouldn't have brought up those glad
memories when you are grieving."

"It's all right. I can't ask you or anyone else to hold their tongue and
never speak of happiness again just to spare me. When I fell in love with
Joe I told him I wanted to play a real part in life, not sit in the audience
to watch and applaud. Well, now I have. I have had a husband and a son
and lost them both, and although it hurts more than I could ever have
dreamed—"

Tears sprang to Emma's eyes, and Gertrude bounded from her chair
and folded her in her arms.

"Yes, cry, Emma, cry," she said, choking on her own tears, and for a
long time the two women clung together weeping.

"You have children," said Emma finally, drying her eyes. "And grandchildren." She spoke without envy or reproach. "Do you know I rejoice
in that? Even though they aren't mine, it lets me believe that in some
way I shall be carried on through them. Is that selfish of me, Gert? Do
you mind?"

"Of course not. Haven't we always been more like sisters than
cousins? And didn't Oren say that when he and Stub were little your
house was their second home? You mothered them almost as much as
you did Glen." Impulsively, Gertrude clasped her hands. "Emma, I will
share my grandchildren with you. Whatever stake I have in them, I give
you half."

"Oh, Gert, what an idea!" Emma brushed away a last tear. "You
always were a silly dear. But you cannot know how much that thought

means to me. I suppose it's only human to want to feel we've left some good behind when we are gone."

They sat a while longer, then Gertrude rose to go. "Will you be all right here alone? Perhaps we should find another hired girl to keep you company and help with the chores?"

"No. Thank you, Gert, but for now I would rather be by myself."

Gertrude nodded and bid farewell. Emma took the teacups into the kitchen, then some inner prompting drew her outside onto the small back porch. It was here that her father Nathan used to sit in his last days, gazing over his eighty acres while the sun set on his land. There was no chair here now, and the afternoon sun was still high, but Emma sat on the step and surveyed her farm.

She felt nothing.

The land was overgrown, ragged with the debris of winter. In her vegetable garden, the dead, yellowed plants Lillian had failed to clear away last autumn trailed in disorder on the ground. Joe's old greenhouse, unused for many years, was an eyesore of grimy and broken glass panes. The orchard, though new leaves would soon appear, still looked gnarled and bare. The chicken coop needed repairs. The barn roof sagged.

Emma looked at it all and felt neither anger nor despair, inspiration nor sorrow. She felt nothing.

"Perhaps it is the shock," she murmured, but in the days that followed, her mood did not change. She saw herself with Glen in New Mexico, hopeful and happy as his condition seemed to improve and he painted in the sun. She saw the two of them with Joe in earlier days, picking apples, strolling along the creek, laughing in the parlor as they helped Joe rehearse for one of his plays. But when she looked around her empty house or gazed over her neglected land, no emotions came. She was sitting on the back porch, a week after Horace's burial, when a knock sounded at the front door. Emma walked back through the house to answer.

"Mrs. McEachran?" A stout, jowly man in a gray suit and red vest doffed his hat. "My name is Vincent Malloy. I knew your brother, Horace Kingsley. So sorry, so sorry." He bobbed his head, the large bald patch on his scalp gleaming through the stringy brown hair he had carefully plastered over it.

"You knew Horace?" Emma repeated.

"Yes, ma'am. So sorry. We were about to strike a deal for your property, him being your agent, when this terrible accident occurred. I regret not having sent you my condolences earlier. It was only when Mr. Kingsley did not show up for our scheduled appointment two days ago and I made inquiries at his hotel that I learned his fate. So sorry, ma'am." Mr. Malloy clapped his hat back on his head and spread his pudgy hands in a gesture of sympathy. "Mr. Kingsley told me you were with your son in New Mexico, and knowing how pressed you were to sell your farm, and this property being to my liking, I determined to come to Livonia and ask if anyone in town could tell me how to contact you. But I see you have returned yourself—of course, you came back on being notified of Mr. Kingsley's tragic passing."

"I came back to bury my son," Emma corrected automatically, and Mr. Malloy's face fell.

"So sorry, ma'am. My condolences." He shook his head and pressed a hand to his heart.

"Did you know my brother well?" Emma asked, curious.

"No, ma'am, can't say I did. Purely a business transaction. That is why I am here today, though I will not stay to trouble you in your bereavement. Simply let me say that I remain interested in purchasing your property, and if you care to sell I would be pleased to negotiate with you or your representative."

"What plans do you have for my farm?" Emma asked. "I'm afraid it is quite run down."

"Oh, no matter, no matter. Clearly, its days as a farm are over. I plan to erect a modern subdivision, along the lines of Rosedale Gardens. Do you know it?" Mr. Malloy bobbed his head, the buttons of his red vest threatening to pop as his stout form swelled in his eagerness. "Soon, subdivisions like this will spread all over your fine little town. It's quite the up-and-coming place. In fact, if you like, you could keep your house and a quarter acre or so and just sell me the remaining land. That way you could partake of all the advantages the new subdivision will offer without moving from this spot. I may even call it 'Kingsley Park.' What do you think about that?"

He beamed, and Emma gave a crooked smile.

"I'd like to think about it."

"Of course, of course. Here is my card." He withdrew a printed card from his pocket and warmly pressed it into her hand. "Call me as soon as you have made up your mind. Good day, good day."

He doffed his hat and bundled himself down the steps to his car, waving as he drove away. Emma went inside, the card in the palm of her hand.

Over the next few days, she was very busy. She cleaned house, raked the yard, cleared the dead plants from the vegetable garden. She visited a lawyer and the bank in Plymouth and paid off her outstanding account at Stringer's. She gave Glen's clothes to a charity, his garments being too small for any of the Millard men. From the watercolors in Glen's room, she selected his three favorites and wrapped and labeled one apiece for Gert and R. Z., Oren and Ethel, Stub and Anna. Emma smiled at her arrangements. Always sensible, always practical, right to the end.

On the last day she went to Stringer's and bought shells for Joe's old shotgun to deal with a fox, which, she told John Stringer, had been visiting her chicken coop.

"By the way, John," she said. "I want to move the piano across the parlor, but I can't budge it alone. Could you stop by tomorrow to lend me a hand?"

"Be glad to, Emma," John replied. "I'll come first thing in the morning before I open the store."

She left and walked to the cemetery. The day was blissful, the trees bursting with tiny green leaves, the sun uncommonly warm. Emma sat on the ground between Joe's and Glen's graves. It was a bit unseemly for a woman her age to deposit herself in such a position, but she liked the solid, grassy feel of the earth beneath her, and she breathed deeply as its rich, warm scent, that smell of softening earth you got only in spring, rose to her nostrils. She imagined Joe's and Glen's arms around her, hugging her, just as she had felt Joe's touch in that tender dream last fall.

She could go on, of course. She knew how to be stoic, how to bear loss and persevere. But her heart wasn't in it, and hadn't Joe once told her that a good actor always knew when to get off the stage? This play was over, and she had acted it the best she could. Now it was time for someone else to take a new role. She stood and planted a kiss from her lips to her fingers and onto each grave.

"I'll be with you soon," she said, and feeling happy, Emma walked home.

Seven

Ethel Millard sat beside her husband Oren and quietly fingered the bracelet of colored stones that encircled her left wrist. They were in the parlor of the Kingsley House, along with Gertrude and R. Z., Stub and Anna, waiting for the lawyer to begin reading Emma's will. Ethel's finger traced a blue stone, and the color made her think of Glen's sky blue eyes. The bracelet was the same one she had tossed into the grass that day of the picnic last September, her ploy to divert Lillian's suspicions when the hired girl intruded on her and Glen sitting in the field. Innocent as their conversation had been, she was glad they had preserved it for themselves. It was her last special memory of him.

"Let us begin," said the lawyer, Mr. Norris Baines of Plymouth. He was a small, elderly man, wisps of white hair floating above his ears, and his voice had a soothing, feathery quality. "I, Emma Kingsley McEachran," he read, "being of sound body and mind—"

Ethel pressed her teeth against her lower lip. Some people would say Emma's mind was not sound to do what she did, and although no one they could name had stayed away from the funeral that morning, the mood was more somber and glum than it had been for Glen. Gertrude was especially distraught, her face pale and ragged from crying.

"This is my fault," she had wept. "I should never have left her alone. And that stupid, superstitious comment I made about death coming in threes. What if that put the idea in her head?" She sobbed afresh on R. Z.'s shoulder, while he tried in vain to comfort her.

Mr. Baines finished the opening paragraph and commenced the division of Emma's estate. The legal language was foreign to Ethel's ears, but the gist of it seemed to be that after her outstanding debts were settled, Emma wished her goods and property to be divided equally among her three closest relatives: Gertrude, Oren, and Stub. How could you divide a farm three ways? Ethel wondered, as vague, sad thoughts flitted through another level of her mind. What if—heaven forbid!—she had lost her husband and children? Would she, could she, have done as Emma did? Ethel rubbed her bracelet, wishing she could leave the room, but she knew her duty as an in-law, and she tried to pay closer heed to the lawyer's words.

"Now we don't know the full extent of Mrs. McEachran's debts, but there is a considerable outstanding mortgage on the property," he said.

"The farm is mortgaged?" Oren shook his head, and R. Z. and Stub looked skeptical. "Emma never told us that."

"Oh yes," said Mr. Baines. He drew another paper from his briefcase. "Mrs. McEachran obtained the mortgage last autumn to finance her son's treatment in New Mexico. That money has been expended, and she was unable to make any repayments. This is the statement from her bank."

He offered it to Gertrude, who sat nearest, but she waved it away to R. Z. as if the matter hurt her too much to contemplate. R. Z. turned to show the others, and Oren and Stub drew close. Ethel glanced to Anna, who hunched her shoulders in uncertainty, as if to say, let the men take care of this. Both women had left their children with Ethel's mother in Detroit for the day, thinking a second funeral in such a short time not good for them.

"So we inherit the farm, but what about the debt?" said Stub. His lips pressed in a doubtful expression. "I'm sure Emma meant well, but I can't afford this, and what would we do with a farm anyway?"

"But we can't let the bank foreclose on it." Oren ran his hand into his thick, dark hair and scratched his scalp, as if trying to coax a solution from his brain. "Emma loved this place. You know what it meant to her. She wanted to pass it on to us."

"To do what with?" R. Z. cast an apprehensive glance toward Gertrude. "No one's blaming Emma for leaving the place in debt, but even if we could pay it off, we're none of us farmers. What with Glen's death, then Horace's, Emma just wasn't thinking straight."

"Gentlemen, please—" Mr. Baines's fluttery voice garnered no notice as the men began to debate.

"We should sell the farm or let the bank auction it," said Stub. "That'll pay off the mortgage, and we'll get whatever is left."

"No." Oren's voice rose, not angry but adamant. "That's not what Emma would have wanted."

"Then she should have told us what she wanted." Stub's voice climbed in proportion to Oren's. "She seems to have planned everything else, drawing up her will, getting a statement from the bank, arranging for John Stringer to find her over some excuse of moving the piano." Stub turned on the attorney. "Did you know what she intended?"

"No, no, not at all!" Mr. Baines put up two frail hands in self-defense. "Believe me, if I'd had any inkling I would have counseled her to turn to her family for help. All she requested was that I draw up her will. She said that with her son's passing, it was the sensible thing to do. But she also left a sealed letter, and if you'll please let me continue . . ."

The men quieted as the lawyer produced a buff-colored envelope. Ethel laid her fingers over her husband's hand. Only this week they'd received word that Oren had gained his promotion at Ford and would soon be transferred to the Rouge River plant. But the three deaths the family had just endured had stolen away the inclination to celebrate. Maybe later, Ethel thought, when all this is resolved. Oren has worked so hard, we can't let his accomplishment pass without notice.

Mr. Baines opened the envelope, and as he extracted the folded sheet, a small white card fell out upon the floor. He retrieved it, pursed his lips in a curious glance, then began to read the letter. Ethel tried to imagine Emma's voice.

"My dear family. I am so sorry for the distress I'm sure I have caused you. Please don't grieve. I'm where I belong—with Joe and Glen—and though others may call my final act a sin, I know it cannot be because my mind is so at peace. By now you have heard my formal will. I made it to be the fairest and most logical disposition of my property. But my true last wishes are contained in this letter, and I believe with Mr. Baines's legal assistance, you may find a way to honor them. Number one—"

Ethel started and felt the rest of the family do likewise. Number one? Here was a woman planning to take her own life, and she penned a letter with step-by-step recommendations? A small smile crept on

Ethel's face in spite of herself. It seemed Emma had been perfectly sane after all.

"—I apologize for leaving the farm in a state of debt. What with our sanatorium expenses, Glen's funeral, Horace's burial, it was more than I could hope to repay in chickens and eggs. It would have been braver to settle this by selling the farm myself, but I could not face the thought of turning over to a stranger the land I have lived on all my life. If you must do so, at least I shall be spared seeing it. Two—"

Ethel almost chuckled. She could hear Emma's voice clearly now, brisk and no-nonsense, laying out her plans.

"—it seems Horace has done us a service after all. Enclosed is the business card of Mr. Vincent Malloy. Horace had arranged to sell him my property, and he is still interested in the purchase. I do not entirely trust him—he wears a red vest—but I don't believe he is dishonest, and if you negotiate smartly you may obtain a good price. Find out how much that real estate company paid for Rosedale Gardens, because that is what Mr. Malloy intends to make of my eighty acres. The sum will guide you as to the amount you should get. But please do *not* allow him to name the subdivision 'Kingsley Park.' I do not want that."

Mr. Baines paused, and Ethel saw R. Z. shake his head in amusement.

"A red vest?" he muttered.

"Don't you laugh. Don't you dare laugh," huffed Gertrude.

"I wasn't laughing, Gert. I was only commenting."

"Well, it sounded like you meant to laugh."

Mr. Baines raised his wispy eyebrows at them and obtained silence. "Three—This is what I truly hope may happen. I think there is one of you who cares for this place as I do, perhaps not as deeply yet, but the feeling is real and in time it will grow. In that case, I leave the Kingsley House and all eighty acres of land to you. I don't expect you to give up your job and become a farmer. I am the last generation of my family born to do that. But Mr. Malloy offered another option, namely to sell him the land but keep the house and a small lot to live upon. This should settle my debts, and to know that the house, at least, has gone to someone who loves it, would give me great content. If you want it, say so now because this isn't a matter to be settled by ponderous thought. It is either in your heart, or not."

The lawyer stopped and peered expectantly, craning his head from Gertrude to Oren to Stub.

R. Z. let out an exasperated breath. "What kind of riddle is this? Do you know what she means, Gert?"

"Is that letter even legal?" Stub broke in. "The will says we're to divide the estate three ways, now she's leaving it all to one of us?"

"Does whoever takes the farm become responsible for the debt?" Anna asked. "I'm afraid I don't understand."

R. Z. and Stub began a fresh debate. Mr. Baines attempted to calm them, accompanying his feathery voice with reassuring motions of his hands. Oren turned to Ethel. A flicker of apprehension showed in his eyes, and his lips were parted as if he'd sucked in a breath and hadn't yet let it out. No wonder, thought Ethel, reading his expression and feeling a strange answering sensation in the pit of her stomach. He's just had a message from the dead.

Her thoughts began to reel, and she glanced around the parlor and gave her head a slight shake. Live here? In Livonia? Yes, it was a fine house for its age, but not modern, no electricity, no facilities, no city conveniences. And what about Oren's job? His promotion? He wouldn't give that up, and the Rouge River plant would be a long daily drive, though she supposed it could be done. But still, why up and move when they were perfectly content in their house in Detroit? And what about her mother? Mama hated the country; she would never consent. Ethel bit her lip. Oren was staring at her, his expression torn.

"She means me," he whispered.

"I know," she whispered back. "What should we do?"

"I don't know."

They clasped hands and looked about them. R. Z. and Stub were bent over Emma's will, the letter, and bank statement. Irritation grated in their voices as Mr. Baines tried to resolve the conflicting documents. Gertrude had become tearful again and dabbed her eyes with her handkerchief, weeping, "This is all my fault." Anna moved closer to console her, her usually perky demeanor deflated and a weary expression pulling down the corners of her mouth. Everyone's trying to bear up, thought Ethel, but we're all sad and tense and tired. These past few weeks have been so hard.

She looked again at Oren. He was glancing around the parlor, his gaze pausing on the wallpaper, sofa, curtains, floor. He seemed to be trying to find in himself some connection to the house, to test the truth of Emma's words. And he did feel it. Ethel could see it in his eyes, suffusing his face and body, an intensifying of memories and emotions he had known so well as a child. But he wouldn't speak unless he knew it was her wish also, and her heart began to flutter in a mixture of protest, hope, and fear. This wasn't fair, to leave it up to her. She'd hardly had to make any serious decisions in all her life. Her mother had taken care of that until she married; then she'd naturally let Oren assume control. What on earth am I to do? she thought. I want to make Oren happy, but I can't desert Mama, can I? And what's best for the children? Let me think, let me think. She heard Emma's voice as she'd imagined it in the letter: This isn't a matter for ponderous thought. It has to come from your heart.

"Laura could climb the big maple tree," she said, and stopped, not knowing quite how the words had popped out.

Oren's head snapped around to her. The rest of the family's eyes followed. Her comment had fallen into a momentary lull in the debate, and the words hung like an echo in the air.

"What?" said Gertrude.

Oren stood. "Ethel and I will take the farm, or the house, or however it's to be managed." His voice started on a waver, then grew certain. "It was me Emma meant in her letter."

"But what about the will?" said Stub. "Aren't we obligated to follow it?"

"And what about the debts?" added R. Z. "I've enough of my own."

"May I propose a solution?" Mr. Baines raised a gentle hand, and this time everyone paid heed as the lawyer explained that Gertrude and Stub could renounce their share in the farm—and the debt—in favor of Oren.

"Then we come up with nothing," said Stub. "Some inheritance."

"No, I'll make up the value to you somehow." An eagerness shone in Oren's face, and Ethel felt herself growing excited. "Mr. Baines could write up an agreement for us."

"But what will you do with the place?" Stub persisted.

"I don't know. I only know Emma meant me."

"And I want Emma's wishes to be followed." Gertrude stood, her voice teary but strong. "You take my share, Oren, and do what you think is right. No, R. Z.," she shook her head to forestall her husband's protests, "this is my decision."

Oren hugged her, then turned to his brother. "Stub?" He spread his hands in a plea.

"Well, I guess that's all right," Stub grumbled, "so long as we all come out fair. You won't catch me riding a plow, that's for sure."

Oren drew Ethel up beside him, and they clasped arms as if to seal a pact. And to hold me up, thought Ethel. She felt giddy, and in a minute she expected a host of complications, things she hadn't even considered, to come flooding in on her.

"I need a little fresh air," she whispered. "I'll just step outside."

Oren grinned and planted a kiss on her forehead, and she made her way out the front door. She stood, hands pressed flat on the porch railing, drawing in deep breaths. Well, now you've done it, she told herself. Are you crazy?

The April sky was cornflower blue, and her thoughts threatened to scatter like butterflies in the breeze if she did not pull them together. She glanced to the crossroads, and there stood the big maple tree, a shimmer of green outlining its branches where the sunlight fell on the new leaves. She stared at it a long minute, absorbing a sense of quiet strength. Then she turned slowly in a semicircle, looking over the Kingsley land, until her back was to the porch railing and she faced the front door. On a table in the living room, Emma had left for them three flat packages, a painting apiece to remember Glen by. Actually, Glen had sent her and Oren a painting from New Mexico just before he died. It was the view, he said, from their cottage, a sweep of rugged mountains and flaming desert canopied by a cerulean sky. Glen had addressed the painting to "Oren and Ethel," but somehow she had the feeling he meant it especially for her.

Her eyes searched the front of the Kingsley House. The day had been full of tossed emotions, and she hardly knew which of them to trust. Already another feeling was coming, rising inside her, and it surprised her when it reached her lips.

"*My* house," she said. "My husband. My children. My home."

She shook her head. It wasn't like her to be boastful, yet the words almost sounded familiar. Had she heard them spoken by someone else, sometime before? I suppose I could give piano lessons to the children here as easily as in Detroit, she thought. And instead of going to the big Rouge plant, maybe Oren could transfer to one of the small factories along the river valley, so he works closer to home. And the grade school, the same one he went to, is right down the road for Laura and Jimmy. We could put in a modern bathroom. I think we'll give the chickens to the Andersons. And Mama—she stopped, cast a quick glance to the maple tree, and drew a deep breath. *If Mama doesn't want to come, she can stay where she is. Oren will like that. I may like that. Imagine, a home of our very own.*

She took a step forward, placed her hand on the knob, and turned it as if for the very first time. The feel of it traveled through her body, and an answering smile came onto her lips. Then she pushed the door open and walked confidently into her house.

Book Six

1948

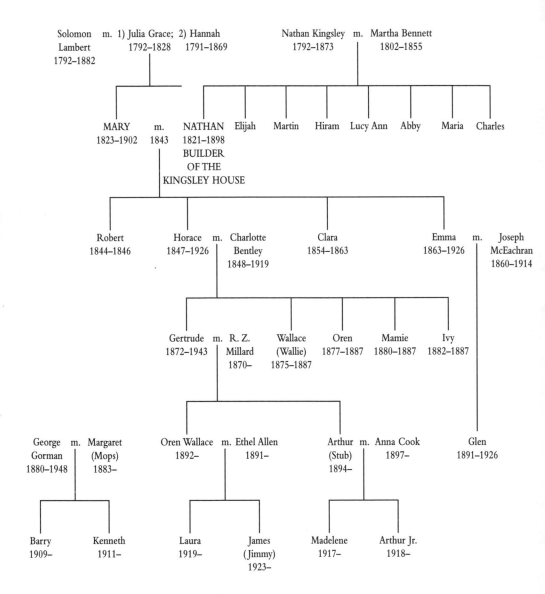

One

"All right, class, let's review what we learned yesterday about how our American government works. Dorothy, please recite the qualifications a candidate must possess to run for the office of president of the United States."

Laura Millard picked up a fresh white chalk and wrote the answers on the blackboard as Dorothy primly announced in her I'm-smarter-than-everyone-else-voice, "You must be thirty-five-years old and a natural-born citizen of the United States. That means you have to be born in this country. Even if you came here from another place when you were just one day old, it doesn't count."

"Thank you, Dorothy."

It was always best, Laura had discovered, to let Dorothy speak first and get her star turn over; otherwise, the pigtailed fifth grader would spend the rest of the lesson with her hand waving frantically in the air and her skinny body fairly rocketing from the desk like a firecracker every time Laura posed the class a question.

"Would you like me to recite the qualifications for senators and representatives, too, Miss Millard?" Dorothy begged.

"No, thank you. That was fine, Dorothy. Let's give someone else a turn."

Laura called on Charles, a handsome redheaded boy, and the class worked its way through the election process, the three branches of government, and the appointment of Supreme Court justices. Although it was only mid-May, and the presidential and local elections not due until November, she tried to incorporate current political events into the daily lesson plan. The town of Livonia faced several critical decisions in the year ahead, the primary issue being whether to permit a horse-racing track to be built within town limits, and the *Livonian* newspaper had become a forum for articles, editorials, and letters to the editor by passionate advocates on both sides of the debate. Laura had told her students they would receive extra credit for any election-related news clipping they brought in and explained to the class. Dorothy, of course, had already accumulated twice as much newsprint as anyone else.

I wish I had a daughter like Dorothy, thought Laura. Yes, she's a little show-off, but so bright, so eager, she practically swallows textbooks whole. The wish fleeted through her mind even as she corrected Tommy that no, it wasn't twelve Supreme Court justices, it was nine.

"Could you be president, Miss Millard?" asked chubby Adam.

"Me? No, I'm not old enough," she replied, a little jolted by the question. Her twenty-ninth birthday was approaching in September. Did she look thirty-five? She patted the tortoiseshell combs that anchored her shoulder-length brunette hair behind her ears. Her hair was fine with a softly permed curl, and the combs were forever slipping out of place. Perhaps a shorter style would be more flattering? Of course, to a ten-year-old, any adult probably seemed—

"No, I mean could a woman be president?" Adam persisted.

"Of course not!" several scornful voices, not all of them male, hooted in unison.

"Yes, we can!" declared Dorothy. "All it says in the Constitution is thirty-five-years old and a natural-born citizen. That means—"

The class erupted into jeers and arguments, a few girls siding timidly with the intrepid Dorothy, the majority of the students shouting her down.

"Class, class! Come to order!" Laura clapped her hands sharply, and with guilty faces the children hushed and squirmed down in their seats trying to look invisible. It was well-known that loud or boisterous behavior was not tolerated by any of the teachers at Livonia Center School, and offenders would find themselves clapping erasers and washing blackboards after the other children skipped home to play.

"Yes, a woman may run for president, although it hasn't happened yet," said Laura. "But let's suppose you could be the head of the town board, the supervisor, here in Livonia for one day. I want everyone to think quietly for five minutes and write down three things you would do to make our town a better place to live."

Five minutes of quiet. Laura released an inward sigh. It was two-fifteen on a Friday afternoon. At two-thirty her class would troop next door to Mrs. Hancock's sixth grade for a special presentation, a talk by a man who had lived in South America for several years. Then at three o'clock the school bell would ring, and she would have survived another week. Not another week of teaching. No, she loved this new position she had started in January, and most of the time the children kept her too busy to feel sorry for herself. But how many weeks had to pass before it didn't hurt anymore, before she stopped thinking of him, before, as her vivacious cousin Madelene urged, she "got on with her life"? Madelene had done it, after all. She had eloped at seventeen, had two children, then divorced her husband when she discovered him in an affair. Now she was engaged again and happily planning a September wedding.

I mustn't get down, Laura told herself, and she forced a smile for the children, busily scribbling their assignment. But what she saw in her mind was a white wedding gown, zippered like a ghost in its plastic storage bag, hanging in her bedroom closet, the dress she had loved and never worn. It had become the symbol of her humiliation, the image to which her mind flashed if even for an instant she cracked open the door of memory. One glimpse and all the sadness she had tried so hard to mothball rushed out, sharp with the scent of rejection. Couldn't he at least have told her before she sent out the invitations, wired her brother Jimmy aboard his ship in the Mediterranean, bought the white dress that hurt so much but was too beautiful to give away?

"Miss Millard, Miss Millard! I'm ready!" Dorothy's hand flapped like a flag in a gale, and she popped in her seat like a jack-in-the-box.

"All right, Dorothy, go ahead."

Laura brought her mind back to the classroom, glad to have been shaken out of the past. Each in turn, the children clamored their suggestions as town supervisor for a day. Pave the remaining dirt roads. Open a bank. Build a motion-picture theater. Give kids a longer summer vacation—this from Frankie, the class clown. Make people be kind to animals. Put park benches down by the river. Have a gumball machine in every classroom—Frankie, again.

"Miss Millard?" A tiny hand wavered into the air. It was Rupert, the smallest child in the class. He had knobby elbows, taffy-colored hair that fluffed around his finely boned head like feather down, and thick metal-rimmed glasses that made him look like a baby owl. I wish I had a son like Rupert, Laura sighed, so sweet and bashful, yet when I coax him to speak, out come the most surprising and poetic thoughts, and I feel as if I've been handed a bouquet.

"Yes, Rupert?" she asked.

"Miss Millard, I would save the maple tree. If I were town supervisor, that is." He pushed his glasses, always slipping down his small nose, back into place with his thumb.

"The big maple tree at the crossroads? What do you mean, Rupert?"

"Well, my father says it's to be cut down to make way for a gas station. But I think it's a very big and beautiful tree, it's the heart of our town, and why can't the tree stay and they put the gas station somewhere else?"

"Well, I—" Laura began, when Adam interrupted.

"They can't cut down our maple! It's the best climbing tree in town."

"We'll stop them!" announced Dorothy. "We'll write a petition. You said citizens could do that, didn't you, Miss Millard?"

"Well, yes, I—," Laura began again, and another ruckus broke loose. She glanced at the clock, exasperated with herself. It was two-thirty, they were expected in Mrs. Hancock's class this very minute for the South America talk, and she simply wasn't doing a very good job of controlling her pupils this afternoon.

"Class!" She made her voice cut through the noise, and they hurried to settle down. "Here's what we'll do. This weekend I'll try to find out the situation about the maple—"

"Miss Millard, if I find an article about it, can I earn extra credit?" interrupted Dorothy.

"Yes, you all may. But first we must get the facts, and then if it seems the tree is in danger, we'll write letters to the newspaper as a project to learn how citizens can express their opinions. But now we must go hear about South America. Line up at the door, please."

They bumped into place, and she shuttled them across the hall with apologies to Mrs. Hancock for their tardiness. The present Livonia Center School was the third one on the site, built in 1930 to replace the old one-room schoolhouse her father Oren had attended. The new building was a handsome red-brick structure with two stories and four classrooms, not to mention such modern amenities as heating, ventilation, and toilets. Livonia now had half a dozen schools bursting with children, for although the suburban building boom expected in the 1920s had been delayed by the Great Depression, by 1940, the population had grown to 8,700 upstanding citizens. Now it had doubled to more than 17,000, and with the war over and the economy booming, still more families were pouring into town. As Laura's pupils tumbled into Mrs. Hancock's room, the desks were pushed aside and the combined classes sat cross-legged on the wood floor. Laura took a chair at the rear of the room.

Mrs. Hancock introduced the speaker, Mr. Barry Gorman, who had recently returned to the United States after ten years in South America. He had flown air-mail planes from Argentina to Panama, mined for gold in Ecuador, and mostly recently helped build a hospital in the Andes Mountains of Peru.

"He is an ADVENTURER!" thrilled Mrs. Hancock, a large, bosomy woman whose exuberance for her profession had not dimmed after thirty years in the classroom. "We are so fortunate to have him come speak to us about our neighbors in South America."

An adventurer, thought Laura, and she gave an inward chuckle at her colleague's dramatic flair. But as Mr. Gorman began his talk, it did seem he had led an unusual life. Not like hers. She had grown up in Livonia, graduated from Wayne University in Detroit, then roomed with several of her college girlfriends in the city as they began their teaching careers. It had been fun and exciting, but one by one her friends got married and moved out, until she was the last one unwed. Then finally she'd met a man, the man of her dreams, and the wedding was scheduled for December. But instead of a gold band on her finger, she had a white wedding dress haunting her closet like a forlorn and unloved ghost.

Let it go, Laura, she ordered herself. Don't dwell on what's past. She glanced out the window to distract herself with a view of the street. Instead she saw a line of gray thunderclouds rolling in. Lovely. As usual, she had walked the half mile to school from her parents' house, and the morning being clear she had not thought to bring an umbrella. At the rate the clouds were moving in, she could expect a thorough drenching just about the time she reached the crossroads, soaking her cranberry-colored suit and the armful of spelling and arithmetic assignments she was taking home to grade over the weekend.

Mr. Gorman was passing around some photographs he had taken of Andean people in their native costumes, and Laura politely turned her attention back to his talk. He was a nice enough man, rather handsome really, a little thin, not tall, but with rich, dark brown hair and a sparkle in his eyes when he spoke of the far places he had seen. His skin was deeply tanned with crinkling lines at the corners of his eyes, and Laura guessed his age as near forty. Instead of a business suit he wore khaki pants, laced hiking boots, and a short-sleeved shirt. On a coat hook by the door, Laura spotted a khaki jacket and a brown fedora, as if he had indeed stepped straight from a South American jungle or at least from the pages of an adventure comic book. But for all his daring exploits, he seemed a little nervous and unsure how to talk to ten-year-olds, and it wasn't until Dorothy—trust Dorothy—asked him if he could speak Spanish, and he offered to teach the students to count to ten, that both speaker and audience found common ground.

"*Uno*," said Mr. Gorman, and "*Uno!*" the children shouted, delighted at the foreign words. "*Dos, tres, cuatro.*" In no time they were up to *ocho, nueve, diez*.

"Thank you, thank you! It was wonderful of you to come, Mr. Gorman," trilled Mrs. Hancock, as the three o'clock bell rang. "Children, how do we show our appreciation?"

A round of applause broke out, and Mr. Gorman mopped his brow, apparently relieved to have discharged his obligation without any crisis arising. Of course, Dorothy wanted to stay and ask more questions, and with a polite thank-you of her own, Laura ushered her remaining students back to their classroom to tidy their desks before departing for the weekend. When she left the school at three-ten, she glimpsed Dorothy, still pigeonholing Mr. Gorman in Mrs. Hancock's room, pummeling him with questions about llamas, conquistadors, and how to say in Spanish, "Do you like to read books?"

On the sidewalk, Laura stopped and drew a breath of rain-scented air. The thunderclouds were overhead now. What are you waiting for? she thought. Go ahead, rain on me. She glanced south along the road to the cemetery where most of her ancestors were buried. At least Grandma Gertrude, who had joined the family plot in 1943, had been spared the distress of seeing her granddaughter jilted two weeks before her wedding. And what would Grandmother Allen have said? Laura could hear her razor voice now: A horror! An outrage! Never speak of it to anyone! Grandmother Allen had died in 1939 and was buried in a Detroit cemetery, having lived in iron-willed isolation in the city after Ethel and Oren defied her and moved to the Kingsley House. So it's really only my parents and myself I've disgraced, Laura thought, and my brother Jimmy, Grandpa R. Z., Uncle Stub and Aunt Anna, Madelene and her two brothers, all my friends . . .

She started north toward the crossroads, past houses and stores, ignoring the passing cars. The white wedding dress was firmly in her head now, it wasn't done with her yet, and so hurtful was the image she hardly felt the first drops of rain.

It's because I'm too tall, she told herself. Five-foot-ten. Taller than her father, her brother, and almost every eligible man she met. It was why she'd given up high heels, though they made your legs look great, in favor of low-heeled pumps like the black ones she wore today. Her height might have been an asset if she were glamorous, a model or an actress, but she was just ordinary-looking, nice blue eyes perhaps, but her skin was slightly flawed from teenaged acne, and although her figure was good, the overall package rarely drew a wolf whistle.

"And you're too smart," Madelene had coached her. "Try not to talk so much about books and history and such, Laura. No man wants a wife who's smarter than he is."

But I can't help it, Laura replied mentally to her cousin. I love books, I love to learn, and her father had been so proud of her when she graduated with her teaching degree, the first person in the family, he boasted, to have a real college education. Oren himself had had to leave high school in the eleventh grade to help support his parents and had studied at night with correspondence courses in math and science to get ahead in his job at the Ford Motor Company. He'd been determined from the start his bright daughter would go one step better, and she still remembered, walking across the stage in her mortarboard and gown, seeing him in the audience with tears in his eyes. Even her brother Jimmy hadn't made it to college, but of course that was because he was four years younger, and the year he turned eighteen, World War II began.

And that was another thing: timing. She had graduated from college just as all the fine young men left for the war, to fight and die. When they trickled back from Europe and the Pacific, weary, injured, and maimed, all they wanted was peace and quiet, a wife, children, a home. The women wanted it, too. No more telegrams from the State Department: "We regret to inform you . . ." No more news reports of trenches, tanks, bombs. No more ration lines for sugar, butter, flour. Put away the medals and citations, the gold stars and purple hearts. All people wanted was a plain, safe, ordinary life—thank heaven for it!—and Laura wanted that, too. But there were far too few men for all the girlfriends and sweethearts waiting to be swept off their feet, and when men had their pick, they didn't want tall, smart, book-loving teachers with flawed complexions, no matter how nice their blue eyes.

The raindrops began to splash down, and Laura, startled from her reverie, shook herself and began to run. She was at the crossroads, and seeing the old maple, she darted across the street and took shelter under its full green leaves just as the sky opened and a torrent of rain poured forth. It would probably have been wiser to make for one of the nearby stores, but the memory of Rupert's concern for the tree seemed to have moved her feet without consulting her brain. Now here she was, her clothes already damp, the children's homework papers clutched to her chest, the rain pelting overhead and threatening any minute to penetrate the leafy canopy and drench her head to toe. Plus, she was standing under a tree in a storm, something she had warned her students never to do just last week during science lesson. Laura stared up into the leaves, feeling like an absolute fool. Why, oh why, had he waited until almost the last minute to say it? Sorry, Laura. I've met someone else. The most wonderful girl in the world. I know you'd adore her. No hard feelings? Oh, and since you won't be needing the engagement ring . . .

"Miss Millard?"

Laura snapped her head toward the road. The tears had been so close to spilling down her cheeks that she was grateful for the sudden cascade of rain that splashed between the leaves and onto her face, concealing her distress.

"Miss Millard? May I offer you a ride somewhere?"

Barry Gorman spoke from the rolled-down window of a maroon Chevrolet stopped by the side of the road.

"Well, I just live . . . I got caught . . ." She pointed up the road toward the Kingsley House, thinking she probably sounded even more foolish than she looked. "Yes, thank you." She hurried to the car and got in. "Thank you. I stopped because my students are up in arms about the maple tree. It's very old, you see, and they've heard it's to be cut down to make way for a gas station." There, that sounded like a plausible explanation. Scientific, even.

Mr. Gorman studied the maple, and a look of regret pinched his face. "That seems a shame. It's a beautiful tree. Why can't they leave the tree and put the gas station somewhere else?"

Laura stared at him in surprise. "Why, that's exactly what Rupert said. One of my students," she added. "We may write letters to the newspaper about it. Anyway, thank you for coming to speak to our school today. I hope Dorothy didn't pester you with too many questions."

"And I hope I didn't bore them." He made a rueful grimace. "I haven't had much experience around children."

He aimed his car in the direction Laura had indicated, and she found her glance stealing toward him. He wore his khaki jacket and fedora, and the packet of photos he'd brought to show the children rested on the

348

front seat between them. Up close, his face showed clean lines and his brown eyes were lighted by golden flecks, as if for each strange, exotic sight he'd seen, his vision had gained a tiny bit of gold.

"I should probably warn you," he added, "you being Dorothy's teacher, that the last thing she asked me how to say in Spanish was 'I love you.' I gathered there's some boy in her class she has a crush on."

"Dorothy? A crush?" Laura shook her head in disbelief.

"I told her '*Te amo*' and '*Bésame mucho*,' which means 'Kiss me a lot.' Now that I think of it," he glanced at her apologetically, "that probably wasn't such a smart thing to tell a ten-year-old. Is this the house?"

"Yes," said Laura, disappointed they had arrived so quickly. Well, it was only a quarter mile, after all.

Mr. Gorman pulled into the driveway and nodded at the pillared porch. "Much older than the surrounding homes, isn't it?"

"Yes, my great-great-grandfather built it for his bride in 1843." Laura smiled, grateful he had noticed. The only good thing about her wedding fiasco was that it had prompted her to leave Detroit and return to her parents' house to regroup in relative anonymity. She made a broad sweep of her hand toward the crossroads. The gesture took in a line of shops fronting the street, and beyond, a tract of new homes in various stages of construction. "This used to be an eighty-acre farm, but when my father inherited it from his aunt there were debts, and he had to sell all the land but our one lot to pay what was owed. The land stayed empty during the Depression and the war, but now it's being developed as a subdivision, Coventry Gardens."

"Well, Livonia seems a pleasant town," said Mr. Gorman. "If I get the job at General Motors, maybe I'll be seeing more of it. Can I help you to the door with those papers?"

"Papers? Oh, no thank you." Laura picked up the children's homework to show she could manage. "I appreciate the ride, Mr. Gorman. You saved me from a soaking."

She smiled, opened the passenger door, and sprinted through the rain to the porch, exchanging a final wave as the maroon Chevrolet pulled away. Inside, she found her mother in the kitchen, taking cornbread from the oven. Ethel had found the recipe in Aunt Emma's recipe box a few months after they moved into the Kingsley House, and Oren had reacted like a boy at Christmas.

"That's it!" he cried. "The same cornbread she used to make when we were kids. Let's try it right away!" It had become a family staple ever since.

"Did you get a ride, Laura?" asked Ethel. "I thought I heard a car in the driveway."

"Yes, Mom." She explained about Mr. Gorman, trying to recall tidbits from his talk about South America that might interest her mother. She should have invited him in, she thought. His photos were right there on the car seat. Photography was one of her mother's hobbies. She could almost hear Madelene chiding her. "Well, how old is he, Laura? Is he married? Where does he live? Was he in the war? Why did he come back to the States? How did he happen to be at the school? Why didn't you let him carry the papers into the house? You could have offered him a cup of coffee."

But it was such a short ride, Laura argued back mentally, accepting the square of hot, buttered cornbread her mother offered. I could hardly get his whole life history in five minutes, could I? Although he had said something about getting a job at General Motors. Did he mean the new GM plant in Livonia on Plymouth Road?

"It was only a friendly ride," she said a little crossly, hardly realizing she'd spoken aloud until her mother turned and asked, concerned, "What did you say, dear?"

"Nothing. My clothes are a little wet, that's all. I better go change."

She walked upstairs to her bedroom and slipped off her black pumps. Well, Mr. Gorman was gone, and she was a good two inches taller than he was anyway. Besides, she thought, as she shrugged off her damp suit, I have other things to do, homework to correct, an investigation to conduct about a possible gas station on the corner, Saturday cleaning tomorrow. And who could Dorothy have a crush on? Handsome, red-headed Charles, I bet. Or maybe Frankie the class clown? I wish I had a daughter like Dorothy and a son like Rupert and another son like Adam . . .

A white shape shrouded in plastic at the back of the closet caught her eye. Or had she looked for it, knowing full well it was there? Maybe I'll just be buried in it, she thought bitterly.

Sorry, Laura, to leave you in the lurch. No hard feelings?

I gathered there's some boy in her class she has a crush on.

Te amo. Bésame mucho.

Why was everyone falling in love except her?

Two

When are you going back?

The question echoed in Barry Gorman's head as he drove from Livonia to the west side of Detroit where his parents lived. Where his mother lived, he corrected, since his father had died the month before. It was his father's 1938 maroon Chevrolet he was driving, still an odd experience. In the remote regions of South America where he had spent the past ten years, transportation was generally a matter of bush planes, riverboats, horseback, or your own two feet. Here in Detroit, the cars were so thick on the roads it was like navigating a river strewn with boulders, trying to keep your place in the jumble and flow. He would much rather cross paths with a puma or meet a twenty-foot anaconda dangling from a tree than confront this traffic every day.

When are you going back?

It was a small boy in metal-rimmed glasses, Barry remembered, who had asked the question, and it was the only one he had been at a true loss to answer. "Soon," he would liked to have said, but "I don't know" would have been more honest. How do you explain to children that sometimes life doesn't give you a choice?

He turned onto a quiet street, parked before a neat brick bungalow, collected his packet of photos, and entered.

"So how'd it go? You ready to lead an expedition of junior scouts to the snow-capped Andes?" His brother Ken nudged him with an elbow. The two men shared the same build, lean and compact, but Ken's coloring was darker, olive skin and jet black hair.

"You're a fine one to talk," Ken's wife Frances interrupted, teasing. She rubbed her hand over her pregnant belly. "You'll be responsible for a child of our own soon enough. But seriously, Barry, did the children enjoy your speech?"

"Hard to tell." Barry took off his jacket and fedora. He knew they looked out of place in the city, but he'd worn them so long that anything else made him feel as if he were dressed for a costume ball. Having to don a suit and tie for his interview last week at the General Motors plant had been close to torture. But at least now he had an edge on the job. The interviewer at the personnel office had gotten a bright idea after reading Barry's South American resume. Say, the man ventured, I have a sister who's teaching her sixth grade class about South America. I bet those kids would love to hear you say a few words. So Barry had said a few words and now, greatly relieved the ordeal was over, he hoped Mrs. Hancock's report to her brother would clinch him a job in the new plant's purchasing division.

Maybe I won't have to stay there long, he thought. At the hospital in Peru, he'd worked to locate medical equipment and supplies, tracking down the right instruments, bargaining or bartering to make the best deals, flying to pick up badly needed drugs wherever they could be found. At GM the purchasing would all be accomplished with a typewriter and triplicate forms. Hardly a challenge, but with the tremendous post-war demand for new cars, the auto industry offered the best employment, and he'd have to consider himself lucky if he got the job.

"Where's Mops?" he asked Ken, using the nickname the brothers had always applied to their mother, Margaret.

"At the neighbor's, having a gossip," Ken replied. He was thirty-seven, two years younger than Barry, and even in casual clothes he always gave an impression of being natty and debonair. "Frances is going to make a meatloaf for dinner, so maybe now's a good chance for you and me to clean up the last few details of Dad's affairs. There won't be time before we catch the train back to Texas tomorrow morning."

Barry nodded. There really wasn't a lot to settle about his father's estate, a modest bank account to balance, some legal papers to sign and mail. Still, as an Irish immigrant in the early 1900s, George Gorman had done better for himself than he could have expected in the old country. He had earned an electrician's license and become a self-employed contractor, often finding work in the automobile industry. Now it looks as if I'm to be an auto-industry man myself, Barry thought. But it wasn't his choice.

"Was Mops feeling a bit more cheerful this afternoon?" he asked, and Ken nodded.

"Frances says you should expect it to come and go for a while. That's how her sister was when her husband got killed at Midway. Of course, Dad's heart attack was a natural death, but it still came without warning. And maybe losing the one you love gets even harder when you're older. I don't know, Barry. All I know is how lucky I am."

Ken glanced toward the kitchen where Frances hummed as she patted the meatloaf into shape. Her honey blond hair waved to her shoulders, and her belly rode high under her apron. Ken grinned.

"Doc's guessing it's going to be a boy. I'll send you a cigar in the mail when the big day comes."

"You do that," said Barry. "You've waited long enough. Or rather, Uncle Sam made you wait."

"That he did."

Ken stretched back on the couch, and for a minute the brothers were quiet. Both had signed up for the army, Ken on December 8, 1941, Barry as soon as he could get back to the States after word of Pearl Harbor reached him where he was gold mining in Ecuador. Ken had been accepted and sent to basic training at Fort Hood, Texas, where he met Frances. They'd corresponded for four years while he served in the South Pacific, then married in 1946 after Ken returned from the postwar occupation of Japan. But Barry had been rejected when his Army physical detected a heart murmur he'd never even known he had.

"But I cut paths through the jungle, climb mountains, fly planes," he explained, incredulous.

"Sorry," the regulation-minded doctor pronounced. "You're not fit for active duty. Next."

So he'd returned to South America where, since there was concern the Nazis had hidden interests, his jungle adventuring was deemed to have some potential defensive and patriotic bulwark effect. He remained throughout the war and probably would have stayed indefinitely but for his father's unexpected passing. Now he had a widowed mother to support, and he needed a steady job with a good income. But what was he to make of himself in this new life?

"You should find a nice girl and settle down," said Ken, and Barry glanced sideways. One look at his brother's beaming face convinced him Ken was merely basking in his own happiness, not trying to read his mind.

"No, I don't think so," he replied. "Besides, I'll be too busy working and taking care of Mops."

"Barry, you know Frances and I would help if we——"

"Ken, no, that's not what I meant."

His brother had spoken defensively, and Barry lifted a hand to signal peace between them. Ken had done his share serving in the war, while he had pleased himself in South America. Now it was his brother's turn to have the life he wanted, the life he'd fought for and earned. Maybe someday Mops would want to move to Texas to be near her grandchildren. Maybe once Ken's new sales job earned him some big commissions, he and Barry could share her support. But in the meantime . . .

"You and Frances and the baby deserve a home all your own," Barry insisted. "Mops and I will be fine. Besides, after just half an hour with those kids today, I'm not sure I'm cut out to have any of my own."

"Wiped you out, did they?"

"It was like being under siege by an army of fire ants."

"You're exaggerating," said Ken.

"Not by much," Barry replied.

Their mother returned a short time later, and while the four of them ate dinner, Mops chatted about her visit with her neighbor. Margaret Gorman was short, plump, and gray-haired, fond of colorful clothes and costume jewelry. She'd dressed brightly today and kept up a smile throughout dinner, but the skin around her sea-green eyes pouched in little folds of sadness. Barry let Ken and Frances make most of the replies. He'd grown so accustomed to thinking and speaking in Spanish that English sounded almost foreign to his ears. I haven't been a very good son, he thought, as he looked at Mops, her face more lined, her skin more dotted with brown liver spots, than the last time he'd paid a visit home to celebrate the end of the war. Sure, he'd written, sent photographs and cards, mailed gifts like the silver napkin rings with bas-relief llama designs that even now held pride of place on the dinner table. His parents, content with their lives, had only once or twice let slip a wistful desire to see him more often. But now it dawned on him that there were more gaps than connections between him and his family, even between him and Ken.

"Anybody care for a walk?" he asked when the meal was finished, thinking that might be a good, family-type thing to do. But Mops wanted to finish knitting some baby clothes for Frances to take home to Texas, and Ken was actually eager to help his wife wash the dishes.

"You go, Barry," they said, so he did.

He walked a few blocks east, then south, no particular destination in mind. Most of the houses he passed were cozy bungalows like his mother's on small, gardened lots. A half mile in any direction brought him to a commercial street, offering grocery markets, bakeries, banks, hardware stores. He felt so out of place. If he were in the Andes now, he'd be halfway up a great mountain, part of the bony spine that snaked along the curve of the continent, a powerful upheaval of earth that pierced the clouds and made your head go light and your heart pump harder with each step upward. The gods lived there, the Indians said, and to fly over them in a plane, around them, between them, like a condor on vast outspread wings, was to lose touch with base reality and exist alone in the world, weightless, unburdened, the land a painting far, far below. He thought of the Andean people, bronze-skinned and black-eyed, distrustful of gringos, even those building a hospital for their own good. Who are you to come here? their faces said. Why do you intrude? He couldn't answer that, except to say to himself, I am in love with places, lost, mysterious places. I need to see them. I need to be here.

Now he felt more at home among the Indians than he did among his mother's neighbors or the eager fellows lining up for positions at the new GM plant. Most were a decade or more younger than he, and although he had had two years of college before the Depression forced him out of school, they had the advantage of the GI Bill and spoke confidently of the degrees they expected to earn going to college at night. In no time they might well be his boss. Should he do that, go back to school, or just do the job well and hope for the best? Maybe if he got hired at GM, Mops would consider moving to Livonia. It would be nearer to work, and despite the sprouting subdivisions like that one near the schoolteacher's house, the town overall was still rural with cornfields and dairy farms and a sense of breathing space. But no doubt that wouldn't last. The soldiers were home, the country wanted stability, houses, and jobs, and Detroit would just keep growing outward, swallowing everything in its path. Hadn't that teacher, Miss Millard, said the maple tree in the center of town was to be chopped down to make way for a gas station?

He walked back to his mother's house. Mops had finished an orange baby sweater and, looking tired, excused herself to bed early. Ken and Frances would take the Chevy back to the hotel where they were staying, returning in the morning with their suitcases packed, and Barry would drive them to the train station. He walked them to the car, noting how Ken, after helping his wife into the passenger seat, the two of them giggling over her protruding belly, practically floated around to the driver's side. I thought, Barry mused, shaking his head, that when a wife got pregnant, *she* was the one who was supposed to glow.

He returned inside, sat on the couch, and opened the envelope of South American photos he'd shown the children at school that day. On the back of each one, a caption and date were penciled in his neat, angular hand, and he spent a few minutes rearranging them, not chronologically, but in an order that pleased his eye. Then he spread them on the coffee table and looked in quiet longing at the places he had left.

When are you going back?

If his father hadn't died, if he'd stayed in South America, what then? He'd have finished helping outfit the hospital in Peru, then moved on. He'd heard there was an airstrip planned in Brazil to fly loggers and miners into the jungle, and after that maybe he'd head up to the oil fields in Venezuela or join a crew on the tramp steamers that plied the Argentine coast. Probably he would just have kept going until somewhere, sometime, he met a natural or unnatural death. Did it matter? Was there anything wrong with that? Weren't there enough happy, eager couples like Ken and Frances to live in the houses and build the cars and make the babies and keep the world going round?

He collected the photos and stored them in the envelope. He'd known when he left South America this time, it might be a long time before he could return. It might be never, because sometimes when you came to a fork in the road, the path you chose never forked again. Barry Gorman glanced around the tidy bungalow, and he thought of all the other bungalows like it that lined the street and of the factory where he would work at some tidy desk, processing papers, dressed in his suit and tie. Who are you to come here? the Indians' faces had asked him when he stepped into their strange land. He asked himself the same question now and got no reply.

Three

How did I get myself into this?

Laura Millard put on a brave smile, shook hands with the elderly gentleman who had paused to lean on his cane at the crossroads, and offered him a mimeographed flyer that declaimed in bold purple letters: SAVE OUR TREE! Below the headline were excerpts from some of the letters written by her students and published in the *Livonian*:

> *This is supposed to be a democracy where everyone gets to vote. But did anyone let us kids vote on chopping down our maple tree? No! We are citizens, too, and we should have a say!*
>
> *—Dorothy*

> *If I were town supervisor, I would preserve the maple tree and also put a trash barrel on the corner so people wouldn't litter there.*
>
> *—Adam*

> *My father says a lot of people want to live in Livonia because it is a nice town and having a gas station on this corner would be convenient. But I think having a maple tree on this corner is beautiful.*
>
> *—Rupert*

"So you're that schoolteacher lady who started all this," the elderly gentleman said. He scrutinized Laura's face. "I recognize your picture from the newspaper."

"Yes, that was me." She gave a game smile as the man frowned at the flyer, folded it into his pocket, and hobbled away on his cane. It was just two weeks ago that she had stopped by Town Hall, made a few phone inquiries, and gently informed her class that the Standard Gas Company had indeed purchased the land at the crossroads and there were no zoning laws or legal restrictions to prevent them removing the maple. But her indignant ten-year-olds had refused to accept the answer.

"We have to change the gas company's mind," said Dorothy. "It's freedom of speech, public opinion, and the right to petition. Remember you taught us that, Miss Millard?"

Of course she remembered. Maybe she had taught them too well. But she agreed they could devote their English lesson to writing letters to the editor, providing every missive was a model of good handwriting, spelling, grammar, punctuation, and sentence structure. The next day she delivered the letters to the *Livonian* in person. With luck, the children might get a few inches of newsprint and their moment of glory on the opinion page. Instead, perhaps due to a momentary lull in local events, the editor had accepted the manilla envelope and Laura's brief explanation with a growing gleam in his eye. The next thing she knew, a reporter and a photographer were in her classroom, followed by a front-page article titled: "Fifth Graders Campaign to Save Livonia Center Maple Tree. Teacher Calls Effort a Lesson in Democracy."

"I'm sure I was misquoted," she tried to explain to Mr. Schultz, the principal, flinching at the photo of her students and herself—oh, why was that lock of hair sticking out from behind her ear?—their classroom walls plastered with crayoned pictures of the tree. Frankie had drawn his bearing bright red apples.

But the principal congratulated her on her innovative teaching methods, and Mrs. Hancock's sixth graders promptly sat down to write letters, too, and soon the editorial page of the *Livonian* was crammed with opinions from people all over town. Not all of them were tree lovers. Some agreed the maple was pretty but pointed out its age and expendability. Others denounced the whole campaign as an effort to impede Livonia's economic development and chided Miss Millard for stirring young students to speak out on issues of which they had no knowledge. There was even an articulate, fair-minded opinion by Mr. Henry Hilberson, spokesman for the Standard Gas Company, regretting the imminent demise of the maple—his company had had no idea, on purchasing the property, that the tree held such a fond place in the hearts of the townspeople—but explaining most persuasively why a gas station smack in the center of Livonia would stimulate business throughout the town.

"What do we do next, Miss Millard?" cried Dorothy, as she and the other children thrust forward to Laura's desk, their hands stuffed with newspaper clippings.

"I don't know," Laura admitted. She was already regretting she'd gotten her students involved. Little Rupert had tears in his eyes behind his glasses as he showed her a letter that proclaimed the tree to be a "darned old nuisance," and Laura longed to cradle him in her arms for a comforting hug. "Let me think about it," she urged, secretly hoping that in a day or two they'd forget. Decoration Day was approaching; speeches, a parade, and picnics were planned. Surely, the excitement would divert the children to other activities. But all week they pestered her, and Friday night, sitting on the front porch with her parents in the balmy evening, Laura gazed along the street to the maple tree and sighed.

Her parents exchanged glances, then Oren spoke.

"Good for you, daughter."

"Good? Dad, I've raised a ruckus that probably won't do any good at all. The gas company bought the land fair and square, and the intersection is mostly stores and offices now anyway. The tree would have been gone long ago if the real estate company that owned the property hadn't gone bust during the Depression." She gestured toward the crossroads where the lofty maple stood in ridiculous isolation amidst a cluster of shiny shopfronts. "And think how disappointed my children will be when all their letters and posters are to no avail."

"I know." Oren patted her shoulder. "But I can't help hoping you'll come up with some way to succeed. Your mother and I fell in love in that maple tree, didn't we, Ethel?"

Her parents traded a tender smile, and Laura felt a pain like a tiny crack in her heart. That's what *I* want, she thought, to fall in love and be married, to grow old in peace and contentment with someone, to have children, oh please, children, and suddenly, because a vision of a white wedding gown began to intrude into her mind, she swore under her breath. All right, damn it, I will save that ridiculous, lonely maple. Why not? It was part of history, part of Livonia; she had climbed it herself as a child. It was important to her parents, her students. Who knew how many other townspeople had loved or quarreled or debated politics or whispered the latest gossip under its leafy branches? What matter if the odds were against them? If she fought for something really hard, no matter how pointless, hopeless, or foolish, maybe she wouldn't have any energy left to think about other things or care that she felt so empty and hurt every time she saw a couple arm in arm or a baby buggy being pushed along the sidewalk.

"Children," she announced Monday morning, "I don't know how much good it will do, but I have a plan."

So now it was the morning of Decoration Day, and even though it was a holiday from school, Miss Millard and her fifth-grade students, Mrs. Hancock and her sixth-grade students, and even the principal Mr. Schultz who, Laura suspected, only wanted to get his picture in the newspaper, had gathered at the crossroads. On the sidewalk before the maple tree, they set up a table, a lemonade stand—Frankie's idea—an American flag, and a display consisting of their tree posters plus some photographs of the maple Ethel Millard had taken in the 1920s. As the unsuspecting residents emerged from their homes and headed toward Town Hall for the opening speeches, they were ambushed by passionate children brandishing purple flyers and requesting every man, woman, and child to sign the petition to SAVE OUR TREE!

"Remember," Laura cautioned, "we must show we are responsible citizens, so don't block the sidewalk or go running around the maple. And be polite!"

"How's it going, dear?" Ethel asked, as she and Oren stopped on their way to hear the dignitaries. She handed over a basket of cookies. "So the children don't get hungry," she explained. "Your father and I will come back to help you as soon as the town supervisor has made his speech." She kissed her daughter, and they went on.

Laura smiled and turned to hand another flyer to a passing citizen. At least, she reflected, she was quickly gaining confidence in fielding questions and comments from the many strangers who stopped to remark on the event. And it was fun to hear the old-timers reminisce about life at the crossroads and in turn to impart a little history to the children who passed.

"I remember when Stringer's Store used to be right next to this tree," sighed one white-haired woman. "They've been gone, what, fifteen, twenty years now?"

"Can't you dig up the tree and move it?" asked a tiny girl, and Laura explained about the roots.

"Do you live near here?" several people inquired, and when Laura pointed up the road to her parents' home, there came answering nods and remarks of, "Oh yes, the Kingsley House."

"You any relation to Horace Kingsley?" one old codger croaked, and when Laura said yes, he was her great-grandfather, the old man har-rumphed and shuffled off, muttering, "Bad job on my porch. Cheap shingles. Bent nails."

"Miss Millard."

Laura looked up and saw a maroon Chevy parked beside the curb.

"Mr. Gorman," she said, trying not to sound surprised.

He opened the passenger door and helped a short, plump woman to alight. She wore a violet print dress, a large cameo brooch, and rhine-stone glasses on her round, friendly face. Her bright green handbag matched exactly her bright green high heels. His mother, Laura decided, noting that today Mr. Gorman wore a blue suit, white shirt, and tie. She liked him better in his khakis and fedora, she thought, and blushed. As if she had any right to be interested in how he dressed at all. Mr. Gorman stopped to greet Mrs. Hancock, who thanked him again profusely for his visit to her class, and half a dozen children clustered around him, happily chanting, *"uno, dos, tres,"* to show how well they remembered their Spanish lesson.

"Te amo. Bésame mucho," whispered a voice at Laura's side, and she glanced down to see Dorothy carefully rehearsing the phrases she had coaxed from Mr. Gorman after his talk. It reminded her that she hadn't yet heard Dorothy use them on any of the boys at school, and she resolved to keep an ear open. Having one of her pupils romance another in a foreign language was one innovative teaching method she doubted Mr. Schultz would approve. Meanwhile, Mr. Gorman was gradually working his way toward her, and Laura found herself wondering how often he had whispered *"Te amo"* and *"Bésame mucho"* to some raven-haired South American beauty as she fluttered long eyelashes at him over her fan.

"Hello, Miss Millard. This is my mother, Margaret Gorman. We came out to take a drive around the town."

"How do you do?" Mrs. Gorman held out her hand. She wore white gloves, and her button face, powdered and wrinkled, creased in a pleas-ant smile.

Mr. Gorman nodded toward the maple. "I read about your SAVE OUR TREE! campaign at the plant."

"The plant?" Laura asked, confused.

"The General Motors plant on Plymouth Road. I got a job there. Started this week." He ran a finger inside the collar of his shirt as if try-ing to insert some space between the starched white cotton and his neck.

"Oh yes, I believe you mentioned that," Laura said.

"They get the *Livonian* there, so I've been reading up on the local news during my lunch hour. Mops, my mother, wanted to see where I work, so we drove by and then stopped to hear the speeches at Town Hall. I didn't realize you had a rally set up here, though."

"Well, it's not a rally actually. Or maybe you could call it that. Would you like a flyer?" Laura thrust a purple paper at him, feeling awkward and not knowing why.

"Thank you."

A drum roll interrupted, and for the next few minutes activity on the sidewalk came to a halt as the parade came marching along the road. First strutted the town supervisor and town board members, then the school board, then the valiant but slightly off-key high-school band. After them came the men in their army and navy uniforms from World Wars I and II, and finally three elderly soldiers, riding in a convertible, who had fought in the Spanish-American War. By the time the parade passed, Laura's parents had returned, and while Oren began explaining to Mrs. Gorman the history of Livonia Center, she found her mother and Barry Gorman had discovered a common interest in the 1920s photographs Ethel had provided for the display. Meanwhile, the crowd of people returning from Town Hall provided a ripe opportunity to gather more signatures for their petition, and with another admonition to her students to "Be polite," Laura and the children plunged into the crowd.

"Miss Millard?"

She turned hopefully, although already her ears told her it was a female voice that had pronounced her name. A slim woman in a tailored gray suit offered Laura her hand.

"I'm Eleanor Bernstein from the Livonia Women's League," she said. "I'd like to speak to you about the possibility of your running for town board."

"Me?" Laura started, gave a little laugh, then paled as the woman's vigorous nod confirmed the words were not a joke.

"We're encouraging female candidates to run for local, state, even national office this autumn. I'm sure you noticed, as the parade passed, that not one of our elected officials wears a skirt." Eleanor Bernstein gave a wry smile and nodded after the procession as it marched out of sight around a corner, the last strains of "America, the Beautiful" wafting off-key from the high-school band. She drew Laura a step aside from the crowd. "We believe it's important to get more women involved in politics. We proved during the war that we can handle military service, factory jobs, administrative work, even heavy labor. We made real economic gains, now we need to continue that effort in the political arena. Are you a registered member of either political party?"

"No," said Laura. Eleanor Bernstein seemed about her own age, and her auburn hair was rolled back from her temples and pinned in a cluster of curls at the nape of her neck. She had an alert, slightly pointed face set with clear gray eyes, and her demeanor managed to be both friendly and businesslike. She spoke in a precise voice that didn't leave much room for pause.

"But you are a registered voter?" Eleanor persisted.

"Yes. I voted for FDR."

"And you are a resident of Livonia?"

"Yes." Laura pointed up the street to the Kingsley House, explaining, for the dozenth time that day, her descent from Nathan Kingsley, her childhood in the house, her six years of teaching in Detroit after college, and her return to Livonia this past Christmas.

"The name Millard also goes back quite a way in this town, doesn't it?" Eleanor continued.

"Yes. My father could tell you that history if you're interested."

She shook her head, not in dismissal, but as if she were moving straight to a more important point. "I'm sure the connection will prove helpful when the time comes. Meanwhile, what I'd like you to consider is this: You're a college-educated, professional woman, you have long-time roots in the Livonia community, you've already generated a good deal of publicity and interest for your maple tree campaign—"

"SAVE OUR TREE!" several of the children clamored in agreement, and Laura shooed them away to the lemonade stand.

"But it's only one tree," she said, feeling if she did not speak soon, Eleanor Bernstein would have her elected before she got a word in edgewise. She found herself both admiring and a little intimidated by the woman's confident manner.

"But it's symbolic of a much larger issue," Eleanor countered. "One of your little pupils there," she pointed to Rupert and paused to smile, "just told me this tree is the heart of the town, and he's right. This crossroads is the geographic center of Livonia, an exact thirty-six square mile township, one of the few in Michigan, or in many other states, I dare say, to have retained its original boundaries from prestatehood days. Other communities around us have expanded or split off sections. Some were swallowed up or partitioned and don't even exist anymore. But Livonia has stayed intact—until now. I assume, even though you've returned here only since December, that you're informed on this business of the race track?"

"I have read the articles in the newspaper." Laura nodded, recalling the basic debate. Several parties were promoting the idea of a horse-racing track, and although most of the churches and some civic groups were opposed, many businesses and citizens favored it in the hope of substantial tax revenues. But what did that have to do with the maple tree and the geographical integrity of Livonia? Rupert had edged closer to listen, and Dorothy was tugging excitedly at her skirt, eager to interrupt with some comment. Trying to hold off the pigtailed fifth grader, Laura said to Eleanor Bernstein, "Please continue."

"Well, unless everyone gets together on the race track issue, the Elm District, where it's to be located, may break away to form a separate town. Other districts could follow suit, each pursuing its own interests. I'm not saying at this point whether the race track is right or wrong, but the board members we elect in November will have important concerns like this to address, and their decisions will affect the future of our schools, our tax base, our jobs. We need women to become involved in this process, Miss Millard, women who could make a difference."

"Miss Millard, you could be the first woman president!" squealed Dorothy. She squeezed Laura's hand, practically dancing on tiptoe, and Rupert's mouth opened in an awed gape, as if already beholding her elevated to the highest office in the land.

"Children, I really don't think I'm qualified for that." Laura made her voice firm. "Miss—, Mrs. Bernstein?" The woman nodded at the latter appellation, and Laura continued. "This is very flattering, but I have no political experience."

"Most women haven't. But we can help."

"And I'm a schoolteacher. I couldn't leave my children."

"You wouldn't have to. Being a town board member isn't a full-time job. But it is a serious commitment, and it would require time and energy." Eleanor dipped into her purse, pulled out a small notebook, and jotted on a piece of paper. "All I'm asking is that you come to our next meeting and learn a little more about the opportunities for women in politics. A number of other potential candidates will be there, so you won't be alone. Here's the time and place." She handed Laura the paper and smiled briskly but warmly. "Now I'll let you get back to your maple tree and your petition, which by the way, I've already signed. I must get on to the cemetery to decorate my husband's grave. Normandy," she added, and Laura's heart gave a lurch as Eleanor walked away.

"My daughter on the town board."

Oren Millard spoke softly, and Laura turned. She had been so caught up in her conversation with Eleanor, she hadn't realized her parents, as well as Mr. Gorman and his mother, had overhead the entire exchange. Oren grinned at Ethel in growing delight.

"Our daughter on the town board," he repeated. "What would you say to that?"

"I would say no one should rush or force Laura into anything she doesn't want to do," said Ethel sensibly, but Laura saw a little smile playing on her mother's lips.

Mrs. Gorman frowned. "You know, in the old country, in Ireland, women always had to do what their father and then their husband told them. But I ran away and made my own choice. I think women should speak up for themselves."

"I had a very similar situation with my mother," said Ethel, and somehow, without it quite being planned, Laura found her parents had formed a triangle with Mrs. Gorman, the three of them deep in discussion, leaving her and Mr. Gorman standing alone.

"It's really preposterous, you know," she said to him, looking for help, as if he might say something to conveniently excuse her from this mess—for it was beginning to feel more and more like a mess—that she'd gotten herself into. "I know next to nothing about politics, I doubt I'd be any good at it, and if I did run, I'd probably come in dead last. I'm not even sure I can save this maple tree, and the thought of how disappointed my children will be is almost more than I can bear. The whole thing may be one lost cause."

Barry Gorman looked at her, then transferred his glance to the tree. Laura hung her head. Well, she had vowed to fight for the maple, and if she were going to be foolish, she might as well be foolish all the way. What did it matter when her whole life felt like a joke? She stared down at her feet. Even in her absolutely flat-heeled sandals, she was still taller than Barry Gorman. She was contemplating her toes, her spirits about as low as they could go, when she heard him speak.

"I have always liked lost causes," he said.

Four

"He seems like a nice man," said Ethel Millard.

Oren made a noncommittal "h'mmm."

They were sitting on the front porch while Ethel flipped through a foot-high stack of piano music, selecting the tunes her students would play for next week's grand Fourth of July celebration.

"And he has a good, solid job at General Motors."

Oren's second "h'mmm" had a hint of an underlying "grrr."

"I think 'Yankee Doodle' should come before 'The Arkansas Traveler' and that 'Battle Hymn of the Republic' should be the grand finale, don't you?"

"Yes."

At least this time he could give his wife a definite answer.

The day-long festivities on the Fourth offered a chance for almost everyone in town to participate, from the high-school glee club to the Livonia Players annual reenactment of the signing of the Declaration of Independence, from his wife's piano students to speakers from the Livonia Women's League, another of whose meetings Laura was attending this very night.

"I know you'd prefer he worked at Ford's," Ethel continued, as if her own comment on the music had not intervened, "and I know you'd prefer he were closer to Laura's age. But really, what other objection could you have against Mr. Gorman?"

"That he's not in love with her."

"Nor she with him."

"Then why on earth are you trying to cook up something between them? Isn't one disappointment like that enough?"

Oren bristled, then subsided. In the thirty-three years he and Ethel had been married, scarcely a hard word ever passed between them, and even a small quarrel made him feel as if the whole world were out of joint.

"I'm sorry," he said.

Ethel patted his hand. "You don't want her to get hurt. Neither do I. But maybe you're being too protective. It isn't fair to judge Mr. Gorman by the way that other man behaved."

"I should have shot that other man," Oren muttered, and Ethel murmured consolingly, "I know."

She went into the house to fix lemonade, and Oren sighed and watched the traffic pass on the road. Life had been good to him. A steady job at Ford—shortly after he and Ethel had moved into the Kingsley House he'd obtained a transfer to the Nankin Mills plant, one of Mr. Ford's small water-powered factories along the Rouge River, just a few miles from their new home. He'd been laid off only nine months during the Depression, and tight as those months had been, he felt luckier than many of his comrades who'd gone unemployed for years, scavenging work wherever they could find it. He'd seen college-educated men go down on their knees and beg for janitor's jobs. He'd seen one man burst into tears when he was turned away. When Oren got his own job back, he and Ethel had taken in for six months an unemployed gardener, creating a makeshift bedroom in the basement so the man would no longer have to sleep in a box by the railroad tracks in the raw winter weather.

"My daughter, my grandchildren, living with a bum in their cellar!" wailed Ethel's mother, Mrs. Allen, who had never forgiven Oren for taking Ethel away to the Kingsley House.

But the gardener, a gentle, toothless, slightly dim-witted man, had been so grateful for his bed and board that when his luck finally turned, he came back a year later and planted beautiful flowers for Ethel all around the house.

Throughout the years, Oren had advanced as a tool-and-die maker at the Nankin Mills plant. One day, early on, Henry Ford himself arrived at the little factory with his friend Thomas Edison. The workers tried to act calm as Mr. Ford proudly explained to Mr. Edison how the factory made the dies that cut the stencils for the famous Ford logo.

"Tell him how fine we can do it," said Mr. Ford, randomly selecting Oren and guiding him toward Mr. Edison.

"We can engrave the letters six one-thousandth of an inch high,"

Oren replied, and Mr. Ford added, "That's just twice the thickness of a human hair. Can you beat that, Tom?"

Oren had trembled with inner excitement long after they left. Today I have met, and spoken to, not one but two geniuses, he thought, and though it pained him a little to realize he could never be like them, he felt an overriding thrill to know that such people existed and that the world could be changed infinitely for the better by the vision of one man. He went back to his work, inspired, and even during the dark days at Ford, the times of violence and strikes, Oren never lost the feeling that he was part of a great era of progress that would benefit all mankind. Now, age fifty-six and a plant foreman, he had only nine years to go to a comfortable, if modest, retirement. Then he and Ethel would take some long car trips—he had a hankering to see the Grand Canyon—always coming back home to the Kingsley House.

From inside, he heard stirring sounds and the clinking of ice as Ethel prepared the lemonade. Over the years, they had made a few improvements to the house—not too much, just to install a modern kitchen and a tiled bathroom and to take advantage of the plumbing and utilities that had gradually come to town. He wished Emma could see it; she had known change must come, yet she would be pleased to know how he had cared for and treasured her gift. Perhaps it wasn't a mansion like Mr. Ford lived in, but it was a good, true home, and here he had done what every man was meant to do, love his wife, raise his children, earn his keep.

He was proud of his son Jimmy, a radio officer in the merchant marine and third in command on his ship stationed in the Mediterranean. Like all the other young men, eighteen-year-old Jimmy had rushed out to enlist following Pearl Harbor but was rejected for a partial hearing loss in his right ear, a defect he'd been born with but that never seemed to handicap him. Undeterred by Uncle Sam's rejection, Jimmy had crossed the Detroit River to Canada and tried to enlist in the army there, only to be turned down yet again. His son had felt ashamed and disgraced, and still determined to serve had at last managed to pass physical muster for the merchant marine. Looking back, Oren was glad for the way it had turned out. Many of Jimmy's high-school friends had died in those strange places—Anzio, Bataan, Guadalcanal—or come back minus an arm, a leg, or a face. In 1941 everyone had thought the war a noble cause, a glorious duty, and yes, it was. But no one had really understood how long, how brutal, how costly in young lives, that glory would be.

Now, Laura. Oh, but he doted on that girl. All the more reason he should have shot the bastard who broke her heart. He half wished he'd kept Emma's old shotgun, but Ethel had insisted he get rid of it when they moved into the Kingsley House. "We're not going to need it, and it's a danger around the children," she said flatly, and of course, she was right. And it wasn't that Laura needed a shotgun wedding, not his daughter. But that man had hurt her, no matter how brave a face she put on it, no matter how she buried herself in her school teaching and now this women-in-politics business. Sometimes Oren still felt like marching to Detroit, calling out that scoundrel, putting up his dukes, and pummelling the you-know-what out of him, although it was far more likely that the scoundrel, twenty-five years younger, six inches taller, and fifty pounds heavier, would have beaten the you-know-what out of Laura's balding, bespectacled, and slightly stout-bellied dad.

"Here you are. This will cool you down." Ethel handed him a frosty glass of lemonade and resumed her seat. Strands of pure white mingled in her once-blond hair, giving it the color of pale sunshine, and if Oren's eyes saw the gentle wrinkles that told her age, his mind simply erased them. "Now," she continued, "as I was saying about Mr. Gorman . . ."

Oren sighed patiently as his wife repeated Barry Gorman's matrimonial qualifications which, as far as he could see, boiled down to the fact that the man was single.

"But he doesn't seem like the marrying kind," he objected. "He's near forty, Ethel. If he had an inclination to wed, he's surely had the chance before now. Instead, he's been off traipsing through the wilds of South America."

"Which means he's got his wild oats out of his system and is ready to settle down. He's already taken an interest in Laura's SAVE OUR TREE! campaign."

Oren gave another noncommittal "h'mmm." Following the Decoration Day rally by Laura's students, Mr. Gorman had indeed written a letter to the *Livonian,* commenting that on the basis of his travels in South America he had come to appreciate the majesty and freedom of open spaces and that people must not be so enamored of progress that they thoughtlessly plowed over natural beauty that should be preserved. It was a nice thought, but the connection, Oren felt, between the jungles and mountains of South America and a single, aging maple tree was a little too far-fetched for most of the good citizens of Livonia to appreciate.

Mr. Gorman had also stopped by the maple once or twice on his way home from the GM plant to say hello to Laura and hear how the campaign was progressing. She, her students, and a few other concerned townspeople had made it a habit to gather there in the afternoons to continue collecting signatures on their petition. Oren had been present on one such occasion, and the conversation between his daughter and Barry Gorman had hardly been of a romantic turn. He asked about her students. She asked after his mother and his job. Then they talked about the weather in an awkward sort of way. A fellow had to be a bit more adept at conversation and compliments than that if he meant to woo a girl.

"It's the maple tree and some notion about preserving the landscape he's interested in, not Laura," he grumbled, "although how any red-blooded man could care about a tree when there's a smart, pretty, unattached girl standing right in front of him . . ."

"So you agree it is possible." Ethel smiled quietly, and Oren opened his mouth as if he'd been tricked.

"But you said she doesn't love him."

"No, she doesn't. Not exactly. Not yet." Ethel gave a calm shrug. "And I agree the ideal thing would be for Laura to meet the man of her dreams and fall head over heels in love, just like we did." She gazed at him, and Oren's heart, as always, melted a little at her look. "But she's already done that, and the man of her dreams let her down. What she wants, no matter how much she pretends otherwise, is a husband, babies, a home. You've heard her referring to her pupils as 'my children,' haven't you? And Mr. Gorman is a good-looking, intelligent, well-mannered man who's come back from South America to take care of his mother. He's the kind of man who makes a commitment, just like you, and if he makes a commitment to Laura, he'll stick by her. Besides, he may think he's stopping by the maple tree to talk about the march of progress in Livonia, but he must at least like Laura or he wouldn't bother. If they can share just one thing together, be it companionship or politics or a notion to save a maple tree, they might fall in love along the way. So promise me you'll give Mr. Gorman a fair chance?"

"All right," he conceded. "But if he hurts her . . ."

"He won't. Now let's say no more about it because here she comes." Ethel nodded up the street where Laura was approaching at a jaunty pace. "But I'll keep an eye out for Mr. Gorman at the crossroads, and the next time he makes an appearance I'll stroll on over. After all, I showed him my photographs of Livonia Center in the 1920s, and he mentioned he has a collection of photos from South America, so it certainly wouldn't be out of place for me to express an interest in seeing them and invite him and his mother to dinner and—"

Ethel stopped. Laura had reached the front walk. She wore a red skirt, a pink blouse, and she'd walked in such eagerness that her brunette hair was bobbing out of its combs. Oren stood. His daughter's blue eyes were shining in a way they hadn't in months, and her face looked ready to burst into a joyous shout.

"Mom! Dad!" She flung out her arms and almost leaped up the porch stairs. "It's happened! I did it! I've officially entered my name as a candidate—the first woman candidate ever—for the Livonia town board!"

Five

Barry Gorman finished his chicken salad and poppy seed roll and turned to his mother, sitting in a canvas lawn chair beneath a shady elm tree.

"Would you like me to refill your plate, Mops?" he asked.

"No, thank you, son." His mother sucked her tongue behind her lower teeth. "These rolls are delicious, but there's a nasty little poppy seed stuck beneath my dentures. Do you think anyone will notice if I slip it out and give it a quick wipe with my napkin?"

"No, go ahead. There's no one close by, and I'll cover for you if anyone comes our way."

Demurely, Mops raised her napkin to her lips, while Barry smiled casually at the crowd mingling on the neatly trimmed lawn of his boss's backyard this Fourth of July. Behind him he heard discreet sucking and swiping noises as his mother swooped in on the offending poppy seed.

"Got the little devil," she whispered, and when Barry turned around, there was his mother politely dabbing her lips with her napkin and waving graciously to his coworkers as they chatted in groups on the lawn.

Barry smiled, glad to see his mother in good spirits. As Frances had predicted, Mops's moods had been up and down since his father's death two months before. But today she was supremely happy, thanks to the phone call from Ken in Texas last night announcing the safe arrival of a lusty eight-pound twelve-ounce boy named David George, the "George" in honor of their late father. Little Davey was squalling in the background even as Ken telephoned from the hospital room.

"I'm going to get you and Frances some earplugs for a baby gift," Barry had joked, and Mops, now that the male identity of her first grandchild was confirmed, was up to her knitting needles in blue yarn. She had even brought her knitting to today's picnic, which turned out to be a smart conversational ploy, for naturally all the other wives, not a few of them pregnant themselves, flocked around her to inquire the reason for her handiwork, which in turn gave Mops an open invitation to brag about her new grandson. So happy did she appear that Barry hadn't the heart to tell her that in July in Texas little Davey probably wouldn't have much need for a wardrobe of warm blue woolens.

The faint buzz of a small plane skimmed overhead, and he shielded his eyes and peered skyward. I wish I were up there, he thought, catching a glimpse of silver wing high against the bright sun. The plane passed out of sight, and he blinked and returned to earth, to the cookout at his boss's handsome brick home in Livonia's Linden Park subdivision. The clipped green lawn and pink rosebushes, the terrace with striped umbrella table and matching chairs, resembled a photograph from one of those suburban trends magazines that came with the Detroit Sunday newspaper. His neatly groomed coworkers and their pretty wives looked almost like models placed decoratively around the set. Barry surveyed them with a mixture of forced goodwill and resignation. They were nice people, all nice people, from his boss Ted Burrows and blond wife Alice to all the eager young couples chatting about the new auto models, their preference in local supermarkets, and the easy-care linoleum floors in their eat-in kitchens. How could he be surrounded by such nice, well-meaning people and feel so completely out of place? Even Mops was doing better at making conversation than he was. He wished he had a shot of tequila, not because he was a drinker, but because just a sip would reinforce the memories: of high, godlike mountains, supremely indifferent to all below, of ancient roads that mired in mud in the rainy season and baked to dust in the dry, of the jungle steam that made you swim in pure sweat as you hacked through the lush, strangling vines, of the clamor of Spanish in the marketplace where smooth yellow mangoes and ripe orange papayas heaped like gold on the vendors' stands.

He let go the memories with a sigh. The day was hot, and though nothing like the South American heat, the summer already promised to be one long heat wave punctuated by occasional and far too brief showers. Barry wore lightweight beige pants and a short-sleeved checked shirt like the other men, and it relieved him to know he'd chosen the right attire. He'd packed a suit jacket and tie in his car just in case. Since starting his job at GM six weeks before, he had acquired five suits—navy blue, dark brown, tan, gray-striped, and charcoal—and five white shirts, which Mops faithfully washed, starched, and ironed every Friday evening. From his father's closet he assembled a collection of striped and paisley ties, taking his cue as to colors and patterns from his coworkers' neckwear. He wore one of his five suits each day of the week, not from lack of imagination, but because his imagination preferred to dwell elsewhere, and by having his choice of clothes ready-made for him each morning, he gained more free time for his mind to roam.

Mops, on the other hand, was perhaps a little overdressed for today's cookout. Where the other women sported cotton slacks or skirts, she wore a dusty rose print dress and open-toed turquoise pumps. A turquoise handbag rested by her side. This was the first habit Barry had really come to notice about his mother since his return: she always wore dresses, never slacks—heaven forbid!—and she always insisted that the color of her shoes and handbag match precisely. These latter accessories were not of expensive quality—Mops couldn't afford the best—but somehow she had taken a notion that if the colors were perfectly synchronized then she had achieved the epitome of style. She also adored costume jewelry, and when one of the young wives mistook the purple glass stone in her ring for a genuine amethyst, Mops didn't trouble to discourage her "oohs" and "aahs" at the size of the gem.

A few more wives had stopped to say hello to his mother, and excusing himself, Barry strolled over to Alice Burrows, his hostess, working up a compliment on her chicken salad. The cookout, although seemingly voluntary, had had something of a "be there and be counted" undertone, and he knew where his duty lay. He was adapting, learning to speak the GM lingo about production quotas and market share, to spend five minutes each morning, no more, no less, at the water cooler, passing an idle comment with his workmates. In a way, Barry reflected, he and Mops were both victims of a recent loss, she of her husband, he of his freedom, and each had to cope with and overcome their particular grief. If he thought of his new life here as a journey to a foreign place and tread cautiously, just as he had at first in South America, he would gradually get the hang of it.

He reached his hostess and said, "Delicious chicken salad, Mrs. Burrows. You have a lovely home." Hardly original, but both statements were true and he delivered them sincerely.

"Why, thank you, Mr. Gorman." She smiled, her even white teeth, clear skin, and coiffed blond hair reminding him of a model he'd seen demonstrating a Maytag washer in a department store in Detroit. It amazed him that although he'd been introduced to her only an hour before, she already knew his and every other employee's and spouse's name. "I hope your mother is enjoying herself?" She nodded toward Mops busily knitting beneath the elm tree.

"Yes, thank you, she—"

Another plane, louder this time, interrupted their talk, and they both stopped to locate the sound. Barry pointed out the small craft, flying low to the west. I wish I were up there, he thought, free to go wherever I please.

"Must be heading for that two-bit dirt airstrip down Joy Road," said Ted Burrows. He had wandered over with several junior employees close at his elbow, and he waved in the direction the aircraft had gone. "Those little planes better be careful they don't cross paths with the big boys at Detroit-Wayne and Willow Run. Alice, did I tell you Barry flew in South America in the war?"

"Did you, Mr. Gorman?" Mrs. Burrows turned toward him and began to inquire about his aviation career. She seemed genuinely interested, not just trying to be a good GM wife, or maybe the two were so intertwined Barry couldn't tell the difference. Either way, before he could answer, several of the juniors piped up, eager to establish their own wartime credentials, and Barry was just as glad to slip unnoticed out of the conversation, if not out of the crowd. A two-bit dirt airstrip. It sounded like most of the no-name airfields he'd flown into and out of in South America, and the location Ted had indicated was only a few miles distant. If the place had a plane or two for rent . . . He glanced over at Mops, sitting in the lawn chair beneath the elm tree. She seemed to be assiduously mopping her mouth with her napkin, and Barry beckoned Alice Burrows aside.

"You know," he confided, "my mother does get a little fatigued in this heat. Would you mind if I excused us to take her for a short drive? It would cool her off a bit before we meet everyone at Town Hall at four o'clock to hear the programs."

"Why, of course, how thoughtful of you to take such care of your mother." Mrs. Burrows sent him off with a friendly smile, and as Barry headed away he heard her making his excuses to her husband and adding in a mock scolding voice, "Why don't you men put your heads together and find Mr. Gorman a nice, helpful wife? There must be an unattached secretary or two in your department."

Barry bent to Mops, still hiding her mouth in her napkin and making small sucking noises. "Another poppy seed?" he whispered.

"Like gravel, those little devils," she replied, snapping her false teeth back into place.

He explained his plan and led her out, adding a few waves to his coworkers. Mops settled into the passenger seat of the Chevy and continued her knitting as they drove away. In ten minutes, Barry located the airport, an overgrown field with one dirt runway, a small wood office building and hangar, both painted a cheery yellow, and a dozen small planes parked at random on the far side of the runway. A bright orange wind sock floated gaily at either end of the field. It was everything Ted Burrows had implied, a shoe-string operation held together by elbow grease, spit, and glue, and Barry thought, *it's beautiful.*

"I'm going to look around," he said to Mops. "Want to come?"

"No, just park in the shade so I can finish my knitting," she replied. She held up a sky blue bootie and frowned at a dropped stitch.

Barry drove the Chevy to a shady spot beside the office. The door was closed, and no one was inside, so he walked across the field to inspect the planes. There were a handful of Piper J-3s, a J-4 Coupe, two Aeronca Champs, an Ercoupe, and an old Stearman biplane outfitted for crop dusting. He wove in and out between them, peering into the cockpits and admiring each design, feeling happier by the minute. One or two of the planes were a little battered, their interiors worn, but most were in good condition and showed evidence of regular maintenance. The star of the lot was a brand-new Cessna 170, its gleaming aluminum fuselage striped with metallic blue trim. How he'd love to take that one aloft!

He returned to the airport office, knocked, and opened the door. The one-room interior was a combination passenger lounge and ticket counter, furnished with three mismatched chairs and a water cooler and decorated with gaily colored posters proclaiming "Scenic Tours $8" and "Learn To Fly!" From the nearby hangar came the thumps and clunks of assorted tools, and Barry made for the sound. Inside he saw an old Stinson and a gangly youth in grease-covered overalls standing on a ladder, wielding a wrench over the engine.

"Hi! Can I help you?" he called, swiping his sleeve across his forehead to mop off the sweat.

"What are the chances of going up for a quick flight?" Barry asked.

"Scenic tour, you mean?"

"No, to check out in a rental plane, if you have any. Here's my license." Barry pulled out his wallet and removed the tattered ticket. "I've been flying in South America and just took a job at the new GM plant." He spelled out his aviation experience for the young mechanic, who introduced himself as Bob.

"Wow, neat." Bob nodded appreciatively at Barry's resume. He looked about twenty, and his bucktoothed grin gave him a perpetually eager expression. "Well, Don, the owner, is due any minute. Ask him about the Cessna 170. It's his pride and joy."

"Thanks."

Barry stepped out of the hangar. A green car had parked beside the Chevy, and a short, pudgy man was chatting amiably with Mops. Barry hastened toward him.

"Hello! Are you Don, the owner?" he asked.

"Owner, manager, tour guide, janitor, yup, that's me. Don Windham." The man held out his hand. He had thinning hair and a deep chuckle in his voice, and when Barry explained his interest, a grin flashed across Don's chubby face.

"So you like my snazzy new Cessna, do you? Yup, she's my favorite bird. She's got everything: polished aluminum construction with fabric-covered wings, six-cylinder 145 hp Continental engine, two-way radio, three 12.5 gallon wing tanks, steerable tailwheel, a completely uphol-stered interior with leather trim. Cruises like a dream at 118 mph." He beamed at his own recital. "Let's go up and if you like the feel of her you can take your mother for a spin." He winked at Mops, who huffed in reply.

"Oh no. You're not getting me in one of those things. I'm too old for loop-de-loops and whatever else it is you plan to do. Find someone your own age to go adventuring with."

Barry kissed her, and she adjusted her rhinestone glasses and went on unperturbed with her knitting. They headed for the plane, and Barry hoisted himself into the pilot's seat. He lifted his hand to his head, an automatic gesture to remove his fedora, and laughed aloud. The hat wasn't there, of course, but he felt almost as good as if it were. Don buckled in beside him, Barry started the engine, and they taxied to the end of the runway. Full throttle, ease back the yoke, and almost instantly the wheels broke ground and they were airborne.

I'm free, Barry exulted as the little plane climbed, *free!,* while Don rambled helpful comments about the trim tab—"Just give it a roll and she corrects like a charm."—the busy airspace around the large air-ports—"Dang DC-3s think they own the sky"—the radio—"If Bob's in the office, we can raise him. Hey, Bob, you there?"—and the rough patch at the near end of the runway—"Just skim over it before you touch down." Barry's body settled into a state of quiet joy. Flying a plane was like riding a bike. You might be a little creaky after a few months out of the sky, but it wasn't something you ever forgot. And while cruising above the flat, green Michigan countryside wasn't quite like swooping between Andean peaks where the emptiness sang like music in his soul, still, he was high, he was soaring, and every cell in his body felt inexplicably happy.

"Say, you know, we're a new outfit here," said Don, half an hour later, as Barry touched down smoothly for a landing. "I got all sorts of plans for this place. Storage for private planes. Scenic flights. Commuter hops up to the capital or over to Flint or Grand Rapids. A flight school. Maybe even some banner towing and skywriting. You ever done that?"

"Not in the Andes," Barry laughed, as he taxied off the runway and shut down the plane.

"Well, I aim to make this little field a sort of everyman's airport, you know what I mean? 'Flying—The Sport of the Future,' how's that for a slogan? Anyway, I know you got a day job and all, but there's evenings and weekends, never know when I could use an experienced pilot on a job. You interested?"

"You bet."

"Then come out again next weekend and let's talk," said Don.

Barry paid for his flight, shook hands, and hurried guiltily back to the Chevy. He'd left Mops alone for almost an hour.

"Did you have fun?" she asked, her needles clicking over a sky blue sweater. "Good. Well, we'd better get on to those speeches at Town Hall so your boss can see you made it."

They drove to Livonia Center, and Barry dropped off his mother and went to find a parking space. The downtown was crowded, although it wasn't quite accurate, he'd discovered, to call any particular area of Livonia "downtown." Instead, the businesses seemed to group around any convenient intersection and spread along the surrounding streets in an orderly bustle. He parked the car and rejoined Mops, who was standing next to Alice Burrows, in time to hear the closing piano chords of "Battle Hymn of the Republic." A bunting-draped grandstand had been erected on the lawn in front of Town Hall, and the crowd stood in a semicircle before the pavilion. A trim, business-suited woman from the

Livonia Women's League introduced herself at the microphone. Speeches, Barry thought, and he glanced to the corner and took a small measure of satisfaction in seeing the old maple tree spreading its giant green umbrella over the intersection. He hadn't stopped by the last two weeks to see how the SAVE OUR TREE! petition was going, but at least there was no sign of imminent danger. He was thinking of Miss Millard and wondering if he strolled over there, might he see her, when the woman at the microphone announced that their candidate for town board, Miss Laura Millard, would now say a few words. Barry's head jerked toward the pavilion at the name. So the schoolteacher had declared herself a candidate. Good for her.

"Really." Alice Burrows rolled her eyes and gave a pretty, exasperated sigh. "What are these women thinking of? Politics is a man's job."

Mops made a little grunt in her throat, and Barry gazed apprehensively at his mother. He saw by her face that she recognized the schoolteacher, and although he felt sure—at least fairly sure—that his mother would not say anything impolite to his boss's wife, he could tell by the way Mops wriggled her rhinestone glasses up her nose that the memory of the pleasant chat she'd had with Miss Millard and her parents on Decoration Day had predisposed her to like this particular candidate.

"Do you think so?" Mops inquired, her tone innocently curious. "I wonder what a woman's job is these days."

"Why to support her husband, of course."

Alice Burrows glanced again at the podium and shook her blond head at the folly of what she saw. Miss Millard had begun speaking about the plans to build a horse-racing track within the town boundaries and how it would affect taxes, traffic congestion, the possible breakup of Livonia into inconsequential communities. The teacher had her facts and figures neatly organized, and the crowd listened politely. Still, she spoke a trifle nervously, and her hand went several times to her hair combs, as if to be sure they hadn't strayed out of place.

Go on, you can do it, Barry found himself thinking, when Mrs. Burrows's smooth voice interrupted again.

"It's true during the war we women had to take on men's roles, but now it's over thank heaven we can get back to normal. I wouldn't dream of working when the men need the jobs to support their families."

"Maybe some women like to work," said Mops.

"As teachers and nurses, certainly," Alice agreed. "Those occupations are naturally reserved for us. And I mustn't forget secretaries. Ted says he could never find his files or get his coffee without them."

Mops smiled, her teeth—her false teeth, Barry thought—showing broadly. But she held her tongue, and as Miss Millard ended her speech to scattered applause, Alice Burrows waved to another couple and prepared to move away. As she left, she added over her shoulder with a little laugh, "Of course, if you're as tall and plain as that schoolteacher, you might as well amuse yourself with politics or charity work. Some girls just don't have what it takes to catch a man."

She sallied off, and Barry felt a stunned sensation in the center of his chest. He'd been listening to Miss Millard's speech with growing interest—he wasn't sure why because as a resident of Detroit he couldn't vote in Livonia—and he'd been thinking how brave it was of her to get up and face so many people—not something he'd ever be good at—and noticing that he rather liked it when her combs did slip and her hair got a little mussed by the breeze—which surprised him because he didn't really think much about women in a personal way—when Alice Burrows made her cutting remark. But before he could even think what to reply, she was gone. Barry turned to Mops, who looked as if she wanted to spit out a whole mouthful of poppy seeds.

"Nasty little devil," she said.

The program went on another hour, but Barry didn't pay it much heed. He found a seat for Mops on one of the park benches placed around the grandstand, then he located Miss Millard in the crowd. She was surrounded by a small cluster of supporters, and among them he recognized her parents, a few of her pupils, and the business-suited woman from the Livonia Women's League who had introduced her. It was a few minutes before she saw him, and he couldn't tell by her expression whether she was pleased to see him or just a bit startled.

"Oh, Mr. Gorman, how are you?" she said. "I didn't expect to see you here today."

He explained about the Burrows' cookout. "I thought your speech was very good. How is your maple tree campaign coming?"

"Well, it's at something of a stalemate. We've collected about all the signatures we can and sent them to the current town board, asking them to try to work out a compromise with the gas company. But this being an election year, none of the incumbents wants to take sides or cause a commotion that might split the voters. And the gas company's position is that—"

She went on for several minutes, and Barry listened, smiling. She sounded more like a candidate off the stand than on it. Perhaps she was just more comfortable talking one-on-one. She wore a tailored navy suit and a red blouse, and it dawned on him that she was, as Alice Burrows had said, rather tall. But plain? He didn't think so, although exactly what he did think about her appearance wasn't entirely clear to him.

"Well, it sounds like your candidacy is off and running," he remarked.

"Yes, I'm so busy, even though school is out, I hardly know whether I'm coming or going." She laughed. "It's exciting, a little nerve-racking. I have so much to learn. I have to start thinking about advertising, getting my name known, but on a very small budget. And it could be all for nothing." She bit her lip, and a shadow of doubt crossed her face. "A lot of people have put their faith in me, and I hate it when I feel like I've let people down."

"Well, I'd vote for you if I could," said Barry stoutly, and her blue eyes met his in undisguised gratitude.

"Would you? Thank you! Just to hear someone say it gives me a little more conviction."

They grinned at each other, until Barry began to feel awkward.

"Well, it was a pleasure seeing you, but I'd better get back to my mother." He winced. *That* sounded stupid. "I mean back to the party we're with, my boss, coworkers . . ."

"Yes, I'd better get back to work the crowd, shake hands, make my pitch, to anyone who'll listen, that is." She nodded vigorously, and one of the tortoiseshell combs in her brunette hair tumbled loose and fell to the ground. They stooped for it together, but she snagged it first, and he felt strangely disappointed that he'd missed touching her hand. *Don't,* he thought, as she reached to anchor the comb back in place, *let your hair go free,* and his hand almost went after hers to stop her. Then he thought that if she were sitting beside him in an airplane with the windows open, both combs would blow away and her glossy hair would tumble and dance around her face like a wayward cloud.

An idea began to take shape in his mind.

Six

Mops Gorman set her red handbag on a kitchen chair, helped herself to a butterscotch candy from the china dish on the windowsill, and turned to unpack the three grocery bags on the table. She had spent this Saturday afternoon marketing with a friend and was glad to return to the coolness of her bungalow to put away her purchases and plan a nice dinner. Barry was at that little airport, flying as usual, but she had long ago given up worrying about whatever it was he did in the air. Besides, Mops had a theory. Since her son hadn't crashed in ten years in the wilds of South America, he certainly *couldn't* crash in the civilization of the United States. That would not be logical, and Mops prided herself on her logic.

But—shouldn't there be more to her son's life than flying?

She sighed and pushed a footstool to the cupboard to stock her canned goods on the shelves. In Ireland, in her youth, Margaret Gorman had been considered a local beauty. Just under five feet tall, she'd had the flame-tinged hair and sea-green eyes of her Celtic people, a flawless complexion, button nose, and a buxom figure that made men think of ripe apples and fresh-mown hay. Her father had been a half-step above middle-class, a minor landowner, and with her looks and spunk she might have upped her station in life even further by the right marriage. But headstrong Margaret had fallen in love with handsome, black-haired George, who had dreams, ambition, and hardly a shilling to his name. They had eloped to America in 1908 and settled in Detroit where the boom of the automobile industry promised plentiful, well-paying jobs. While George worked hard, proud of his self-sufficiency as an electrician, she raised their two boys, and altogether life in America suited them. Once in a while, when times got hard, Mops wondered what her life might have been had she stayed in Ireland instead of following her heart. But even now, aged sixty-five, a plump, gray-haired widow with brown liver spots dotting her once flawless skin, she never regretted her decision. Nothing in the world could ever be so grand, so sublime, as to be swept away by a wild and glorious love.

Now if only that would happen for Barry. Even a nice, steady romance would do. His younger brother Ken, dashing and black-haired like his father, silver-tongued into the bargain, had always had a way with the ladies, and only that wicked war had delayed him and so many other young men from living happily ever after with the girl of their dreams. But Barry had never shown much interest in females at all—nor males; yes, she knew such goings-on existed though no moral person should ever acknowledge them. No, it was simply that even as a child Barry was a loner, his nose buried in adventure books, his imagination longing for the day he'd emulate his fictional heros. So although he'd made a stab at college, then dropped out to work as a grocery stockboy to help the family through the Depression, once the national recovery began, he was off on his quest. He wrote them letters from Panama, Ecuador, Peru, always managing to find work in remote places and sending rare gifts that Mops treasured and displayed all over the house. How many of her neighbors owned a pair of Venezuelan maracas, the hand-carved black gourds filled with tiny pebbles that rattled like a miniature hailstorm when you shook the wood handles? Who else on their street had an alpaca rug from Bolivia spread across their bedroom floor, its geometric pattern dyed bold red and black. Did any of her friends possess a mysterious silver medallion, engraved with ancient Inca symbols, or a beautiful brass-studded, leather-covered bench detailed in Andean scenes? My, what a big box that had been! And was there any-one at all in Detroit, in the whole state of Michigan, who could boast of having a genuine shrunken head from the Amazon jungle grinning front and center on their living-room wall? Well, she could.

Mops folded the empty grocery bags, took out her cookbook, and searched for a dish to please her son. Since the war, many new, enticing foods were appearing on the grocer's shelves, and salads concocted from a variety of fresh fruits and vegetables were especially popular. Following her cookbook's urgings to "Be creative!" she had invented one last night, a colorful affair of green lettuce, sliced red radishes, and ripe yel-low bananas in mayonnaise. Barry said he'd never tasted anything quite like it, and that was surely a compliment considering all the exotic foods he'd sampled in his journeying. She picked a recipe for turkey noodle casserole and began to gather the ingredients, timing the meal for his return at six o'clock. In addition to Saturdays, he went to the airport one or two nights a week after work, always asking, "Mops, are you sure you don't mind?"

"No, you go," she assured him, glad for the consolation he'd found in flying. She felt sorry he'd had to return to the States on her account. She had simply never expected her George to die so suddenly; they were supposed to last together until the end. If she'd ever learned a trade or had much schooling, she might have found a way to support herself, though it was unlikely anyone would hire her now at her age. But like most girls of her class in the old country, she'd gone straight from her father's house to her husband's, and she rather admired these modern young women, like that schoolteacher, Miss Millard, who could support themselves and earn money like a man. Meanwhile, she had her neighbors to chat with, her favorite radio programs in the afternoon, shopping, housekeeping, and more baby clothes to sew, knit, and crochet for her rapidly growing grandson. You could keep busy or you could get old, and the devil take her if she'd toss in her towels.

She was lifting the turkey casserole from the oven when Barry walked through the door.

"Well, I think it's about ready to go," he said.

"What is?" She beckoned him to the table, poured milk into his glass, and spooned casserole onto his plate. He helped her into the seat opposite before taking his chair. "What's ready to go?" she repeated, as they commenced their meal.

"The banner-towing. This is good casserole, Mops."

"Thank you. What banner-towing?"

"The banner on the back of the plane. We've been practicing for weeks, and we'd get better performance if the air weren't so hot and muggy, but we've got it down to a system now." He took a pen from his pocket, fetched a sheet of paper, and began sketching. "The letters are interchangeable, see, each five feet high by three feet wide. They're sewn onto strips of canvas with bamboo rods at either end, and you clip the rods together to spell out the message. You attach a towrope at the front, then mount the loop of the rope between two upright poles beside the runway and spread the banner along the ground. The plane takes off, circles the airport, and comes in low as if for a landing. Instead we let out a hook, snag the towrope, and pull up sharp to peel the banner off the ground. It's weighted so it straightens as soon as it's in the air."

Mops rolled her eyes, but reminded herself that this being civilization, her son's safety was assured. "And what does the banner say?"

"It can say anything you want, providing the message isn't too long." Barry took a swallow of milk. "Don thinks its best use will be for advertising. It could say 'Shop at A&P,' for example, or 'Buy Clover Dairy Milk.' "

"And the business owner would pay you to fly this message all over town?"

"Exactly. Thousands of people would see it, and because it's new and eye-catching, it would get a lot of attention. I was thinking it could also work well for a political campaign."

"Such as?"

"Such as LAURA MILLARD FOR TOWN BOARD, although that's a little long. Maybe just MILLARD FOR TOWN BOARD would do it."

Glory hallelujah! thought Mops. He's noticed a woman after all. Then her impression changed as he began another diagram to demonstrate how the length of the banner, the power setting, the cruising speed, and a number of other factors she couldn't quite follow figured into the process.

"Wait a minute," she interrupted. "Does Miss Millard know about any of this?"

"No." Barry looked surprised. "But she mentioned at the Fourth of July program that she needed an inexpensive way to get her name spread around town. This seems like a good solution. Since we're still experimenting, Don said I could try it a few times for free."

"Don't you think you better call Miss Millard and ask her?" Mops clucked her tongue against her dentures. "That was the Fourth of July, this is the beginning of August. Have you even spoken to her since then?"

"Well, no. I had to make sure it would work first."

"Then you better call her. What if she doesn't want her name flown all over the sky? Maybe she has other plans."

"Call her?" Barry stopped chewing his dinner and looked at his mother, and Mops thought that if she had one of her handbags handy, she would have whapped him over the head with it.

"Yes, get her number from the operator, phone her, and explain your plan." She spelled it out in careful steps. Three months since her son had returned from Peru, and it still didn't seem to penetrate his skull that if you wanted to communicate with someone you picked up the telephone receiver and dialed them. Did he think he had to wait for a river raft or monkey mail or however it was they passed messages in those remote corners of the world? More important, didn't he realize he was talking about a nice, eligible young lady who might be happy to hear from him? How could she have raised such a dunderhead?

"Call her on the telephone," Mops instructed. "Explain the situation. Invite her to the airport to see the banner and give her approval. And tell her I'm coming," she added, as she pushed Barry toward the phone. This was clearly too important to let her unromantic son muck it up.

Seven

On the Saturday night that Barry Gorman phoned, Laura was sitting at the kitchen table of the Kingsley House with Eleanor Bernstein and half a dozen other members of the Livonia Women's League. They were poring over the latest newspaper articles about town politics and jotting notes for their campaign strategy when the phone rang. Laura excused herself to the living room to answer it. She returned ten minutes later wearing an expression that managed to appear dazed, amazed, surprised, and happy, all in one.

"What is it?" Eleanor asked, and the other women quickly suspended their chatter at the hint of something afoot.

"I've just had an offer to have my name, my candidacy, advertised in the sky." Laura shook her head, the idea still not quite real in her mind. She sat down to explain, amidst her friends' excited cries of who, how, when, where?

"And it's free?" asked Lorraine Demske.

"Would you ride in the plane with him?" demanded Jean Voss.

"This is great!" said Betty Rhodes, while Ruth Harris wagged a teasing finger. "I remember seeing you speak to him on the Fourth of July. He's good-looking, Laura."

"Now just a minute." Amused but firm, Eleanor brought the group back to order. "I agree this sounds like a fantastic opportunity, but we have to consider all the implications. Is this really the best advertising strategy? Some voters may love it; others may call it a nuisance and unsafe. If there were any kind of accident, if the banner broke loose or the plane crashed, the whole thing could backfire in our faces. And even if it's free at first, how much will it cost later on? Suppose we can't afford to keep it up, but our opponents can? They could steal the idea as the election neared, and we'd lose the advantage."

The women broke into a vigorous discussion, while Lorraine, the group's secretary, busily jotted notes on a lined pad. Laura let them talk. Eleanor was the natural leader, and early on Laura had asked her why she didn't run for town board herself.

"Because I'm not only female, but Jewish," Eleanor explained with a matter-of-fact shrug. "That may be asking a little too much of the voters our first time around. My turn will come. Right now, I can do more behind the scenes as an organizer."

And organize Eleanor did. Of the seven women in the Kingsley House that night, two others besides Laura had tossed their hats into the ring at Eleanor's urging. Betty Rhodes and Jean Voss were running for school board, and all the women pulled together to help each other campaign, feeling that a victory for any one of them would be a victory for all. Eleanor seemed to work dawn to dusk, and Laura wondered sometimes if her commitment had been born of her own need to keep busy, to overcome the grief of her husband's death at Normandy. But there was also no denying that Eleanor possessed a genuine talent for politics. Maybe, thought Laura, when you've lost something you wanted with all your heart, you start out just trying to fill the empty space. You feel it crying inside you, like a hungry child begging to be fed, so you feed it whatever is handy, whatever keeps it quiet and brings a moment's peace. If you find the right means to nourish it, the crying and aching slowly ease, and in their place come purpose and content. Instead of emptiness, there's fullness again, maybe not in the form you anticipated, but enough to let you carry on and be happy, just like I'm trying to do. If you're lucky, like Eleanor, it can become a whole new life.

Laura smiled at the group around her, grateful to be part of their circle. Aside from the excitement of the politics, she was having fun, yes, real fun, in the company of these women. They ranged in age from twenty-two to thirty-nine, in occupation from homemaker to attorney. Three were married, Lorraine was engaged, and only Laura and Ruth were still patently single. But it was like having girlfriends again, like the days when she'd roomed with her college classmates in Detroit before they slipped off one by one to wed. So when the debate around the kitchen table ended with the consensus that the sky banner was a bold stroke worth trying, Laura wasn't unhappy when Ruth made another teasing remark about Mr. Gorman's good looks, and Eleanor, apparently considering the business portion of the meeting closed, let the discussion disintegrate into a girlish gabfest.

"He wouldn't call, Laura, if he weren't interested," said Lorraine, and her friends chimed their agreement.

"But why would he wait so long, since the Fourth of July?" she protested, feeling compelled to make at least a show of resistance. "And he made the offer sound purely mechanical, like an aviation experiment. Besides, he's bringing his mother."

"Oh no, a mama's boy," groaned Jean. "Let me tell you about the trouble my sister had, marrying a man like that."

For the next half hour, the women analyzed, scrutinized, inspected, dissected, and debated every aspect of Mr. Barry Gorman's physical, social, and financial attributes, while Laura alternately basked in and tried to dissuade their eagerness and Lorraine mischievously took full notes of the proceedings.

"I hope this isn't going into our official records," Laura pleaded at nine-thirty as the women laughingly concluded their meeting and rose to leave.

"It's not," Lorraine assured her. She tore off the lined sheet and handed it to Laura with a wink of her eye. At the bottom of all the scribbled pros and cons regarding Barry Gorman, Lorraine had written in large block letters: DON'T LET HIM GET AWAY!

Laura washed their coffee cups and went to her bedroom on the second floor. Her parents were in Detroit for the evening, visiting Grandpa R. Z., Uncle Stub, and Aunt Anna, and she had the house to herself. Stretched on the bed, she tried to read a magazine, but her thoughts refused to focus on the words, and more than once she found her eyes traveling to her closet door. Finally, deliberately, she went to the closet and opened it. From the rear she brought forth the plastic-shrouded wedding gown and faced it, a tremble in her heart. The hurt was still there, but not as painful, not as deep, a sign that she was doing a good job, between her teaching and the politics, of filling the empty space. But now a new danger threatened, a glimmer of foolish hope, a longing she didn't want to define. Don't be ridiculous, she told herself. You hardly know him. But he wouldn't have called if he weren't interested, would he?

The next day, Sunday, she drove to the little airport on Joy Road, seven miles from the Kingsley House. Since Mrs. Gorman was coming, Laura had invited her parents along as well. It felt safer that way, and her mother, in particular, seemed pleased that Mr. Gorman had called. She made several less-than-casual references to his South American photos, hinting how much she would enjoy seeing them at some future date. Her father appeared more wary, alternately muttering about wild oats and scoundrels and how just because a woman ran for town board, no man ought to take it into his head she couldn't bake a decent cornbread.

Mr. Gorman and his mother were already at the airport when the Millards arrived, and he and the airport owner, a short, jolly man named Don Windham, set about showing them the plane and explaining how the banner-towing worked. The older people followed the lesson with interest, and Laura noticed her father gradually warming to Barry Gorman as the mechanics of the project began to intrigue him. But having heard the same information on the telephone the night before, Laura found her mind focused less on airspeed and altitude than on the pilot. Ten years older than me, she thought, and he's seen so much of the world. He'll think me uninteresting, naive, a homebody. I'll probably say something stupid and scare him off forever. Maybe he won't like the way I wear my hair, or my lipstick or perfume. Maybe I should have worn a skirt instead of slacks. What if he asks me to go up in the plane with him? I've never flown in my life. What if I faint or get sick to my stomach? What a lovely impression that would make. Especially when I'm already two inches taller than he is. Couldn't I shrink somehow? Maybe I shouldn't have painted my fingernails. He might think that's racy. Do the South American ladies wear slacks? Do they flirt, do they bring their parents along on dates? Is this even a date at all?

By the time Mr. Gorman and Mr. Windham displayed the lettered banner they'd prepared, Laura's stomach was in such a flutter she felt as if she'd swallowed a whole flock of butterflies. Then for one split second all the butterflies halted in midflight. MILLARD FOR TOWN BOARD proclaimed the banner in big, huge—oh, gigantic—red letters, and the next instant, as the enormity of having her name spread sky-high all over the town of Livonia struck her, the butterflies in her stomach went into such a maelstrom of flight she had to clamp her mouth closed for fear a storm of frantic, winged creatures would beat up her chest and burst out her lips.

"Now we're going to take off and you folks can just sit back and relax," Mr. Windham informed them. He led them to chairs positioned in the shade by the hangar where they would have a clear view of the runway. With a final wave he and Mr. Gorman got into the plane.

"How brave of your son to be a pilot!" said Ethel. "And what is that you're knitting, Mrs. Gorman?"

In seconds, the two mothers were off and running in an easy conversation about their families. Laura tried to second-guess what was happening inside the plane. She could vaguely see Mr. Gorman and Mr. Windham talking and nodding in the cockpit, and she wished she could hear the men's voices. It was bad enough not knowing if she were on a date or not, bad enough that her name was about to wave in five-foot high letters all over town, and then on top of it wondering if Mr. Gorman and Mr. Windham were now saying things like "A bit on the tall side, isn't she, Barry?" and "Yes, but don't you think she has nice legs, Don?"

The engine revved to life and settled into a steady rumble, the wood propeller an invisible blur. Then the trim silver plane—Mr. Gorman and Mr. Windham, Laura noticed, both referred to it as a bird—began to roll along the runway. One second it was on the ground, the next instant it lifted into the air, and the transition was so effortless, so graceful, Laura almost felt as if she had witnessed an act of magic. The noise of the engine—perhaps the wind was blowing it away—had all but ceased, and with the sun glinting off its silvery wings, the little craft climbed above the trees like a songbird sprung from a cage. In a minute it disappeared against the brightness of the sky.

"Now they'll circle around the airport, swoop down between the support poles, and hook the towrope," explained Oren, as if he'd supervised the process a hundred times.

"Here they come!" Ethel jumped to her feet and pointed excitedly.

"No, that's a bird," said Oren.

"Are you sure?" Ethel asked.

"I'm afraid I don't see it at all," said Mrs. Gorman, squinching up her nose and placidly continuing her knitting from the comfort of her chair. "Oh yes, I do. There it is."

She pointed, and Laura stared. A small silver speck caught her eye, a dot against the blue. For a few seconds it seemed to hang motionless, growing gradually larger, until a sense of forward movement attached itself to the shape. Then in a whoosh came noise, a winged outline, and the plane skimmed above the poles, snagged the banner, and immediately angled skyward. The banner peeled off the ground and rose into the air behind the plane like a long red tail.

"Oh!" Laura gasped, her knees half-buckling at the sight. MILLARD

FOR TOWN BOARD blared the banner, and she thought, What have I done? I'm in for it now. The whole town will be staring up at it thinking, thinking— But what they might be thinking didn't much matter because her father, her mother, and Mrs. Gorman were all on their feet, shouting, clapping, and cheering, "Hooray! Hooray!"

"Wow! Look at that!" Oren pointed proudly as the bold silver bird with its extravagant red plume flew off to the north. "Now they'll crisscross Livonia until everyone sees it."

The three parents resumed their chairs, chatting in great animation, while Laura sat beside them not knowing whether to be ecstatic, embarrassed, elated, or just plain terrified at who knew what consequences might result from this mad endeavor. It was a full hour before the plane returned, and in all that time she barely managed to add more than an "uh-huh" and "yes, indeed" to the conversation. Some candidate I am, she thought. My tongue feels permanently stuck to the roof of my mouth. When the winged shape finally reappeared, it coasted over the field, released the red banner beside the runway, and circled back again for a neat landing. Laura let out a heartfelt sigh. At least there'd been no crash, no MILLARD FOR TOWN BOARD draped across the Livonia Center intersection while the plane dangled upside down like a broken-winged bird in the maple tree. The plane taxied back toward them, and as Laura stood to await its return, Bob the mechanic came running from the office.

"Miss Millard! Phone call for you!" he cried.

Laura hurried inside to hear Eleanor Bernstein practically whooping into the phone.

"Laura! Laura! My phone's been ringing like a five-alarm fire! Everyone in town saw it. A few of the calls were negative—cranky old fuddy-duddies who don't like airplanes period, and a few more of the usual women-should-stay-home-and-have-babies complaints—but everyone else thinks it's the most fabulous thing since canned peas!"

By the time Laura got off the phone and returned outside, the plane's engine was off, and Mr. Windham and Bob were on the field, folding the banner. She ran to Barry Gorman, her hand outstretched.

"Thank you! I've just heard from our organizer that your banner was a big hit!"

"My pleasure." He grinned, an exhilaration in his face that made the gold flecks in his brown eyes gleam. He patted the plane. "It felt great. The balance was perfect."

Oren pulled his checkbook from his pocket. "Sign us up for another flight. As the proud sponsors of this candidate, her mother and I want a repeat performance as soon as possible."

"No, no." Mr. Gorman pushed away the checkbook, looking embarrassed. "I told Miss Millard the first few flights were free. This helps advertise our business as much as her run for office. Isn't that right, Don?"

"Oh yeah, right indeedy," Don agreed. "No charge, Miss Millard. No charge."

"But there must be something I can do to thank you," said Laura, and before she could withdraw the words, realizing suddenly that they could be misinterpreted in any number of ways, Mrs. Gorman spoke up.

"Have you ever flown in a plane, Miss Millard?" she asked, a bright smile on her round face. "My son loves company when he flies, don't you, Barry?"

Laura turned to him, her mouth half open, and from the merest corner of her eye, she thought she saw Mrs. Gorman nudge her son with the lavender purse that so neatly matched her lavender shoes.

"Yes, sure I do," said Mr. Gorman, half startled, but also looking as if he might have thought of it himself given enough time. But Oren was suddenly worried. Was it safe? Didn't he need a qualified copilot like Mr. Windham along? Ethel opined that perhaps it might be nicer to all sit down and look at photographs, while Mrs. Gorman waved her short, braceleted arm and broadly assured everyone that flying in a civilized place like Michigan was as safe as a car ride to the corner store. Meanwhile, all Laura could think of was Lorraine's parting message: DON'T LET HIM GET AWAY!

"I'd love to go flying," she announced. "Next weekend? Same time?"

And so it began, the month Laura would think of later as a time when she had been happy and unhappy, puzzled and pleased, calm, flustered, brave as a tiger and scared as a kitten. They decided to fly the banner weekly on Saturdays at 2:00 P.M. when people were most likely to be outside enjoying the summer weather. Laura showed up at the airport, took a deep breath, climbed into the plane, and off they went. Whether she actually enjoyed the flying, she couldn't truly say. Half the time she was in the air, her heart was in her throat, silently praying the plane wouldn't crash, the engine quit, the wings fall off, the banner break loose or snarl in a tree. The other half of the time her heart was in her shoes, thinking, he isn't interested in me at all, it's the flying, the excitement. I'm just a convenient weight in the passenger seat to balance the load. And the other half of the time—which proved how confused she was, because obviously there couldn't be three halves to her heart; even her fifth graders would catch her on that one—her heart was in her head, a strange place for a heart to be, thinking, what do I say to get him to like me? What do I do? He must enjoy having me around, and after three weekends of flying he still insists there's no charge. But it was noisy in the cockpit and hard to talk while Barry concentrated on the flying, and although they were on a first-name basis now, the closest he'd come to paying her a compliment was when she pointed out another small aircraft converging toward them, and he said "Nice spotting" as he altered course for safety's sake.

Meanwhile, about the only place Laura's heart wasn't was in her campaign, although it didn't really have to be. The banners—which they changed weekly to maintain interest and which most lately read LIVONIA NEEDS MILLARD—seemed to be covering the campaign trail better than she could ever do on foot. The *Livonian* had rushed a reporter out to the airport to write an article after that very first flight and followed up with a new photo each week. The Women's League, led by Eleanor, had begun fund-raising to ensure the airborne advertising could continue once the free flights ran out. Strangers stopped her in town, remembering her SAVE OUR TREE! campaign, still at a stalemate, and declaring they'd seen her banner and the newspaper pieces and how brave she was to go aloft. If only they knew, thought Laura, how my knees shake before each takeoff. Then why am I doing this? she asked herself. And that was the most difficult question of all.

"I was in love once," she said, confiding the whole story to Lorraine one night on the phone. It sounded far away now, an event that had happened to someone else, but useful as a caution not to make the same mistake. "I know how love feels, and this just isn't the same."

"Are you sure?" teased Lorraine. "Maybe it's not the flying that makes your knees shake. What do you talk about when you're in the air?"

"Not much. It's noisy, and mostly we point out the sights and stick to our route so people will know when to look up and see us. He has let me hold the controls a few times, so I guess he trusts me a little bit."

"Well, you must be pretty cramped in that cockpit. C'mon, Laura, don't you ever touch?"

"Lorraine, if we do, it's hardly romantic. All I can think is, 'What if I haven't used enough deodorant?' "

"Okay, then what do you talk about on the ground?"

"His job, my job, the usual. Actually, he doesn't say much about his work. I get the feeling he'd rather leave it behind on the weekends."

"Does he ever pay you compliments?"

Laura related the incident when she'd spotted the other plane.

"No, I mean personal compliments," Lorraine persisted.

Laura thought hard. "Last week, when we were flying, I opened the window to see what the wind felt like. It blew the combs right out of my hair, and he said, 'Oh, leave them out. It's pretty when the curls fall around your face.' "

"There, you see," Lorraine crowed. "That's a compliment."

"But he's never said anything else like it."

"Well, he's obviously not a talker. Maybe he lost his tongue in the jungle. You can't have everything in a man. How does he feel about children?"

"Children? Lorraine, I can't ask him that."

"Well, maybe you better, Laura. Maybe you're going to have to be the one to make the move. Because if you leave it up to him you'll just keep flying in circles from now until doomsday. Is that what you want?"

No, Laura thought, that's *not* what I want. I need to know where I, where we, stand. A lot of people seemed to have her and Barry half-engaged already, her friends at the Women's League, Don the airport manager and Bob the mechanic, both obvious in their attempts to play Cupid, her own parents and Mrs. Gorman, who had mailed Laura a rather strange-sounding recipe for a salad that featured sliced bananas and radishes and which she claimed was one of her son's favorites. Even the *Livonian* reporter, who continued to chronicle the adventures of "Laura Millard—High-flying Candidate" in weekly installments, had hinted in the latest article that there was more than politics in the air.

So are we in love or aren't we? Laura pondered, as she hung up the phone. I have to know, because I've made commitments to people, to run for office, to save the maple tree, and next week school starts again. If my heart isn't in any one place altogether, I'm going to let everyone down.

She drove to the airport that Saturday, a hot sticky day, wearing light blue slacks and a short-sleeved white blouse. She didn't wear the combs in her hair, but she didn't wear lipstick or perfume or her absolutely flat-heeled sandals either. She wore sensible shoes that neither exaggerated or minimized her height, because she wanted no tricks, no feminine wiles—not that she really thought she had any—no seduction. She wanted an honest answer, so he might as well see her just the way she was.

The plane was ready to go when she reached the airport. This week's banner read simply VOTE FOR LAURA, since, as Barry explained, her name was now so well known they might as well make it short and sweet.

"But another pilot touched down a half hour ago, and he reported thunderstorms to the west." Barry pointed, and Laura saw a faint darkening, like dirty cotton batten, creeping onto the horizon. "They look slow moving, but I don't want to take any chances with you in the plane."

Because you care about me or because you'd rather have an experienced copilot along, Laura wondered, but that wasn't the way to get the discussion started.

"I'd say you've got a good hour or more," said Don, as he mopped his forehead with a checked handkerchief. Both he and Barry were sweat-stained from their work preparing the banner on the field. "Besides, it'll likely turn out to be nothing. We've had these dang heat waves on and off all summer, and every time we get a promise of a good downpour, it drizzles out before it gets here."

"But that pilot saw lightning." Barry continued searching the sky, which above the airfield was a hazy blue.

"Well, we're not going far," said Laura. She'd picked up enough about flying by now to speak with confidence. "If we go up and there's any hint of turbulence or clouds moving in, we just come back down, right?"

"Right," said Don. "So the sooner you get going, the better."

They climbed into the cockpit, took off, and circled back to hook the banner on the tail. Then they headed over Livonia, the message VOTE FOR LAURA sailing proudly behind them. Barry seemed preoccupied, constantly glancing westward and checking the instrument panel, but the air was smooth, and Livonia being only thirty-six square miles, it didn't take long for the silver bird—even Laura thought of it as a bird now—to make its first pass over the town. As she sought a way to broach the subject on her mind, they flew over Livonia Center and her glance fell upon the schoolhouse. I've got it, she thought.

"Do you remember my student Dorothy?" she asked, shouting a little over the engine noise. "Pigtails, very bright. You told her how to say *Te amo* and *Bésame mucho*."

"Oh yeah." Barry laughed. "Cute kid. She in your class again this fall?"

"No, Mrs. Hancock has her for sixth grade. But I forgot to tell you: I finally heard her use those expressions. It was the Fourth of July. You and your mother had gone. There was a fireworks display after dark, and I came upon Dorothy just as she was whispering her secret into one lucky little boy's ear. You'll never guess who it was."

She tried to make her tone amusing, flinching as she did so because it sounded like flirting, something she knew she wasn't good at. And she felt a sudden hurt recalling the scene, although at the time she had rejoiced in it. Why couldn't it be that easy for her? Why couldn't she know what she felt and then say it, letting loose the wonderful words, whispering them into one special ear, while bouquets of sparkling fireworks bloomed overhead, shedding their colored petals into the velvet summer night.

"It was Rupert," she said. "Rupert with the glasses, my little owl. His eyes got wide, his face flushed red—I could see it even in the dark—then he puckered his lips, closed his eyes, and kissed her on the nose."

Barry chuckled. "Good for him. But you know, that Dorothy's such a pistol, I wonder she needed Spanish to communicate at all. Why didn't she just speak her mind?"

And why don't you? she thought. But Barry was busy, sighting ahead for a barn where they always made their turn, and though a sudden feeling of doom pressed on her, Laura pushed on anyway.

"Exactly," she said loudly. "If people have something to say, they should just come out and say it. Otherwise, it leads to gossip and speculation and misinformation being spread about. Like that article in the *Livonian* about our last flight." She paused. Don had clipped and posted every article about their exploits on his office bulletin board, and Barry surely must have read the reporter's comments that implied they were having a romance in the air. But he was frowning at a crackling noise on the radio, and exasperated, Laura plunged on. "Well, that writer tried very hard to link us romantically, and although I'm sure she was only trying to juice up her story—Eleanor says they do that all the time—well, who knows how many people read it and are now taking it for a fact? All my friends at the League are teasing me about it, and my mother keeps hinting about seeing your South American photos—as if she's trying to set up a date or something—and your mother sent me your favorite salad recipe—did you know that? They all seem to think we ought to be engaged by now, when I'm sure that's the farthest thing from either of our minds, isn't it? Isn't it?"

"Madre de dios!"

His tone was so violent and unexpected that tears started to Laura's eyes, and even though she didn't fully understand the Spanish, she thought, *Well, damn you, too, Barry Gorman,* and then, *Why don't I just fling myself out the door of the plane this minute?*

Then she saw what he saw, for all the while she'd been barreling on, trying to make him say something, anything, he'd been slowly circling back to the west. There on the near horizon towering black thunderheads loomed like angry dragons, and the first rumble of thunder reverberated in the air. The plane shuddered in its echo.

"Barry! Come in!" Don's voice yelped over the crackling speaker. "It's blowing up faster than hell! Get her down quick!"

"I see it!" Barry shouted back. "What's the wind on the field?"

A loud burst of static garbled Don's reply.

"What should I do?" Laura searched frantically over the instruments, her hands wavering above the controls.

"Don't touch anything! Sit tight!"

They were only ten minutes from the airport, the longest ten minutes, Laura thought, of her life. Ahead, wicked forks of lightning stabbed to earth, and as the plane strained into the oncoming rush of wind, the sky grew grayer around them, and bumps of turbulence began to rock the wings.

"What's the wind?" Barry yelled again into the mike, and this time Don's voice came back. "Thirty-five and gusting! Rain a mile west, closing fast."

"We're full power, but we've got turbulence!" Barry shouted, and Laura gripped her seat as another bump tossed them upward and the plane struggled to recover. From that moment on, she didn't speak, didn't blink, just stared and prayed. She could see the airport, a bare, brown patch in the distance, but it seemed a thousand miles away, and each bump and quiver sent a fresh jolt of terror from her feet up to her skull. Her stomach began to churn, and she clapped a hand to her mouth to fight back a rising wave of nausea. Slowly, slowly, the plane fought its way into the wind, raindrops splattering against the window. The runway was dead ahead, and as they dropped toward it, gusts buffeted them from side to side. Please, Laura prayed, get us down, get us down. Beside her, yoke and throttle gripped firmly in his hands, Barry maneuvered for the landing. He released the banner as soon as they were over the field, then skimmed the plane to meet the earth. We're safe! Laura exulted, as the wheels touched ground, but a violent gust lifted the right wing, throwing her against him, and for an instant the plane careened out of control.

"Mierda!"

Barry shoved her away, his hands and feet fighting to regain command, and she slammed against the door as the plane swerved and thudded back to earth. A momentary shock and anger rushed over her, but they were down, they were down, the banner crumpled on the ground behind them, and Barry taxied quickly toward the office, reached over and pushed open her door.

"Get inside," he yelled. "There's lightning on the field. I have to secure the plane."

Laura ran. At least, she tried to run the short distance to shelter. Rain pelted and soaked her; her stomach was knotted with cramps. Don and Bob raced from the hangar, and as they passed her Don shouted, "You all right, Laura?" She nodded. Not until they were past did she pause, double forward, clutch her gut, and throw up.

She stumbled into the office and found a tissue to wipe her mouth. Through the window, she saw the three men scrambling to tie down the plane. Laura began to shiver. Her white blouse was plastered to her wet skin, and her hair was a damp, tangled mop. My parents, she thought, they'll be worried sick, and she reached for the phone on Don's desk. As she lifted the receiver, a bolt of lightning hit the ground just beyond the runway. It crashed against the earth with such a jolt that she dropped the phone and clapped her hands to her ears to muffle the blast of thunder that followed. When she picked up the receiver again, the line was dead.

Barry, Don, and Bob came in from the field, panting. All three were as drenched as if they'd just crawled out of a swimming pool.

"That was a close one." Don wiped his dripping forehead with his handkerchief, a useless gesture since the handkerchief was as soaked as the rest of him. "We got the other planes secured before you touched down."

"But we didn't close the hangar doors," Bob remembered, and with a "Dang it!" from Don, the two ran out again.

Laura stared out the window of the little airport office. The rain was cascading down as if Niagara Falls had opened above their heads. All around them the wind howled, lightning danced, and angry booms of thunder sounded. In minutes the parched yellow airfield had become a sea of liquid mud, the rain riddling the earth like a barrage of enemy bullets. Along the dirt runway, now a river of brown water, came a

glimpse here and there of something red and bedraggled as the VOTE
FOR LAURA banner was thoroughly, mercilessly beaten into the mud.

"I'm going home," she said.

Barry shook his head. "You can't go out there. This storm is dangerous. Wait here till it's over."

"No. The phone's dead, and my parents will be worried."

"Then I'll drive you."

"No, thank you. You've given me enough free rides already." Her
voice was stiff, foreign, and she felt like a twisted rope that at any minute
would fray and snap. "I think I'll do better if I just keep my feet firmly
on the ground."

"I know, I know." Barry's face was anguished. "We should never have
gone up today. I'm sorry, Laura. It's my fault—"

He reached toward her, but she turned, bolted out the door, and
strode blindly to her car, getting soaked, getting in, slamming the door,
and driving off before her tires could become mired in the fast-spreading
bog that Don called a parking lot.

I thought I was going to die.

She sniffed, determined not to lose control, although she could feel a
sense of aftershock setting in. How much bigger did the writing on the
wall have to be before she got the message? The very heavens had
opened to show her exactly what they thought of her ridiculous
dreams. She'd barely opened her mouth to suggest the possibility that
she and Mr. Gorman—he'd ceased to be Barry now—might even
remotely consider matrimony, and a deluge not seen since Biblical times
had poured out its wrath on her. As for her political ambitions . . . In
her mind she saw again the bold red VOTE FOR LAURA banner drowning
in mud and disgrace. What hubris to think she could govern a town
when she couldn't even manage her own life. The only reason she was
still in the race was to keep seeing him.

"Oh!"

The hurt of the realization hit her like a rock in the chest, and she
clutched the steering wheel to keep her grip. So that was it. What a
fraud she was! She drove recklessly toward Livonia Center, the wind and
rain whipping her car almost as brutally as they'd attacked the plane. All
she wanted now was to be home. As she rounded the corner toward the
Kingsley House, she saw two raincoated figures, her mother and father,
hurrying down the porch steps toward their car, no doubt headed for
the airport in search of her. She honked her horn, saw them jerk
around, then clasp each other's hands in relief. Oren hurried Ethel back

onto the shelter of the porch, and they waited there together as Laura pulled into the drive and made one last dash through the rain to join them.

"I tried to call, but the phone line at the airport went dead," she began, as they hugged and patted her all over like a child they were searching for bruises.

"You're soaked," said Ethel. "Get inside at once, get out of those wet clothes and into a hot tub."

"Yes, I'll—"

They stopped and turned. For a minute, an eerie white glow illuminated the black sky above the crossroads, then like a twisted sword a gleaming streak of lightning stabbed down. Ethel screamed. Oren made a choking sound. Laura rushed forward to the porch railing just as the lightning struck the topmost branch of the maple tree. It blazed down the great trunk with a shriek and a shudder that seemed to cleave right into the earth. For one silent moment the tree stood intact, then in a boom of thunder that made Laura's ears explode, the old giant split asunder and crashed into the crossroads, its mighty branches spread over the deserted street like embracing green arms.

Ethel, in the doorway, stood in shocked silence, one hand gripped on the knob, her shoulder pressed against the frame for support. Oren stared, half protesting, "no, no," and shaking his head as if mentally commanding the scene to rewind.

Laura had pitched forward, catching the front porch pillar, but stumbling onto her knees all the same. Tears filled her eyes and spilled down her cheeks, as her mouth silently echoed her father's denial. Then the rain lessened, the wind gave a soft shrug, and with a mocking laugh, the storm blew away.

Eight

Barry Gorman pulled into the driveway of his mother's bungalow and turned off the engine of the car. In all his years of adventuring and flying he'd had a few close calls but never a serious accident. But today, though the plane was down safely, no one injured, and the storm already blowing its way out of the state, he felt as if he'd just walked away from a devastating crash. He had a sense of wreckage strewn all around him, of unreality and loss, as if he really had died and just hadn't caught on to it yet.

The bungalow was dark, as were all the other houses in the neighborhood. He'd seen few lights anywhere on his way home but plenty of downed utility lines and fallen trees, especially the maple tree at Livonia Center. When Laura had driven away from the airport, he stood a minute in confused silence, not knowing what to do. Then with a quick explanation to Don, he set off after her car. She was already out of sight, but her house wasn't far, and all he wanted, he told himself, was to make sure she got home safely. He was just south of Livonia Center when he saw the lightning bolt strike and split the tree, and a pain shot through Barry's chest as he felt its agony. The maple sprawled over the crossroads in dying benediction, a sight at once awesome and helpless, then the leafy branches gave a last shudder and lay still. Barry sat in his car, stunned, while from the houses and shops lining the street, people rushed out to stare. They whispered among themselves, but no one spoke out loud or stepped any closer. The trunk of the tree had collapsed onto the road, and although its branches had touched down on several neighboring buildings, those inside emerged shaken but unhurt. The buildings themselves appeared undamaged, no broken windows or caved-in roofs, as if the tree had fallen in death with a deliberately soft touch.

Gradually, the people began to circulate and chatter, their initial shock past. There was no crossing through the intersection, however, and Barry turned his car and drove a rectangular route to approach Laura's house from the north. The crossroads had been clear of traffic when the tree fell, so he felt no momentary panic that her car had been in its path, and when he neared her house, yes, there it was, parked in the driveway. He thought of going in, to explain, to apologize, but suddenly felt he had no right, and worse, wasn't wanted. So he drove slowly home to Detroit and went into the house to find Mops.

She was sitting by the window, squinting in the grayish daylight as she put the finishing stitches on a set of baby pajamas for little Davey. The welcoming smile dropped off her face at the sight of him.

"What happened?" she demanded, and Barry realized his expression probably looked as damp and dejected as his clothes.

"I don't know. We went flying, and we cut it too close getting down before the storm." He sank into a chair and made an angry sound, inwardly berating himself.

"You went flying? In this weather?" Mops blinked her eyes behind her rhinestone glasses and set aside her sewing in dismay. "When they said on the radio a storm was approaching, I thought you and Miss Millard would wait in the office until it was over. All this time I was picturing the two of you sipping coffee, having a pleasant chat, really getting to know one another. . . ." She sighed, as if reimagining the cozy scene, then she snapped, "You're lucky this is civilization! If this had been the jungle, you would have crashed for sure!"

"I know." Barry let out a heavy breath. He had heard his mother explain her theory that civilization equals safe flying to several of their neighbors, and since it seemed to magically relieve her of worry, he had not attempted to tamper with her logic. But the word "crashed" reminded him that was still exactly how he felt, and instead of ebbing, the sensation grew stronger as he recalled the way Laura had parted from him.

"It was my fault, Mops. The sky was clear, she wanted to go, but I still should have said no. What if she'd gotten hurt? I think it really frightened her, and now she doesn't want to fly anymore. She said I'd given her enough free rides, and she'd do better to keep her feet on the ground."

He grimaced, and for lack of anything else to focus on, his eyes landed on the baby pajamas his mother had been stitching. The garment was sunshine yellow with a teddy bear pattern and bright green trim, an incongruously cheerful object in the semigloom of the leftover storm.

"So now you've gone and scared her." Mops clucked her tongue against her false teeth, a noise, Barry had discovered, that could convey a multitude of moods from mild irritation to high dudgeon. This seemed at the middle of the scale. "Well, at least that's easily fixed. Miss Millard doesn't have to go in the plane with you, does she? Next time you tow the sign, and she can watch from the airport. Or maybe she's worried you mean to start charging her for the flights."

"I wouldn't do that." Barry's face tightened in protest. "I pay Don for the fuel, and I offered to put in free flying time on his scenic and charter flights for letting me use the plane."

"Have you told Miss Millard that?"

"No. I didn't want her to feel she was under any obligation to me."

"But maybe she feels that anyway, you doing her this favor week after week, and her not knowing how to respond. Does she know *why* you're doing this?"

"Sure, to promote the airport and Don's business."

"No, no, no. Does she know why you're *really* doing it?"

Barry stared at her, uncomprehending, and his mother's tongue clucking increased to such a pitch it threatened to pop her false teeth right out of her mouth.

"Because you're in love with her!" she shouted. "Didn't you know that? Haven't you even hinted it to her?"

For a minute, Barry's jaw worked without any words emerging.

"Are you sure?"

Mops threw up her hands. She huffed, puffed, clucked, muttered, and tossed up her palms two more times for good measure.

"Of course you are! You like her company?"

"Yes."

"Her looks?"

"Yes."

"And she's smart and nice and fun?"

"Yes."

"And there's no one else you'd rather be with?"

"Yes. I mean, no. I mean, you're right."

"Then when are you going to do something about it?" Mops picked up the teddy bear pajamas and shook them in his face. "The whole country is falling in love and getting married, and you sit there like a bump on a log. It's you and her I should be sewing these for!" She thrust the pajamas into his lap.

Barry stared at the cheerful yellow garment. It was made of some soft, fuzzy fabric with sewn-in feet and snaps down the front, and the printed teddy bears wore big red bows and held cherry lollipops in their paws. He didn't know what to think, and he didn't know what to feel, and that was how it had been for most of his life. His thoughts and emotions seemed to be locked in a box inside him, and though he tried from time to time to work it open, it was like prying at a keyhole with a bent paper clip or the point of his jackknife, hearing an occasional tantalizing click, only to have the lid stay resolutely closed. He just didn't have the key, didn't know if one even existed, and maybe the reason he'd always felt more at home in a foreign country was because he was a stranger to himself. In Peru or Bolivia, he didn't have to blend in or try to figure himself out. The natives knew he wasn't one of them and would have despised him if he pretended to be. But he couldn't be a stranger any longer, he had to live here now and fit in, and after these past few weeks with Laura, he'd come to like the feeling of not being so alone.

"I've never been in love before, Mops," he said quietly. "I thought it was supposed to be like a thunderbolt"—he winced at the bad choice of word, considering the storm they'd just been through—"or a head-over-heels kind of experience like it was for Ken and Frances. That's not how I feel about Laura."

"No," said his mother reasonably. "It would be nice if you did, but it doesn't have to happen the same way for everyone. I expect Miss Millard isn't head over heels in love with you either."

"She doesn't care for me at all."

"Of course she does. You think she goes flying with you every week-end for her health? Besides, even the few times I've seen you together, I can tell."

Barry shook his head. The conversation he and Laura had had in the cockpit was coming back to him. At the time he hadn't given it his full attention, being preoccupied with the flying and a creeping worry that the storm might overtake them. When he'd turned the plane back east and seen the towering thunderheads, her words had vanished from his mind. But now he remembered.

"Mops, it's you and her parents and friends and the newspaper that have us being in love and half-engaged. And believe me, she wasn't happy about it. She said it was gossip and misinformation, and she was sure marriage was the farthest thing from either of our minds, wasn't it?"

"Wasn't it?" Mops echoed his tone of voice, then paused. She clucked her tongue against her dentures, a thoughtful sound this time. "You mean, she asked you?"

"Asked me what?"

"She asked you if marriage was the farthest thing from your mind. And you answered—?"

"I didn't. That's when we got into trouble with the storm."

"Ahhh." Mops let out a long sigh, as if it were all very clear to her now, and Barry had an odd feeling that it was also becoming clear to him. "She was giving you an opening," Mops said, "a chance to say how you felt about her."

"And I didn't answer," he said glumly. "There wasn't time."

"And if there had been time? What would you have said?"

"I don't know. That I like her, that she's fun to be with, a good copi-lot . . ." Barry's voice trailed, and awkwardly he began snapping and unsnapping the teddy bear pajamas, still in his lap. This was not the kind of speech he was good at, was totally unpracticed in, and he half wished Laura spoke Spanish because that might almost make it easier.

"Not very romantic," Mops agreed, "but it's a start. I got her into the plane that first time, but for heaven's sake, Barry, you're thirty-nine years old, and I can't do everything for you." She reclaimed the pajamas from his lap and resumed her stitching. "Little Davey will have to wait. I'm saving these for you and Miss Millard. If you feel what I think you feel for her, you'll get on the telephone this minute."

But he couldn't call her, because the phone was dead, and two days later, although power had been restored to most of the other suburbs, Livonia Center was still blacked out due to the massive tangling of phone and utility wires caused by the demise of the maple tree. Which meant, Barry thought, that he could either write Laura a letter—a prospect he dreaded since he was even less adept at written words of affection than spoken ones—or he could stop by her house one day after work and risk offending her and her parents by his unannounced visit. He wavered until Friday. Saturday's weather was predicted to be pleasant and sunny, perfect for flying, and he envisioned himself in the plane, far above the earth, the wind streaming above and below him, lost in his own world. But the vision didn't bring him the usual sense of joy, and he knew it was because the seat beside him would be empty. That evening after work he drove to the airport, and in the reassuring disarray of Don's office he picked up the phone and dialed Laura's number.

He thought he opened the conversation pretty well. He apologized for the storm incident, invited her to come to the airport and watch from the ground while he did the next flight, and assured her there was no charge. He was just getting to the hard part, working up to saying that he really looked forward to seeing her, when she interrupted.

"I really thank you for all you've done for my campaign, Mr. Gorman." Her voice trembled, but she pushed on, as if the words must come in one fell swoop or not at all. "It's true I was very scared when we got caught in the storm, but I was the one who pressed you to go, and I'm sure it was your flying skill that enabled us to land safely. So please don't blame yourself. But I've decided to drop out of the race for town board—you can read about it in tomorrow's issue of the *Livonian*—so I won't need to go flying anymore. I'm sorry. I'm sorry I took up your time. Goodbye."

She hung up, and Barry stared at the buzzing receiver. Wait, he thought, you didn't let me finish. I didn't get to say the right words. I was getting close. If you'd only given me a few more minutes, I might have found them. He hung up the receiver and sat down. It was the nearest he'd ever come to unlocking the box inside him. Now the latch slipped closed again, and the keyhole went dark.

Nine

The headline in the *Livonian* looked even worse than Laura had imagined:

MILLARD WITHDRAWS FROM TOWN BOARD RACE

The words accused her in big black letters spread across the front page, and below them was her picture, the smiling head shot her campaign had provided early on to the newspaper to accompany articles and press releases. It looks like I'm happy about this, she thought. She had never felt more miserable in her life.

"It's all right," Oren assured her. "We're proud of you just for trying, Laura."

"You can't do something if your heart's not in it," Ethel added. "Listen to your heart." She exchanged glances with her husband and beckoned him toward the back door. "Probably you'd like to be alone a while. We'll be working in the vegetable garden if you need us."

"Thanks."

Laura managed a weak smile as her parents left, then she read again the article reporting on her departure from the political scene. For the most part, it repeated the information she'd provided in her press release, stating that she had reassessed her candidacy and priorities and had concluded that her true mission in life was to be a devoted teacher to her students. Being in the classroom, instilling knowledge, helping young minds learn and grow was her greatest joy, she had written, and she feared that the time required to do an effective job as a board member might compromise her duty to her children. Moreover, she wrote, there was another female candidate ready to take her place, a woman who was even more experienced, more qualified, and more deserving of election.

"Eleanor Bernstein," the newspaper quoted Laura, "has been the driving force behind encouraging and aiding women to enter the political arena in Livonia. There is no one more knowledgeable about the issues or more dedicated to serving the interests of our town at this critical juncture in its history."

Miss Millard, the article continued, thanked all those who had shown an interest in her campaign and urged them to throw their support behind Eleanor and school board candidates Betty Rhodes and Jean Voss. Below the article, with only a slightly smaller headline, was a second piece titled ELEANOR BERNSTEIN ENTERS RACE.

Laura allowed herself a small smile of comfort. At least something good had come of this. Her friends at the Livonia Women's League had been dismayed and protesting when she told them her decision, and her heart ached as they tried to talk her out of it. She was letting them down, just as she'd feared to all along, and even after they'd accepted her choice and rallied to the idea of Eleanor stepping in, Laura felt deeply that she had betrayed them. It wasn't only that she'd quit the race, but that she'd entered in the first place under false pretenses. She'd been trying to fill that gap, that hollow, hurting space inside her, and though she might have carried on the campaign and even been elected, she knew that wasn't the real answer to the loneliness she felt. She bit her lip and read the remainder of the lead article. Since she'd "declined to be interviewed," the reporter had, as usual, juiced up the story by speculating that Miss Millard's personal life was the real reason for her quitting the race. All those romantic "tête-à-têtes" in the air with a certain handsome pilot must be leading somewhere, the reporter slyly concluded.

"Well, they're not," Laura said aloud, and got up from the kitchen table where she'd been reading. It wasn't his fault. It wasn't her fault. They just weren't right for each other. If he had any feelings toward her, he'd have said something by now. She'd given him enough opportunities, hadn't she? Laura hugged herself, knowing that wasn't quite fair. Sometimes it had seemed he wanted to speak, but the noisy cockpit of a small plane was hardly conducive to romantic chitchat, and besides, Barry needed all his concentration for flying. She felt guilty even now that she'd tried to force him into that intimate conversation when his instincts were already grappling with the dangers of the approaching storm. By the time he'd telephoned last night, she'd had such a heartbreaking week, disappointing her friends and drafting her withdrawal statement, that she was in no mood to talk to anyone.

Laura wandered to the living room and looked out the window toward the crossroads. It had taken half the week to clear away the maple tree and restore the power lines, and throughout that time people had wandered to the site almost like pilgrims drawn to a shrine. The newspaper article on the tree's demise quoted one Livonia centenarian as swearing the tree had been there at least since his youth, and now the people came to pay homage, to preserve a last look as the old giant was hacked apart and carted away. Laura had gone once, the sound of the buzzing chain saws bringing tears to her eyes, and by chance she'd encountered there half a dozen of her students, including Dorothy and Rupert. As if at some unspoken signal they ran to her and hugged her, brave Dorothy crying the hardest of all. So here again, she'd let everyone down, although she was hardly responsible for a random lightning bolt. But she was the one who had encouraged the children to care about the tree, and now they grieved at its loss. Meanwhile, the crossroads looked foreign, empty, the familiar splash of green gone from the scene as unkindly as if some vandal had slashed out the center of a well-loved painting. Only the wide stump in the ground remained, and the Standard Gas Company was bringing in its heavy equipment on Monday to rip out the tree's roots and commence the excavation for the underground tanks. Yet for all the hurt, Laura knew the answer wasn't to teach her children to stop caring.

The rumble of a small plane caught her ear, and automatically she searched upward, a habit she'd fallen into since that first flight with Mr. Gorman. *That might be him*, she'd think, and even when it happened during the work day, when she knew he must be at his job, she felt a little thrill of happiness to hear the familiar sound or spot the glint of sunlight on a plane's wings. She couldn't see the present plane from the window, but she followed its path with her ear as it continued westward. Laura glanced at her watch. It was exactly two o'clock on Saturday afternoon, the time she usually met Barry at the airport, and the thought that she might be there right now, sitting beside him in the cockpit as they prepared for takeoff, made the emptiness inside her seem to cry out loud.

She shook her head, denying it, ignoring it, and returned to the kitchen for a glass of milk. Thank heaven, school started this week. She'd be busy again, teaching, correcting homework, and after school she'd continue to work behind the scenes to help Eleanor, Betty, and Jean win their run for office. But most important, she'd be back with her children, getting to know a whole new crop of fifth graders, their quirks and hidden talents, their voices and waving hands. She hoped she got another Dorothy, another Rupert, Frankie, Adam, and Charles. If only she didn't have to let them go at the end of each year. How much nicer if you could keep the same students from kindergarten on up, like an old one-room schoolhouse. Then they'd be with you so much longer, almost like children of your own. But sooner or later they'd have to leave. . . . Laura gave an angry tsk of her tongue. She was trying to fill that hole again. Maybe she'd just better accept that it would always be there.

Another plane buzzed near the house—or was it the same one? the engine sounded similar—and she thought, *He's flying low.* Should she drive to the airport, see if Barry was there? The temptation must have been in the back of her mind all along because when it popped out, somehow it didn't surprise her. And if he were there, what would she do, what would she say? She could, and should, apologize for the abrupt way she'd hung up on him last night, then see where he took it from there. But suppose he didn't take it anywhere? And what if he wasn't at the airport after all? She distracted herself with a more practical thought, wondering if Don Windham might be getting complaints about the noise from that low-flying plane. Although how could people protest a little engine noise when they were about to have a gas station on the corner? If they wanted progress, noise would be part of it, and if they wanted a horse-racing track and new homes and businesses and to incorporate as a city—all the issues Eleanor had said would be crucial to the election—then the good citizens of Livonia would have to expect more traffic and congestion and all the other benefits of city life.

I wonder what it was like here long ago, thought Laura, when my great-great-grandfather Nathan built this house? How would it feel to look out and see a barn and eighty acres sown with wheat, potatoes, corn? There was no recalling such a scene from her childhood; by the time her parents inherited the house, most of the crops were already gone and the farm had returned to overgrown land. And Nathan Kingsley didn't even have that to start. It was all forest when his family arrived, and they had to clear each acre, cut each tree by hand. What a sight it must have been when this house arose, timber by timber, from the ground, a young husband's proud gift to his new bride.

A third plane buzzed over the house, and a pang filled Laura's chest. It seemed ironic and not a little cruel that her thoughts should have traveled to a bride and groom just as a plane was flying overhead. Or was it the oncoming noise of the engine, heard in her subconscious before it reached her outer ear, that had led her mind down that tricky path?

I want to go to the airport, she thought, and suddenly she felt like a child, wishing, wishing, wishing with all her might. I want to ask him if likes me, even a little bit, if he wants to come over for dinner or maybe go for a walk or do something like a real date. I want to know if he's ever thought of marriage or children or what we might be doing six months from now. I want to know if there's an empty space inside him, like there is inside me, and if maybe we could fill it for each other.

"Laura?" Ethel came through the back door, and Laura started out of her thoughts. "I think there's something wrong with this plane outside. It keeps flying over the house, trailing a sign, but the words on it don't make any sense. And this last time it passed over, it waggled its wings." Awkwardly, Ethel imitated the motion with her arms. "Should we call the airport? Do you think it's Mr. Gorman? Could the plane be in distress?"

"I'll come see."

Laura hurried out with her mother. Her father stood in the vegetable garden, brownish dirt stains on the knees of his pants, squinting up at the sky.

"There, Laura." He pointed, but the plane was already off to the westward and all she could see of its trailing banner was a faint red streak.

"It seems all right," she said, finding a bit of amusement in the fact that her parents seemed to think her few flights with Barry Gorman had made her some kind of aviation expert. "I don't know why it would waggle its wings, but if it's in trouble, it would make for the airport, not keep passing over town."

But that was exactly what the plane was doing. At the end of its westward path it made a graceful turn and skimmed back toward them. *It might be him,* Laura thought, the reflex leaping once again to mind, the little thrill of happiness, followed by a tug of pain. I *will* go to the airport. *I have to know.*

She waited one more minute for the plane to cross their line of vision. Its flight path was slightly to the south, so the banner should be easy to read. The shape grew, its silvery wings and tail emerging from the sun, the hum of its engine growing louder, flying low but straight and level, as if the pilot had no doubt about his course. Then the wings did begin to waggle, little up-and-down motions, as if the plane were waving hello. She'd never seen that before, and for an instant she was almost too busy puzzling over the odd maneuver to read the bold red letters the bird carried as its tail. When she did, Laura gasped.

"There, you see," said Oren, "the words don't make sense."

"Yes, they do." She began to laugh, then to cry, then to laugh a little more. "Mom, Dad, I have to call the airport. Once he knows I got the message, he'll come down."

"What message?" Oren began, but Laura had already turned to run toward the house. She dashed inside and dialed the phone. A few minutes later she strolled back outside.

"It's okay," she said, as the smile on her lips spread over her whole face. "Don radioed him and told him I saw it. Don said it's a good thing, too, because Barry planned to stay up there till he either ran out of fuel or the sun went down. He'll come to the house as soon as he lands. But I asked him to make just one more pass overhead. I don't expect I'll ever get a proposal quite like this again."

"A proposal?" Ethel threw her arms around her daughter. "Is that what it is? And will it make you happy?"

"Yes, Mom. It will."

"Well, I still don't get it," grumbled Oren. "How can it be a proposal when it doesn't even sound like English?"

"It's not, Dad. It's Spanish. Look, here he comes."

The plane angled toward them, then straightened, so the words on the banner stood out clear against the blue sky. From the backyard of the Kingsley House, Laura waved up at the cockpit, and the plane tipped its wings in salute. If people want to say something, they should just come out and say it, she had told him. And so, in his own way, Barry Gorman had.

Laura raised her hand to shade her eyes and follow the path of the bird in the sky, the bird with the beautiful tail:

TE AMO. BESAME MUCHO.

Epilogue

1993

"Who is that, Grandma?"

"That's Horace Kingsley. He was, let me see, your great-great-great grandfather. But I'm afraid he wasn't a very nice person."

"Who is the lady in the long dress?"

"That's his sister Emma. She married the farmhand, Joe McEachran—there he is beside her—and they inherited the Kingsley House from her parents, Nathan and Mary."

"Where are they?"

"Oh, I don't have any pictures of them, dears. It was too long ago. You'll have to imagine how they looked."

Laura Gorman sat on a wood bench and turned the pages of the album in her lap. Her six grandchildren clustered around her in the July sunshine, ice cream from their heaping cones dribbling down the little ones' chins. She'd begun the album years ago, gradually adding bits and pieces of family history as a faded letter or a long-lost photograph came to light. And the more she studied the pages, the more she understood these people, these lives. She looked into the faces in the photos, and the set of a jaw or the tip of a head told her an emotion, a subtle trait of character, a secret buried deep in the heart. She read between the lines of a legal document or gazed at a wavering signature and knew more than the words themselves said.

Of the photographs, none dated much earlier than 1900 when a few formal portraits, a one-time luxury for a farm family, opened the gallery. Laura paused at one of Charlotte and Horace, Charlotte's haunted stare in strange contrast to the twinkle in her husband's eye. A wedding photo of Gertrude and R. Z. caught a hint of triumph in the bride's smile.

Another picture showed two young boys in sailor suits, one serious, one mischievously grinning—Laura's father Oren and his brother Stub. Around 1915, amateur photographs appeared. That was the year her parents had wed, and Ethel, with her camera, began recording their visits to the Kingsley farm. Many of the photos were surprisingly good, and there was one set in particular, when the whole family had gathered for a September picnic, that Laura especially liked. She stopped for a moment at a shot of Emma and her son Glen, his arms wrapped fondly around her shoulders, her hands pressing his hands tightly to her heart. Laura herself was in those photos. She smiled at the wide-eyed little girl with the cap of brunette hair and turned the page.

"Now let me find the pictures from the day the house was moved. Here, look. See how they carried it behind the truck, sitting on those big beams? It was only November, but I still remember how bitter cold it was. Your Grandpa Barry took these photos."

Laura bit her lip. Barry had died only six months before, and she was still trying to adjust to her widowhood. Funny how she looked skyward—an old habit returned—every time a small plane flew overhead. But although the loneliness would probably never quite go away, she didn't feel the great emptiness, the crying ache in her heart she had expected. She felt lucky.

"Grandma?"

"Yes, sweetheart?" Laura brushed her hand to her eye. The sensible, brown-haired granddaughter, the one who liked to organize everything, was tugging her sleeve.

"Grandma, you weren't listening. I said, how did they keep the house from falling off the truck? Did they tie it with ropes?"

"No, no ropes, but do you know I was worried about that very same thing?" Laura peered through her bifocals and pointed at a photo. "I thought, What if the house slides off right in the middle of the street? Yes, it is silly, but of course that didn't happen. The house's own weight kept it in place. Grandpa and I kept tabs on it all the way, and now here it is."

She looked up from the album, and all the grandchildren's eyes followed suit. Before them stood the Kingsley House, resplendent in a fresh coat of white paint, sunlight sparkling off the windowpanes. It was a beautiful house, it had always been a beautiful house, so simple and self-sufficient and no bigger than was needed to serve a family well. And there was something fine embodied in it, a belief that when you built a house with your own hands and farmed your own land, you made a lasting place for your family to be born and live and die and for the next generation to be born in turn.

A sense of pride filled Laura, and was quickly replaced by gratitude. After Oren died in 1974, Ethel had insisted on staying in the Kingsley House alone. But her mind began gently slipping backward, and when she started to talk as if Oren were still beside her—not unusual, perhaps, after a marriage of almost sixty years—Laura had brought her mother to live with her and Barry until her death in 1983. Ethel had been so pleased when Laura told her the house would be preserved.

That was sixteen years ago, when the Kingsley House had been one of the first buildings moved to this site, the fledgling Greenmead historic village, established on land that had once been another pioneer farm. She had felt both the excitement and risk of it—the money to be raised, the volunteers needed, the tremendous amount of work to be done. So easily it might all have fallen through, and the house abandoned here on bare land. Instead, it was now kept company by a dozen other historical structures rescued from throughout the city: a Methodist church, a one-room school, the Quaker meeting house, a general store, and a handful of kindred homes that had survived from the century gone by. The village was still very much a work in progress, as painstaking restorations slowly returned each structure to its original state. The land, too, was in progress, planted with shrubs and saplings that promised future greenery and shade. Yet already the village had begun to achieve its goal of recreating a crossroads community from Livonia's past.

But it was the Kingsley House that was the center of attention this summer day, as the ice-cream social on the front lawn celebrated the house's one hundred and fiftieth birthday. Restoration had made it new—and old—again. The tiled bathroom and modern kitchen had been removed, the pegged wood floors refinished, the walls painted and papered in colors and patterns of pre–Civil War vogue. A sofa and horsehair chair graced the parlor; the living room held a wood rocker, table, and reed chairs. In the kitchen, a bucket of logs sat beside the antique cast-iron stove; in the bedroom, a patchwork quilt covered an old-fashioned rope bed. There were even signs of some prosperity—a lace tablecloth, silver candlesticks, an ancient sewing machine—and vases of fresh flowers to brighten the rooms. If Mary Kingsley had walked through the door, she would have gazed around and thought proudly, *My house, my parlor, my home.*

"Did you ever live in the house, Grandma?" asked the tall, handsome grandson, dark blue eyes glinting in his sharp face.

"Oh yes, when I was growing up and again for a while when I taught at the Livonia Center School. Then I met your grandpa, and we had our wedding in the parlor, and afterward we lived nearby and visited often."

"Don't you wish you lived in the house now?"

A small finger stroked the photo album, and Laura smiled down at the youngest grandson with the wistful blue eyes and sandy hair and ears that stuck out a little. She thought a moment before replying. The answer came to her with a touch of surprise, as if she should have known it all along.

"I *do* live in the house, and so do all the people who came before. That morning the truck carried it away I felt all mixed up, worried and hopeful that it could really be saved, but sad the farm just wasn't there anymore. Do you understand? I didn't want anything to change, even though so much already had. But at the end of the day when the house arrived here and they set it on its new foundation, I had a sudden feeling everything would come out right. The house carried its history with it, like a book carries a story inside. Look with your heart, and you'll see the people who lived there. You'll feel the impression each one left behind."

On the front porch of the Kingsley House, volunteer guides in period costumes were greeting visitors at the door. On the lawn, families chatted over ice cream or strolled off to see the rest of the village. Laura closed the album, took a packet of tissues from her purse, and began to wipe her grandchildren's sticky chins. Her daughter, sons, and assorted spouses laughed in conversation nearby. The luminous July day was a perfect gift for the Kingsley House on its one hundred and fiftieth birthday, and Laura rose from the bench and shepherded her grandchildren forward.

"Come," she said. "Let's go into our house."

Author's Note

When my mother, Laura, first showed me the album of photographs and documents she'd assembled on the Kingsley House, I didn't quite realize what I held in my hands. It was enough to pore over the pictures and put faces to names. Here were my grandparents Oren and Ethel in a family grouping taken in 1913; the camera had caught the engaged couple tenderly holding hands. Here was my great-grandmother Gertrude, the only one of five siblings to survive the diphtheria epidemic of 1887–88, her eyes serious beyond their years. Here was Horace, my great-great-grandfather, the scoundrel of the family, looking smug in his handsome overcoat. The more I gazed at the photographs, the more tidbits of family history my mother recalled, the more intrigued I became. I started to like these people, to feel I knew and understood them. Then one day, it hit me: This wasn't an album; it was a novel sitting in my hands.

What spoke to me most deeply about the Kingsley House and its inhabitants was that these were the real people who built America, not by drafting laws or waging wars, but by literally building it, one house, one barn, one community at a time. Nathan Kingsley, my great-great-great grandfather, who erected the house in 1843 in Livonia, Michigan, for his bride Mary, could neither read nor write. Yet he built a house of classical symmetry in the Greek Revival style on land that ten years before had been wilderness. The stones for the foundation he plowed from the fields; the lumber came from trees on his forty acres of land. Nathan, twenty-two, laid every board, fixed every shingle, by hand. When I began writing the novel, I was disappointed we had no photograph of Nathan, or of Mary. Then I discovered I didn't need one—the house itself told me about the man.

I also had little in the way of written family history. The Kingsleys were not rich or prominent. They never engaged in the kind of newsworthy deeds that would have earned them a mention in contemporary reports. Nor did anyone in the family ever keep a journal. But from my mother and other relatives came kernels of stories, and imagination, backed by research, did the rest. In a way, the scarcity of source material was an advantage; unburdened by a mountain of facts, I was free to invent episodes, shape personalities, spice the plot. In some cases, I let characters live longer than the dates on their gravestones allowed. I liked them too much to let them go. I also contrived to have the Kingsley House remain in my family's possession until 1977, when it was moved to Greenmead, a historic village in Livonia. In fact, the house had to be sold when the widowed Emma and her ailing son Glen could no longer keep up the farm. Emma must have felt terrible about that; in the novel, I found a way for her to pass the house on.

In writing fiction, there has to come a moment when the characters speak to the author, and it is their voices, not yours, telling the story. Looking at those photographs in my mother's album was what first awakened my ancestors' voices in my ear. For all the interweaving of fact and fiction in the novel, I have tried to be true to their spirit. Often their stories needed little embellishment; the very simplicity of their lives made their joys and tragedies more dramatic than anything I could devise.

I love the people in my book. I hope they would approve.

Arliss Ryan
September 1999